THE WAY TO VALHALLA

The Way to Valhalla

Brendan Martin

(A story inspired by actual events)

JANUS PUBLISHING COMPANY LTD
London, England

First published in Great Britain 2009
by Janus Publishing Company Ltd,
93–95 Gloucester Place,
London W1U 6JQ

www.januspublishing.co.uk

British Library Cataloguing-in-Publication Data
A catalogue record for this book is available from the British Library

ISBN 978-1-85756-720-5

Cover Design: Janus Publishing

Printed & bound in the UK by PublishPoint,
a service from KnowledgePoint Limited.

Dedication

The Way to Valhalla was inspired by real events in Africa, the Balkans, Ireland and the South Atlantic and the author's experiences as a professional soldier.

This book is dedicated to Sue, Natalie and Kate

To die in battle, sword in hand was the greatest honour a viking warrior could aspire to.

It would earn him his place at the table of the god of war Odin, in 'Valhalla'.

Contents

Acknowledgements

Jeannie Leung for her confidence and belief and everyone else at Janus. And a very special thank you to Claire Pickering for her tireless work, professionalism, advice and endless patience.

Author's Note

This book was inspired by real events. However, the events described in these pages should not be construed as a true reflection of those events.

Statements expressed in the text represent nothing more than my own thoughts, observations and opinions. It is not a historical record and with the exception of the South Atlantic phase, much of the geography and many of the names of those who may have been involved have been altered as a matter of prudence on my part, not least because some things are best left unsaid!

I wrote the book to entertain, so read on. Explore its different dimensions, draw your own conclusions, but above all enjoy it!

B. M.

The Quitter

When you're lost in the Wild, and you're scared as a child,

And Death looks you bang in the eye,

And you're sore as a boil, it's according to Hoyle

To cock your revolver and ... die.

But the Code of a Man says: "Fight all you can,"

And self-dissolution is barred.

In hunger and woe, oh, it's easy to blow ...

It's the hell-served-for-breakfast that's hard.

"You're sick of the game!" Well, now, that's a shame.

You're young and you're brave and you're bright.

"You've had a raw deal!" I know — but don't squeal,

Buck up, do your damnedest, and fight.

It's the plugging away that will win you the day,

So don't be a piker, old pard!

Just draw on your grit; it's so easy to quit:

It's the keeping-your-chin-up that's hard.

The Way to Valhalla

It's easy to cry that you're beaten — and die;

It's easy to crawfish and crawl;

But to fight and to fight when hope's out of sight —

Why, that's the best game of them all!

And though you come out of each gruelling bout,

All broken and beaten and scarred,

Just have one more try — it's dead easy to die,

It's the keeping-on-living that's hard.

Robert Service

The Characters:

ALICE FEARON WARNER — The other half of a most unlikely friendship

ANDY KILBRIDE — Special Branch

ANNE QUIGLEY — PIRA security group volunteer

BIG BRENDAN — Jimmy Curtis' father

BILLY FEANY — Jimmy Curtis' best friend

BILLY MCNIEL — Otherwise known as Father Benedict

BOB — Landlord of Queens Hotel, Aldershot

CAPT. NIELSON — Covert ops in Northern Ireland

CHRIS SCHOLLONBURG — Contract soldier/mercenary

CLANCY — Owner/landlord of Clancy's Bar

DECLAN — Terrorist

DICK KAMINSKI — Contract soldier/mercenary

DOHERTY — Loyalist terrorist

EAIMON BLAIRE — Fledgling PIRA volunteer

EMPEROR EDI — Leader of rebel group from Jackson's Crossing

FATHER DALY — Priest/teacher from Jimmy Curtis' childhood

GUS GRILLO — Contract soldier/mercenary

HAROLD CARSON — Protestant farmer

JAMES EDWARD BRINTON — PIRA volunteer

JANE — Covert operator

JIMMY CURTIS — British Paratrooper/contract soldier

JIMMY QUEEN — UVF Commander

JOE MCKENNA — PIRA volunteer

KENNY ROYALS	Guard commander
KENNY SALWAY	Friend of Curtis
KONSTANTINE ALEXANDR KASHITSKIN	British double agent (turned by MI6)
KURT WILLT	Contract soldier/mercenary
LEO VAN RIJN	Contract soldier
LIAM	Declan's brother/terrorist
MR WILLIAM MOKESE	Greedy man (who should have known better)
MISS ROBBINS	Veterinarian
NEIL KILBRIDE	Special Branch
PATRICK TOMMELTY	Smuggler
PAUL	Company medic
RENÉ VOSS	Curtis' close friend/contract soldier mercenary
ROISIN RAFFERTY	Informer and source for NI RUC Special Branch
SAM	Dog
SAM MULLEN	PIRA volunteer (Army Council)
SEAMUS FALLON	PIRA volunteer
SEAN	PIRA volunteer
TERESA CURTIS	Jimmy Curtis' sister
THOMAS	The tracker
TOMMY MCGUIRE	PIRA volunteer
WILLY FALLON	Contract soldier/mercenary

Bread and Butter

When you're wounded and left on Afghanistan's plains,
And the women come out to cut up what remains,
Jest roll to your rifle and blow out your brains
An' go to your Gawd like a soldier.

Rudyard Kipling; *The Young British Soldier*

It was hot in the hide. The man lay motionless, peering through the bramble cover, which had been his home since he had slid quietly into its hollowed-out centre two nights before. The drop-off had gone well.

The van, with its electrical wholesaler's livery, had slowed but not stopped in the narrow lane called Carrickstricken, which wound its way near the border between Northern and Southern Ireland.

The driver had quietly counted down as he approached the point in the lane where the well-rehearsed drop would happen.

'Ten ... nine ... eight ...' he said as he knocked down the gears.

'Bridge coming up.'

'... seven ... six ...'

'All quiet here.'

'... five ... four ... three ...'

'Ten miles an hour now, no traffic.'

'... two ... stand by ... one! Go!'

With one fluid movement, the man had opened the rear doors, slid onto the road, weapon in hand, day sack on his back, closed the door of the still-moving vehicle with an inaudible click and melted silently into the cloak of the South Armagh night.

Dropping into the roadside ditch, he crouched, listening, watching and waiting. The van continued its uninterrupted journey along the lane until finally out of sight. Nearby, a fox screamed; in the distance, a dog replied and a muffled human voice berated the animal. The smell of burning peat crept across the landscape and nestled in the man's nostrils. Then he was alone.

He was comfortable with that – "alone" was his friend. He much preferred his own company to that of larger groups of men he had worked with in the Green Army, before he had been persuaded to take on the challenge of his present employment.

He reached inside his windproof pocket and produced a small, thumb-sized betalight, which he held close to the OS map that lay across his knee. The light glowed but produced no beam as he quickly confirmed his position and intended route to the target. Replacing the map and betalight, he waited for a further ten minutes before moving south towards the border, stopping regularly to watch and listen.

He had made good time and arrived within 200 yards of the target, where he cached some of his equipment before moving off again to continue with his task. He made a 360-degree sweep of the small stone house, which had become the centre of his attention. He looked for routes in and out, covered approaches, best vantage points, signs of visitors, but most of all for the least obvious but most advantageous position for his OP. He found this in the bramble cover that had overgrown a thick sandstone wall which had long outlived its purpose.

Now, it gave him some reasonably robust cover from fire and the thick brambles afforded him cover from view.

Satisfied that he was well hidden inside his cocoon, he made some final adjustments to the chicken wire, which now made up the walls and ceiling of his hide, interwoven with bramble from the undergrowth. He had needed to remove a substantial sandstone block from the wall to afford him a clear view of the target, which he used as an improvised table and which now accommodated his mini binoculars and night viewing aid. He moved imperceptibly, easing the pressure off the three stun grenades which he carried inside his jacket. In addition, there were two smoke grenades: one red, the other green. The latter would be used later, to mark a safe LS for the Special Forces pilot, who would extract him if required. His main weapon of choice was the Heckler and Koch G3, his backup, which was holstered and strapped to his left hip, was a Browning High Power, cocked, safety catch applied, just as the G3 had been since leaving his base location.

He surveyed the area, maintaining a level of awareness developed only through long and repeated exposure to sensory deprivation, combined with an absolute dedication to his craft. It was 16.00 hours and the August sun beat down. A bumblebee fumbled with a wild flower, not 6 inches from his nose.

It was six hours earlier that the boy had arrived, walking with nonchalance achieved only by someone with something to hide. He decided the boy must be new at the game; eager to impress his local heroes. He'd be the same as many others who'd gone before, seduced by the words of rebel songs sung in bars and homes throughout his community. If he got this right, there would be more jobs – better jobs – and eventually, if he was good enough, he'd take the oath, and then he, too, could kill the Brits and push them out of his land. The boy had been watched for some months by the local Provo IO and was one name in a long list of possible recruits to the cause.

Background checks had revealed no reason for concern, for the IO and the briefing, which he gave to his OC, concluded that the boy might be used as a courier. Subsequently, a junior Provo commander was tasked with inviting the boy to carry out his first job for the movement. The boy's name was Eaimon Blaire. He was 15 years old, unemployed, and he'd almost wet himself with ill-concealed excitement when the Provo had told him what was required. Three weapons would be delivered to him that very evening. There would be ammunition, gloves and balaclavas in a small shoulder bag. He was to take the weapons to a small stone house south of Forkhill, where he was to place everything under a large flagstone outside the front door, leaving no sign of his having been there. Once done, he was to leave the area and speak to no one about his involvement. He was left in no doubt about the consequences if he failed to comply. He was to deliver the goods in two days, before 10.00 hours.

That evening, the goods arrived at the back door of his terraced house; three loud knocks followed by disappearing footsteps signalled their arrival. By the time he'd opened the door, the bundle lay at his feet and there were no signs of life. He quickly picked up the bag and placed it in the cupboard under the stairs. His heart beat fast as he paced up and down, wringing his hands nervously, having checked the bag a dozen times at least throughout the night.

Later that evening, he'd called at his girlfriend's house in the next street and they'd gone on an extended spell of under-aged drinking in a local shebeen in Drumintee. He'd been unable to contain himself any longer and he'd blurted out the details of his new career as a freedom fighter, an all-round hard man, to Roisin Rafferty, his girl.

He had only known her for two months of her sixteen years. Her SB handler, however, had known her penchant for cash for the last three years. She was the cousin of the IO who had originally spotted Eaimon Blaire's potential as a courier and she was valuable for that very reason.

She moved in circles that occasionally threw out snippets of intelligence, which she passed on "at a price" to her branch handler.

The latest "snippet" was the reason why the man in the bramble hide, not 30 yards from the front door of the stone house, had photographed the drop made by Eaimon Blaire just six hours earlier.

The man, however, had remained in situ for a further ten hours and once he was confident he had the cover of darkness on his side, he carefully withdrew to a position 500 yards north of his hide and relayed his situation to his own base station. He stated his intention to move to the prearranged PUP between Bog Road and Forkhill SF base, giving his ETA and forgoing the heli pick-up in favour of the mobile QRF from the detachment.

All went as planned and he was soon on his way back to base, where he would brief his own superiors, members of the intelligence world, SB and a representative from "the troop" as the permanent SAS team in the province was known. Plans would be drawn up and studied before a decision would be made on what sort of OP would be mounted to counter the proposed use for the weapons.

That same night, a technical attack was mounted on the weapons cache by an operator from the Det. After the meeting at TCGS, the operator had taken less than fifteen minutes to insert the electronic tracking device into the butt of one of the weapons before withdrawing, undetected.

Early Days

Oh you are a mucky kid,
Dirty as a dustbin lid.
When he hears the things you did
You'll gerra a belt from your Da!

Stan Kelly; *Liverpool Lullaby*

He spent the first seven years of his life in a one-bedroomed terraced slum in Blackrock, Dundalk. His father Big Brendan, a merchant seaman and a brutal individual, spent most of his time away from home and the thankless task of bringing up four children alone fell to his all-enduring mother, who took in laundry to pay the bills.

The home was little more than derelict. Plaster barely clung to the walls, where pervasive damp had taken its toll over the years; it smelt of rot and decay and was constantly cold. Jimmy shared a bed with his mother, two sisters and a brother – he was the youngest of four. By the time he was 3 years old, his sister Colleen and his brother Curragh were both dead – the girl succumbing to tuberculosis and the boy to pneumonia. Jimmy and his surviving sister Teresa suffered constantly from colds as a result of their abysmal living conditions. At night, as they lay beneath several layers of old coats on a damp mattress, they would play a game, guessing how much bigger the mushrooms in the corner of the ceiling would grow overnight. Arguments would often ensue over who would get to wear the old army overcoat in bed or who didn't want to be next to the wall to avoid the running condensation. In the end, it was always Jim's mother who would suffer for the kids.

Downstairs, one small room contained a dresser – part of his mother's dowry – and an old Victorian mirror, hung on a large rusty hook. To its right, hung a portrait of the Pope in an ornate gold-leafed frame, which was regularly taken down and cleaned with due reverence; especially when the priest, Father Daly – a true martinet of the Catholic religion – was due a visit on Friday evenings after school. The picture was the most valuable article in the house.

The room also housed a bare wooden table and four chairs and a worn leather armchair – his father's – where no one dared sit, even when the big man was away at sea. There was also a threadbare, home-made rug, which lay in front of an empty hearth. A picture of Christ's Crucifixion hung both above the family bed and next to the Pope in the parlour. The front, downstairs window, with a large diagonal crack, looked out onto the 40-ft high wall of the cotton mill; the back window overlooked a cobbled yard, through the centre of which ran an open sewer drain. In summer, the stench permeated the home along with the resident rats. In winter, it ran freely with human waste and boats made from sticks by Jimmy and other kids along the block, who used it as a shipping lane; occasional heavy rain providing the means to race and bet on the winning boat. The currency was invariably that of stolen apples from the orchard in the grounds of Brendan Fearon Manor House on the edge of town.

Many a day would see young Curtis with his arse hanging over the drain and his trousers round his ankles, suffering from his latest attack of the "skitters" (the runs), brought on by an over-indulgence of baking apples; an attack leaving him no time to cover the extra 3 yards to the half-walled, roofless outdoor toilet! Helped along by a liberal dose of invective from his mother and dog's abuse from the other kids, young Curtis could only grunt and groan and take solace in the fact that it would be someone else's arse hanging in the breeze next time.

His first day at school also heralded the return from sea of Jimmy's father. He always arrived unannounced, came into the house, spoke to no one and looked about the place. His mother tripped along dutifully behind him, awaiting her orders, and then he would be on his way to the bar. Clancy's was his favourite and none there would cross the big seaman. He never spoke when he could hand out a punishing blow to some unfortunate's jaw instead and many had fallen foul of his fiery temper. He would drink until two or three in the morning and then come lumbering home, expecting his food to be served on arrival and woe betide Jimmy's mother if it wasn't produced.

Family folklore indicated that Jimmy's father and grandfather were two horns off the same goat. Both were loners and sound beatings were delivered with great gusto to the women of the house on a regular basis by both men alike. One such incident, witnessed by Jimmy, took place one evening, when Big Brendan, Jimmy's father, had ordered Jimmy's mother to have his food on the table at 8.00 p.m., but then subsequently turned up an hour late. When Jimmy's mother had protested, having duly delivered the meal on time, the big man had calmly picked up a large carving fork and had stabbed Jimmy's mother through the hand, pinning it to the table. He had then finished his meal in front of the whimpering woman, after which he had delivered a parting belt across her face, before leaving the house and returning to sea, leaving Jimmy and his sister the unenviable task of releasing his mother and dressing her wounds. Jimmy's grandfather had done an almost identical thing to his grandmother not three months earlier and not for the first time, either. But that was Jimmy Curtis' world and he didn't complain; it merely shaped and moulded him and prepared him for the future he could never have foreseen.

School also brought young Jimmy into conflict with his mentors – the nuns and priests of Black Rock Catholic School – and it had set the tone for the next two years. Turning up at the school, alone, with the names of Sister Anna and Father Benedict scribbled on a piece of paper in preparation for the historical event, he wondered what the day would bring ... and he wouldn't have to wait long to find out.

Young Curtis had arrived late and he spent the first five minutes waiting in the austere corridor outside Father Benedict's office, before deciding that a trip to the local pond for a day's fishing presented a far more attractive alternative. So off he went, satisfied that his close encounter with a life of enforced education was not for him.

However, an hour and a half later, he was ambushed and captured by Father Daly armed with a shaving leather and cane, he was projected the 500 yards back to the school on the end of both weapons. By the time he arrived back, his ears were bright red and throbbing owing to the several belts around the head which he'd received, accompanied by six or seven bright, shining weals across the arse ... the first of many.

But beatings had also been part of Jimmy's life and he took them defiantly, refusing to cry. Big Brendan had meted out far worse to Jim for as long as he could remember. So Jimmy learned to treat his religious beatings with contempt. His challenge to these authority figures simply enraged them even more, inviting further physical punishment, especially from Father Daly who, from that day on, would take a personal interest in young Curtis' demise ... or so he believed.

Daly promised to, 'Beat the badness out of you, Curtis, you wee heathen.'

But young Jimmy knew, even then, that they were just beating it further in.

Days, weeks and months passed; nothing changed. Jimmy would be frogmarched from school to home following a beating from Father Daly, only to be met by Big Brendan, who would hand out yet another for being beaten in the first place. But it wasn't all bad; Jimmy's best friend Billy Feany lived in almost identical circumstances three doors along the block and they'd been partners in crime ever since they could walk and talk.

At first, walking in itself had presented somewhat of a problem for Master Billy, who wore calipers, having contracted polio at 4 years of age. But the little lad had clunked, clanked and squeaked along behind Jimmy during their many and varied adventures. When the other kids ran on and out of sight, it would be Jimmy who would stop and wait for the puffing, panting Billy.

In due course though, the calipers were removed and he was left with a severe limp and one leg much thinner than the other. And so the inseparable pair would often be found stealing apples together, poaching trout from Brendan Fearon Manor or generally getting up to any and all forms of skulduggery.

On such occasion, Master Billy arrived, suitably attired with the Feany family communal wellington boots, which he reverently insisted on wearing on the wrong feet, believing that it helped him run faster. It was something to do with wind "persistence", an extremely valuable asset when stealing apples, often from under the nose of the game-keeper, who was not averse to letting an intruder have a couple of barrels of rock salt in the arse from his trusty shotgun.

Such were the perils that faced the two amigos on a regular basis and one fine day in the summer, that very fate had befallen the pair and Feany caught an arseful. His screams and wails had Jimmy in a fit of hysterical laughter which, infectious as it was, soon contaminated Feany and they were both captured, helplessly wriggling, hanging upside down on the fence, laughing uncontrollably.

'Well,' said Feany, gasping for air, 'it looks like we're both in the shithouse now, Curtis.'

Feany, meanwhile, couldn't sit down for a week.

When they were together, time raced by in a blur and hardships shrank into a series of unfortunate encounters in the background of their lives.

Another favourite pastime of theirs was fighting the imaginary English, usually in retaliation for the potato famine; but any reason was good enough when you came from the same Republican background as the boys. The scene of most of these reprisals was the old stone quarry lake, long since disused, which had a thickly wooded island in its centre. The kids would often swim out or access it via a causeway about 2 feet wide, which ran straight and true 6 inches below the surface onto the island. In the overactive imaginations of the kids, this usually supported an English stronghold, ripe for attack and destruction.

During one bright, clear september day, having been paid handsomely by Clancy for the three large sacks of horse manure, Jimmy and Billy waited to watch the start of the local hunt.

Clancy had wanted the manure for his roses and he'd paid handsomely for it. The riders and horses would gather outside Clancy's Bar with the foxhounds; Jimmy had always thought how grand they'd looked and he'd loved the dogs, too. Armed with a fresh meat pie from Mrs O'Callaghan's shop and a stash of apples, the boys had set forth on that day's adventure, attacking the English and capturing the fort in the lake.

Slapping their hips in time with their feet, to imitate the sound of their horses, roaring and whooping and brandishing swords fashioned out of twigs, in no time at all, they were at the lake. Jimmy reached the causeway first, splashing into the shallow water and immediately beginning to skewer two Englishmen. Billy roared in behind, slashing and parrying, thrusting and stabbing.

'Onward, onward. Kill the English!' they screamed and roared.

Halfway across, Billy shouted, 'I'm wounded, I'm wounded!'

Jimmy turned to see Billy stuffing a snotty hanky down his shirt to stem the flow of imaginary blood.

Then, bellowing to Jim, Billy shouted: 'Fight on; fight on for Ireland.'

Jimmy turned in a spray of blood and water. Spurred on by the wounded Billy, young Jimmy bounded forwards again, cutting down a dozen or more English before reaching the old oak in the dead centre of the isle - the site of the English stronghold. Once again, up in the branches, victory was theirs.

'Yeaesss!'

Triumphant, Jimmy sat in the bole of the great tree. Still no sign of Billy. He'd be away, as was their tradition, being fixed up by a sympathetic quack – an act they had often staged so as to meet up again later or the next day, to relate stories of how they had avoided deadly groups of escaping English to live and fight another day.

An hour later, Jimmy made his way home, excited at the prospect of hearing Billy's escape story the next day. Along the lane, he passed the chapel and the fields, where Ned Cromer kept his cart and horses. Their heads lolled over the gate, towering above Jimmy, and he fed them an apple each. Then, reaching up, he rubbed them both on the nose before walking on.

He reached Clancy's Bar just before ten o'clock. Walking across the cobbled street in a world of his own, the door of the bar suddenly burst outwards and hung by one hinge as a man crashed backwards into the street, landing on his back with a thud and a groan. It was Eanis O'Malley, a well-known bully and roughneck. He was from farming stock and was strong and well-built, years of hard work having toughened his ways. But he was no match for the man who stood above him silhouetted in the doorway. Filling the frame as he stepped over the fallen O'Malley and straightening his cap, Big Brendan paused and looked at his son.

'Come here, boy,' said the big man.

Jimmy walked towards his father, who turned him to look at the unconscious O'Malley.

Brendan put his hand on Jimmy's shoulders and said, 'Look at this, lad; it's the only thing that matters.'

Young Jimmy frowned quizzically and returned his father's steady gaze.

'What do you mean, Da?'

'Last man standing, lad, that's all!'

It was Brendan's way of saying, "Don't end up like this!" It was the closest thing to advice Jimmy's dad had ever given him and the boy would remember it forever. There were never any hugs. Jimmy had no recollection of his father ever having given him a hug – just the words, "last man standing". They turned and walked home in silence, past two policemen standing in the shadows, who knew well to keep a safe distance from the big man.

Big Brendan ordered his wife to fetch a bottle of Bushmills as Jimmy went up to his bed. His ma followed him up and tucked him in, whilst Jimmy spoke about the day's adventures with Feany; embellishing his story with plenty of "fucks". His sister Teresa listened and giggled as they both drifted into the land of nod.

During the night, Jimmy heard grown-ups shouting and doors being banged, but he'd decided he must have been dreaming. But the next morning found him walking back down to the old quarry lake, only this time Big Brendan was at his side.

When they arrived, it was a hive of activity. Women, kids, men and, strangely enough, police – seven or eight of them – some in civilian clothes. Jimmy looked along the causeway to where two men in the water were passing something upwards – treasure, thought Jimmy and his heart leapt, but there were grown-ups in his line of view. They were making their way closer now and as they reached him and his father, he peered around the two men in front of him: a uniformed copper and a suited man carrying a briefcase – the local doctor – then behind him came Mr Feany Snr … It was then that Jimmy saw the reason for them being there as in his arms lay the limp, lifeless form of his son – Jimmy's best friend – Billy Feany.

His eyes were half open and his skin was a pallid grey; his tiny, thin arm waving gently in time with his father's footsteps. His head lolled back, a strand of weed crossing his cheek.

Big Brendan said to Jimmy, 'Take a good look, lad, it's all that matters.'

There was a pause and then Jimmy replied, 'Last man standing, Da!'

Once again, Big Brendan was cryptically telling Jim, "Don't end up like this!" But, as usual, there were no comforting hugs or that compassion thing that Alice Fearon Warner often talked about.

It was over a week before Jimmy spoke again, but when he did, it was quickly established that the dead boy, far from slipping away to receive the medical attentions of a sympathetic quack for his war-wounds, had simply slipped from the causeway as he and Jimmy had "fought their way across". He must have got caught below the surface in the thick weed bed and drowned.

Jimmy had walked home none the wiser and for the rest of his days, he would hold himself responsible; unable to come to terms with the fact that he could have done nothing.

At his friend's funeral, Jimmy Curtis stood behind the adults, listening to the priest and the tears of those around him. At the end of the service, he pushed his way between the coat-tails, which smelt of moth balls, and the sea of legs, walking in the opposite direction like an incoming tide. He stood beside the grave stone, with its simple inscription:

> Billy Feany Killed in an Accident
>
> Aged 7 Years

But Jimmy Curtis' mind decided that the inscription really said:

> Billy Feany Killed in Action,
>
> Fighting the English

His little friend would be happy with that – and so was Jimmy Curtis. He turned and walked away with a salty taste of tears on his lips and the sound of the grave diggers at work behind him. He was alone; but "alone" would become his friend.

Jimmy spent many long hours sat in the bole of that great oak on the island, remembering the fun that he and his little friend had shared during their short lives together. And he spent a great many more held in the arms of Mrs Alice Fearon Warner in front of the great fire in the manor house. It was her gentle way that helped Jimmy come to terms with the loss of his friend, but he never would accept that he could have done nothing to prevent it.

As time went by though, his loss became easier to bear and he gradually returned to the carefree lad he had once been before the accident. Even his devil-may-care attitude came back to the fore, especially at school – when he was there – but deep inside, he missed his little friend terribly.

But life goes on and so it did for Jimmy Curtis and it was to Alice that he turned more and more for support. She read him stories from Dickens and she helped him to read and write; she taught him the virtues of good manners; she cooked him meals and mended his clothes, saying, 'Tell your mother not to be offended, Jimmy; she'll understand what I mean. You're a good boy, Jimmy, and don't let anyone tell you otherwise.' She also taught him the meaning of compassion and warned him never to laugh at other people's misfortunes. 'Remember that, Jimmy. There's always room for compassion.'

'What's "misfortunes", Alice?' Jimmy asked.

'Well,' she would say, 'your little friend, Billy; he had a problem with his legs, didn't he, Jimmy?'

'Yes,' Jimmy replied.

'Well, that's something he couldn't help; it just happened. Life's like that, Jimmy. Sometimes, things just happen, things we don't like, that's a misfortune. Do you understand, Jimmy?'

'Yes! Yes, I do. But you should have seen him when he got those wellies on. Holy fuckin' Jesus! He was like shite off a fuckin' shovel!' he guffawed.

'Jimmy Curtis! Sometimes, even I think you're a lost cause!' said a reproving Alice.

'Sorry, missus,' said Jim, covering his mouth with his hand to hold back the giggles.

And so it went on. But when the time came to leave, Jimmy never got the chance to visit and say goodbye. He wrote – more so as he got older – but never once did he mention his job as a soldier. We'll talk about all that when it's done; no need to worry her now, he thought. But it was not to be, for he never saw her again.

Jimmy remembered her always with great affection, knowing he'd remain eternally grateful for all she had done for him. He never knew and nor did she ever tell him why she would have taken to that snotty-nosed little urchin who stole her apples and ran about with the bloody nose or cut lip and bruises and no arse in his trousers. But now he was a man and worldly wise, he knew it was simply compassion … and Jimmy knew all too well that there was always room for that.

A New Start

*"One crowded hour of glorious life
is worth an age without a name".*

Sir Walter Scott

Following young Feany's death, Big Brendan never returned to sea. A month later, the big man was pushing a two-wheeled cart along the road towards the port, with the family's possessions piled on top. Jimmy's mother walked alongside, with Jimmy and Teresa tripping along behind. They were all moving to England – to the City of Liverpool – that's all Jimmy knew. But life was to improve for them all. The seaman's mission in the city had helped Brendan secure a job on the docks and the family were to stay with a relative near Dock Road.

They arrived at their new home two days later and Big Brendan started work almost immediately. Jimmy's mother took a job in a local laundry, which paid 2 pounds 10 shillings per week. Jimmy and his sister started in a mixed Catholic school, but this one was run by teachers and not by priests or nuns, whom Jimmy had come to despise.

In spite of his poor attendance and his behaviour being less than favourable, his level of education improved considerably and he could soon read and write competently. Nevertheless, his inherent free spirit often drove him to choose life away from school and frequently, he would absent himself for several weeks at a time. There were plenty of things to do and Jimmy fully immersed himself in docklands life, learning by the day and often living by his wits.

It was taken for granted that lads from the area would almost certainly end up as seafarers. He accepted this and looked forward, eagerly, to whatever adventures lay ahead. But that was the future; right now, there was skulduggery afoot and he loved it.

Post-war Liverpool was, and still is, a lively place and if you lived along the dock road as Jimmy did, you could see the whole world in a day. Once a great sea port in the days before left-wing trade unionists stirred up so much industrial unrest, the port itself eventually closed as a result of constant strikes and walkouts. Jimmy and his mates often sat down near Mann Island at the pier head, close to what has now become a tourist attraction and home to Granada Television at the Albert Dock, to watch shipping from all corners of the earth queuing up to unload and load their precious cargoes before shipping out to their next destination. It could be anywhere from Kristiansand in Norway to the mysterious Orient. Even as late as the sixties, the world was still a big place and Jimmy's imagination would take him aboard ships en route to Russia or the South Sea Islands.

Seafarers of all nationalities could be seen around the dock road, drinking in bars, fighting in the street, rolling about as drunk as lords, but they always found their way back aboard ship – like fuckin' pigeons, thought Jimmy. Occasionally, Jimmy and his mates would coax one or two to play a game of pitch and toss, bouncing coins off a warehouse wall: nearest was the winner. Sometimes, the kids would grab the money and run like fuck or pick the sailors pockets and be off like a shot.

Jimmy thought he'd robbed a fortune on one occasion. His surreptitious foray into the depths of one drunken sailor's reefer jacket had produced a wad of notes he could hardly carry in one hand. Running like the wind and convinced he'd become a millionaire, he'd galloped breathlessly down alleys, over walls and through yards, until he'd arrived at Huskisson Dock and safety. Climbing through the window of a bombed-out, derelict building, he'd squatted down to count the hoard.

During his great escape, he'd managed to buy three or four sweet shops and several cars, and one of those posh washing tubs for his ma – the leccy ones – and a pair of boots for Big Brendan. But his dreams were dashed and torn asunder when he'd started to count his stash. His fortune, in Chinese Yuan, had turned out to be worth about 15 bob! He fucked and cursed and tore up the notes then, laughing to himself, he thought, ah well, easy come, easy go. Still, it was worth it just for the "great escape".

There was a great sense of community in the area where Jimmy lived, but you had to fight to survive. It was just the nature of things at the time. All disagreements were settled with one's fists; no one ever involved the police. It simply got sorted and life went on as before.

Jimmy once saw a nun roll up her sleeves to take on one of the wives in the street over nothing more than a sarcastic remark about the woman's teenage daughter. They were allowed to slug it out for several minutes, before being separated by the local priest and the woman's husband, who sent both women packing and then proceeded to the local pub to discuss the fighting prowess of both antagonists over several pints of Guinness and whisky chasers.

But there was more to fighting than just fat lips and broken noses. If you knew where to go, you could fight for money. There was no shortage of hard cases around, who were only too happy to fight for beer money; others fought to feed their families and some to find a way to a better life. With purses of £20 for a win, this king's ransom could put them well on the way to that so-called better life. Some men financed a family move to Australia, Canada or the States with the winnings from these fights. Whereas others just liked to fight and true to form, Jimmy's da was one of those men.

He was big and broad-shouldered, with natural strength and power, but best of all, he had a jaw like granite and he could take a belt from the best and yet still go forward. That's how he fought – never attempting to block the blows – he just took them and "it was like hitting a side of beef", one of his opponents had once confided in Jimmy.

'He's a hard man, your da, boy. It'll take someone special to put him away.'

Like the other men, each would strip to the waist and fight bare-chested. There was none of this ten rounds and we'll decide the winner; they just fought toe-to-toe, until one lay on his back, unconscious. They fought without gloves and Jimmy had once watched Big Brendan fight three men, one after the other. He had knocked them all senseless and won £60 plus a £10 bonus. In his day, he was a tough, uncompromising man, who took no prisoners.

The people of the dock area were hard-working, mainly Roman Catholic folk of Irish origin. They knew their place and asked no quarter. They had pride and good hearts and they would give you the shirt off their backs, but cross them at your peril. An assault on their sensibilities was an assault on them all and the perpetrator would pay dearly for that.

A spate of housebreaking caused great concern amongst these poor people, who already had little of any value, apart from the sentimental kind. The eventual ending of the burglaries coincided with the discovery of a very dead body in the local canal. The wife of the deceased, his mother, children and grandfather were hounded out in abject disgrace. Hence, don't shit on your own doorstep. It was a cruel response, but it maintained a sort of status quo in and around the back-to-back terraces of the docks and Scotland Road areas of the city.

The ferries that cross the Mersey from Liverpool to Birkenhead and Wallasey were, and still are, manned by merchant seamen and the boats provide passage from one side to the other for people travelling across to the Wirral or into Liverpool to work in the city or on the docks. The deal was that you hop onto the boat on one side and pay for the journey when you got off on the other. Though, Jimmy and his mates knew that if you were fleet of foot and possessed the stealth and cunning of a hungry fox, you could spend the whole day travelling backwards and forwards without getting off. Great fun for anyone possessed of an adventurous spirit. Jimmy and the boys fervently believed they were fooling everyone. It didn't occur to them for one moment that the men they thought they were fooling had themselves played the same games as kids, and maybe even their fathers before them. No doubt they allowed themselves a wry smile as they were "tricked" by these skilful brigands. Life goes on.

By the time he reached 14 years of age, the school had had enough and he was invited to leave; so he did. His father fixed him up with a job as a deckhand and his first trip to sea was on a tramp ship called *The Mandarin,* which took him away for nineteen months, giving him a chance to see the world and grow up. Jimmy was already old beyond his years when he first set out and "Jimmy the boy" became "Jimmy the man". At least that's what he thought!

Further trips on the ships *The Oxfordshire* and *The Rena del Mar* followed and another eighteen months at sea saw out his three years that he'd promised himself. He signed off, intending to take work on the docks with his father. But Jimmy's move to England had brought him into contact with cousins and uncles he never knew existed. Most were seafarers, but one or two were soldiers and it was one of these – John – who caught his imagination with tales of conflict worldwide, where his regiment, the "Paras", had left their glowing references. And so the decision to become "a man at arms" was made and in January 1971, Jimmy joined the army and moved to Aldershot to become a paratrooper.

It was six hard months later that he joined the 2nd Battalion Parachute Regiment, heralding the start of something different for Jimmy Curtis. Following tours in Northern Ireland, exercises, the routine in the barracks, courses of all sorts, demolitions, signals, fieldcraft, support weapons, sniper cadre's, driving courses, promotional courses and brief periods of R & R or breaks for leave, he was eventually promoted to Lance Corporal – and then, in due course, from Section 2 i/c to Section Commander. A couple of months at the battle school in Brecon, South Wales, combined to fill the first six years in the battalion, which began to mould Jimmy into the type of individual required to soldier in the Paras. He devoured the courses which, in time, gelled together to teach him his craft. He learned quickly and was intensely interested in world affairs – especially anything that involved other countries' armed conflicts around the globe.

He felt, as did many other soldiers, that Northern Ireland was not essentially a job for professional soldiers; or at the least, not the Paras.

After all, the regiment was considered to be the very best of the teeth arms in the best army in the world. So why weren't they being used in conflicts worldwide? The yanks were at it as usual – all over the world.

And whether you like them or not, from a soldier's point of view, wherever there's a scrap, you'll usually find the Americans "doing the business". Curtis admired and respected that, even though the Yanks manufacture many of the world's conflicts themselves (one of the dozen or more security and intelligence agencies found in the USA; for example the CIA being allegedly responsible).

The Belgians were at it in The Congo; the Legion had their war in Chad; there was war in Central and South America and the Rhodesians and South Africans were at it along their borders, also. But not the Brits – what a waste, thought Jimmy. And for all his love of the regiment, he was getting bored. He wanted more – he wanted the real thing – he wanted war.

Curtis knew deep within himself that all the self-praise, all the pats on the back in the boozer extolling the greatness of the British airborne forces, didn't add up to a kick in the bollocks, unless you were killing the fucking enemy! The Paras were, and had been for years, a wasted, valuable asset and as far as he was concerned, that was criminal.

It didn't take him long to decide what had to be done. It seemed simple to him – study the form – pick a war – pack his bags – and go. And that was exactly what he did.

Africa screamed out to him; anarchy reigned supreme. In turn, White minority rule had ended in South Africa and Rhodesia; the Black majority in both lands had taken over power, but had been unable to maintain control. They, in turn, had collapsed and tumbled into chaos, leaving a void filled with feuding and warring factions. White ex-rulers, Black communist groups, Cubans, Russians, freeloading ex-soldiers, even religious zealouts. Criminal organisations with nothing but personal gain on their minds; mini armies run by organised crime.

Then there were others, with their own agendas; and warlords with their own heavily armed militias.

And so it was into this maelstrom that Jimmy Curtis threw himself and by fair means or foul, he found himself working for a faceless force – not Black majority, or overthrown White – but a third and unseen force with its own agenda, which directed operations and which looked after the bill and that suited Curtis just fine. He asked no questions and he fought for two and a half years in return for the opportunity to answer his own questions – to test himself in conflict.

He knew only one thing about his faceless masters – that they were fiercely anti-communist and, as far as Curtis was concerned, that was good enough for him. He wasn't concerned with the great scheme of things or the politics; he went to soldier and that's what he became: a contract soldier, mercenary, soldier of fortune – whatever you cared to call it. Curtis would stand or fall; only time would tell. Jimmy Curtis had crossed the Rubicon!

Curtis continued to mull over time gone by – people, places, operations and Africa. A vision of the setting sun sat in the centre of his conscious mind and he remembered the Dark Continent like a magnet.

He loved Africa and he smiled as he saw his old friend Schollonburg; he even heard his South African accent. Then, crossing the void in his mind, he was back there with him; back with Schollonburg, René Voss, Leo van Rijn, Dick Kaminski and the rest; back under an African sun.

Things That Go Right; Things That Go Wrong

"Have a plan,
Execute it violently,
Do it now!!"

General Douglas McArthur

The problem the PIRA planners were faced with was knowing which route the wages truck would take to get to its destination. Physically stopping the vehicle and then getting its two rear security guards to open the back and hand over the £350,000 cash, they didn't see as a problem, as they already knew the method they would use to achieve that. The problem they were faced with was knowing which of the four routes the vehicle would take after it had left the bank in Belfast with its cargo of wages for the pharmaceutical company. Information regarding pick-up times from the bank, the amount of money on board, the number of guards and even their names had come from a sympathiser who worked as a clerk at the bank.

But the route was chosen by the vehicle commander alone once the money was on board and the vehicle was on its way; a simple method of preventing prior knowledge reaching anyone interested in pre-planning an ambush. The PIRA had been watching the run for a whole year and, on each run, they had carefully tracked the vehicle as it had travelled along each and every course that was available to it; alternating between them but setting no particular pattern. In the end, they decided to place ambush teams on each route at points where the vehicle had no means of making a last-minute change. This way, they would be certain to achieve their aim, whichever route it took.

Tommy McGuire read through his plans once again; his three accomplices listened quietly as he covered each point for the third time.

'Right, boys, it's at this position that the vehicle passes the point of no return.'

He pointed at a place on the OS map, where the road took a 90 degree left turn then, 250 yards on, it passed over a small stone humpback bridge across a culvert. Just before the turn on the left-hand side stood a derelict stone barn.

'This will be your firing point, Seamus!' He moved his weapon slightly as he indicated the spot. 'The device will be in situ here.' He pointed again to the bridge. 'And the command wire will be run along this dry stone wall back around the bend.' He traced the route with a toothpick into the barn, where Seamus Fallon would be positioned.

'You have a clear view of the bridge from here.'

Fallon nodded in agreement.

'Now, this is how it's going to happen.' He pointed again to Fallon to continue.

'Right,' said Fallon. 'I'll be here, watching the bridge from the back window.'

'OK,' acknowledged McGuire. 'What next?' He pointed to the next man, his driver Declan.

'We wait till the target passes the barn and once it negotiates the bend, we pull out of the barn and follow.'

'OK. Next,' he said, pointing to Liam, Declan's brother.

'Right,' said Liam. 'We stop here, just before the bend, and wait for Fallon to blow the bridge before the van can pass. We remain under cover till the dust settles – twenty to thirty seconds – then, round the bend, stopping behind the van, we turn our vehicle around ready for the off.'

'Excellent!' exclaimed McGuire. 'OK. It's at this point we leave our car and approach the rear of the van on foot,' he smiled. 'These guys are going to be shitting themselves by now. Right, you two cover the rear, they won't open up without some persuasion; they're ordered not to and they'll feel safer inside – but not once they see this little beauty.'

He pointed at the 20 lb charge of Semtex already made up and ready to go. 'I'll show the driver this and give them one minute to open up. We've been around long enough now for them to know we mean business. Any questions so far?'

There were none.

'Once they open up,' continued McGuire, 'we'll use them to load the money into our car. Then, the guards go back into the van, we set the charge to detonate two minutes later and that's the end of them! By which time we'll be at least a mile away – high and dry.'

'Very nice.'

'Excellent.'

'Yeah, no problem, McGuire,'

The team congratulated him as he rolled up his map.

'Right, boys, ready to move at 04.00 hours tomorrow. All we have to do is hope they choose our route.'

At 04.00 hours the next morning, as arranged, the ASU made its way through the darkness with Declan behind the wheel. By first light, the group were in situ in the barn ... watching and waiting. If the van chose their route, from their slightly elevated position in the firing point, they would have a clear view of its approach from about three quarters of a mile away. If all went as planned, they could expect it to arrive at 10.00 hours.

They waited – 09.00 hours came and went, whilst 15 miles away at the bank the guards took on their cargo. The commander then signed the docket and they were on their way. The route the commander chose was a rural, narrow, winding road, bordered by blackthorn hedges atop dry stone walls. It was a clear day without a cloud in the sky and Tommy McGuire's heart leapt as he looked across the fields with his binoculars and saw the dark blue Mercedes van on its approach.

'Here she is, boys – get ready.'

They leapt to their feet, picking up their weapons as Fallon grabbed the firing pack and quickly tested the circuit for the dozenth time.

'No problem,' he told himself. He leant his own personal weapon against the wall and shouted a subdued, 'Good luck,' to the others as they made for the car.

The van trundled closer, now only 200 yards away.

McGuire had his weapon beside him, as did the others, and on his lap he carried the 20 lb Semtex charge, with its parkway timer ready to go.

Declan started the car just as the van passed them and approached the bend. As it disappeared from sight, he gunned the engine.

'Good luck, boys!' exclaimed Liam as the car pulled out onto the road.

'We won't need luck once these bastards get a good look at my little persuader,' McGuire said, laughing as he indicated the Adidas grip which housed the bomb.

They covered their ears. Then, came the huge explosion as Fallon pushed the button and the bridge disappeared in a flash. The ground shook and huge granite stones flew in all directions as debris rained down everywhere. The van skidded to a halt, teetering on the edge of the 20-foot crater, which immediately began to fill with water. A huge black cloud billowed skywards, with great sods of earth landing everywhere; the crater smoked and all around, wildlife was stunned into deathly silence.

Tommy, Declan and Liam jumped from their car, which Declan had neatly turned around ready for the getaway. McGuire dashed to the front of the vehicle, his masked face leaving the driver in no doubt as to whom he was dealing with.

He pulled the plywood from his bag; on it, printed clearly, were the words: You have 60 seconds to open up or I detonate this! He held up the bag and pointed.

The man in the driver's seat paused for a moment. Then, looking over his shoulder, he spoke through an intercom to the guards in the rear. Turning back to his tormentor, the driver gave McGuire a nervous thumbs-up.

McGuire nodded and then ran to the rear of the van to join his men. There was a short pause, then a click. The ASU stood confidently at the rear, smiling behind their masks, and then the doors sprang open.

There was a simultaneous burst of automatic fire that was so intense it lifted all three Provos off their feet as dozens of bullets struck home; all three were dead before they hit the ground.

At the barn, Fallon was unable to decipher what was going on, but a sharp "Pssst" from behind him sorted that out. He spun round, coming face-to-face with another masked man, who immediately emptied a full magazine from his MP5 into the terrorist, stitching a line of wounds diagonally from hip to shoulder, ramming him against the wall of the barn. He slid to the floor, already a corpse.

Back at the van, the SAS team were checking the bodies and their commander was confirming that McGuire's bomb was safe. Twenty minutes later, the area was under control of the RUC and a company from the Scots Guards had a cordon in place. The SAS troop was long gone.

The SF had been able to mount a successful operation as a result of excellent intelligence and the tracking device on Eaimon Blaire's weapons, which had been inserted under the butt plate of McGuire's weapon whilst it was still in the hide at the stone farmhouse that Jimmy Curtis had been watching, south of Forkhill.

From that moment on, the location of the weapons and anything that was said within 20 foot of them was broadcast directly to intelligence; the operation to nail the would-be robbers was mounted accordingly. Arrangements were made by SB to swap the SAS team vehicle with the official guards' en route. The rest was history. PIRAs pain was clear and it lay in the road and in the barn for all to see. Sometimes, however, it went right for PIRA and the roles were reversed – it was the nature of the beast.

It was the end of the road for McGuire's ASU and their murderous activities along the border. And for Jimmy Curtis, there was a tremendous amount of satisfaction in that. But the fight went on and Jimmy would continue to play his part.

Beginnings

A little gain, a little pain,
A laugh, lest you may moan;
A little blame, a little flame,
A Star Gleam on a stone

Robert Service; *Just Think*

Round-faced, with grey humourless, piggy eyes, her hair was snatched back forming a neat, round bun contained in a tight net. She was 5 feet 4 inches tall, dressed in a flower-patterned dress, worn beneath a grey buttoned-up, cable-stitched cardigan. A neat white starched, collared shirt was held closed at the neck with a silver butterfly brooch, which had small rubies adorning its wings. She wore thick brown woollen tights and sensible, highly polished, flat-soled shoes; all this contained a rotund body and she looked for the world like a primary school headmistress. She chain-smoked stumpy Hamlet cigars, which had stained her oversized teeth yellowy-brown over the years.

A couple of her assistants were hard-looking men in their forties, who wouldn't have looked out of place behind a plough and horses. The third, a more studious-looking individual, was sat taking notes slightly behind and to the right of Roisin Rafferty, who was sat bolt upright, tied to the wooden chair by her ankles, thighs and wrists; the latter of which were pulled behind her back and secured by half-inch leather strips, which had been soaked in water.

They had been in place for eleven hours now and Roisin's hands had turned blue; indeed, her fingers had taken on the appearance of grotesque, discoloured sausages. Another strip of leather, knotted every 2 inches, had also been soaked in water and was tied like a bandanna around Roisin's shaven head. She was completely naked and the heat produced by her body had the effect of drying the leather and as it did so, it tightened as it shrank. Her head felt ready to explode and in her pain-induced delirium, she prayed that it would.

Roisin had long since told her tormentors what they wanted to hear, but her prolonged agony served only to satisfy a desire to inflict suffering. Cigar smoke hung in the air and it was raining outside. A black-and-white TV flickered in the corner of the room; the weatherman talked of strong winds and rain across the province ... and the disappearance of a 16-year-old girl from Drumintee in South Armagh.

'That's it, then; this wee bitch has said all she's going to say.'

The headmistress' voice was matter-of-fact. She stared coldly at Roisin. The girl's naked body silently heaved and shook, blood pooling at her feet on the plastic sheet, placed there for this purpose. In the blood were her severed toes, which had been removed by the headmistress using tin snips. Her face was battered, bruised and swollen; both lips were split and her top front teeth had been snapped off at the gum. Her knees were swollen to twice the norm as a result of the Black & Decker drill used to destroy her knee caps and leg joints, which had served to successfully encourage her eventual complete cooperation.

She had ranted of her three-year career as a SB informer, touting on her people, the organisation and its volunteers. Although she was not a member, her tiny snippets of info, which she duly passed to her SB handler, had served, along with many other source snippets, as random pieces in the intelligence jigsaw. Alone, seemingly meaningless, but together, producing a great panorama in the world of agents, double agents, handlers and field operators. That is how it worked; each side watching the other in its endless quest for answers. One of Roisin's answers had described her evening in Drumintee with her boyfriend Eaimon Blaire and his "declaration of intent" regarding the weapons.

She had teased him about it, saying he was only a boy and not tough enough for the world of the Provos, in the end declaring her feigned disbelief of his story. Instead, she was seeing pound signs rolling around in her head as she'd made a mental note of every detail.

Curiously and unexpectedly, she talked of her relationship with one Joe McKenna and his extra-curricular siphoning off of black cab funds in Belfast. Funds which belonged to the movement no less.

Treachery, thought the headmistress, we'll be looking into that in due course!

Roisin's information was passed on by means of a dead-letter-box system of communication to her handler and she, in turn, received payment. The better the quality of the information, the higher the price.

Every detail of her confession was meticulously noted by the studious man and would reach the Provos' chain of command, along with the headmistress' recommendations. Roisin herself had, of course, served her purpose and would receive the summary justice reserved for all touts – a bullet in the head.

The headmistress took a long draw on her latest half-smoked cigar. She leaned forward and in a surprisingly gentle voice, close to Roisin's ear, she said, 'There, there, love. No more pain; no more pain, Roisin. It's over now,' she lied. Roisin's head lolled back and she coughed out another sob.

Still bending forward over the girl, the headmistress took another long draw on the cigar, smiled a warm smile, blew away the grey ash and stubbed the red hot ember into Roisin's half-open eye. It fizzed, and then popped; the girl stiffened and then blacked out.

The IO who had spotted Eaimon Blaire's potential had been sent to pick him up and deliver him to a volunteers house in the village of Meigh, where he was ushered into the kitchen and was quickly made aware of Roisin's treachery. No holds would be barred. He'd be made to see the damage she'd done and the terrible threat which vermin like her posed to the cause; the only way to deal with vermin was to trap and kill them.

Blaire was mortified, but the deal was this: Blaire's way into the movement – into his dream – was clear. He – Eaimon Blaire – would hood and shoot the wee bitch, to show his commitment. He would kill Roisin – his girl – the informer, the traitor.

They told him how they knew he'd talked, telling him that they'd put it down to his inexperience.

'We understand, Blaire; just do this job and we'll put it all behind us. Then you'll be able to call yourself a Provo volunteer – you'll be one of us.'

Blaire nodded, his mind in turmoil; the next few seconds were a blur because there, in the front room of the house, sat Roisin. Blaire hadn't realised she'd be there, in that very house. As he was ushered into the room, he stopped dead. Shock and surprise overwhelmed him, but he was pushed hard in the back, which took him a further two steps inside. His mind was racing to make sense of the scene which now confronted him.

'Here's the wee bitch, Blaire. She'd be the one to tout on you, to get you lifted and to throw you to the SAS, the Det or SB.'

Then, a weapon was pressed into his hand from behind and, close to his ear now and full of malevolence, he heard the voice again.

'It's ready, Blaire. Just do it. Do it! Point and fire. Do it, lad. Do it now!'

Blaire did. Some invisible force made him raise a trembling arm and, clutching the 38 – pausing – he fired.

Roisin's head was snatched back in a spray of blood and bone. A moment later, the second shot rang out. But this time from behind the boy and the body of Eaimon Blaire was thrown forwards by the impact of the bullet, which struck him in the back of the neck. His corpse fell in a heap at the feet of Roisin, his girl.

The headmistress lowered the weapon. It was number eighteen for her; eighteen executions and she'd relished every one! The television flickered in the corner of the room, *Onward Christian Soldiers* rang out; *Songs of Praise* had just begun.

'That's it; job's done then!'

She peeled the rubber gloves from her hands and dropped them onto the pile of severed toes in the blood and urine on the plastic sheet.

The studious man gathered his notes as the two bodyguards wrapped the bodies of Roisin and Blaire in the plastic sheet; one made a brief call, arranging the clean-up of the room, and the other arranged the removal of the corpses for disposal. Then, with the headmistress in the lead, the four left, pausing in the doorway just long enough to check the street.

It was deserted outside, except for three small girls, who laughed and giggled as they played hopscotch on the pavement. The headmistress smiled and patted one on the head as she made her way to the car.

'Careful now, and don't stay out late. It's not safe,' she said.

She carried a briefcase, held close to her chest. Then all four were in the car and away. She sat in the front passenger seat, drumming her fingers on her knee, content in the knowledge that the interrogation of the girl had, indeed, been fruitful. Roisin had sprung into the limelight several months ago when her IO cousin had become more and more suspicious of the girl's regular and increasingly extravagant spending sprees on her shopping trips to Dundalk and Belfast. That in itself wouldn't normally draw any unwarranted attention, but considering she was an unemployed country girl with no visible means of income, her cousin had decided he simply had to ask himself the question: how was she was doing it?

His position as IO in the organisation, combined with his naturally inquisitive nature, led him to take the next step. Involving several trusted volunteers working on a round-the-clock surveillance operation in search of the answer, Roisin had eventually been seen on three separate occasions, visiting her dead letter box in Bog Lane, Jonesborough. On the third occasion, after she had visited the spot, a volunteer had lifted the lid on the buried milk churn, revealing a folded plastic bag containing an envelope, inside which were details of low-level PIRA activity for her handler. It was photographed and returned to the churn by the volunteer. The copy was then forwarded, by secret means, for scrutiny. From that moment, her fate was sealed and so, eventually, was Eaimon Blaire's, along with Joe McKenna's.

She'd been taken by four hooded men as she'd walked home from church on a Sunday morning; thirteen hours later, she was dead, along with Blaire. McKenna, too, had been fingered and arrangements were made to deal with him in the most beneficial way.

The clock was ticking and the security group still had work to do. Pillow talk between Roisin and her boyfriend and McKenna, with the bottomless wallet, had been their downfall. He'd told her about the black cab scam and his friend Brinton's involvement and she, in turn, had told the security team. She'd also given details about the passage of weapons at the farmhouse, which she'd sold to her SB handler, thus enabling SF to plan and mount an operation to "iron out" the PIRA plan for the weapons.

The result would be an interesting journey for both Brinton and McKenna. But that could wait for now. The fate of these two may well fall into the headmistress's hands. She, alone, knew of the imminent changes regarding her own position and she would relish the opportunity to decide their future.

Greed had become the architect of McKenna's demise. His own involvement in the black cab scam didn't end there. There were other things as well: the skimming-off of the takings from their illegal drinking dens, like the green hut in the Ardoyne; and protection money from shops and businesses in his domain, where he'd taken his cut and did very nicely, thank you; but now, unknown to him, the cat was out of the bag. His friendship with the girl, Roisin, the informer, also guaranteed his "guilt by association" as fellow informer.

Soon after, both he and Brinton were summoned to a meeting in the Free State. This was normal procedure for men in their position and whilst the day drew near, arrangements were made for their journey.

Rememberings

Just think! some night the stars will gleam
Upon a cold, grey stone,
And trace a name with silver beam,
And Lo! 'twill be your own.

Robert Service; *Just Think*

Having updated his chuff chart, he lay back on his bed. The ceiling fan in Curtis' room spun slowly; hypnotically, he watched it turn. His belt order hung by the shoulder straps over the end of his metal bed and a large black 58-pattern mug of freshly brewed tea steamed on his metal bedside locker. Below his bed were two pairs of non-regulation boots.

Above him, on the wall – close enough to touch – hung his weapon on a home-made rack. On the shelf on his bedside locker, stacked neatly, one on top of the other, were four empty magazines. He'd just finished transferring the rounds into the four full mags stacked next to the empties, a practice which he'd employed each time he'd returned from an OP. This practice rested the magazine springs and ensured that they retained the capability to feed rounds from the mag up into the breech; the first of which was always a tracer, for target indication, followed by five armour piercing. Then the rest; 7.62 ball.

The familiar odours of cheeseburgers and fried onions from the Chogi Shop mixed with the smell of gun oil hung in the air. His equipment was prepared for a quick move and it was sleepy-time for Curtis. In his mind, he travelled through time, sifting through the moving pictures thrown up by his subconscious: people, places and things he'd seen. His training had been hard, relentless, compassionless and selective.

Then there was his parachute training at RAF Abingdon, which was very laid back; very civilised and very professional. Jumping from the balloon, he heard the words of the dispatcher echoing in his head, 'Up eight hundred, four men jumping'. Then, 'Step forward number one into the door of the cage,' followed by the command, 'Go!' Day and night, he'd made jumps from the C130 Hercules transport aircraft, receiving his wings on completion of the eighth jump at Weston-on-the-Green DZ. Their wings had been handed to them by some middle-ranking RAF bloke; no fuss, took about five minutes, then it was on the wagon and back to camp.

He grinned. The fucking Yanks would have had bands and drums, music and crowds, and some steely-eyed general with a strong handshake telling them how well they'd done. Not us though – not the Brits – we were altogether more subdued; no big deal. What a contrast – and Jim liked it!

His thoughts wandered: a funeral of a friend – one of many; but he shut it away. Then his thoughts strayed to his training again: all that work, time, money, all his ability and nothing but police action and internal security. What a waste, thought Curtis. Fuckin' lamentable! He wasn't the only one. Many left the Paras through feeling wasted.

Then there was the school in Ireland: the priests, the nuns and the regular beatings. More and more memories raised their ugly heads: with beatings from Father Daly, who didn't like Jimmy – the contemptible, defiant and uncontrollable Little Jimmy with his cripple friend. He had often been beaten by him; then beaten again by Big Brendan, his Da, for being caught in the first place. All his formative years loomed large in Jim's memory.

He found work in the province in general quite boring these days. Maybe he'd have a shot at something more specialised? Maybe even the SAS selection or the Det, perhaps. The Green Army had far too many restrictions placed on it now. He decided that what he was doing now was really a job for the police and he was a soldier. It was mind-numbing: the endless patrols, VCPs, police checks and guard duties, followed by more patrols ... routine, routine, routine. The early tours were by far the best; 1971, '72 and '73, operation motorman, internment, lots to do and a far better chance of a kill.

Contact with the enemy was, indeed, rare these days. A more professionally rearranged PIRA had seen to that with the four-man cell system, giving it an infinitely more secure structure; unlike the early days in the Campaign, when every man and his dog carried an Armalite and used it. All this, against the backdrop of huge riots and civil unrest, which went on for days and weeks at a time, involving thousands of people. By 1972 alone, he remembered that there had been over 10,000 shootings and 1,400 bombings; most of which were in Belfast and Londonderry alone. A huge fucking mess, but worth it, he remembered. Plenty to keep them occupied. Enemy action by '72 had claimed 467 lives.

He thought about his childhood in the Free State. What a fucking performance that was. Nearly as wild as 1972 in the north, he smiled.

There had been bombs in the Free State when he was young; like when the boyos blew up Nelson's Column in Phoenix Park, Dublin. But all in all, his childhood had been terrorist free. He'd had the Church and school to contend with instead back then. Although both organisations played a large part in his life, there had always been time for his favourite occupation of getting up to no good with his best mate Billy Feany. Curtis smiled warmly, remembering his little mate.

Billy Feany was funny as fuck and at 7 years of age, his inspirational leadership in the field of arch skulduggery was unsurpassed in the area. He was a constant source of amusement to Jimmy, who only had to look at the lad to burst into hysterical laughter.

Young Billy had a lazy eye as well as a duff leg. The effect was that whenever he looked at someone, he had to turn his head to the left to get a good view and when he did so, for some unknown reason, he always opened his gob and grinned. Some people found this infuriating in the extreme and if Billy didn't like the individual he was speaking to, he would over exaggerate the act – just to wind them up.

When he spoke, he did so at great speed, which added to the difficulty many had in understanding him. Jimmy, on the other hand, had no problem at all, because they'd spent so much time together. But an exchange of words between young Feany and most adults would result in the said grown-up responding with a blank look to one of Billy's replies or statements. This, in turn, would have to be translated by Jimmy in order to achieve any level of success in the field of human communication.

It was just as well, because Billy, being the hard-faced little twat that he was, often squeezed the odd profanity into his statements or replies. But he did so at such speed that it was obvious by the recipient's expression that they thought they'd heard "I'm very well thank you, Mrs Fat Twat O'Riley", but couldn't be at all certain if their ears were playing tricks; especially when they had to contend with the distraction of Feany's seriously wandering eye and a grin like the village idiot. So, by the time they'd decided which to believe, young Feany and young Curtis would be long gone, pissing themselves with laughter as they went.

It was following one notable conversation with Mr Carson, a gentleman of the Protestant persuasion, that Billy had decided that a degree of retribution was in order. Having experienced several of Billy's oratories in the past and having grave suspicions about the content, Carson had decided that just in case his own suspicions had been correct about the veiled abuse in Billy's replies, he'd give Billy a smack in the chops. He'd delivered this with a rolled-up newspaper, landing several sharp blows to young Billy's head and body with severe intent, pointing out to the lad that he was a cheeky wee shite who probably didn't know his own father.

'Ahh, ya fuckin' auld fucker! I'll tell me da!' was Billy's reply; knowing full well that he wouldn't, as the result would be further abuse.

So they'd made good their escape, with young Curtis laughing like an eejit and young Feany rubbing his ears and promising all forms of revenge, which included the murder of Carson, his family and anyone he'd ever known. The desire for revenge at any cost burned like a naked flame in the heart of Feany and so he schemed and planned for weeks to get back at "that auld fucker, Carson".

In the end, he came to Jimmy with his plan of attack, a grin a mile and a half wide and two buckets of paint: one orange and the other green. The operation was to go ahead that very night and Jimmy's job was to act as lookout at the county showground, which was set up for its annual display which was due to start the following morning.

The annual county fair was a grand event that drew people from miles around to feast and drink and watch the local breeders show pedigree animals of all types and breeds. There were ducks, pigeons, geese, dogs, cats, cows, donkeys, sheep, goats, rabbits and more. Flowers were shown in abundance and one huge marquee was given over to food alone – rich pickings to be had for the bold Jimmy and Billy!

The larger animals drew most attention from the crowds, as they were shown in the various fenced compounds as the owners looked on, awaiting the judge's decision. Much valuable silverware could be won, with extra monetary prizes to be had. But the best prize of all in the countryside community was "prestige". To be acknowledged as one who "knew his beasts" was praise indeed, and most sought this above all other rewards. To fail or to produce a "duffer" for show could, and occasionally did, result in years spent in the stock and poultry wilderness, in which snide comments in the bar or barely concealed giggles at jokes made at one's expense could be heard. And whilst meaning little to the outsider, it meant everything to the show-people.

Young Curtis performed his job as lookout the night before the show as young Feany limped into the darkness of the tentage, stabling and stalls with his buckets of paint. He returned a good forty-five minutes later with a triumphant look on his face; but try as he may, Jimmy couldn't prise out of his friend what he'd done. 'You'll see in the morning, Jimmy,' was all he would divulge.

The morning came, heralded by a clear blue sky and a bright, warm sun. Crowds gathered and the atmosphere grew. The smell of cooking and livestock mingled with chatter and laughter. Winners and losers of various categories and breeds began to be announced and as the day approached noon, an announcement that the goat show was about to begin was heard.

Mr Carson, Feany's "best mate", stood proudly to one side, confident he would take the title as he had done for the past four years. Yes, he was, indeed, a giant in the world of the goat breeder and he bristled with pride and arrogance as he waited, thumbs hooked into his waistcoat pockets, for the foregone conclusion to be announced. Several animals were walked through the pen to words of approval, or not, from the watching crowd, which had now grown to a mass.

Then, off to the left of the entrance to the pen, came the announcement that the goat now showing was a 3-year-old Nubian, bred by Harold Carson, last year's winner. The crowd brimmed with anticipation. Carson seemed to inflate as his ego worked overtime. But then the announcement was cut short by a cough and a snort down the loudspeaker, which was followed by a buzz from the crowd, giggles, derogatory statements and roars of laughter as Gwendoline, the prize Nubian goat, was led into the ring for all to see. Resplendent in her new colours of green, white and orange stripes – the colours of the flag of Southern Ireland and "Feany's Revenge".

There was no sign of Carson's ego, now the colour of a beetroot, as veins stuck out in his bulging neck, his eyes widened and blinked, his mouth opened and closed, but nothing came out. He turned on his heel and bowled his way through the crowd in abject rage; then, tripping over a horse trough, he was reduced to a laughing stock as he disappeared from sight, ignominious.

Doing the Business

For it's Tommy this an' Tommy that, an' "Chuck him out, the brute!"
But it's "Saviour of 'is country" when the guns begin to shoot; [...]

Rudyard Kipling; *Tommy*

The big man was delivering a set of orders for an assault on the enemy training camp. Jimmy Curtis' old unit had no name; it existed to fight a war of attrition in the enemy's backyard: it was mercenary and its faceless gold and diamond-rich masters paid the bills. Curtis would have done it for free – his preferred currency was war.

In the aftermath of the collapse of both Black and White governments, Curtis fought its war in the explosive void which remained; its enemy was anyone who perpetrated the violence for whatever reason, but especially in the name of communism. Therefore, the assumption amongst the men was that it was sponsored by the White government in exile, or by a third force. Its assumed intent was to regain power. In the meantime though, its primary aim must be to quell the anarchy.

Curtis' group was company strength; its commanders and SNCOs were South African and Rhodesian. Other ranks were a cross-section of nationalities: Brits, Portuguese, some German, French, Belgian, a couple of Croats, even a couple of Poles. Schollonburg's orders followed the standard British Army format for a deliberate attack on an enemy location. The detailed tasks paragraph indicated that Curtis would accompany Schollonburg plus one to carry out a final CTR, to confirm that all was as expected prior to the assault.

The company, having been inserted by several helis, went to ground in its various platoon formations and waited in silence, allowing the surrounding nature to return to normal. Eventually, crickets and cicadas began to chirp and buzz again and the soldiers' night-vision adjusted to the darkness.

After a brief, O Group, with the Coy HQ element, and the platoon commanders returned to their platoons which had been left under command of platoon sergeants. In turn, the platoon commanders reaffirmed with the section commanders that there had been no change to the overall plan and that they would move off in five minutes time heading NW to begin the 10-mile approach to the LUP.

It was decided that One Platoons would lead, with coy HQ to the centre rear, and Two and Three Platoon behind left and right; the point section, led by a pair of Black Rhodesian trackers, moved off with the main body following on. Communication was by hand-signals only with the unit maintaining radio silence. It took the unit five hours to cover the distance to the LUP. The soldiers, all seasoned professionals, moved like wraiths through the bush, silently scanning the terrain for any sign of threat from the enemy force as they pressed on regardless.

Some 800 yards from the main enemy camp, the trackers picked up the ground sign; it was clearly a much-used route both into and out of the camp. Boot prints and tyre tracks of all types marked the way. Suddenly, an engine spluttered into life from the direction of the camp and almost immediately, headlights began to approach along the track. The Land Rover contained a driver and a front-seat passenger, dressed in the same garb. Jim Curtis moved quickly but carefully forwards with the remaining members of the point section. A rapid decision was required in order to silently remove the threat, using crossbows.

Back in the vehicle, the occupants were careless. They felt safe, far away from any perceived threat, and they spoke loudly to each other over the sound of the engine as they crawled along the rutted track. Curtis carried one bow, the Belgian, René Voss, sported the second. The men had only seconds to issue QBOs, make the weapons ready, take up fire position and engage the enemy from the cover of some scrub at the side of the road.

Voss fired first from a range of less than 30 feet. The bolt from the bow covered the distance in a flash, and, entering the driver's left eye, it travelled upwards through the man's brain, exiting through the top of his skull and disappearing into the wilderness. Curtis fired a second later – the bolt striking the passenger above the left ear. The man slumped sideways, head in the driver's lap – the driver remained upright, still clutching the steering wheel as the vehicle ground to a halt, engine still running.

The trackers leapt forwards, dragging the two men from the vehicle and bundling them into the back. The driver made posturing movements as head-injured people often do whilst the brain fights to overcome irreversible damage. Then one of the trackers grabbed him roughly by the hair and, twisting the man's head so as to expose the nape of his neck, he drew a blade from his belt order and placed the tip against the man's neck – just below the base of the skull – and rammed it home, severing the spinal cord. The man joined his friend in death.

Already, others were cutting scrub and the vehicle was pushed some 50 yards off the track and was camouflaged. The whole episode had taken less than fifteen minutes and the unit was ready again. The track became an axis and followed an almost straight line into the camp, which was rectangular in shape. The entrance, at the 6 o'clock position, was manned by two guards carrying shouldered AKs. They stood inside a small bunker constructed from 50-gallon oil drums, ammo boxes and timber – a wooden barrier barring the entrance. An unstable single-storey tin guardhouse stood adjacent to the bunker. The perimeter of the camp was made up of accommodation buildings, similar in construction to the guardhouse. There were four on either side and in the 12 o'clock position in the rectangle stood a slightly more elaborate building, which doubled as HQ and accommodation for the officers, the obligatory "Soviet advisers" and mercenaries. On each corner of the camp stood sentry posts; the centre of the site was open, bare earth. In front of the HQ buildings stood a flagpole made from a long, slim tree trunk that had been stripped of its bark and painted in stripes of green and red; at the top of the pole hung the green and red flag – limp in the still night air.

The sound of muffled voices came from the accommodation buildings and the unmistakable sound of a conversation in Russian came from inside HQ, accompanied by the clink of glasses, guffaws of laughter and the sobs of a young girl.

The night sky was inky black, studded with a myriad of stars. The air was cool and all seemed well in the world of the enemy. The company commander had confirmed that the area around the earlier ambush site would become the LUP and the men went firm in all-round defence.

After a short time, the fire support teams moved off to prearranged positions comprising two MMG teams and two mortar teams. The mortars moved off together and set up to the SE of the target and the MMGs moved to a small hillock some 250 yards to the SW.

In the meantime, one section, the two trackers – now dressed in the uniforms of the dead enemy from the ambush – the ex-Belgian Para Commando René Voss, Jim Curtis and two ex-RLI soldiers, Chris Schollonburg and Leo van Rijn, prepared for their next task.

The recce team all spoke good English and had worked together for many months. The trackers carried the crossbows, which were folded down and slung over their backs, plus a Belgian FN and four grenades; as did the rest of the section. In addition, Curtis carried two smokes and the Rhodesians carried two WP each. They all carried six fully charged magazines in their fighting order, plus one on their personal weapon.

Slung across each man's back was a 66 mm LAW and 9 mm side arms carried in shoulder holsters completed the armoury. All weapons were made ready and safety catches applied. Schollonburg commanded the section and although their task was reconnaissance, they were ready to fight if necessary.

Schollonburg issued a brief based on air photos and the model created from personal model kits carried by the NCOs. String, ribbon of differing colours, small wooden blocks and coloured plastic discs all combined to show tracks, bushes, buildings, obstacles, routes in and out, etc. Terrain was created with mounds of soil and sand, with grass and leaves indicating areas of bush. The model was about 5 feet by 4 feet and it represented a 3D image of a map. A north pointer in the top left-hand corner provided orientation and a scale marker at the bottom right indicated size.

The plan was simple and the team would approach the threat from the south, stopping at the FRV about 150 yards from the target. Here, Voss, one tracker and Van rijn would go firm to provide a base of fire. The bush began to thin out considerably here, so movement became quite restricted. They did, however, find good cover in a dry water course, which afforded them a clear view of the south side and of the entrance to the camp. From here, they could, if required, provide fire support for the other half section in the event of contact or compromise on the target.

The rest of the team, one tracker, Curtis and Schollonburg, would box the target, gathering all the relevant information as they moved around: enemy strength, morale attitudes, equipment, weapons, sentries, stag changes, camp cleanliness and tidiness, whether or not the enemy appeared disciplined and much more. Previously unknown obstacles, new constructions and perceived ability to respond to attack all combined to present a view of the task in hand.

It was 23.00 hours when the recce began the box, noting first the size of the camp at 250 yards long by 100 yards wide. Apart from the two guards on the front gate, plus fixed sentry posts with one sentry in each, there was just one roving sentry, who wandered at will throughout the camp, smoking and occasionally stopping at accommodation blocks to chat to his friends. He carried an AK47 and wore a belt around his combat jacket with one ammo pouch and a water bottle. His clothing was camouflaged and bore origins of France and was topped off with a floppy hat.

The recce took three and a half hours and once satisfied, Schollonburg and the rest of his team returned to the FRV, picking up his fire support team and moving back to the company at the LUP.

Virtually everything had been as expected, with one exception. Schollonburg had noted the presence of a helicopter on a recently installed helipad to the north/rear of the HQ.

On arrival at the LUP, the Coy commanders received all the relevant information from Schollonburg and his team and then briefed the company accordingly, tasking platoons; One Platoon would assault forward left, Two Platoon forward right. They were to sweep through the camp from south to north, clearing the buildings as they went using SA fire and grenades. Then Three Platoon, less One Section, were to bring up the rear. Coy HQ would stay central; One Section were responsible for the HQ building. Prisoners were not an issue – none would be taken – the unit was to fight through the position, killing as they went.

The LOE was 50 yards north of the HQ buildings and it was here that they would reorganise and elements would move back through the camp, confirming all the enemy present to be dead as they went. Once this had been achieved, all buildings would be destroyed, along with any militaria in situ.

The assault began at first light. It was preceded by a deception barrage of smoke from the mortar fire support team dropping rounds to the north of the camp. As the company began its attack from the south, the MMGs engaged targets at will. The smoke in the north had the effect of drawing the attention of the enemy towards that direction. Half-naked men ran from the huts and were immediately cut down by small-arms fire and buildings were cleared in quick time. But it wasn't all one-sided, for One Section lost two men dead during the assault on the HQ building.

Curtis found himself with nothing to fire at not fifteen minutes into the assault. Having cleared the last hut on the western side of the camp, he dropped to one knee and watched One Section enter HQ. Shots rang out and grenades exploded as he noted the background sound of the helicopter starting up. He heard shouts in Russian and Portuguese; then, suddenly, out of the side window of HQ, a child of about twelve was projected – hands tied in front of her. Almost immediately, she was joined by the rolling figure of a Russian, dressed in Soviet combat kit; his dive and forwards roll brought him up next to the girl. Curtis fired. The man yelped, a round drilling through his right leg just above the knee, but still he didn't stop; he roughly grabbed the child's tied wrists and, swinging her around his back, arms looped around his neck, he half ran, half stumbled towards the chopper. With the child like a human rucksack, shielding him from the fire, they both disappeared out of sight.

Curtis could not pursue as he would have infringed on One Section's assault, so he waited. The shooting was sporadic now and he registered the change in the heli engine noise and knew it had taken off. For several seconds, the sound of the disappearing heli faded and then, just as quickly, it returned. Flying fast at about 50 feet, it appeared before him, moving due south above the camp – too fast to engage. Curtis could see the laughing face of the Russian through the open side door of the craft and, perched in the doorway in front of him, was the girl. Curtis' mind, working in double-speed now, took in the scene.

Then, suddenly, the child was falling; tumbling. There was a thin, high-pitched squeal as the human projectile, legs flailing, hurtled towards the ground; the Russian had pushed her out. She hit the flagpole about three quarters of the way up and there was a sickening thud as the child's torso separated into two distinctive parts, the pole snapping beneath her weight. She hit the ground not 20 yards from Curtis. Hands still tied, her legs continued to kick for three or four seconds; then she was still.

The shooting had stopped and the sound of the heli had faded to nothing, but the laughing face of the Russian didn't. It remained, burnt into Curtis' memory like a brand; he would remember it always – even when he tried to forget.

The attack left thirty-four enemy dead. All were piled in the centre of the camp and burnt. The buildings, too, were put to the torch. Weapons, ammo, explosives and equipment were piled together and destroyed with explosives. As the company withdrew, the men filed past a small grave marked with a wooden cross, marking the resting place of the dead child – their one concession to humanity.

The men passed out of the camp, through the only standing structure left. The entrance barrier stood untouched and sitting as if watching on the flat top of an oil drum stood the severed heads of the two enemy sentries – lifeless eyes staring out, seeing nothing. Both trackers had had family members murdered in insurgent attacks and it was the trackers who had visited the sentries.

Curtis looked at the grizzly sight. His face registered no emotion as he spoke quietly to himself.

'Dulce et Decorum est Pro Patria Mori.' Providing you're not the one doing it, of course.

They continued their walk south to the PUP. Many of the men wore beards, haircuts were non-regulation and clothing was loosely similar: camouflaged shirts and trousers with combat boots. Fighting order consisted mainly of a belt with two or three water bottles, two ammo pouches and a utility pouch with a survival kit. Escape kits were, in most cases, secreted in their clothing. All carried knives in sheaths and a Swiss Army utility knife was also a useful tool. Every man carried a prismatic compass plus a Silva.

The company continued its march south. Night drew in and the setting sun dipped behind the rolling hills. All that remained in the distance to mark the company's visit to the enemy camp was a column of spiralling smoke, climbing high into the African sky, pointing like a huge grey-brown finger towards the heavens.

The night cloaked the land in a great veil of darkness, but the men pressed on and sections alternated at the point of the company to lead the group. Soon, it was the turn of Schollonburg's team to move up front, ready to move off. Their preferred formation for moving through the bush country was to have the two Rhodesian trackers up front, with the point man looking for signs as well as leading the way.

He carried a short-barrelled, pump-action shotgun – the preferred weapon for all point men working in close country, which suited the "shoot and scoot" tactics employed by the men at that time. An area weapon, it provided a greater chance of nailing the enemy with an instinct shot in a head-on contact. Then came the point man's cover man, then Curtis covering left flank, followed by Voss, right, Van rijn, left and the tail end Charlie was Schollonburg, the section commander, right and rear. The formation was what they termed as "tight and prickly" and it provided good all-round defence both on the move or static and it gave them the best chance to fight their way out of a contact if necessary.

About 5 to 10 yards separated the men in the section, depending on the bush, and they moved about 50 yards ahead of the main body. Contact between the sections was by hand signals and, as usual, radio silence was maintained until things went "noisy".

However, that night there would be no shooting to split the shroud of darkness. They moved on, always watching, listening and feeling their instincts. Their destination was an LUP in a shallow ravine that ran across a low embankment in the centre of a river, which ran either side of the feature, creating a natural moat and an ideal defensive position.

The embankment, although low, was still slightly elevated and it provided an excellent 360-degree view of the surrounding terrain. The ravine, no more than 20 feet at its deepest, sported graduated sides, which enabled lookouts to attain ideal OPs without exposing themselves to any interested parties. Scrub topped the gully, providing more natural camouflage.

The team, marching on compass bearing, aimed off to hit the river about half a mile south of their objective, intending to enter the river and then turn left and wade, chest-deep, along the water course to the LUP.

It was at a point 100 yards from the river that the point man stopped the section and gave the hand signal to say that he and his cover man were about to move forward to recce the riverbank. The section closed up and moved slowly forward towards the scrub at the edge of the river; there were about one and a half hours left till daylight. The section stopped again and the point man and his cover began the last tentative moves to the river's edge.

The point man took two steps into the head-high, thorny scrub and half-turned towards his cover man, gesturing downwards to a huge, steaming pile of dung. The cover man acknowledged with a nod and the bush exploded in a huge bellowing, snorting roar of lethal aggression as through the undergrowth, like a runaway train, crashed a massive Cape buffalo, head-down, filling the world with its murderous intent. It hit the point man square in the chest, ramming him backwards against a tree; the trunk of which snapped asunder, killing the man outright.

Continuing out of sight through the scrub in a cloud of dust and sand, stamping and snorting its half a ton, it disappeared; then, silence. Second's ticked by. Curtis stood, riveted to the ground; the beast had passed within 3 feet of him on its lethal charge.

Voss responded first, running to the aid of the tracker; but it was too late. The full weight of the beast behind its 4-inch-thick skull had shattered the man's frail chest and innards; he was stone-cold dead. Blood welled up in his mouth and poured onto the sand.

Voss turned to Curtis and asked, 'How do you like your buffalo?'

Stifling a grin, Curtis replied, 'Rare!'

The whole incident had lasted no more than ten seconds, but the loss of the tracker was a blow to the unit. He was a valuable, talented and experienced operator with a wealth of knowledge and bush skills; but it highlighted once again, to everyone in the team, that the dangers of operating in Africa don't just come in the human variety.

The tracker's body was put into a waterproof Bivvy bag and floated along the river to the LUP. The remainder of the journey was uneventful and the company was met at the LUP by a four-man Special Forces team from the Rhodesian regular army.

They had secured the RV the night before and they'd brought in reports and details of tasks and targets for the company to hit over the following weeks. How and when, would be decided by the OC and in the meantime, the Company would enjoy a well-earned rest in the relative safety of the ravine.

'Jim ... Jim ... Jim. Wake up. Time for scoff.'

He rubbed his eyes and sat up on his bed. 'What time is it?' he asked his fellow operator Billy Martin.

'Twenty past seven. You've been asleep for eighteen hours, you lazy git. Come on, let's get breakfast – then the boss wants to speak to the team.'

Curtis quickly washed, cleaned his teeth, picked up his G3 and walked to the Portakabin, which contained the cookhouse. Bacon, eggs, fried bread, mushrooms, tomatoes and toast; all washed down with three black plastic mugs of tea from the urn. Then it was back to his bunk to pick up his notebook and pencil and a couple of maps, colour-coded in shades of orange-Protestant, green-Catholic and yellow, mixed areas, before going on to the briefing room for the next job.

The brief always started with an overview of life in the province: incidents, deaths, bombs, robberies, riots and terrorist activity in general. Then, once the general update was complete, the next job was outlined.

The boss spoke for several minutes about the links between the Georgian mafia, who had been spreading their wings throughout Europe. He outlined the Provos and the Georgian mafia's wish to extend gun-running operations into the Irish Republic, whilst at the same time cultivating their "friendship" with a view to enlarging an already sizeable cocaine distribution network into the British Isles.

A rep from Box then took over the brief, citing first the usual requirement for absolute secrecy. Once he'd made his point, he continued by outlining the smuggling routes on a world map from Afghanistan and Baluchistan and an arduous route through Africa, before going north, along the west coast, through the Namib Desert to the sea.

Here, he explained, it was transferred into microlight aircraft and flown west, before being dropped at sea, where it was to be retrieved by divers onto fishing boats. These would then follow the Gulf Stream north, through the Bay of Biscay and along the Portuguese coast to the south-west coast of Ireland, where it would be floated ashore at night into a small cove on the Dingle Peninsula. It was here that it would be retrieved by PIRA and logged by Southern Ireland anti-terrorist team's surveillance. It would then be accompanied on its journey by road to its hiding place in north-western Southern Ireland (Connemara) by the PIRA. Several deliveries would probably have arrived already. The weapons were part of the demand made by the PIRA as part of the agreement to open up trade on behalf of the Georgians quid pro quo.

The Georgians would deliver the drugs at a price and the PIRA would sell the drugs at a profit. As a sign of goodwill, the Georgians would be encouraged to include an additional consignment of weapons with each delivery. Freely available in Georgia, it was a small price to pay and it made good business sense, enabling access to the vast profits available from drug sales. And so the carousel turned; everyone was happy, especially Box.

Because they had a man on the inside, political asylum was his payment for defection, with immunity from prosecution, a new identity and a new life. The man from Box didn't divulge anything to the team about their source; it wasn't necessary at that point. Box wanted what Box craved – information – for it fed the beast; and they got it in abundance from their man.

Konstantine Alexandr Kashitskin – an ex-Russian Special Forces, military adviser to SWAPO in Angola, and veteran of the conflict in Afghanistan – had cultivated his own friendships amongst tribal leaders and enemies of the Soviet state. They, in turn, relied on Kashitskin for their own profits, who was well placed to offer his help and expertise; his own brand of free enterprise at a price, if you like, quid pro quo.

When the conflict had come to an end in Afghanistan and Kashitskin had returned to his mother country, he had covertly kept his contacts in Kabul and it wasn't long before he had been able to "arrange" another – and a much more lucrative – endeavour in the form of a posting to Africa, where he, under the direction of his masters in Moscow, had begun to pass on his expertise. Tempered with aid in the form of military training and finance for the Marxist organisations waging war along the borders of both Rhodesia and South Africa, he offered support for these people's armies in their struggles to overthrow the White supremist governments that ruled in both countries. Of course, Russian support for their cause was a thinly veiled ruse, using native Black armies to do Moscow's bidding; the end game was not Black or White domination of the Dark Continent, but Russian.

The domino theory in action: take one country and the neighbour will soon follow.

Up until the end of the Cold War, these methods had served the Soviet bloc well and all had benefited greatly; all except those who deserved it, that is. The world of equals never did exist – nor ever will exist – in communism; someone is always more equal than the rest.

Curtis hated the communists: in Russia, it's the party members, cardholders with their dachas and big limos; in Africa, it's the politicians who spirit away millions to Swiss bank accounts; and so on around the world, where the Russian communist path to power lies, paved with bribes and corruption and control of the masses. Where those with power beget power and nations starve for the want of a bowl of rice or a bag of maize, this was the true cost of communism and Soviet world domination.

Kashitskin was, meanwhile, passing information to Box about the drug provision and weapons hauls in which he, himself, was involved.

His defection to the West would be his payment from the Brits, but in the meantime, his interest in supply and demand would supersede both his orders from Moscow and Box requirements in the UK. He was feathering his own nest in advance; he wanted financial security in place before he finally jumped ship and his new best friends on the PIRA Army Council were only too happy to help.

And so Lieutenant Colonel Konstantine Alexandr Kashitskin, model soldier, product of the Patrice Lumumba Peoples' Friendship University in Moscow and an expert on African affairs, became Kashitskin gunrunner/drug dealer, traitor to the great Soviet nation, defector to the despised capitalist West, and he wallowed in the thought of his approaching Western decadence.

Curtis sat watching telly in the TV room in the SF base in Crossmaglen; Reginald Bosanquet was reading the news summary. He wondered why these people never seemed to have an accent. You never heard one that spoke like Tarbuck or Alf Garnet, although one or two of the women readers did resemble Garnet, he thought; but still no accent – strange!

Anyway, according to Reginald, there were floods in Bangladesh. Build your house on stilts then, thought Curtis. Then there were robberies across the Province, fuel shortages, unrest in Yugoslavia, and factory closures in the North of England. He outlined the declared intent by trade unions to mount a series of one-day strikes, beginning the following week and timed to coincide with the next public holiday. Guaranteed to cause maximum disruption to anyone who didn't deserve it and at a time when union leaders and officials often had a background in the CPGB and were suitably situated to carry out the wishes of their own masters. Jim always believed in a Soviet connection with the British trade unions and probably in government circles as well. Their aim? To weaken and undermine Western society and governments through political and industrial unrest. He recalled Philby, Burgess, Maclean, Blunt, Cairncross (the Cambridge Five) and even Harold Wilson, the ex-Prime Minister. Now there's a fuckin' Red if ever there was one, thought Curtis.

He wondered why it was allowed to go on. Surely the SIS was aware? It was beyond him why they didn't just "deal" with the problem. The simple answer, thought Curtis, was probably that the lunatics were already running the asylum.

And Yugoslavia, thought Curtis; now there's a fuckin' place. You didn't have to look far in those parts for signs of skulduggery. There were whole groups of small states in the Balkans that had been criminally captured and were being run by politicians who were criminals by any other name – allegedly. Then there's Burma and The Golden Triangle – drugs and ethnic cleansing by the military. Crazy!

Curtis knew that in the Balkan society, the gun-toting mobster, especially one with political aspirations, is often widely revered and respected; even being treated like a film star in some cases. Once in power, they have the mechanics of state government to help them ply their often murderous and lucrative trade, which can range from cigarette smuggling to trade in human beings – people trafficking – or gunrunning and it can pass through generations of the same family.

He pondered over what leaders of so-called law-abiding nations like the UK and USA thought of it all. They must surely be aware but did little to combat the scourge and in many cases, they even continued to maintain trade and diplomatic connections. This annoyed him – for what it was worth – and he thought to himself that if these so-called "good nations" put as much effort into ridding the world of the pond-life as they do into political correctness – covering their own arses and counting their votes (a currency for which they will gladly get down onto all fours and kiss anyone's arse); and then of course, there was the avoidance of upsetting the neighbours – then surely we wouldn't have half the problems we've got now. The politicians, once elected, cease to represent the wishes of the people who put them there and they begin to address their own agendas instead. Self-serving, backsliding, reptilian gits, thought Jim.

Reginald was on to state pensions now, before moving on to the sterling work of the Neasden Fire Service in rescuing a 12-year-old tabby cat from a field drain.

Of course, the SIS did have their own little black book, thought Curtis. It must be bursting at the seams with names of bods just crying out to be whacked. He knew only too well how easy it was to dispatch any given individual or group, so why not for the greater good just "whack 'em and go" as it were? No doubt that would be construed as dirty tricks by our whiter-than-white masters – at least publicly, anyway. He smiled to himself and thought that a little direct personal retribution never hurt anyone.

As Reginald said "good night", Curtis remembered the oil man – Mr Mokese – another man who couldn't draw the line. The oil man was greedy. Historically, he'd involved himself in all manner of scams to make money over and above that which he was handsomely paid for in his job in the oil world. His dirty dealing with the criminal world eventually brought him into contact with subversives with a far more serious and dangerous agenda. Mokese's problem was that he couldn't make the distinction between low-level criminals and committed terrorist organisations and this would become the architect of his demise: "big boys' games, big boys' rules" as it were.

Mr Mokese

We spread out in the open: it was like a bath of lead;
But the boys they cheered and hollered fit to raise the bloody dead, [...]

Robert Service; Bill the Bomber

The interim periods between operations provided an opportunity for resupply, debriefs, administration and intelligence updates, and proposed future operations, which would normally be delivered by SASF teams operating locally or by means of a dead letter box. Targets would come in many forms and the company was constantly kept busy with a seemingly endless supply of tasks. One such rest period heralded the arrival of an SF team but this time, they were accompanied by an individual dressed not in the usual military garb, but in robust, outdoor clothing of the type worn by walkers and serious explorer bods.

The OC spoke briefly to the SF team commander, who handed over the usual leather pouch. He was introduced to the mysterious civilian, who spent an hour and a half with him, obviously talking at length about something of considerable importance. Curtis knew, of course, that they'd soon be briefed as per normal, but was intrigued by the arrival of the stranger nonetheless. He soon decided he must be a "government man". Still, he would just have to wait and see.

Curtis was sitting on the remains of an old termite hill watching Voss and Van rijn in conspiratorially mischievous conversation as they, too, sat watching a platoon commander wander off, shovel in hand, to do the necessary behind a small bush. The officer stopped behind the bush and was in the process of undoing his denims, when Voss and Van Rijn, also carrying spades, stood up and, at a half crouch, crept towards the unsuspecting man. As they got close, they slowed, lowered themselves onto the ground and slithered the last few feet on their bellies.

Once close enough, Van Rijn, with the stealth of a stalking leopard, silently pushed his spade at arm's length under the arse of the straining man. Catching a large turd, he withdrew as Voss caught another. Undetected, they returned to their original positions and sat there, giggling like children. Curtis watched them highly amused.

The officer duly finished his task and turned to bury the evidence. A stunned look spread across his face, followed by several rapid checks down the inside of his trouser legs and the inside his shirt, followed by several circuits of the bush, looking for the amazing disappearing turds. Voss, Van Rijn and Curtis were in fits of laughter and soon the officer was presented with his missing property. Any further trips to the bush were treated with much greater caution and respect. But he was never allowed to forget the incident and the story earned Voss, Van Rijn and Curtis many a pint in Cape Town's bars.

In due course, the team were called forward for their briefing on the next job. It was outlined by the OC, who explained that the civilian visitor, "Who shall remain nameless, because he wouldn't fuckin' tell us what it was", may well have been a representative of one official department or another! As a result of a long and extensive security op, he had discovered the identities of several individuals marked for "disposal" owing to their subversive activities and threat to national security. Of interest to the teams would be one Mr Mokese – a high-ranking executive in the oil industry.

It seemed that Mr Mokese's extra-curricular activities had, for some time, been in the provision of safe houses for activists operating against the sovereign states of South Africa and Rhodesia. And so, in short, he had to go. How and when was up to the team, who had been provided with an extensive description of the man's movements that he stuck to on a regular basis; his friends, associates, bars he frequented, his gambling habits, his favourite tipple and the fact that he was a married man with five children aged between seventeen and twenty-eight. The 28-year-old, following in his father's footsteps in more ways than one, was likely to accompany Mr Mokese on his father's favourite pastime of whoring and drinking into the wee small hours on Saturday and Sunday nights, without exception, in Leonardsville – a small shanty town west of "Gill-O-Gill". He had his favourite group of good-time girls in The Star hotel and his frequent and regular visits to them would be his demise.

There were two teams that were given the task of negotiating this particular problem. The first, led by Schollonburg, consisted of three others: René Voss, Leo van Rijn and Jim Curtis. The second, led by Gus Grillo, consisted of Kurt Willt, Billy McNiel and a Russian-speaking Pole named Dick Kaminski – one of Curtis' mates from 2 Para.

The target at the hotel stood on a crossroads, which opened out into a square about 40 yards by 40 yards. The only roads in the small shanty town led out – north, south, east and west – one from each side of the square. Buildings of wood and corrugated iron lined each road and served to house the population of about 200.

The square itself provided a meeting place for locals. There were shops and bars and two hotels; one – The Star – owned and run by the local "madam", would become the centre of the team's attention. It stood on the north side of the square. None of the streets leading off the square were lit up, but the electric lighting that did exist was served by a 27 KVA generator that was housed at the rear of The Star in a large wooden shed.

The Star Hotel was well attended by the townsfolk and it was also a favourite haunt of the local government troops from the barracks, 10 miles distant. The backbone of the town consisted of the four main streets, crossing in the square, and they had the effect of turning the town into four segments. Other buildings had grown up in each quarter – in no particular order – producing a hotchpotch of alleys and dead ends. Rubbish was strewn all around and sewerage ran openly in the narrow streets, with children playing amongst the rotting waste.

It was decided that Gus Grillo's team would form a loose security/early warning cordon around the intersection and the square, whilst Schollonburg's team would deal with the target. Using the cover of darkness, the teams would simply walk into the town, stopping short of the illuminated square, where they would hunker down and watch and wait until the time was right for Schollonburg and his boys to do the job of booby-trapping the oil man's car.

It was agreed that the lights in the square would pose somewhat of a problem; therefore, Curtis, once the ball was rolling, would nip around to the rear of The Star and simply cut the power by switching off the generator. This would give Voss and Van Rijn the very short period of time required to tag the car – the Merc saloon – which they expected to find parked in its usual place at the front of the hotel. Schollonburg would direct operations from nearby, maintaining radio silence until things went noisy. The withdrawal would follow a different route out back to a final RV; then, after a head count, there would be a complete withdrawal from the area.

The two teams studied the aerial photographs of the town, which clearly showed, in finite detail, all the required information that they needed in order to carry out the mission: the square in the centre of the town, with its four roads radiating out, The Star hotel, the generator shed and the little tin huts, which served as homes for resident townsfolk.

Schollonburg sat on one side of the photo, which they pored over, and the remainder of the men sat opposite in the shade of a large acacia tree. The demon sun climbed through its arc across the vast blue African sky. A small Scops owl peered down from a branch above the group of men as if overseeing Schollonburg's presentation.

Schollonburg spoke in his rough-throated, South-African accent, clear, concise, confident. 'Our route in will follow this re-entrant which will, with darkness, provide cover from view. Then we will continue through this segment and almost up to this side of the square.' He used a long, thin pointer fashioned from a piece of cane to trace the route.

He stopped just short of the square, with the pointer on what was clearly the shape of a derelict car in the bottom of the re-entrant. 'This,' said Schollonburg, 'is the final RV for the route in.' He turned to Gus Grillo.

'When we reach the RV, Grillo, your team will peel off and slip into our loose cordon. Ensure your boys remain in the unlit area – give me two clicks on your pressel switch to confirm you're in place. OK?'

Grillo nodded. 'No problem, boss.' He spoke in a deep, southern Texas drawl.

Kurt Willt, Billy McNiel and Dick Kaminski also nodded in agreement.

Schollonburg turned his attention to Curtis. 'Curtis, once I've had the nod from Gus, you'll move off and take care of the jenny. Voss, once the power goes off, you and Van Rijn make your way directly to the target which, all things being equal, will be parked in its usual spot.' He held up two crossed fingers. 'Outside the hotel, Voss, you'll deal with the car. Waste no time once you're complete. Move straight back through me. I'll be here.'

He pointed again at the photo to a cluster of shrubs beside a small wooden outbuilding which overlooked the square. Then he turned back to Gus Grillo.

'Once the boys are back at my location I'll give you three clicks – that's the signal to bring your guys back, too. Once we're complete at the RV, we'll extract to what we consider to be a safe distance and wait for the fireworks. In the event of a compromise or contact, we'll fight through and extract as best we can. Any questions?'

'Fire support?'

'Yes. Two 81 mm mortars on call from H + 01?' asked Curtis.

Schollonburg nodded. 'Any more?' he asked?

'Can we nip into The Star for a pint before we leave?' said Van Rijn, pan-faced.

Everyone laughed and moved off to prepare for war. Van Rijn and Curtis sat with Voss, chatting casually about the imminent demise of Mr Mokese.

Curtis spoke as Voss listened. 'We used to use a charge called a "normal" to target charge or the standard SAS charge for general demo. It consisted of a 5 lb block of plastic which could, of course, be set up for electrical initiations, or flash, or various forms of booby-trap RCIED – or, using a safety fuse, light up, move back and … bang! The point is that it was a manageable-sized charge with many uses. Everyone carried a block, so it gave us the capability of collectively disposing of say a reasonable sized structure; or conversely, something as small as a car. Obviously, we'd use movement-operated initiation or pressure for that – what do you think, Voss?'

Voss cupped his chin in his left hand with a studious expression on his face. After a few seconds, he spoke. 'I'm going to use pressure-pad, victim-operated initiation for this, boys.'

Curtis and Van Rijn nodded in agreement and Voss got to work. It took him thirty minutes to produce the device, which would end the life of Mr Mokese in just a few short hours. He placed the device inside a plastic container – Tupperware type – for transportation. Once preparations were complete, the teams ate a meal of cold rations and then received a message from Coy HQ giving the ready to move for 23.00 hours. That gave them six hours' rest before the off. They slept soundly.

The teams were woken at 22.00 hours in time to have final refreshments before they moved off. Kit and equipment was double-checked and at 23.00 hours on the mark, Chris Schollonburg led the two teams out en route to the town. They were little more than an hour distant from their target and they had covered the 4 miles without incident. As they neared the RV, they moved tactically, making not a sound; each man covered an alternate area of fire, giving all-round protection. They stopped at the wreck of a VW camper van at the base of the ravine, where both teams then closed up. Schollonburg's team taking up the 12 to 6 position and Gus Grillo's the 6 to 12. Lying and crouching, they remained within touching distance of the next man – waiting, listening, watching – allowing their senses to take in the sounds of the town at night. Local to them were household sounds, where dogs barked, and music emanated from the hotels and filled the square; then there was the smell of sewage mixed with the smells from fires fed by cow dung. Schollonburg turned to Grillo and formed a circle with his thumb and forefinger and then held his hand to his eye like a spy glass, beckoning Grillo towards him and pointing with a flat hand on edge to the head of re-entrant.

Grillo joined him and the two commanders moved purposefully through the 30 yards to the top of the slope. Once in place, they went off, leaving the remainder of the team behind. From their new position, they could clearly observe the huts. There, across the square, was The Star hotel, with its brightly coloured red, yellow and blue veranda in full view.

The sounds of drunkenness and revellers reached Schollonburg's ears and both he and Grillo smiled as they registered the presence of a large Mercedes saloon. He confirmed it as the target, having checked the registration number with his binos. After fifteen minutes, Grillo returned to the teams and picked up his section and then they moved off to put their lazy cordon in place. It was ten minutes past one in the morning – the rest of the men waited patiently, at risk in the darkness.

Then, twenty minutes later, Schollonburg heard two clicks on his radio and Curtis moved off in an anticlockwise direction to deal with the jenny. He carried an FN assault rifle with a round up the spout and the safety catch was on auto. Any hostile engagements would receive a quick burst of three – shoot and scoot – relying on surprise and his aggressive response to give him the time to "catch the bus".

He passed the backs of huts with people snoring happily just inches away. Skirting a property where a large, white dog appeared in front of him, Curtis stood, stock-still, weapon pointing at the animal that had appeared before him. He reflected that the mutt must have been a tough guy in its own right, because it cast him one of those "what's your fucking problem, arsehole" looks, before cocking its leg, pissing against a fence and then disappearing into the night as it continued on its way.

Cow dung smoke still hung in the air and it cloyed with the pungent smell of raw sewage. Wherever he looked, the barrel of his weapon pointed as he moved and scanned the route. Then, just ahead, human sounds stopped him in his tracks. Deep concentration etched on his face as he tracked the sound to the back of a large truck – an open-backed flatbed. Slowly, like a wisp of smoke in the still night air, he moved towards the grunts and moans. As he came up alongside, it was obvious that the occupants were oblivious to the world outside their own sweaty fumblings. Curtis smiled and drifted past towards the sound of the jenny, now only 75 yards away.

A few yards further on, he stopped and listened again. No change – life was being lived – so he pushed on, aware that the closer he got to the sound of the jenny, the less chance there was of him being heard; but he was also aware that there was less chance of him hearing anyone else. He did a quick circuit of the shed, which was open at one end. Then, with one last look around to get his bearings, he slipped inside.

Taking out a betalight, he moved close up to the side of the jenny and locating a large cable, he followed it up to its connection with the main body. Above the connector was a large dial and just above that were a series of three other dials, with small black needles jumping between graticules on their faces. Holding the betalight close, he inspected the rest of the control panel, before moving slowly around the side of the machine.

Curtis glanced up and froze – his FN automatically brought up into the aim position. Standing before him, side on, were two men. Unbelievably, they hadn't seen him. He stood, stock-still, as the two men started to relieve themselves against the wall of the hut, chatting away to each other, his hair bristling on the back of his neck. Although he was confident he could take them out in an instant, he was also intensely concerned that he would compromise the op at such a late stage.

Seconds passed and then the men turned and left; he breathed again and continued with his work. He decided that he would go down the route of restricting the fuel flow to the motor to stop the engine running. This would be less suspicious than pulling out a cable or switching it off when someone inevitably came out to check the jenny during the blackout. He quickly discovered a fuel line, took a Leatherman from its pouch and clamped the pliers onto it. There was a pause of about fifteen seconds, which seemed like an eternity to Curtis, and then the engine spluttered, coughed and fell silent – the lights in the square died and music in the hotels ceased. Human voices became clearer, speaking in Portuguese.

There were shouts of dismay in the darkness, but already, René Voss and Leo van Rijn were on their way across the square to the car. Curtis had arrived just ahead of them. Voss reached the driver's side of the vehicle and Curtis and Van Rijn covered him from the bonnet and boot respectively. Voss had the door open and the booby-trap in place with the door closed again in under two minutes. Then, all three running on adrenalin started on their way back to the RV. But, suddenly, as they took their first steps back towards Schollonburg's position, two wagonloads of enemy troops arrived in the square. Obviously here for a "boys' night out", they were fully armed, as was the norm in these parts, and completely unpredictable.

The vehicles, by chance, had stopped on both sides of the square, blocking the proposed exit route for Schollonburg's group. Schollonburg remained in situ. Surveying the situation, he watched as the troops debussed and using his night viewing aid, he saw Voss, Curtis and Van Rijn start across the square, before doubling back towards the jenny shed and out of sight.

Where the fuck did this lot come from? thought Schollonburg. Then, from the direction of one of the main streets, he heard shouts in Portuguese, followed by a short burst of automatic fire.

Recognising the type of weapon, Schollonburg spoke to himself, 'One of ours.'

More shots followed. This time, the distinctive sound of an AK47. Then there were three or four more bursts and yet more shouts.

Schollonburg flashed a glance back towards the direction of the car and the hotel, but there was no sign of the boys. It was turning to rat shit. The rest of the government troops were drawn towards the sound of the shots.

Schollonburg decided to take an incredible risk. To draw attention away from the rest of the team, he made the decision to leave the safety of his cover and walk casually out into the square. With enemy troops on at least three sides and within yards of his position, he fired; first left, then in front, then right, shouting, 'Over here ya' fuckin' Commie bastards. Over here!'

As fate would have it, at that precise moment, the jenny kicked into life again; the square was filled with light and Schollonburg was centre stage, with his arse hanging in the breeze.

Undeterred and with complete disregard for his own safety, he stood firm. Many of the government troops turned to face the sound of his taunts and others disappeared out of sight in the direction of the first shots.

In the meantime, Schollonburg had produced two grenades from a pouch, pulled the pins and calmly rolled them in the direction of the two closest clusters of troops. He then raised his FN and fired several more bursts in the direction of the rest; three or four of the stunned troops fell. The rest still hadn't reacted to the appearance of Schollonburg and remained riveted to the spot; others dived for cover.

Time to go, thought Schollonburg – a huge understatement – and as he turned and ran back into the darkness, the first grenade exploded … then the second. Enemy bullets whizzed and cracked around him. Spurred on by the explosions and the cries of the wounded, he upped the pace. A bullet smashed into the butt of his FN – a second clipped his right ear. Less than thirty seconds had passed since he had first stepped into the square.

Curtis, Voss and Van Rijn had witnessed Schollonburg's performance and they knew exactly what he was thinking and the risk he was taking for them, but there were too many government troops between them and Schollonburg to be able to rejoin him. They moved stealthily around the back of The Star, Curtis in front, followed by Voss and then Van Rijn. Having turned away from the brightly lit square, they were almost blind in the darkness.

Rounding the side of an outdoor toilet, which they could smell before they reached, Curtis walked slap bang into Kurt Willt. He'd been wounded in the jaw, but was still in the firefight. Curtis muttered several expletives in the darkness. Enemy troops were firing indiscriminately now and bullets flew everywhere, one smashing against a brick upright not 6 inches from Curtis' head – he ignored it.

Curtis spoke briefly to his three team members. 'Best we split into two pairs, boys, to lengthen our chance of getting out.'

Just then, there was an ear-splitting explosion as the windows in the hotel disappeared and showered the men with glass. Voss looked into Curtis' face and returned his beaming smile.

'Job done,' said Voss. 'Mr Mokese must have decided to leg it – big mistake!'

Leo van Rijn and Kurt Willt made up one pair; Curtis and Voss the other, the tempo of the action building by the second. They had just decided on who was going with whom, when voices in the darkness not 20 yards away spurred them into action. Curtis and Voss spun round and fired bursts into the night and they were rewarded with the sound of someone's pain. Van Rijn and Willt disappeared off to Curtis' right.

Voss and Curtis ran straight across the street and crashed, headlong, through the front door of a one-roomed house; both rolled across the floor, knocking over a small wooden table – its kerosene lamp falling onto the floor, starting a fire. Curtis snatched up a blanket from a rickety iron bed and smothered the flames. Then, jumping to his feet, he lifted the wooden door back into place and pushed the bed hard up against it to keep it in its frame.

René Voss immediately turned his attention to the only occupant of the house – a man in his thirties, tall, broad-shouldered and seemingly nailed to the floor, shook with fear. Voss grabbed the man by the throat with his left hand and growled at him to keep quiet, his voice deeply threatening.

Outside the hut, the enemy troops moved about, smoking dope and talking amongst themselves. The smell of hashish drifted through the night. Some fired wildly into the buildings but remained blissfully unaware of the two men inside. Just then, a bullet hit the iron bedstead and ricocheted out through the roof.

Curtis peered through a crack in the wooden wall and could just make out the form of Kurt Willt being dragged into the centre of the street. The others ran on through the night, stopping occasionally to face back down the route they had just taken, waiting for ten or fifteen minutes at a time to ambush any would-be followers. None came. Later, back at the RV, one by one, the rest returned ... all except Willt, that is.

'They've got Kurt,' Curtis hissed to Voss.

They watched helplessly as he was surrounded by troops, who had wasted no time on formalities. He was already wounded and unable to follow Van Rijn, for he had become separated from Van Rijn as they had made their bid for freedom. He was finished off with a shot to the head and his body was set alight in the open for all to see. Van Rijn was nowhere to be seen and nor was Dick Kaminski. It was this same fate that Voss and Curtis were trying to avoid as they'd forced their way into the house and had taken its only occupant hostage. Government troops still walked up and down outside, literally inches away.

Once again, the man attempted to speak, but Voss, not one to waste words, with a second warning put a stop to any thought of speech – good, bad or indifferent. He was still grasping the wide-eyed man by the throat with his left hand as he drew back his right arm and with a fast punching motion, he smashed the barrel of the snub-nosed 38 Smith & Wesson straight into the man's mouth, splitting both lips wide, knocking out several teeth and gouging a large gash into the roof of his mouth with the weapon's foresight. Blood gushed over the weapon and down Voss' arm. It had the desired effect though, for the man was silenced. Curtis smiled a cold smile; he always enjoyed watching professionals at work.

They remained in the house for a further three hours, hearts pounding, sweating profusely under the intense pressure of the possibility of imminent capture and death. But, eventually, Willt's body ceased to burn, the troops moved away and the man on the end of Voss' 38 lost consciousness, enabling Curtis and Voss to make good their escape. Although they had twice virtually walked into government troops who had taken to firing at any movement in the darkness, they were able to exfiltrate the town, with no idea as to the fate of the others.

It was an experience neither wished to repeat, but they had achieved their aim – the oil man was dead … they hoped.

It wasn't their custom to pat each other on the back. Jobs well done or otherwise were taken as read and the men committed all to memory.

Very close bonds were formed through the quiet acceptance of the bravery shown by the men such as Chris Schollonburg on the night the oil man died.

Boasting or talking out of turn about personal attributes were frowned upon and, indeed, actively discouraged, which had the odd effect of carving out a body of individuals who were, in fact, unassuming overachievers in the world of soldiering. They got on with it, put it behind them and then looked to the future. Losses such as that of Kurt Willt were sad – occupational hazards – and had shown that the men wouldn't always have it their own way, but life went on regardless – "nature of the beast" – and the future brought more work in the way of their craft.

Voss, Curtis, Van Rijn and Schollonburg sat talking of anything and nothing as they waited for the arrival of a resupply of rations. They expected another seven days' worth, which would see them to the end of their present operational tour of duty in the bush; then they would have a month off on full pay, before their return to duty.

'I'm starving, Voss. Have you got any scoff?' said Curtis.

'Yeah. I've got some biltong here, mate.'

'Ooh, fucking super!' replied Curtis, full of sarcasm. 'I'd rather eat me own arse!' was his stock answer when Voss offered it to him.

'Rather you than me,' said Schollonburg.

They all laughed.

Half an hour later, the rations arrived along with a further security update and a new task for the boys. The rations were distributed and each individual broke down their packs to make them easier to carry.

Some swapped items with each other; others, not so fussy, kept whatever their packs contained. Once again, the constant routine of personal administration, so important to the efficiency of soldiers in the field, continued. Equipment was exchanged with the admin flight and platoon sergeants redistributed ammo. Weapons were cleaned on a daily basis; whether fired or not. It was all part of the natural order of things for the professional soldier.

Nobody chased anyone to stay on top of their jobs. Each individual was expected to stay on top of their own personal admin, self-discipline was the order of the day and anyone who fell short of the mark was shown the door. Indeed, the unwritten rule was that he would remove himself, rather than fail to maintain the standard expected of each and every man. Off-duty soldiers were expected to keep their work private and to themselves; to remain the quiet soldier.

Just before last light, the arrival of a runner at Schollonburg's section heralded the start of another O-group, which Schollonburg attended. He returned an hour later and told Curtis to let the boys know he would be briefing the section in the morning at 09.00 hours, after scoff.

The night passed without incident and at first light the four two-man-standing patrols returned from the cardinal points of the compass, where they'd remained 100 yards out from the main body all night, waiting and watching for any sign of the government troops that they'd encountered in the town. None came.

The X-factor had kicked in in the town in the form of the enemy troops, but the teams were well prepared to fight through that sort of event, either in teams or as individuals. The loss of a comrade in the profession of arms has a sort of non-effect. Among groups of seasoned, professional soldiers, death plays a constituent part in everyday life. As long as there is a live enemy, the threat of one's own demise remains a constant reality.

Professional soldiers though, don't live in fear of the end; they simply respect its presence and carry on regardless. Indeed, it is a state of mind found only in the military and then, only amongst what are generally known as teeth arms, Airborne Forces, Special Forces, etc., and their own brands of black humour reflect this spirit and carry them forward. This is not to say that fear is not present; it is, and plenty of it. But soldiers learn to overcome and suppress fear in order to maintain self-control and thus operate effectively.

It was whilst in the relative safety of the base camp during a Chinese parliament that further details emerged regarding the capture and eventual death of Kurt Willt; as well as the parts played by other individuals such as Dick Kaminski.

Kaminski and Curtis were old friends back in the UK. Both had soldiered in the British Army's 2nd Battalion Para Regiment in various operational areas across the globe; Curtis, as a member of Patrol company. And it was to Curtis that Kaminski was explaining his ex-fill from the town.

It transpired that when the government troops had arrived in the town, they had done so in the two large Hino trucks, which all had witnessed in the square – but it now became clear as to why no one had heard them until it was too late for Grillo's early warning to be effective. Rather than drive the trucks into the town, the enemy troops had taken to freewheeling the vehicles down the incline into the town. This meant they could switch off the engines of their vehicles and allow the slope of the road to give the vehicles the required momentum to carry them down the 500-yard-long, gentle slope into the square.

Willt and Kaminski had, indeed, seen the trucks appear like apparitions out of the darkness and, left with no other option at that late stage, they had taken the only course left open to them and fired a couple of bursts at the vehicles to alert the rest of the boys. Fire had been returned and Kaminski heard Kurt, who was only a few feet away, yelp. Both he and Kaminski had immediately split up and began to ex-fill. Dick explained that it must have been then that Kurt had run into Curtis' group at the rear of the hotel.

The boys nodded their agreement, noting that shortly after that had been the explosion and Van Rijn and Willt had split from Curtis and Voss. Van Rijn stated that "the shit was flying now" and he had almost immediately lost touch with Kurt in the darkness.

Again, Curtis spoke, outlining his and Voss' close encounter in the house and the witnessing of Willt's death. Dick Kaminski came up with one more piece of good news though. Finding himself cut off with no immediate way out through the enemy troops – who now seemed to be around every turn – he slipped, unseen, into the cab of the nearest Hino truck. Here, he waited just long enough until he felt that he could start the vehicle, drive it across the square, past Schollonburg's hiding place, and jump out at the top of the slope, leaving the wagon to roll the 30 yards down the re-entrant slope, crashing into the VW camper wreck at the bottom.

For good measure, he had pulled the pin on a WP grenade, leaving it inside the cab as he jumped clear. It had exploded, turning the cab into an inferno, and so, in one fell swoop, it had reduced the enemy's transport assets by 50 per cent and he had escaped in the process; completely reversing his fortunes. Something good always comes out of something bad. Indeed, no matter how dire your situation may seem, there is always something else you can do, especially when operating with people with a daring, bold and adventurous spirit, reflected Curtis. Kaminski's actions epitomised this concept.

The group echoed a collective desire to continue to damage the enemy wherever they believed they were safe. They were effective, and the enemy knew it. But, before any further plans were produced, Gus Grillo made clear his feelings that he was going nowhere until he had retrieved the remains of Kurt Willt. He needn't have worried, because he simply upheld what the rest were thinking. They all agreed this would take priority without delay. So, with the OC's blessing, plans were made.

That evening, one of the standing patrols that had been deployed to give early warning of enemy movement returned to camp with one of the townsfolk. He'd been found wandering in the bush ... or spying.

When he was questioned, he said he had been away visiting a sick aunt in "Boraville" and on his return, he had discovered the town deserted. He said there had been bodies in the square but no soldiers, either dead or alive. He could find no signs of his family or his friend and he had fled into the bush, fearful for his own safety. He made several references to the Russians in town.

The men were very sceptical and suspicious of the man's story, but it was decided that they had to keep him in "protective custody" during the return to town. If his story turned out to be genuine, he'd be held until the unit extracted. If not, then his future was likely to become a very short one.

They asked the man to tell them what he believed would be the best and safest route to take back to the town and he explained, in detail, which way they should go. The men listened carefully and then took a totally different route, bringing the man along with them for insurance.

They kept him secure by means of a rope noose around his neck. The rope ran down his back, where it secured his hands, then went down again to his feet, which were both tied in loops, leaving him a short length in between to enable him to take short steps in a sort of shuffling motion. The remaining length of rope, about 10 feet, was held by the next man in line.

Gus Grillo gave the brief. It was his job, so he led it, once again using the aerial photo that Schollonburg had used to brief the boys for the Mokese job. Grillo used his pointer to outline the route in; this time, using a different approach.

'We'll move off at last light,' said Grillo. 'This time, we'll box the town and come in from here.' He indicated a row of improvised telegraph poles, which ran in the direction of the distant garrison. 'But this time, I'm going to go from this feature, here.' He pointed at a rocky knoll about 100 feet high. Because of their familiarity with at least some of the town, Grillo opted for Schollonburg's team to accompany his.

'Chris, when we reach the knoll,' which lay about 600 yards from the edge of the town, with commanding views of the area, which was easily defended, at least for a short period, 'I intend to observe the target, until we decide it's safe to move in and pick up Willt, OK?'

Schollonburg nodded.

'While I'm observing, I want you and your boys to move down towards the town and collect any info you can. Don't enter the lit area.

I need to know specifically about troop movement, but record anything relevant. I want you back here on the knoll no later than an hour before first light. We'll maintain radio silence until it goes noisy, or unless you have something vital to let me know.'

Gus Grillo needed to go into every little detail in order for the teams to understand his requirements. Radio silence would be maintained as he had said and the mortars would be on call from H+01. The mortars were, at present, recording targets in preparation for any fire missions they would receive.

Grillo led the two teams out at last light on the circuitous route that he'd outlined on the brief. The team's new "best friend" from the village shuffled along as best he could. He tripped and fell on numerous occasions, but the gag he was wearing concealed his groans as well as any urges he may have harboured to shout out. As it transpired, his story seemed to be true and he was later released, much to his obvious relief.

Kaminski held the rope and walked patiently behind the struggling man. The night was oppressively warm and black-grey cumulonimbus clouds filled the night sky with the darkly foreboding threat of storms.

It wasn't long before the threat became a reality and sheets of rain lashed the landscape, soaking the men to the skin. It poured down their kit and equipment, running in rivulets from their weapons, where it pooled on the ground and ran into rivers along dry water courses. Fork lightning lit up the night sky, silhouetting the men against the backdrop of the bush.

Like spirits in the night, they moved on, slowly, purposefully, seemingly oblivious to the elements which enveloped them in the cloak of the African night. There was another flash of lightening and Curtis allowed himself a smile as he saw, to his left, a pair of Dik-Dik standing huddled together in the downpour.

Just after midnight, they reached the knoll and went firm in all-round defence amongst the boulders and scrub; still the rain hammered down.

Grillo and Schollonburg sat talking together, their hushed tones inaudible over the sound of the downpour. After about half an hour, Schollonburg returned to his team.

Closing them in, Curtis, Voss and Van Rijn huddled together in the shelter of a large boulder to listen to Schollonburg's brief.

It was Curtis who spoke first though. 'Am I on the right patrol here?'
'Why?' asked Schollonburg, waiting for the punchline.
'I didn't order one with rain!'
They all laughed. The rain meant nothing to them – it was part of their life.
'OK, boys, we'll move off in thirty minutes. So, if you want anything to eat, you've time now.'
The team ate strips of biltong and oatmeal biscuits and drank water from their water bottles. Then, at 01.30 hours, they moved down from the knoll in the direction of the town. Curtis led the way, followed by René Voss and Leo van Rijn, and Chris Schollonburg brought up the rear, communicating, as always, with hand signals. As they neared the town it became obvious that something "stank in the state of Denmark".
No sounds emanated from the place; there was no music and neither was there the usual smell of cow-dung fires.
Moving ever closer and becoming ever more cautious, they came to within 100 yards of the square. Curtis held up his hand to halt the team as they went to ground, covering their arcs of fire. Schollonburg moved up close to Curtis, who was peering through the driving rain, scanning the town for signs of life. He gestured to Curtis to move forward again and get a closer look.
Curtis gave the thumbs-up and off he went. It was at times like these that Curtis fully expected, with each careful step forward, to feel the impact of a round through the chest. His heart pounded and he could feel a pulse beating in his temples; intense concentration etched across his face. But nothing happened. He reached the edge of the square and absorbed the scene with the gradual realisation that the town had been deserted slowly dawning on him. But still he didn't relax. He walked on for a further twenty minutes, before turning back to the team in the darkness and the now dying rain.
Reaching Schollonburg, he said, 'There's no fucker there, mate.'
'What?' said Schollonburg.
'The fuckin' place is deserted.'
'Odd,' said Schollonburg.
'Fucking odd,' said Van Rijn.
'Very fuckin' odd,' said Voss.
'OK,' said Curtis, 'we're all agreed.' A serious look now on his face. 'It's very, very, very fuckin' odd!' he grinned.

Schollonburg decided to send Voss and Van Rijn back to the knoll with the news of the deserted town. They would then lead Gus Grillo and his team down to meet them and it would be over to Grillo again to decide how he wanted to play it.

In the meantime, Schollonburg and Curtis would box the town to confirm its status. They began the box moving clockwise, passing familiar places: the back of the hotel, the outdoor toilet, the flatbed wagon where Curtis had his close encounter and the house where he'd met the white dog. A few yards further on, they met the white dog again, but this time there was no unpleasant growl, because the white dog was dead, several gunshot wounds clearly visible on its lifeless form.

Curtis beckoned to Schollonburg and they moved on, gazing through windows and open doors as they went. But there was no sign of life anywhere.

'It's like the Mary fuckin' Celeste,' suggested Curtis.

'Very fuckin' odd,' intoned Schollonburg.

The generator ticked over helpfully and as they reached the rear of The Star, they'd done a full circuit. The sound of broken glass from the blown out windows crunched under their feet on the only hardstanding in town.

Schollonburg gestured to him to move in to the hotel, pointing towards the open back door; light from inside bathed the open yard at the back.

As they stepped inside, a large cooking range could be seen in the kitchen with pots of burnt, blackened food smoking away on the burning hob. Through the kitchen and into the main bar area, tables and chairs were in disarray; glasses, some still containing drinks, sat on the tables and at the bar; others lay on the wooden floor.

Once past the stairs that led up to the bedrooms, they passed through the front door, which opened out onto the veranda, and it was here that they saw the first sign of human occupation. On a low wooden bench sat the mayor of the town; his wife next to him and between each pair of feet, perched on the floor, were their two children. Like his and hers, aged about ten, both had a single gunshot wound like a third eye in the centre of their foreheads, which matched that of their mother and father. Short lengths of rope held the four corpses in the sitting position for all to see.

'A statement,' said Voss.

'Aye,' said Curtis, his reply full of dual meaning.

It broke the ice, though, and the men relaxed slightly.

They moved out into the square at the bottom of the hotel steps and stood looking at the shell of the Mercedes. The walkie-talkie crackled into life. It was Grillo and the rest of the boys. Schollonburg spoke briefly and called them forward, directing them through the hotel to join him at the car. On arrival, the men stood impassively, looking at the car and its charred contents.

Inside the hotel, Dick Kaminski and Billy McNiel finished checking the other rooms and quickly confirmed that it was, indeed, deserted. A decision was made not to enter any more buildings for fear of booby-traps.

'I think we best get on with what we came here for,' said Grillo as he moved away in the general direction of Willt's last known position, as described on the Mokese debrief by Curtis.

'Is he dead?' said Curtis, a large, mischievous grin cracking his dusty, stubbled face as he surveyed the scene before him.

He was looking at the result of one and a half pounds of PE that had been placed strategically in the oil man's car, which smoked and smouldered, even after the rains. Doors had been blown off, the roof bellowed out like a huge steel balloon, the windows were gone, along with most of the left-hand side of Mr Simon Mokese's body – his head hung down his back, still attached by a strand of tendon. Curtis was talking to Voss, who was stood beside him – it was Voss' handiwork and he was mightily chuffed.

'Well, is he dead?' asked Curtis again.

'Hang on. I'll feel for a pulse,' said Voss. At which point he feigned the act and turned back to Curtis. 'He's stable!'

Then, another voice was heard from behind; this time it was Van Rijn. 'No change in his condition then?'

'No, he's still dead,' said Curtis, to guffaws of laughter.

'Nice work, Voss,' said Schollonburg. 'What did you use?'

'Basic pressure pad below the seat; one and a half pounds of PE4, victim operated.'

'Ho, ho, ho. Dr René Voss – world leader in haemorrhoid cures,' jibed Billy McNiel.

Everyone turned away from a job well done and walked in the direction of Willt.

Then Curtis turned to Voss and said, 'I'm fuckin' starving again – let's eat.'

'Roger,' said Voss, 'I've still got some biltong here,'

'Excellent,' replied Curtis, again full of sarcasm. 'I'd rather eat me arse – in fact, I think I will this time.'

They followed Gus Grillo to the corner of the square and turned right along the street, where the corpse of Kurt Willt lay in the mud. Black and charred, it was unrecognisable as the Willt they'd all known – the laughing, joking Willt, always ready for mischief, always ready to help.

Curtis and Voss walked to the left and pushed open the door of the house they'd hid in the night before. It fell in, with a creek and a bang.

It was dark inside, but they could just about make out something in the corner of the room. As their eyes adjusted, they saw before them the corpse of the man they'd introduced themselves to the previous night. Thousands of flies buzzed and hovered in the heat. He was curled up in the foetal position – lifeless.

Turning back towards the street and the rest of the team, it was Grillo who spoke first. 'We'll carry him back to the knoll and bury him on the top. We can't take him with us, so we'll camouflage the spot and maybe at some stage, someone will be able to retrieve his body.'

The boys nodded in agreement. So Kurt Willt was carried in a poncho the 600 yards back to the knoll, the men taking it in turns to share the load.

Grillo and Willt had been close friends – Kaminski, too, and the boys knew they'd make someone pay.

It was Dick Kaminski who started to dig first and as he struck the ground with the first blow of the pick, lightning lit up the night sky and the rains returned, great, growling rolls of thunder filling the air, now alive with static. The ground at the top of the knoll was hard with rock and shale but, undeterred, the men, in turn, dug on.

Curtis was now standing, thigh-deep, in the grave, which had filled with water up to his ankles. Schollonburg erected a poncho over the toiling men as they continued with Willt's tomb. Curtis was on his knees now, swinging the pick.

René Voss, Billy McNiel and Leo van Rijn kept watch as work continued – out in the night, a lion roared, drawn close by the smell of death.

Finally, after three hours of hard digging, they'd got down over 6 feet and so they agreed that that should be sufficient to deter the wildlife from disinterring the body.

As the rain continued, the men stood for some minutes, covered in the red clay mud from the African earth. Then, Grillo and Kaminski picked up the body of Willt and placed him onto a spare poncho, which they wrapped around him and tied with Para cord. They then placed that inside another and repeated the process. Once done, Kaminski climbed into the grave and Curtis and Schollonburg lowered the large green cocoon down to him. He cradled the body in his arms and gently lowered it to the floor of the grave. Then, Schollonburg pulled Kaminski out. Again, the men stood in the driving rain – silent. Then they swapped places with McNiel, Van Rijn and Voss, who continued the task of filling in the grave back in. No markers were left and the grid reference was recorded for future reference, to pass to the family of the dead man.

Daylight began to return and still the rain continued, heavier now. Once Kurt Willt was committed to memory, the men moved down from the knoll in single file. As they reached the bottom, Schollonburg held out his arms like an aircraft wing; his weapon grasped in his right hand, and the teams fanned out into arrowhead formation for the move back to base camp.

Jim Curtis smiled to himself, he was thinking about the two sweaty bodies in the back of the flatbed the night they'd tagged Mr Mokese's car. He wondered what stage the proceedings were at once the shit had hit the fan! He started to giggle. Voss looked at him and grinned – it was infectious – and one by one, the others broke into broad-mouthed grins, then giggles, and then all at once, they began to laugh. They had no idea what they were laughing at, but it seemed so funny that at one stage, Kaminski found himself rolling about on the floor with his legs in the air. It was several minutes before they could gather their composure and be on their way again. It was an unusual spectacle, given the context, but then they were unusual people.

'Very unprofessional,' Schollonburg commented later.

Curtis agreed but had to walk away to avoid another attack of the giggles.

But life had returned to normal for the men and soon, they'd be coming out for a rest. First, though, there would be the small matter of a bridge and its imminent disappearance!

Grillo and Kaminski, on the other hand, wanted someone's head on a plate for the death of their friend Kurt Willt and they'd have their revenge no matter how long it took. Everyone understood – no one questioned their motives. The rest just accepted that someone would pay.

Curtis' memory flashed back and forth through the rooms in his mind. Doors opened and closed with ease; others had to be forced; and some he slammed shut after the briefest peep. Then, visions of one particular journey loomed large.

The Journey

That night is speeding on to greet
Your epitaphic rhyme.
Your life is but a little beat
Within the heart of Time.

Robert Service; *Just Think*

During the early to mid 1970s, the IRA experienced a split in its ranks. The leadership decided that the armed struggle could not and, indeed, should not be sustained indefinitely and so opted for a long-range plan of a political fight to win its overall aim of a united Ireland.

Many of its members agreed, but a considerable number, many from the more urban areas, disagreed but knew that an armed conflict with the British was untenable. And so, whilst not openly admitting that they couldn't win the military conflict, they would, behind the scenes, pursue a plan to take over and then dominate all organised crime in Ireland and so maintain the power base.

Their leadership, in general, would have no part in crime of any sort choosing, instead, to follow their goal by political means only. And so they turned a blind eye to those members who opted to follow the route of organised crime, insisting they knew nothing of their criminal activities, to maintain that future power base. The governments of Britain and Southern Ireland also opted to turn a blind eye, or at least to pay less attention than they should have. In return, the PIRA would indulge and commit fully to the peace process.

Both governments failed completely to appreciate the lengths to which the PIRA would go to achieve its aim to dominate organised crime and subsequently move from sophisticated terrorist organisations to sophisticated criminal overlords, and this may be how it happened ...

*   *   *

75

James Edward Brinton spoke in hushed tones to his fellow conspirator Joe McKenna. They were travelling along the Dublin Road on their way to visit one Sam Mullen, who sat on the PIRA council, along with its other five members: four men and one woman. She was a newcomer with an impressive CV.

Brinton, at 34 years of age, had spent the last eighteen years of his life as a member of one Republican movement or another and the last six years as a sworn-in member of the IRA. His rise in the organisation had been meteoric and was achieved firstly through his youthful enthusiasm for the cause and later, as a result of "things done". "Things done" included the assassination of prominent figures – the latest victim being a High Court judge who, not three weeks before, had been dropping his wife at the hairdresser's in the Armagh town of Newry for her six-weekly hairdo.

He'd calmly walked alongside the couple as the judge had escorted his good lady along the busy pavements to Cute Curls Salon and, as the lawman had moved to open the door of the shop, Brinton had stepped forward, smiling as he did the job for him. The judge had returned the smile in thanks and had stepped to one side; his wife had done the same.

Brinton allowed her to enter and as she did, he closed the door behind her, turning to the judge, saying, 'You're very welcome, Judge. Now, here's my second good deed for the day ...'

Producing a pearl-handled, nickel-plated Colt 45, he'd aimed it directly at him.

The Judge stood, mortified, but only for a split second, as Brinton had fired two bullets into his chest, followed by a further five rounds into the fallen man's head. Passers-by had dived for cover. The judge's wife stared, transfixed, through the glass door at the prostrate form of her now late husband, while two small girls screamed and sobbed not 6 feet from Brinton, clutched to the breast of their terrified mother. A milkman had dropped a crate of milk, its contents mixing with the blood of the judge on the pavement. A man on a motor scooter had crashed into the back of the milk float, his attention ripped away from the road ahead by the chaos before him. And at centre stage, Brinton had calmly replaced the Colt in his shoulder holster and, turning to face the judge's wife, with a broad smile, he had given her a polite wave as if greeting an old friend, before calmly walking to his getaway car, to be driven into anonymity. This last act triggering unearthly wails from Mrs Judge, now inconsolable in her grief.

Brinton had then disappeared into the busy traffic and hasn't been seen since.

It was one more kill for the movement; one more blow for the establishment; one more step towards a united Ireland; one more tick in the box of Brinton's CV – ruthless, focused, determined, daring, cool, cruel – "The right man for the job".

Brinton, his rank now "Commandant Force" in PIRA parlance, was Brigade Commander of South Armagh Brigade PIRA. Newly installed, he was considered to be an A-list terrorist by MI5, SB and British Army Intelligence – one of the top five most wanted men in the province; the passenger in the car with him being another. Both were Belfast men who, unusually, had been moved south to control and coordinate operations against the Brits in the fight to dominate the battlefield of South Armagh.

Their appointment was testament to the high esteem in which both men were held by the army council – at least that's what they'd told themselves – in an area generally considered on all sides of the conflict's divide to be frequented by the most militarily professional, ruthless and able PIRA brigades north or south of the border.

They'd been summoned to a meeting of considerable importance – they supposed – by Mullen, whose farm lay near the village of Forkhill.

His own local surveillance and intelligence team would warn him of the imminent arrival of his two subordinates. He would then drive the short distance to the village along Carrickstricken, where he'd cross the South Bridge. Then, turning left on Main Street, he'd pass the Forrester's and Patrick Tommelty's house – a local smuggler and sympathiser – on the left, with the barracks on the right. Continuing south, where the Main Street became Carrive Road, past the Carrive Road/Sheen Road junction, up the hill and so over the border into the "Free State" at Dungooly Cross Roads. Here, the tractor would be exchanged for a "staff" car and Brinton and McKenna would join him, leaving their vehicle, along with the tractor, in the barn of a sympathiser until later that night, when both vehicles would be driven to pre-arranged PUPs near the town of Dundalk.

Selected individuals would return them north with no police "trace", whilst other arrangements would be made for the return journeys of Mullen, Brinton and McKenna, using hire cars from the south – or not!

Both men believed in the movement and both also believed in a bit of free enterprise on the side, especially McKenna. Brinton loved to speak of its heroes from the past: of De Valera, Michael Collins, 'And,' said Brinton, still in hushed tones, 'my grandfather, who fought in the Easter uprising in 1916. The leaders were all executed by the fuckin' Brits, the bastards. They've been executing us ever since. B-Specials, the bastard Black and Tans, dragging true Irishmen from their homes and shooting them in front of their bairns.'

His grandfather had again taken part in the campaign against Brit cities between 1938 and 1945 and he had also offered a safe haven to the Germans in World War II. He'd fought here on the border in the 1956–7 campaign, but it had failed. Although, he always said, 'One lost game doesn't mean it's over, lad. We'll play them again with a bigger ball one day, ha, ha, so we will.'

'Jesus, Jim, how many times are you going to tell me that fuckin' story? We need to look to the future – take the fight forward – we need to take control of other forms of finance, anything and everything.' McKenna was referring directly to crime.

'Yes, yes, I know, I know,' replied Brinton impatiently. 'But we should never forget those who've gone before, right? We have a duty to continue what they started.'

'I'm aware of that, but let's concentrate on the work at hand. I wonder what they want?' said McKenna. 'Must be important for Sam Mullen to call for us. I'm in favour of moving the campaign to the mainland – hit them where it hurts most.'

'That's been tried before, Joe.'

'I know,' replied McKenna, 'but with the right people and the right finances –'

Brinton cut him short, 'Let's wait and see first, shall we?'

It had started to rain as they'd turned away from the village of Drumintee, past The Three Steps pub, where they'd captured the Brit spy Capt. Nielson, towards Forkhill. On the outskirts of the village, a patrol from the army base at Forkhill was stopping every few vehicles and questioning the occupants. They waited in the queue, but were waved on when the car in front was pulled over. Both men looked straight ahead and drove on. In the village, they crossed North Bridge and then turned left on Main Street, past another foot patrol. Both made mental notes. In front of them, a red Massey Ferguson crossed South Bridge and turned south. They followed on behind, heading towards Dungooly Cross Roads and the "Free State".

As they crossed the border, both men relaxed slightly knowing they were, to some degree, on "home ground"; although they wouldn't feel safe until they were much further away from the border.

They were well aware of the agreement – between the Brit government in London and the Irish government in Dublin: to allow British troops to cross the border whilst in hot pursuit or after a contact. The PIRA, whether they cared to admit it or not, were paranoid about the activities of units such as 14 Int. Coy, the SAS, E4A from the RUC SB and the Para Brigades pathfinders. All highly effective and professional covert operators who, the PIRA believed, inhabited every bush; they were also convinced that they operated south of the border.

These units were responsible for the many "silent" victories the SF achieved over the enemy in the Province, saving many lives and preventing the destruction of vast amounts of property through bombings, etc.

They had been told that their destination was Dundalk. The address, memorised by both men, was "Kevin Barry Drive". Previous and future meetings were, and would continue to be, held in different locations and once at the address, they'd be directed to their final destination.

The road wound its way south-east through rolling countryside; twice, they'd been held up by flocks of sheep and cattle being herded along the narrow lanes to new grazing. While Mullen accepted this patiently, the city-boys, already on edge over the impending meet, sat in the Vauxhall Cavalier impatiently tapping feet and drumming fingers. They travelled on, south-east, towards Dundalk.

About 5 miles short of the town's outskirts, they stopped at a pub called The Dancing Man. Parking the car outside, they entered, leaving the keys in the ignition.

'God bless all here!' exclaimed Mullen.

The bar was deserted except for the owner, who made a brief phone call and then asked what they wanted to drink. A peat fire glowed warmly in the hearth; turf, smoke, beer and old leather smells hung in the air. All three opted for Bushmills Irish. The owner served up doubles, which they quaffed, and they were immediately served with three more – no money changed hands.

Mullen spoke first. 'How's the weather, Sean?'

'All's well in the east.'

Mullen nodded his approval. Then, beckoning his accomplices with a nod towards the corner of the bar, the big man turned and all three moved and sat down at a wooden table surrounded by four chairs. An aluminium ashtray and a couple of Guinness mats lay on the table.

Mullen faced the entrance, while Brinton and McKenna sat with their backs to the corner, facing the bar. A small whippet lay curled up in front of the fire, paying scant attention whilst scratching a bald patch in its brindle fur.

As was his habit, Mullen spoke in hushed tones, interrupting Brinton's gaze, which had settled on an oil painting of Michael Collins that hung above the bar. On its left was the Irish tricolour – green, white and gold – in the centre of which had been sewn a flame-shaped piece of silk in orange and white – the eternal flame of Republicanism; below it were the words: *Sinn Fein*, the Gaelic; meaning: Ourselves Alone.

This, all contained in a wooden frame and glass. The date on the frame was 1922.

To the right of the Collins was a sepia-coloured photograph of three men dressed in boots and trench coats, with belts tied around the waists; oversized flat caps completed the outfits. The men all carried 303 Lee Enfields; British Army issue. Probably captured during a raid on a barracks, thought Brinton, fascinated. Grandfather could have been there, too, with these very men, he thought. The caption at the bottom of the photo read: Jones, Wilson and Martin, members of a flying column murdered by the Black and Tans, August 1921 at Mullingar, West Meath, in an ambush. To the right of this was a photograph of Pope John Paul.

'The eternal flame burns brightly hereabouts, but not all Irish hearts beat for the cause, as you well know,' whispered Mullen into Brinton's ear. 'The need for security is now greater than ever if we are to take the fight forward and to that end, a great deal of thought has been given to the way we finance our operations and face the future. Changes at the top – referring to the inclusion of a woman on the Army Council – have brought with it the wind of change for us all and you'll be hearing more of this in due course.'

The city boys were intrigued and Brinton started to speak, 'What kind –' But the raised paw of Mullen cut him short. 'About the size of a spade and calloused in keeping with the rest of his huge frame.' The smell of bacon cooking drifted into the bar. He stood, his 6 feet 4 inch frame almost touching the smoke-stained ceiling. Turning to the bar, he said, 'God bless all here.'

The owner nodded in response and then all three men were on their way, stomachs rumbling.

Outside, the Vauxhall Cavalier was gone. Replaced by a Volkswagen Passat estate, the keys were already in the ignition. Mullen squeezed himself into the driver's seat, sliding it back as far as it would go.

McKenna and Brinton climbed into the passenger and rear seat respectively. Then Mullen drove slowly away.

After about a mile, Mullen noticed that they had company; a Southern Irish police car, the Garda, were following behind. He continued his journey at 35 mph, keeping a weather-eye on the police.

Then, five minutes later, the police turned off and disappeared.

Mullen satisfied himself that they had no interest in the Passat and pressed on through the rain. The lush countryside of County Monaghan, gleaming like a jewel, enveloped the car. Green, jade and emerald, with silver ribbons of rivers and streams, glittering discs of lakes and ponds and drystone walls, crowned with blackthorn and hawthorn, partitioned the patchwork of fields and enclosures, where sheep and cattle grazed.

Now and again, they passed small stone cottages; some occupied and painted. Doors, surrounded by climbing roses and thatched roofs, shunned the persistent rain. The roads were, in many places, unkempt and neglected, with potholes every few yards, and at one point, they drove through a ford alongside the remains of a wooden bridge – long since fallen into decay – which was slowly being swallowed up by the stream and washed away piecemeal. As if mourning the bridge's demise, standing alongside was a small stone shrine containing a statue of the Blessed Virgin Mary, hands clasped in prayer, surrounded by rotting posies of flowers, a teddy bear, a small child's shoe and a doll – tiny offerings left with prayers by local folk.

The further east they travelled, the lighter the rain became and soon it stopped. The low, brooding grey-black rain clouds gave way to a deep azure-blue sky. House martins dipped and scythed through the air and two large buzzards caught Brinton's attention up ahead, above a large oak. He gazed out, disinterested, with a city boy's eye, as they spiralled around and upwards, riding the thermals, harried by crows.

Mullen marvelled at the gift of flight and saw, from a countryman's view, so much more than Brinton. Indeed, he had voted against the appointment of Brinton and McKenna on the very basis that to operate in rural Armagh effectively took a true countryman – someone at one with the countryside, someone with the place in his bones – not townies, used to the big city and crowds, with the noise and the traffic.

He had argued that they were a different kind of people, almost foreign. But he was overruled and had to succumb to the greater power.

He'd heard McKenna and Brinton were good men, who had both proved their worth. But he also believed in horses for courses and he reckoned these were the wrong nags for Armagh. Still, he was professional enough to know that even in his position, he wasn't party to the whole picture. He would continue to play his part in the great scheme of things: for the struggle, *Sinn Fein*, "Ourselves Alone" and the *Eternal Flame*.

County Monaghan stretched south-east to County Louth, bounded to the north by the border area of South Armagh and County Down; colloquially known as "bandit country" by the Brits. To the south lay County Cavan with Louth to the east.

Brinton wrinkled his nose at the smell of a muck spreader in a field to his right. Mullen, seeing his reaction in the mirror, grinned.

'The road to righteousness smells of shite, eh, Jim?' he laughed.

Brinton held a hand over his nose and mouth. McKenna mirrored him. Mullen shook his head and drove on.

About a mile further on, the road rounded a sharp bend and dipped below an avenue of ancient hawthorns, which had grown together to meet above, forming a natural tunnel of about 50 yards long and, because of the bend in the road and the dip, they had, in effect, disappeared from sight both at ground level and from the air. Mullen pulled the car tight over to the left-hand side of the road, behind a white Ford Transit.

He climbed out of his vehicle and walked to the driver's side of the van and spoke through the window to its occupant, who appeared to hand Mullen a letter, which he quickly read and then placed in his pocket.

McKenna and Brinton watched as the van driver dismounted and walked back to their car, accompanied by Mullen. The man, dressed in a blue boiler suit and woollen hat, climbed into the passenger seat of the Passat and Mullen gestured to McKenna and Brinton to get out and follow him to the van. This, they did without question.

Mullen opened up the back, ordering them to jump in. Closing the doors behind them, he climbed into the driver's seat and, executing a neat three-point turn in the confined space of the lane, he pulled away in the direction from which they'd come.

Looking out of the back windows of the van, Brinton saw the Passat continue on its journey towards Dundalk. Then, suddenly, the van was back out into daylight and on its way west, in the opposite direction; the whole operation had taken less than two minutes and was part of the usual deception and counter-surveillance precautions employed by both sides in the conflict.

In the back of the Transit, they had company. Sitting on a bench behind the driver's seat sat another man, also dressed in a blue boiler suit, only this man wore a black balaclava. Brinton noticed the man's large frame and his piercing blue-grey eyes; cold eyes. Without speaking, the man produced a further two balaclavas from a pocket in his boiler suit. He pointed first at Brinton and, without a word, beckoned with his right hand for Brinton to join him on the bench.

The man pulled the blue balaclava over Brinton's head and then put a pair of Amplivox ear defenders over the mask – the eyeholes at the back – then he firmly shoved Brinton back towards the rear of the van. Brinton felt his way back to his seat. The same process was repeated, with McKenna also receiving a black mask, and thus the two men continued their journey, blind and deaf.

In the driver's seat, Mullen grinned broadly. An hour later, the van rumbled to a halt and both Mullen and the boiler-suited man climbed out and walked to the rear doors. McKenna and Brinton had dozed off in their desensitised world.

Mullen and his accomplice took an elbow each and guided first McKenna and then Brinton out of the van and positioned them, facing each other, at the side of the road. They had stopped in a thick wood.

The heady smell of pine hung in the humid air beneath the trees and silence prevailed. Deep drainage ditches bordered the road on both sides; a low rumble of thunder rolled across the sky.

After a short while, Jim Brinton's ear defenders and balaclava were pulled from his head. His sight was blurred for several seconds but as his vision cleared, he saw, standing 3 feet in front and facing him, the masked figure of his long-time friend Joe McKenna. Standing beside McKenna was the man in the boiler suit, arm extended, fist grasping what Brinton instantly recognised as a Tokarev, which was pointing straight at McKenna's head. No sooner had his mind taken in the information than the man squeezed the trigger and the soft-nosed hollow head round hit McKenna in the right side of the head and exited, exploding out on the left; the flattened round removing the face from the cheekbone to the crown of the skull, along with its contents. Something wet hit Brinton in the face. The dead McKenna tilted in slow motion, before dropping sideways into the peaty water of the 5 feet ditch.

Gripped roughly by the scruff of the neck, Jim Brinton was bundled back into the van by Mullen as the boiler-suited man covered the corpse with branches. Then, rejoining Mullen, the journey continued with James Edward Brinton in a state of shock and mortal terror in the rear, struggling desperately with a myriad of questions racing through his mind and fighting for an answer to what he'd just witnessed.

Mullen recognised this and spoke into the interior mirror of the van.

'Your friend was a traitor; later, you will find out why.'

Brinton tried to speak but as he wiped McKenna's blood from his eyes, he couldn't form the words.

Mullen continued, 'A wee girl called Roisin Rafferty from Drumintee fingered him. The security group interrogated her on an unrelated matter – she poured her little heart out, the wee bitch – but don't worry, Jim lad, there are no plans to send you on the same journey as McKenna – at least, not that I know of.'

It was a classic PIRA execution serving two clear purposes: one, to dispose of a weak link – a spy, a tout, a traitor, someone who should know better – call it what you will. And two, to reinforce to those who remained the absolute will of the organisation to dispose of any threat to its existence and to terminate with extreme prejudice any such threat, either real or perceived. It was emphatic.

'If you want to play big boys games, you'd better be prepared for the big boys rules. Roisin wasn't and neither was Eaimon Blaire.'

The clock ticked; time moved on and so did the van. Brinton felt nausea welling up and was sick in the back. The psychological trauma of witnessing the execution of McKenna, along with the uncertainty of his own future, was proving too much for him.

During his time in the movement, Brinton had himself committed several executions, but had had time to steel himself from those. They didn't come out of the blue like this one. What the fuck was going on? he wondered to himself; and in growing desperation, he began to shake.

Mullen spoke over his shoulder and Brinton jumped at the shock of the unexpected words.

'Right, Jim lad. Get your hood back on, boyo. Not long now.'

Brinton hesitated and Mullen, once again seeing his plight, reiterated his statement that there was nothing to fear.

Brinton gained little solace from the big man's words. Instead, he slipped on the reversed balaclava and let his thoughts drift to the silent boiler-suited killer seated next to Mullen. The man hadn't spoken a word since they'd met in the back of the van. Not a yes, aye, nor a kiss me arse.

The thought of his presence made Brinton deeply uncomfortable. Then, the van stopped. Brinton stiffened and waited.

Both front doors opened and then banged shut. Footsteps approached the rear of the vehicle and the doors were flung open; Brinton gasped.

Strong hands took him by the arms, guiding him out of the vehicle onto a concrete surface. His legs buckled and he fell to his knees but was roughly brought back up to his feet. He was standing in a concrete-covered farm-type yard; a stone wall enclosed a small pen inside which clustered a dozen or so sheep. There were two men stood amongst the sheep, one holding a large, wishbone-shaped electric stunner, which he closed on each side of a sheep's head, sending a shock through the animal's brain. It fell to the floor of the pen, twitching, and was immediately seized by the other man. Gripping it between his legs, he pulled the beast's head back and slit its throat from ear to ear. Turning to its rear end, he then pushed a sharp meat hook through its leg – between the hock and tendon – and pulled on a chain shackle, lifting the animal clear off the ground, free to hang above a large trough into which its blood gushed.

This was the sight that greeted Brinton as the balaclava was unceremoniously ripped from his head. He remembered immediately that the body of the Brit spy Capt. Nielson, whom they'd captured at The Three Steps pub in Drumintee, had been brought to a place just like this to be disposed of after his interrogation and murder. Brinton himself had been involved in that. Nielson had been a hard bastard, tough as hell, thought Brinton, and he had told them nothing; even when they'd blow-torched his feet before hooding and shooting him. In the end, only a handful of people knew he'd been fed piecemeal to the pigs and one of those was Brinton; another had been left in a ditch less than an hour ago. Jesus, thought Brinton, was that what this was all about?

There were two others and he knew where one of them was; he'd seen him in Belfast just yesterday. The other, a woman, had been on the security group and no fucker knew where or when they would appear. The Brits had relentlessly pursued the answer as to the mystery of Nielson's disappearance and Brinton wondered whether they'd been getting too close for comfort of late. Was this the organisation cutting its links with that particular job? Severing any connections by the disappearance of those involved? He knew only too well the mechanics of these things. The best guarantee of a closed mouth was a dead owner. He knew there would be no way out – there would be endless, desperate hours of remorseless interrogation; although he couldn't imagine what answers they would seek from him. He had, by now, resigned himself to the idea that the end would come soon and he sought solace in the memory of his grandfather as he always had when things became rough.

But then, a firm shove between the shoulder blades brought him back. It was Mullen again.

'C'mon, Jim. Wake up. Time to meet the Pope,' he jibed.

Brinton forced a half smile and started to walk, his feet like lead.

He was ushered on, past the slaughter pen and past rows of hanging animals, all at different stages of slaughter. They passed on through a long barn, in the corner of which was the entrance to a breeze-block enclosed staircase. Climbing the stairs, they came, after three flights, to a landing, which was carpeted and laid out like a waiting room. There were two easy chairs and a low, square coffee table with several magazines: *Irish Life, Modern Agriculture*, etc. On top of the pile was a copy of the *Belfast Telegraph*. The front page headline spoke of a visit from Pope John Paul and a sideline trumpeted the news that the bodies of a young man and woman had been found on the main Newry to Dublin railway line on the Kilnasaggart Bridge near the South Armagh village of Jonesborough.

The area had been cordoned off by the military and the clearance op was under way. The clearance, according to the report, was likely to take a further two days. The report cited unconfirmed speculation that the bodies were those of the missing Drumintee girl Roisin Rafferty and her close associate Eaimon Blaire. Police had warned their families to expect the worst.

Roisin, thought Brinton. Roisin? That, he was sure, was the name Mullen had quoted when he'd said, 'A wee girl called Roisin from Drumintee fingered him.' So they'd removed her as well; but who was this Eaimon Blaire? Brinton asked himself. But, of course, that was irrelevant. Even though Brinton didn't realise it, Blaire was just a pawn – a nobody that no longer existed.

The man in the boiler suit stood in the corner of the small room, towering over Brinton. Is he guarding me, or keeping me company? Brinton couldn't decide. He chose to venture a question, 'Can I get a drink? I'm choking with thirst here.' He had tried to interject some confidence into the question but immediately knew it had sounded like someone waiting to die.

The boiler-suited man didn't speak but simply raised an outstretched arm, hand mimicking a gun, pointing first at Brinton and then he swung it to his left and stopped, with it indicating towards a mini fridge in the corner on a small table.

Brinton got to his feet, walked the three paces to the fridge and opened the door. Inside, there were three large bottles of sparkling spring water. He grabbed one like a man finding an oasis in the desert, cracked it open and poured, gulping the whole of its contents, non-stop. Dropping the empty bottle into a waste bin, he took out another and, turning back to Mr Boiler Suit, he saw that the man was already gesticulating back at Brinton's chair. He sat down. He's guarding me, thought Brinton, answering his own question.

At that moment, the door next to the fridge was opened by yet another boiler-suited man who, along with Brinton's escort, led him along a corridor lined with photographs on an agricultural theme: tractors, combine harvesters, open fields with great round hay bales.

The corridor terminated at another door, where all three men stopped and Mr Boiler Suit Number Two knocked. There was a pause and then the door opened into complete blackness. Brinton was shoved firmly forwards into the darkness and the door clicked shut behind him. He heard a key turn in the lock. He stood, blind in total darkness, blinking. Then, like a startled deer, Brinton jumped as strong arms gripped him by the elbows, cannoning him several paces forwards to a chair, where he was unceremoniously forced down to await his fate.

He sensed someone standing to his rear and if he could, he would have seen two men, both armed. The members of the army council had achieved their own brand of greatness by being careful; hence, the unconventional arrival of Brinton. He sat, waiting. Then, without warning, a light was switched on above and to his front. From the darkness beyond and above the lamp came the disembodied voice of a woman speaking, which Brinton thought must be through what sounded like a speaker or intercom of some sort.

'Your reputation precedes you, Mr James Edward Brinton. Born 1 July 1950. Twinbrook Gardens, Twinbrook Estate, West Belfast. Youngest of three, your two brothers Michael and Shaun were killed by their own bomb two years ago almost to the day. We've outgrown that sort of thing, you understand, Mr Brinton?' More professional and more technically adept.' The voice was full of contempt.

Brinton listened intently to the voice from the darkness. It betrayed no emotion and no compassion, even at the mention of Brinton's brothers, who now lay in Milltown Cemetery – or what was left of them – in the plot laid aside for fallen volunteers.

The voice continued, 'Mother: Mary Theresa Cecilia Brinton – née Martin. Father: Patrick Joseph Collum Brinton. Both deceased.'

There was silence as the seconds ticked by. Brinton strained to see into the darkness beyond the light, but couldn't.

'You've been "chosen", along with your friend, the traitor, McKenna, to come here today, but both for very different reasons. Clearly, the reason for McKenna's visit was demonstrated en route. For you, though, it was an unpleasant but necessary sojourn, however brief, through the world of the traitor. A demonstration intended simply to remind and focus your attention; to concentrate the mind on the one thing that, above all others, keeps us one step ahead of the Brits – security. Security at all levels preserves our survival. It ensures our very existence.'

'Do you understand that, Mr Brinton?'

The interrogative took Brinton by surprise. It was a man's voice now, coming from beneath his seat.

'Yes, yes. I do entirely understand.'

'Then you have no further need for concern. Now, we can get down to business. How's the leg?'

It was a man's voice again, only a different one from the right.

'Nasty wound, that. Any long-term effects?'

It had been four years since the injury he'd received during a firefight with the Brit Paras in the Ballymurphy area of the city. He'd been spirited away across the border to Donegal and had spent the next six months recovering under the watchful eye of a doctor from the "city of the tribes". It had been a pleasant period in his otherwise hectic existence, which was over all too soon, and he was catapulted straight back in at the deep end as Battalion Commander West Belfast Brigade PIRA.

Then the voice of the woman spoke this time, 'Mr Brinton, your pedigree, as you may well imagine, is well-known to us. Important positions occasionally have to be filled or created. In your case, it would be the latter. Are you with me, Mr Brinton?'

He was trying to concentrate but finding it difficult.

'Yes. Yes, I am. Of course I am; it's just –'

The voice cut him short.

'Good. Now, pay very close attention to what I have to say. The movement is in, shall we say, a transitional period', pondered the voice. 'Yes! Transitional.'

'Transitional. Many meetings have been held with government representatives from both Dublin and London. To cut a long and complicated story short, both are prepared to turn a blind eye – although neither would care to admit it publicly – to the organisation's extra-curricular activities in exchange for our full cooperation, commitment and participation in peace talks to end the armed struggle … a struggle we cannot win.'

There was another pause for effect. Brinton's jaw dropped. He couldn't believe what he was hearing. He was being told, ultimately by the nerve centre – the heart and soul of the movement – that they had agreed to surrender the armed struggle. To give in. To throw it all away. To turn tail. To run. To fade away – he felt like a slowly deflating balloon.

Then the voice again: 'Outwardly, the struggle will continue – probably for many years to come – but in the end, there will be capitulation. It is up to the movement to make preparations to move from armed struggle to political struggle in the time we have left, but there is another road we must take to preserve our power base. Control of organised crime throughout the whole of Ireland is now our undeclared aim. We will achieve this by stealth and cunning. We will be ruthless in our endeavours; failure is not an option and you, along with others, will be at the cutting edge of our new crusade. You will, to a greater degree, be allowed to expand and pursue on behalf of the movement in any way you see fit. That does not mean you will have "carte blanche" to operate any little sideline, like the black cab scam you've been running back in the city, and your own personal endeavours alone will ensure you survive.'

Brinton stiffened. How in God's name did they know about that? He fought the urge to reply.

'Yes, Mr Brinton. We are well aware of your activities in that direction. Roisin saw to that. By the way, your account in Jersey has been closed. Yes, we are aware of that, too, and the balance of £257,614.22 has been donated to a worthy cause – our cause. There is nothing we don't know, Mr Brinton. Enough, wouldn't you say, to warrant severe repercussions.'

He knew full well what he was being told. He was going to go forward with his new career; success was his only option – as criminal overlord – or there would be plenty of room in the ditch next to McKenna. So, McKenna, his long-time friend, had touted on him. His extra-curricular activities – Roisin – and their pillow talk was now public knowledge – via the security group – and Brinton's black cab secret was out of the bag, thanks to McKenna.

'Yes,' replied James Edward Brinton, feeling like nothing more than a whipped dog. Jesus! Can no one be trusted? he thought. He'd been caught out, picked up by the scruff of the neck, shaken around and cast to the ground.

'So you know as much in this direction as necessary and now all that is to be done is for you to go forward in the world and succeed. Yes – succeed. Or else … well … I'll leave the rest to your own imagination. But remember this, Mr James Edward Brinton, you took a solemn oath some years ago and you've strayed from it. It will not happen again,' said the voice, with such venom that Brinton shrank back in the chair.

'You will be scrutinised day and night, during waking and sleeping hours, and even in your dreams. The movement will know your worth.'

And then, blinded by light, he was spun around, hoisted to his feet and frogmarched from the room, down the stairs and out into the open air. Before he knew it, he was back in the van and on his way again, on the roller coaster of shock and confusion that had become his world that day.

Brinton wanted to ask endless questions of Mullen, who continued to drive west, back through County Monahan. The scenery flashed by and he fought the urge to speak. He felt deeply uneasy about the presence of the cruel-eyed, boiler-suited man, who had dispatched McKenna, still silently seated in the front of the van.

But it was Mullen who punctuated the silence with the first words spoken since Brinton had been catapulted from the darkened room.

'Everything you've experienced today, Jim-boy, has been for a reason. To focus and concentrate your mind on your duty from now on; and, of course, to demonstrate the consequences if you fail the movement again. You've been blessed with two lives, lad, and the first has already been flushed down the pan. You're into your second now and it hangs by a tenuous thread. You're still with us; one, because of your successes in the past, and two, because of your obvious intellect. The combination of the two, along with your many other attributes, combine to make you a considerable asset to the movement; but, be in no doubt that you are most definitely not indispensable and if you make the same old mistake again – or even a new one – you will be off the planet in the blink of an eye.' The van came to a standstill and Mullen turned and looked over his shoulder at Brinton. 'Understand?' Brinton nodded and Mullen's hard face cracked into a broad grin. 'Good! Then we're friends again. And now I'd like you to meet your new "best" friend.'

He turned, with his huge, right paw opened upward, and gestured towards Brinton's boiler-suited companion. Brinton turned to face the cold-eyed killer and as he did so, the man pulled the balaclava from his shaven, square-jawed head. Steel blue-grey humourless eyes stared straight through Brinton. A jagged scar ran from the bridge of the man's nose down across his left cheek, ending in the stubble at the corner of his mouth. His steady gaze didn't waiver. Mullen urged the two to shake hands.

Lt. Col. Konstantin Alexandr Kashitskin, former Russian SF, now retired, had a strong grip.

'He works with us now. There'll be a couple of days hereabouts. Time for you to rest yourself. Time to plant the seeds of progress. Out you get, Jim-lad; knock on the door and wait.'

* * *

Brinton jumped out of the van, which drove away, leaving him standing alone at the garden gate of an archetypal Irish cottage.

Whitewashed walls, thatched roof and leaded windows, with turf smoke spiralling skywards in the still air. After his experiences in the first half of the day, it felt surreal.

He gazed at the front door; the horseshoe that looked back at him was nailed at eye level below a shiny brass bull's-head knocker. He walked along the path, the setting sun on his back – still warm. Night-scented stock and dwarf nicotiana bordered the path and a well-established wisteria, with its lilac blooms resembling bunches of ripe grapes, clung in large clusters along its searching tendrils as it felt its way around the shape of the house. Scent from the flowers magnified itself in Brinton's already heightened senses. A wave of exhaustion washed over him and he craved sleep.

At the doorstep, he raised a heavy hand and grasping the brass bull's head, he knocked three times. Soon, shuffling footsteps approached and the door opened to reveal the tiniest lady Brinton had ever seen; her attire – all lace and frills – reminded him of widow Tallan's housekeeper in the film *The Quiet Man*. Without giving Brinton time to speak, she said, like a loving, old aunt, in a broad Donegal accent, 'Ah, yes, yes, yes, come in, come in. You're expected.'

She stepped aside and Brinton, towering above her, walked into the house, bending slightly to avoid banging his head on the low wooden beams.

'This way, this way,' she said as she led him through her parlour into a bathroom, blocked with steam from the bath that was full of foaming, hot water.

There were some clean clothes folded neatly over the back of a chair and a large blue bath sheet hung across a brass radiator. The strong smell of lavender filled Brinton's nostrils, massaging his mind, and he swayed on his feet. A tiny voice from behind him suggested he take his time and relax in the welcoming pool.

'There'll be good food and a soft, warm bed when you're done. Now, go ahead and fix yourself up. Just drop your old things in here,' said the woman, handing him a large, clear plastic bag. 'Everything – shoes and all now.' Then she was gone, closing the door behind her.

Brinton took a deep breath and started to undress, stuffing his clothes in the bag and dumping it in the corner.

Slipping into the bathwater, he luxuriated in its hot, comforting cloak. A pulse in his temple thumped and his head ached. Forcing himself to stay awake, he considered everything that had happened that day, concluding that he'd been more than lucky to end up in a hot bath as opposed to McKenna's present abode. He'd been caught out, filleted and but for the grace of God, he'd have gone the same way as McKenna.

He considered the dozens of men and women in and around the movement, who'd been dispatched, disappeared, removed and suicided for far lesser misdemeanours than his own. He was only here now, according to the disembodied voice at the meeting, because of his past performance and intellect. He had value; his parents had been right after all, he thought, when they'd constantly extolled the virtues of hard work and the benefits of obtaining a good education. He'd done just that and completed a degree in the University of Belfast, gaining a first in Political Sciences.

He knew he possessed a good level of business acumen and it would be this that would project him and the movement forward from the realms of the sophisticated terrorist organisation to sophisticated criminal overlords, controlling all organised crime across Northern and Southern Ireland, just as the army council had commanded. It would be through a myriad of fronts, ranging from the successes of the black cab business, VAT fraud and dodgy disk sales in Belfast, to the fishing industry in the south, smuggling along the border, shops and services of all kinds.

Pubs and clubs would be used to launder dirty money from DVD sales, robberies and multimillion pound deals with African and Colombian drug barons through extremely secret, versatile and ruthless, worldwide smuggling networks. And so the seeds were sewn and politicians did, indeed, look the other way or pay far less attention than necessary, giving instructions to SB to cease the use of well-placed informers, citing their use as ethically wrong in view of the ongoing peace process; unbelievably naive. Whilst doing so, they failed cataclysmically to realise the depths to which the PIRA, - driven organised crime would undermine society, as PIRA had no such qualms. Its arms have, indeed, grown long and they reach into virtually all corners of crime.

The politicos concentrated far too closely on the peace campaign and totally underestimated the ability of the movement to change in other directions in order to maintain its hold on power. This metamorphosis would ultimately cost both governments far more than the conflict itself and not just financially. It would force them to move from armed conflict to a far more widespread and serious fight to control the apparently insurmountable trafficking of drugs and people worldwide. Hardened terrorists would be given freedom from jail and prosecution; many would be released as a result of government deals.

And it was against this backdrop that James Edward Brinton came to select his underlings and then control and coordinate ops overseen, albeit from a distance, by the very satisfied and vindicated army council.

Several loud knocks on the door brought Brinton out of the sleep that had eventually overtaken him.

'Right, missus, I'll be there now.'

Some ten minutes later, he was sitting at a perfectly laid table in the small front room of the cottage. The stone floors were highly polished and spotlessly clean. An open fire glowed with burning turf and alongside stood a blackleaded open range cooker, which was no longer in use. The stone walls, 2 feet thick, were plastered and painted white; photos of the family variety adorned the walls. Pope John Paul gazed down benevolently from within a frame above the open fire. The window, bordered by perfectly hung, real lace curtains, looked out over a neat rear garden, beyond which stretched the open countryside of Southern Ireland. The window seat sported a thick, hand-stitched cushion, covered in green and gold paisley-patterned cloth. In the centrepiece of Brinton's table was a small vase of dwarf nicotiana; the heady fragrance of their blossom hovering and mixing with the smell of burning turf. The table was laid for two people, each setting with a place mat, knife, fork and spoon. The cutlery, Brinton decided, was more than just of the everyday variety, which you normally found at most people's tables; there was quality here. It was solid silver and beaded of the highest standard, which spoke volumes to Brinton. He was a well-educated, working-class man, but he knew style when he saw it and this little old lady had it in spades.

The grandfather clock in the corner chimed 4.00 p.m. and continued its comforting tick, tock, tick and the crockery displayed on the handmade cherry wood and maple dresser oozed value. Brinton could hear his host moving about in the kitchen, cooking and humming to herself. 'Not long now, not long now,' she repeated, as was her way; and Brinton smiled to himself.

She appeared from the parlour and holding a box of matches, she proceeded to light candles in various parts of the room; all now in single silver candelabras, except for the table, upon which stood a double, supporting two of the pink-coloured, fragranced, barley twist variety.

'Lavender,' said the lady. 'Very therapeutic – I make them myself.' Then she disappeared into the kitchen again, only to return with two large plates filled with the most welcome meal Brinton could remember: pork belly, black pudding, white pudding, three eggs, sausage, fried bread, fresh tomato, soda bread and bacon; all piping hot. He dived in.

The westering sun threw out a shaft of light through the leaded window, gilding their faces as they looked at each other across the dining table. It glinted on the ornate candelabra, showering the room with dozens of cascading, faceted reflections like many precious stones.

The woman was studying Brinton and he felt like an open book in her hands. He blinked and she returned to her food without speaking.

Unbelievably and uncharacteristically, he found himself wondering if she could read his mind, such was the intensity of her gaze; but then he shook himself out of it and followed her lead, tucking into his meal again and washing it down with several large mugs of Earl Grey.

Brinton sat recovering in a large, leather-studded armchair next to the glowing fire, wiggling his toes inside his new woollen socks. The woman sat opposite, knitting quietly. Brinton stared at her diminutive frame; then decided to venture a tentative question or two. He spoke conspiratorially.

'Who are you, missus? Where am I? I know I'm in the south, but this sure as shit isn't Dundalk.'

She stopped knitting, letting her gaze settle on Brinton.

'I'll thank you not to use that sort of language within these four walls, Mr Brinton. There's a time and a place for all things, but this is neither the time nor the place.'

Feeling like a little boy who'd been caught with his hand in the sweetie jar, Brinton ventured what he immediately felt was a totally inadequate, 'Sorry, missus,' and fell silent again.

Several seconds passed before she spoke again.

'I'm 92 years old with a history of my own. Earlier today, you stopped at the bar called The Dancing Man. Whilst you were there, you took some interest in a photograph of three men hanging above the bar.'

Brinton pictured the scene in his mind.

'The inscription spoke of the deaths of the men in the picture, killed in an ambush at Mullingar. Murdered by the Black and Tans, 1921. I believe I'm correct, Mr Brinton?' she said, injecting a question into the statement.

He nodded in reply.

'One of the men in the picture was my husband. You may continue to call me "missus"; there are many other things which are better left unsaid. I'm a sympathiser, Mr Brinton, and that's all you need to know. As far as your whereabouts is concerned, well, you're here and that's enough, too.'

She continued to return Brinton's gaze and then began her knitting again. Without looking up, she sent the big man to bed and off he went on his trip to the land of nod, suitably chastised, none the wiser and feeling like a 12-year-old. What a fucking day, thought Brinton.

He was wakened from a coma-like sleep by the "missus" woman, who presented him with a hot cup of Earl Grey. The aroma of bacon wafted into the room and stirred his senses. He swallowed the tea and having washed and dressed, he wandered into the parlour and took up a place at the table, which was suitably decked out in its own inherent style.

Within a couple of minutes, his breakfast was served and he ate heartily. Once he'd finished, he took up his now favourite place in the leather armchair next to the fire and prepared for his next session of chastisements.

She joined him, bringing with her the knitting she'd started the previous day.

'Mr Brinton, you'll be leaving in a few hours' time; someone will pick you up and you'll be taken away from here. You're to mention nothing of your stay, or the events leading up to it. You're to forget me, this house and anything you've done here – do you understand? If you have any questions, you'll be given a chance to voice them later. That's all there is to say on the subject. So, shall we say six o'clock, ready to go?'

'That's fine,' replied Brinton, knowing instinctively that any enquiries would be met with a blank response. 'I'd like to thank you for your help, missus!'

'No need for thanks,' she replied. 'I do this for the cause and for my husband – God rest his soul,' she said, crossing herself. 'So put it all out of your mind entirely.'

They were the last words that passed between them. Six o'clock came, the van arrived – blue this time, a Toyota – Mullen was driving with Kashitskin in the rear.

'Right, Jim lad. I want you to know that Konstantin is our very well established link with Georgia; the source of one of the products you'll be responsible for distributing. His commitment to our relationship is unquestioned. Our aim, and his, may well be fundamentally different, but our continued cooperation has, and will for the foreseeable future, remained mutually beneficial to say the least. We must continue to cultivate that relationship for as long as is necessary, quid pro quo. His background in Russian special ops has been extremely advantageous to us in both training and operations. On a separate level, his links in international trade shall we say, have been, and will continue to be, of great value.'

Mullen, an astute man, could see in Brinton's face mistrust at the very least and so he qualified his latest advice.

'This is a professional relationship, Jim boy, and you must put all personal differences behind you regarding McKenna's demise. You will look to the future. McKenna had to go. The fact that Konstantine was the one to dispatch him was simply a matter of prudence to ratify his commitment to our relationship. It is what it is – nothing more – nothing less. Perhaps you cannot see it yet, but remember this: there is a conflict in every human heart between good and evil, right and wrong. However, human beings are still eminently capable of holding fundamentally opposing views, whilst still maintaining a mutually successful professional relationship. This is the road you must take. Clear?'

Brinton's answer was succinct.

'Yes. Clear.'

His decision was made for him. Several years into the future were mapped out for him and he would follow the plan to the letter until the day of the talking dog! McKenna had paid with his life. Brinton would repay through successful business ventures. Not a bad deal, considering the possible alternative.

Lt. Col. Konstantine Alexandr Kashitskin had made the move to Ireland as part of his planned defection to the West, arranged by Box.

Unbeknown to the PIRA, he was their man. His controllers in the West – Box – had long since made him one of theirs, "turning him around", with the promise of immunity and a new life in the West, in return for his "cooperation in the shape of information". The information he could provide in this case was that pertaining to the movement of weapons and drugs via the PIRA into the UK and wider Europe. His journey had brought him, over many years, from Russian Special Forces, through postings in Africa as a military adviser to SWAPO, ZANLA and ZIPRA. During a time of disillusionment, he had made his decision before being approached to defect; so, when it actually happened, he was ready but largely on his own terms.

Feathering his own nest on the way and preparing a safe and financially secure future, he siphoned off funds from drug deals originally set up between Afghan warlords; then later in Africa, where he'd been perfectly placed; and most recently in Europe. More lately, making himself available in various fields to the highest bidder. That bidder was now the PIRA, with whom he sustained a mutually beneficial relationship. But this latest relationship was one taken up at the insistence of Box, who saw an excellent opportunity to get a man inside the magic circle.

Kashitskin sat in the back of the Toyota van with Brinton. The two new "best friends" eyeing each other with thinly disguised mistrust; Brinton remembering Mullen's more recent words. He knew Mullen was right, of course, as none of this was personal. It was business. And now, in his new career as businessmen, that's the way he would treat their relationship.

Kashitskin gazed out of the window of the van and unconsciously massaged his left knee. It always hurt more in rainy weather and here it rained and rained – not like Africa, where the climate seemed to help. Thinking back, he remembered the day he'd picked his injury up: the surprise attack by the contract troops on the training camp, his narrow escape from HQ and the thwack of the round as its impact had knocked him over. The girl he'd used as a human shield; his flight to freedom in the helicopter; throwing the girl out; watching her tumble to her death below. A thin grin spread across his hard face, but his eyes showed no such emotion. She wasn't the first he'd dispatched – not by a long chalk – either directly or indirectly. No, she wasn't his best work at all. She'd served her purpose as home comfort for the men in the camp and had been treated no better than a dog; taken with several others from local villages to be used and abused, then discarded, anonymous.

During his time, he'd overseen butchery on a grand scale and he wallowed in the absolute power it gave him. His encounters with the contract troops had been many and varied. And their aggression, flexibility and willingness to do whatever had to be done – without the restriction of rules and regulations – had eventually pushed the guerrillas over the edge and into oblivion. For the guerrillas, it was an ignominious end. But for the indifferent Kashitskin, it was water under the bridge; the passing of another phase in his life and one step closer to the West.

In Africa, he had been recruited by the resident MI6 headhunter in Mombasa, Kenya, whilst on leave there long ago. And he'd been convinced by his handler, who had by fair means or foul discovered Mr Kashitskin's zest for the better things in life, which he'd come to acquire through his dealings with various underworld personalities. Notably, the local mafia.

His option was to work for the West, or to discover the delights of falling into the clutches of the Kenyan police authority, who took a very dim view of any connection – to a lesser or greater degree – with the illicit drugs trade. At least that was the public persona they portrayed. Behind the scenes, corruption reigned supreme.

Realising he was hooked, he came without too much persuasion to fall in line with Box, which was actually what he'd planned and to whom he had been passing a constant stream of information ever since. Box had eventually moved him into his new position, alongside the Republican organisation, and he had continued to pass vital snippets to British Intelligence, whilst at the same time providing the PIRA with its own requirements.

Military advice and training – his extra-curricular activities – continued apace and everything was rosy in the garden.

The Talking Dog

The worm turns!

(Anon.)

James Edward Brinton made himself available for a long and fruitful series of intelligence interviews by SB as a result of being informed by Inspector Neil Kilbride of his impending "removal" from the movement. Removal from the movement meant removal from the planet, just as he was warned by Sam Mullen all those years ago. Kilbride, now Brinton's saviour, had become aware of the PIRA's intentions regarding Brinton as a result of an audacious op involving SB, E4A and the Det, which resulted in a highly successful technical attack aimed at the army council itself.

The operation involved long-term surveillance of one of its members, who happened to own a large black dog named Sam. Both Sam and his owner were inseparable, to the degree where the beast lay across its owner's lap whilst he drove his car; it shared meals with the man at the dinner table and it slept in the same bed. Intelligence reports indicated that the ageing dog was in poor health and had, in recent times, begun to spend more and more time at a local veterinary centre, sometimes overnight, in order to receive treatment for severely arthritic hips.

It would not have been impossible to place an acoustic device in the man's house, but it would have been extremely difficult, given that the target, in his elevated position in the movement, was scrupulously careful – bordering on paranoia – regarding his own personal security. However, it would be relatively easy to gain access to the veterinary centre during one of Sam's residential stays.

So, sixteen days into the surveillance operation, the target was triggered leaving his home in the South Armagh village of Cullyhanna, en route to the vet with the unfortunate Sam. The operator from the Det, working in conjunction with others, followed the target and she confirmed the destination on the man's arrival. A further surveillance team already in place at the vet's continued the static watch and confirmed the man's departure forty minutes later – without Sam.

The local area had been placed out of bounds to the Green Army. Satellite patrols from the Det and the troop provided security for the entry team, which would enter the target at approximately 02.00 hours the following morning.

Jim Curtis and his fellow operator moved silently across country towards the target; both wore civilian clothes, sturdy boots and black anoraks and they carried shoulder-holstered MP5s and Glock pistols with extended magazines. Both carried four stun grenades plus two more HE grenades each.

Curtis carried a number of keys, which had been cut as a result of the veterinary surgeon's keys being surreptitiously removed from her bag during a recent shopping trip. They had been copied, cut and returned to the woman's bag before she had left the supermarket, without her having the slightest idea that they had even been touched. Outrageous sleight of hand being just one of the operator's many and varied skills.

In addition, Curtis' partner carried a set of lock picks for use in the event of encountering a lock for which they possessed no key. The Northern Ireland technical team responsible for the colloquially named "funnies" required by the Province's various intelligence teams had manufactured a tiny voice-activated transmitter in the shape of a dog's name container – identical to the type which many people attached to their animal's collar. The small cylinder was about 2 inches in length with a screw top and it was about the thickness of a biro and hollow. The top could be removed and the animal's details inserted. It was then clipped to the dog's collar. NISS had produced one with their usual flair and imagination. Their ability for innovation had become world-renowned in the sphere of surveillance equipment. Anything was possible for them; for example, they could, and sometimes did, produce cameras that looked like bricks or even acoustic listening devices in the shape of sheep droppings. In effect, this tiny piece of surveillance equipment would replace the real thing and the technical attack would be complete once fitted to the dog. All that would be left to do would be for a surveillance team to remain within 500 yards of the target and to listen in. Anyone who spoke within 20 feet of the animal would be broadcasting direct to British Intelligence via the dog and the Det.

In addition to human surveillance, strategically placed listening and recording devices were placed in or near the man's regular haunts to broaden the scope for surveillance. The digital video recording equipment had once again been produced by NISS at the request of Curtis and it was he who had sited the equipment.

Now, he and his companion Jane were themselves being filmed by their own equipment as they walked hand in hand along the country lane towards the vets. A Dutch barn loomed large in the darkness on the left-hand side of the lane and 50 yards further on was the vet's house.

The vet, a single woman in her fifties, lived a solitary existence and to all intents and purposes, she had no close relatives to speak of in the Province. However, the SB check on her background had revealed that she had an elderly aunt still alive and active on the Republican scene, handing out the usual posters extolling the virtues of the hunger strikes in the Maze Prison. She also carried out collections in Irish pubs and clubs in the UK, but that was as far as her commitment went and apart from that, she lived a peaceful life in a Birmingham suburb.

The vet's house, a small, two-bedroomed bungalow, stood next to the detached surgery where she worked during the day, with a staff of two; one of which was a kennel maid, who worked part time during the mornings from 06.00–09.00 hours and then 16.00–18.00 hours. Her duties included feeding and exercising the inmates, administering certain drugs where required, changing bedding areas and washing down kennels. Afterwards, she would drink a cup of tea with Miss Robbins, the vet. Then it was off home for a day in front of the telly, until 15.30 hours, when she would return to the vet's for a replay of the morning's tasks; after which she would secure the surgery; the vet herself having already finished work at 18.00 hours, at which point she went on call for any local emergencies that the farmers on her books may provide.

The second staff member was the receptionist, who worked from 09.00–17.00 hours, carrying out the usual clerical duties commensurate with her job. It was she who had greeted the female operator from SB's covert surveillance team E4A three days earlier, masquerading as a student from Belfast University doing a thesis on rural veterinary care in the Province. She had, with the blessing of the vet, received a detailed tour of the practice, along with a thorough brief on its operation, followed by a very pleasant afternoon of tea and sandwiches.

Prior to the tour, the vet had made a call to the university to confirm the operator's claims. The call had been intercepted by pre-placed technicians who, in the guise of university staff, confirmed the operator's story.

The visit had enabled the operator to provide a highly detailed description of the premises, including the location of the Chubb alarm panel inside the cupboard in the kitchen above the sink; and then there was the code, which had been conveniently written on a piece of sticking plaster inside the door.

All the details arrived in a timely fashion along with the operator, who delivered a detailed brief to Curtis and his companion to enable them to produce their plan for the op.

As they reached the open driveway of the vet's, they turned right off the lane and walked straight around the left-hand side of the surgery, where they knew they would find the porch and the entrance door.

There were no security lights at the property; people felt it unnecessary in the local community.

Curtis took the bunch of six keys from his jacket pocket and, selecting a brass door key, he inserted it in the lock and turned the key to the right. It met with slight resistance and then completed its turn.

The door opened into the porch and the pair were inside in a couple of seconds, with the door closed and locked behind them.

Through the next door, Curtis stepped to the right and waited, looking back out of the reception window through a crack in the blinds. Jane immediately turned left – avoiding a row of chairs on her left and a free-standing coat rack – past the receptionist's counter on the right, with its display of veterinary literature, computer console and swivel chair. Then, she continued purposefully through the next door into the kitchen, quickly locating the cabinet containing the intruder alarm panel, where she punched in the code to cancel the alarm. Both operators stood quietly, watching and listening.

They waited a full five minutes before Curtis joined Jane in the kitchen and signalled with a nod to proceed to the animal care area.

Inside, were revealed three kennels, two of which were empty and the third of which contained Sam, who sat with a quizzical look on his bewhiskered face. Opposite, and separated by a glass cubicle, was the small animal care area: four rabbit hutches, two glass tanks for reptiles and another glass-fronted container housing a large, nasty-looking ferret.

Curtis turned his attention to Sam and produced a couple of pork sausages from his pocket wrapped in cling film. He took one out and pushed it through the wire of the front of the kennel to an eager Sam, who swallowed it in one. Sliding open the bolt on the kennel door, he slipped inside and proceeded to fuss the dog, quietly stroking and patting him, and scratching him behind the ears. He took out another sausage, broke it in half and fed it to the dog, then quickly undid the dog's collar and handed it out through the kennel door to Jane. Then, turning his attention to the dog, he continued to quietly fuss the animal.

Jane worked quietly on the collar, first comparing the ID tube on the collar with the replacement they'd brought. Once she was happy, she removed the original and replaced it with the transmitter and then passed the collar back to Curtis. He checked her work, then, careful to replace the collar the correct way around, he patted Sam on the head and fed him the remaining half sausage. Stepping out of the kennel, he slipped the bolt shut and, turning back to Jane, gave her the thumbs-up.

Following her back through the kitchen, she reset the alarms and both operators slipped quietly out into the porch, pausing only briefly to peep through the window, before slipping outside and locking the door behind them.

Outside, a mist was falling; the air was damp and nothing moved in the night. Jim Curtis and Jane walked back along the drive and then turned left along the lane, passing the barn on the right and the vet's house on the left.

About 50 yards further along the track was a small sandstone bridge, bordered by low walls of about 3 feet in height. The mist had thickened to a fog now and as the two operators reached the centre of the bridge, they quietly hopped over the wall on the left-hand side into the adjacent field and stood with their backs to the stone bridge and waited.

They said nothing but continued to watch, both instinctively covering 180-degree arcs each, listening intently to the sounds of the night. Twice, a barn owl swooped silently out of the mist, patrolling its own war zone in search of prey to feed its hungry young.

Jane looked at her watch and held up two fingers, indicating the amount of minutes till the pick up. Curtis knew it must be 02.43 hours.

Both operators climbed back up in time to meet the car, which stopped on the bridge with the rear, nearside door open ready to accept them. Then it was on its way, with its passengers collected in ten seconds, en route to its base location.

The "talking dog" spoke for several long weeks, divulging the PIRA intent to carry out several large-scale ops against military and civilian targets in and around South Armagh and other points in the Province.

Sam, the talking dog, passed away in late October and was cremated that same day, having carried out some sterling undercover work for British Intelligence!

Brinton, in the years between being installed by the army council as the tour de force vis-à-vis the establishment of PIRA-controlled organised crime, had, indeed, become a great success in the field. Taking over established syndicates where necessary and creating new set-ups and disposing of individuals or groups that foolishly offered any form of resistance to the will of the organisation.

It was Sam, the dog, who had thrown out the snippets of information, indicating that Brinton had served his purpose and having been used to excellent effect, he was now to pay for his transgressions in the past. His black cab scam was never going to be overlooked as he'd been promised on the day that McKenna had met his end. That would be seen as weakness in the organisation and it had never shied away from punishment killings to make its point.

And so Brinton was turned and became "supergrass" and he faded into anonymity. But, the all-seeing eye of Republican terrorism continues its endless search for revenge in the form of a bullet for Brinton and others; revenge to feed the Eternal Flame.

Curtis knew it was good, sound intelligence that would win the war in the shadows, carried out by the covert operators working in the Province. The success of the talking dog would be measured in lives saved and enemy operations thwarted and he wondered how Southern Ireland would fare should the conflict spill over into the south. All things were possible. It certainly could happen – he knew that. It was the way of the world.

A good example was the failed attempt using Cuban anti-communist expatriates to overthrow the Castro regime. They had been trained, financed, armed and supported by the CIA. But the "Bay of Pigs" Enterprise – as it had become known owing to it being launched in said bay in Cuba – fell on its arse for various reasons and failed. Win some, lose some; Castro's still with us, one of life's survivors. Though since the collapse of communism in the East, he's no longer a mouthpiece for Russia in the West. Neither does he enjoy the military and financial support that he once did.

Jimmy hoped it wouldn't happen – not yet, anyway – he had bridges to build back home if he could and he'd begun thinking more and more about how he would do this. Then he found himself thinking about another bridge – a real one – it was a world away and it was on fire!

The Bridge

Then it's Tommy this an' Tommy that, an' "Tommy 'ow's yer soul?"
But it's "Thin red line of 'eroes" when the drums begin to roll—

Rudyard Kipling; *Tommy*

Curtis and Voss moved like wraiths – they had done this before – both deeply focused on the back of the sentry, who leaned against the low pile of boxes which doubled as a sentry post. It stood at the edge of the ravine at the side of the railway line and the line lay across the bridge, which spanned the ravine and cut short a road journey which would normally take five days. By train, it took six hours and served several towns and three garrisons along its route.

The sentry hummed to himself as the two men moved slowly and purposefully closer. René Voss held his 38 revolver in his left hand; Curtis, his backup in its holster on his right hip and his FN slung across his back, barrel downwards. In his right hand, he gripped a fighting knife with an 8-inch blade and a brass wrap-around knuckleduster incorporated in the handle.

They were 15 feet away now and the sentry was oblivious; he continued to hum the African lullaby. A light breeze blew along the valley and into the faces of Curtis and Voss. They were 5 feet away now – close enough to smell the man's sweat – two more steps, silently bringing death.

René Voss, one arm's length from the sentry, was now pointing his 38 at the back of the man's head; he glanced sideways at Curtis and nodded. Curtis looked like a man with his eye on the prize. Voss raised his right arm level with the 38 and, touching his thumb and second finger together, 6 inches from the sentry's left ear, he gave a clearly audible

109

click. The sentry snapped his head round to the left and in a flash, Curtis had swung his right arm around in a sweeping arc, aiming to strike the sentry just below the angle of the jaw on the right-hand side of his neck with the point of the blade. But the first blow struck bone and skidded upwards, opening the man's cheek wide. Curtis struck again. This time, the blade penetrated the sentry's gullet and met resistance. Curtis forced it home and 2 inches of the blade exited between his upper and lower jaw, bursting out through his left cheek, severing his tongue. He whipped his left arm around, cupping his hand over the man's face; the blade slicing into his left index finger as he did so. He didn't feel a thing. With all his strength, he punched forwards and outwards with his right fist, opening up the man's throat like an oversized gaping mouth, at the same time pulling him backwards onto the ground, taking the full weight of the sentry as they both hit the earth with a thud. The impact knocked the wind out of Curtis, but he remained with both arms wrapped tightly round the struggling sentry in a vice-like grip.

Great gouts of blood gushed all around, pouring over Curtis as he wrapped his legs around the kicking, choking, vomiting, dying man's thighs. Curtis was strong, but he still had to grip the man for a good two minutes as his life's blood literally poured over them both and onto the mud. Gradually, the man's struggles faded and became weaker and then finally, he was still. Curtis lay for a moment panting and then he pushed the corpse off himself and looked towards René. His friend was intent on the local area, looking for more business. There was none.

Curtis sat drenched in blood, recovering from the exertion and pondering over the fact that it wasn't easy killing a man who doesn't want to die – the blade still grasped in his right hand.

'Next time, let's just shoot the fucker, eh, René?'

Curtis was an awful sight, perched next to the corpse on the ground, covered in the man's blood.

Voss looked down, first at the stiff, then at Curtis.

'I hate it when that happens,' he grinned, referring to Curtis' generous covering of gore; parts of which were beginning to clot and congeal.

Curtis grinned, too, now inspecting the cut on his own finger.

'So do I,' he replied and then stood up, gripping the sentry by the scruff of the neck as he dragged him the 20 yards to the edge of the ravine. Then, after a quick body search, he pushed him over.

Voss remained standing at the guard post, looking back along the track away from the bridge. Curtis joined him, wiping his face with the back of his hand as he bent down to pick up the sentry's weapon. It was an AK47 and he checked the safety lever, removed the magazine and pulled back the cocking handle, ejecting a round. He turned the weapon on its side and looked into the chamber. Happy it was clear, he released the action, then the safety, and squeezed the trigger – there was a dry click. Placing the magazine back on the weapon after replacing the ejected round, he checked the safety lever was back on. The weapon was now in the "made safe mode", with a full magazine – thirty rounds. Just cock – aim – safety off – fire!

He took his own weapon from round his back and, whilst René kept watch, he field-stripped and quickly cleaned the FN, which was dirty following his struggle with the sentry. It only took a couple of minutes as the dirt was superficial mud from the ground near the post. Once done, they were ready to continue.

René had returned his 38 into its holster and he was holding his main weapon of choice now. He preferred the FN, just as Curtis did. It was robust, reliable, accurate in the right hands, had an automatic capability, a folding butt and spares were readily available; in addition, it suited the "shoot and scoot" tactics employed by the teams. Finally, when someone was hit with one of its 7.62 mm rounds, they stayed hit; so that was it then. In soldier parlance: the dog's bollocks! Both men were happy with their lot.

Curtis checked his watch and Voss continued his vigil, gazing back along the track which, after about a quarter of a mile, curved to the right and into the bush, out of sight. Both Curtis and Voss knew that a mile further on, Kaminski and Grillo were in place, ready to give the signal on the small walkie-talkie, short-range radio, when the troop train was on its way.

The bridge was of a sturdy wooden construction and it was guarded by enemy troops. Van Rijn, Curtis and Voss had been in place nearby for two days, watching the routine of the troops over the whole period. The single sentry had changed every two hours, on the hour. The sentry they had negotiated at the post had been in place for five minutes when he had died. That had been a half hour ago now, so they had less than an hour and a half to rig the charges on the bridge before the arrival of a new guard. The train was due in an hour, so that cut the time down again. But the men were confident that they had enough time to rig a main charge, using the 150 lb of plastic they'd carried to the target, along with the DET cord, twin-flex cable and DETs. Curtis would use an electrical initiation to do the business.

They'd come to blow the bridge but last-minute intelligence had offered up the juicy bonus of the troop train, which was intent on bringing more of the enemy into the area that the boys were tasked to control.

They got to work along with Van Rijn, who had moved forward to join them from the cover of the bush. Voss kept watch, monitoring the radio traffic as well as looking for trouble. Alongside him lay three 66 mm ATK weapons. Curtis produced a roll of white Cordtex. Then he lay a poncho on the ground and put the roll on one end, placing the firing cable on the other. He collected the plastic from Voss and Van Rijn, plus his own, and placed it in the centre. Next, he took a plastic container from a pouch on his belt, about the size of a cigarette packet, and placed four more on his hat. He gently pulled one end and the black box separated it into two equal-sized parts; one part contained six detonators, each of about two and a half inches long, aluminium, sealed at one end with the other hollow; about the diameter of a cigarette. It would be into the hollow end that the safety fuse – itself a low explosive – for a flash initiation, would be gently pushed if used. But he also had the option of knotting the cord, which would also do the job instead of a DET.

He placed the DETs down on the poncho to his right. To his left, he placed a small canvas bag of fifty junction clips then, walking to the edge of the ravine, he reaffirmed his earlier findings, whilst studying the structure of the bridge. It was a rather naive and rudimentary structure which relied, for its strength, on a criss-cross series of timbers projecting upwards from the floor of the ravine, some 80 feet below. The timbers were of varying sizes, the thickest of which were about 10 inches in diameter.

These stood vertically at the top of the structure and ran from one side of the ravine to the other, at 10 foot intervals. They were boxed-off at the top with railway-sleeper-sized beams, though they were of greater length overall; this created the base along which the tracks were laid.

Curtis decided to attack the vertical timbers over a span of four uprights with an additional charge on the side of the track, above each upright. His aim being to cut the steel track at the same time as blowing the supporting timbers below it over a length of about 40–50 feet, dropping the train into the ravine, causing maximum damage in the process.

For this to be successful, it would require sixteen explosive charges on the ring main, all detonating at the same time. The firing point would be the far side of the ravine. Curtis had noted that the firing point he had chosen gave him a direct, head-on view of the train as it approached. This presented a small but potentially catastrophic problem if not addressed.

From the firing position, looking directly at the front of the approaching train, he couldn't judge, with any accuracy, the exact position at any one time of the train on the bridge. If he detonated early, the train may be able to stop. Too late, and at least some of the train and carriages may still make it across. Curtis thought for a while and came up with the simple expedient of sticking a "thin" branch, with a small cluster of leaves on top, on the centre of the track, 15 yards before the charges. He now knew that he could focus on the branch with his binos and as soon as the front of the engine knocked over the branch, he would immediately press the tit, leaving no time for the train to stop; and so the work went on.

Curtis laid out a large loop of Cordtex about 120 feet in circumference. He then cut eight separate lengths, each 6 feet long, and laid them together on one side, after taping the ends to prevent loss of the explosive content. He placed the junction clips in his top left-hand shirt pocket. Making up eight separate 5 lb charges, he earmarked them for the track and then made a further eight 10 lb charges for the uprights. Checking his Leatherman on his belt, he took the coiled Cordtex forward onto the track and laid it in between the tracks in an elongated loop, avoiding any sharp bends or kinks in between the rails above the section of uprights marked for attack. Then, taking the 6 feet lengths of DET cord and using junction clips, he attached one end of each length to the mainline loop and passed each length under the track, so it hung over the sides of the bridge alongside each one of the eight uprights.

Both he and Voss then started to carry the charges along the track and set them down at intervals, where they were to be attached. Voss produced a drum of baling wire – 18 gauge – which Curtis would use to attach the plastic; about twenty-five pieces of pre-cut plywood, about the size of a shoebox lid and a quarter inch thick, to tamp the charges in place. Jim cut a further eight lengths of Cordtex about 18 inches long for the rail charges.

Moving clockwise round the loop, he placed, tamped and attached the rail charges; then, attaching the DET cord with an H-shaped junction clip, he joined the DET cord to the main line, both for the uprights and the track. Next, he climbed down the side of the bridge, attached and tamped the larger charges to the uprights – this time, knotting the ends of the DET cord in favour of the DETs, which he saved for future use. Then, pushing the knots into the plastic, he checked they were secure and, climbing back onto the rails, he repeated the process with the track charges.

Both he and Voss, now working backwards towards the firing point, picked the point to place the branch marker. This done, Voss signalled to Van Rijn to join them with the poncho, etc., whilst Curtis attached an electric DET to the twin-flex wire. Once Voss and Van Rijn had moved back and gone to ground, he attached the DET to the Cordtex end of the mainline loop, which he folded over 4 inches at the end and taped in place.

Then he uncoiled the rest of the twin-flex, laying it carefully in the recess of the rail and then running it back to the firing point. Attaching the ends of the wire to the power pack terminals, the ambush was complete. With twenty minutes to go, they waited patiently for the call from Gus Grillo.

Grillo and Kaminski lay in the shaded cover of the bush which lined the side of the track. About 10 yards further on, away from the track, the bush had been cut back to give a clear field of fire around the small garrison, which housed about 100 enemy troops. Grillo and Kaminski had been in situ for about the same amount of time as Curtis and co. and were observing the routine in the garrison.

They had noted earlier in the day the arrival of the troop train, bringing with it approximately a further 100 troops, who were sitting and standing around with their kit and equipment, obviously waiting for the order to board the train for their onward journey. Earlier in the day, Grillo and Kaminski had watched as they had slaughtered a bullock and butchered it in the open. The beast had then been passed out in man-sized portions, wrapped in large leaves, and it was these portions of meat that they were now cooking and eating with their maize. The smells of meat and spices drifted the 40 yards from the garrison to the two men in the bush and both responded with rumbling stomachs.

At intervals, a couple of guards would walk past their position in the bush, completely unaware of their presence. At one point, the guards stopped not 5 feet away from the men and relieved themselves into the bush before continuing on their way. Grillo and Kaminski had also registered the presence of a group of about twenty Cuban military – probably "advisers" – Fidel Castro's donation to the fight.

Just before last light, there was a buzz of excitement amongst the troops and then shouts and orders in Portuguese, followed by, more interestingly, Russian voices. Dick Kaminski, who spoke Russian, noted the presence of at least three, but there was one who stood out. He was obviously in charge and when he spoke, the people jumped. He was a big man, thickset, broad-shouldered and square-jawed, with a shaven head, and had the men been closer still, they would have registered his steely-grey, hard, humourless eyes. Yes, hard, cruel eyes and an unblinking gaze, which swept back and forth across the troops in front of him – now standing rigidly to attention.

He barked orders in Russian and a small, stocky black soldier in an olive green uniform translated into Portuguese. The troops were picking up weapons now and they were stuffing half-cooked food into their mouths; others shouldered their packs and the train driver stoked the engine. More orders now, and then the troops began to board the train; one man stumbled in front of the large Russian and was rewarded with a vicious kick in the ribs, quickly followed by another to help him on his way.

'Seems like a nice boy,' Kaminski noted.

Grillo nodded, noticing that the rest of the troops were now all but on board – some hanging onto the outside, others sitting on the roof.

The large Russian was last to board the train. Grillo and Kaminski observed one more thing about the man – he walked with a limp. Unknown to them, they were watching Box's man on the inside. They were looking at Lt. Col. Konstantin Alexandr Kashitskin at work, making friends and influencing people; the limp had been courtesy of Jim Curtis at the SWAPO training camp attack.

The train began to move and as it did so, Kashitskin jumped off and stood, hands on hips, Mussolini-style, surveying the train as it slowly picked up speed to begin its onward journey.

'Delta One, this is Delta Three, Ball Boy. Over,' Grillo whispered into the radio mike.

There was a short hiss of static and then came Voss' reply. 'Roger, Ball Boy. Out!'

Grillo and Kaminski began their careful ex-fill; Curtis, Voss and Van Rijn prepared for action.

Each man checked his personal weapons and side arms. Voss handed the other two a 66 mm each. Curtis flipped off the end covers and strap from his weapon and then extended it, which just about doubled the length. The sight flipped up automatically, showing the leads and graticules on its Perspex form. All that remained was to shoulder the weapon, extend the safety catch and then, having checked the rear back-blast area was clear and having given the "standby" warning, aim and depress the rubber trigger and "Bob's your uncle". The weapons were a backup, incase the demolition charges failed. They wouldn't be as effective as dropping the train and its passengers into the ravine, but they'd make their ears ring and give Curtis and co. time to catch the bus.

Curtis, Voss and Van Rijn heard the train before they saw it. The old black Beyer Garratt 482 plus 284 locomotive chugged relentlessly forwards like a great 80-tonne iron buffalo, seemingly unstoppable. A huge, belching plume of black-grey smoke vomited forth from its stack and was immediately whipped back above its coal tender and four carriages, cloaking its passengers in a film of smoky, oily soot. On the engine footplate stood the driver, head sticking out of the side window, gazing forwards along the track. His footman shovelled spades of coal tirelessly into the furnace to build up a greater head of steam.

Curtis watched intently. Voss and Van Rijn peered in the opposite direction, away from the oncoming train. It came into view now in the fading light like a huge grey-black spirit, looming larger and larger. As it negotiated the bend, Curtis guesstimated its speed to be at 30 to 40 mph, but he couldn't be sure; then he pushed the thought aside as he focused entirely on the simple act of watching the front fender knock over the branch marker. Pausing his finger over the tit, he glanced over his shoulder and registered Voss and Van Rijn lying low, hugging the ground, hands over ears, mouths open. Just seconds now, and the train came on and on, over the edge of the ravine and onto the bridge.

Curtis' world shrank to a tiny place: just him, the ravine, the bridge and the train; and now the bridge and the train; now the train; now the marker ... then it was gone!

A one second pause, he pushed the tit and then fell flat. There was an ear-splitting, earth-shattering explosion, a mega-flash and white-hot clouds of thick black smoke. Huge jagged shards of wood several feet in length scythed through the air, whistling over the men at the firing point and up and down the ravine, high into the air.

Flames licked at the timbers of the bridge; 40 feet of track had disappeared and through it all, the Iron Buffalo thundered on into the void, spilling downwards into the gaping mouth of the ravine, dragging after it the four coaches full of human debris – down and down, as if in slow motion. There were screams of fear and pain, then – boom – followed immediately by a second explosion as the steam train split, showering all around with white-hot steel shrapnel. The carriages crashed, one after the other, onto the locomotive at the bottom of the ravine, collapsing in on it; bodies torn, crushed, thrown and ripped asunder in a huge, obscene display of death amongst the fire and timber and hissing, twisted steel and iron.

Something came rolling, spinning, tumbling, at great speed between the rails towards the firing point, halting just 6 feet short of the men. All three gazed at the naked, steaming torso of a human being, devoid of head, arms or legs. Their ears buzzed and rang from the sound of the attack, but all three could still hear, above the noise of the hissing engine in the bottom of the ravine, the sounds of lives ending.

They calmly gathered their equipment and moved off along the track, away from the Valley of Death. Behind them, 150 yards along the ravine, a huge steel engine wheel spun slowly round and round, like a child's toy. The cries of the dying echoed and faded into the night.

The night sky around and above the bridge glowed as the remaining timbers caught fire, blazing, spluttering and crackling. Clouds of sparks and embers spiralled skywards into the night sky. Voss, Van Rijn and Curtis stopped to rest 5 miles from the scene of the ambush. They had turned south-east off the line and moved 500 yards into the bush as they went to ground in a small depression and waited. Curtis checked his map and confirmed their location. Voss and Van Rijn checked his findings and agreed. They rested for a further thirty minutes and then moved on, marching throughout the night, resting for five minutes in every hour. Then an hour before first light, they crawled into some thick scrub and waited for daylight.

*　　*　　*

Throughout the night, they had covered a distance of 33 miles and now they felt safe enough to talk amongst themselves.

'You know when that big lump of meat came skidding along the track towards us – it took me several seconds to realise what it was,' reflected Voss, not to anyone in particular.

'Yeah, he wasn't half shifting for a man with no legs though,' jibed Curtis.

They all chuckled quietly. Curtis was stripping bark from a branch. He gathered together the small slivers and pushed them into a small canvas bag, to be used later when it had dried out for kindling. The others watched.

'Be fuckin' careful with that thing,' said Van Rijn, pointing to Curtis' fighting knife. 'You'll have someone's eye out.'

'Yeah,' said Voss. 'Remember the sentry?' he said in a pseudo-scolding tone, wagging his finger at Curtis.

Once again, they fought back the laughter.

The sun rose above the horizon, touching the land with golden solar fingers, massaging the hard black hills with its warmth. It was a new day in Africa and the soldiers passed like wood smoke through the acacias. Each step bringing them closer to their base.

Gus Grillo and Dick Kaminski were itching to make the enemy pay for Kurt Willt and they'd been knocking about a few ideas between themselves. Whilst they were watching the garrison on the railway line, they'd come up with some options they wanted to talk about. One thing they were adamant about was that no matter what they decided, they would be taking a very personal interest in extracting a copious helping of direct, personal retribution for Willt.

'Now, Curtis,' said Kaminski. 'We'll talk in more detail later, mate, but Grillo and I fancy a shot at the ammo compound at the garrison back there. There are some interesting command personalities thereabouts and we think we can get in, do the compound and remove one or two of the top bods; maybe even a Soviet or two.'

Curtis listened. Grillo cut in.

'It would probably be an independent job, Curtis, and we'd need some help.'

'I'm in,' said Curtis, without hesitation.

'No problem, mate. Give it some more thought and we'll take it from there. Voss will want in, too, but leave him to me; I'll speak to him later.'

It was getting hotter now and a silvery heat-shimmer bathed the land. The men had estimated they had about 6 more miles to go before they reached the RV, where the rest of the Coy would be waiting.

They arrived at 11.30 hours and went immediately to Coy HQ element, where they were met by the OC. They were the last team to return; the others were performing the usual routine in defence, personal admin, weapons cleaning, sorting of kit and centralising rubbish, which was always carried with them and never left behind anywhere. Some teams were cooking meals in mess tins; others slept. Not a single weapon was more than an arm's length from anyone.

Curtis took it all in as a matter of course and bathed in the fact that he was surrounded by true professionals. He admired them all deeply and considered the people most close to him. His team comprised of Schollonburg, the patrol commander, who was a tall, broad-shouldered South African man, a veteran of regular army service in the SADF – as tough as they came – who suffered no fools lightly. He was a professional in the true sense of the word and an excellent role model for any newcomer to this conflict.

Indeed, Curtis and others would often advise any newcomer to the company to "watch Chris Schollonburg" if you wanted to do well in the bush. Watch him, copy him, be like him in your personal skills and attitude; blend this with your own personal attributes – the good ones – and you'd do well. Put simply, that meant survival.

Curtis admired Chris Schollonburg immensely and they got on well. From Schollonburg's point of view, he loved to soldier and he, too, loved true professionals. To allow any of your personal military skills to slip was like a personal affront to him. But he was so well respected by the rest of his team that they would have died of shame rather than let him down – or, indeed, themselves.

There was another side to Schollonburg, too – like many others. He had once carried an injured Dik-Dik for ten days, splinting the creature's broken leg until he could take it to a bush vet and guarantee its survival. Curtis could understand this display of kindness from people who were often considered cruel enough to eat their own young, because he was so much a part of this world himself.

It permeated his very soul and it took that sort of involvement to understand it. The men were often misquoted, misrepresented and misunderstood; and always by people with a preconceived idea about contract soldiers. This didn't bother Curtis or any of the others though, for they were completely committed to each other, the job and soldiering and if anyone had a problem with the way they operated, then they should pick up a weapon, throw a 90 lb pack on their backs and get out into the bush and do their own fucking dirty work.

Curtis' thoughts drifted to Van Rijn. Leo van Rijn had come to South Africa to get what he wasn't getting enough of in the Belgian Para Commandos. Although he'd seen action in the Belgian Congo, he wanted a greater commitment to soldiering than he was getting there. So he signed off and flew to Cape Town with an ugly bloke called René Voss.

Leo was a real harum-scarum lad of 5 feet 7 inches tall, wiry and strong. He was an excellent mountaineer, who'd taken part in two Everest expeditions, the second time failing in his attempt on the summit because of foul weather. Unlike Voss, his fellow commando, Leo had a permanent grin on his funny little face – a grin that disguised a ruthless streak a mile wide. Van Rijn would have eaten the Dik-Dik, but then Schollonburg would have eaten Van Rijn, pondered Curtis, who found himself on the edge of one of his now famous giggling fits.

'What the fuck's up with you?' said Voss in Curtis' right ear, snapping him out of his dream world.

'What? What?! What's up?'

'You've got the fuckin' village idiot look on your fuckin' face again!'

Curtis just laughed and dreamt on.

Kurt Willt had been another South African who everyone liked; his warm personality and constant willingness to help, combined with an uncontrollable urge to perform practical jokes, made him a magnetic personality. He was a great loss to the team and had been a hard act for his replacement to follow. Of course, he wouldn't just be replaced; there would be a Chinese parliament, which would be overseen by the OC. Firstly, the new guy would have to be a willing participant; then, the remaining members of the team would vote on his inclusion. After that, he would either be in or out, but there had to be 100 per cent agreement on his inclusion. This was vital when working in such small teams, in order to avoid conflict of any sort. It was tried and tested, and it worked. So the opinion was if it's not broke, don't fix it.

Curtis himself was an enigma. He was an intensely shy man who loved solitude – he'd carried out several ops alone for this very reason – but he also enjoyed the company of the others. He spoke little and believed that if you've got nothing to say, then don't say anything. For this reason, amongst the teams, he was often referred to jokingly as "the Quiet Soldier" which, in a way, contradicted his mischievous sense of humour.

It would be many years after his return from Africa before he would learn of the high esteem in which he was held by the people around him. It was his friend René Voss who enlightened him on the subject during a weekend of heavy drinking and war stories and, as always, Curtis had listened while Voss talked, reminding him of the many things he had forgotten. Curtis had stated on many occasions, 'I don't remember,' or, 'did I really do that?'

'Yes,' replied Voss. 'You did great things and thought nothing of it!'

This was praise, indeed, from the great René Voss. Curtis had looked mildly surprised, the darkness in the bar disguising his blushes as he'd replied simply, 'Didn't we all?' unwilling to accept any accolades.

René knew Jim as well as anyone was able to and so he decided to twist the blade into his aloof friend.

'Oh yes, yes. It's true, young man,' said Voss, clucking like an old mother hen.

Curtis was becoming more and more uncomfortable and Voss was loving it. Indeed, any thought of even the slightest hint of praise made the shy man feel intensely uneasy. But Voss went on regardless.

'Schollonburg, Van Rijn and I were talking about you behind your back. They send their love, by the way,' he said, planting a big sloppy kiss on Jim's cheek.

'Fuck's sake!' said Curtis, wiping his hand across his face.

'And you were liberally toasted and described in the following manner: stand by – quiet, unassuming, daring, unflappable, focused and sometimes reckless, to a degree bordering on the crazy.' Voss grinned. Then, in genuine tones, he continued, 'But, above all, you were always there – yes – quietly there.'

There was a pause and Curtis stared into his empty glass.

'So, here's to the quiet soldier!'

Voss raised his glass and tipped the contents down his throat.

Curtis looked up and said, 'Fuck off, you Belgian twat. I'm off for a piss.'

It took longer than usual; Voss' words had moved the Quiet Soldier to tears.

The OC listened intently as Schollonburg and the boys spoke about the last op, about the bridge and Willt, the town, the Russians, the garrison and the estimated number of enemy dead; probably 200. A good result and special congrats were directed at Curtis for his work on the bridge. After the debrief, the OC listened patiently to Grillo and Kaminski. He knew his men well and he would, in due course, see that the full story of Kurt Willt's demise reached his family. He would, if possible, deliver the details personally as was his habit, ensuring accuracy and continuity.

But for now, there was work to do. Grillo and Kaminski had echoed their wish to whack the ammo compound at the garrison. The OC had agreed, knowing instinctively that the boys needed to get the desire to avenge their friend's death off their chests.

It also had the added bonus of disposing of a legitimate target. They wouldn't be expected back so soon by the enemy. But the OC wanted something in return for his blessing on the op. Talk of the Russians had stirred his imagination and he, as well as the rest of the teams, wanted to know what had happened to the people in the town, so he required a prisoner. From a prisoner would come information, one way or another! A Russian or a Cuban would do nicely and Grillo and Kaminski would bring him two!

> 'It is better that people should wonder why you don't speak, than why you do!!'
>
> Benjamin Disreili.

Fireworks

Cry havoc, let slip the dogs of war

William Shakespere; *Julius Caesar*

The sketch map that had been drawn by Gus Grillo during their task to watch the garrison near the bridge was being transformed into a model in preparation for the brief to be delivered by Schollonburg.

Kaminski built the model, helped by Curtis. It showed the garrison in detail, with its clusters of buildings and the railway track running north–south and crossing the ravine, where Curtis, Voss and Van Rijn had been at work the previous day at their bridge.

This time though, the teams would be concentrating on the ammo compound and the accommodation block. It was here that Grillo and Kaminski hoped to snatch their prisoner, whilst Curtis, Voss and Van Rijn dealt with the ammo compound.

The accommodation block was of wooden construction and it stood 50 yards to the east of the ammo compound. Between the two buildings lay the water supply in the form of a low-walled pond. It was about 20 by 20 feet square and 3 feet deep. The pond was kept topped up as required by a small pump, which channelled water from a local stream. The area throughout the garrison had been cleared of all vegetation out to a distance of about 80 yards and so, once inside, the men would be in clear view of anyone who may be watching out for an attack.

The men who sat listening to Schollonburg on the brief had no intention of carrying out a conventional assault on the garrison. The plan was simple. They would travel on foot, until they reached the ravine over which Curtis' bridge had passed. Aiming to intersect the ravine about 800 yards east of the bridge, they would enter it and move along its base, until they reached the remains of the bridge. At this point, they would split into five teams. Teams One and Two under the command of Grillo and Willy Fallon respectively, would be responsible for the accommodation block. Team Three, commanded by Voss, would deal with the ammo compound, and the fourth, commanded by Schollonburg, would command the op, coordinate fire support and provide a section on the target to keep the enemy occupied, whilst the teams on the compound and accommodation did the business.

During the briefing, Grillo and Kaminski made the point that the front gate of the compound was guarded at all times by one guard, who rotated every hour and was overseen by either Cuban or Russian advisers.

Dick Kaminski suggested to Jimmy Curtis that an explosive entry would probably be required to open the iron-barred gate. Curtis said he'd make arrangements for that probability.

'It won't take a big charge. I'll sort it,' said Curtis.

The accommodation block had, at its front, a sandbag and oil drum guard box, housing one guard, who rotated on the hour, as did the guard on the ammo compound. Roving patrols consisted of two men on foot, who patrolled the perimeter with no particular routine or route. Schollonburg indicated that he would deal with the roving patrol. He then spoke to Kaminski.

'Kaminski, you'll be attached to Voss' team. If these people are commanded by Russians, as we suspect, it's probably best if we use your ability with the language to achieve the element of surprise at the compound.'

'No problem, boss,' replied Kaminski. 'I mean, *da da!*'

'That means, getting Curtis close enough to the gate to deal with it and get inside. Once we're here, you blow the gate and we'll start taking heads!'

The teams all nodded in acknowledgement.

'Kaminski, once you've introduced yourselves and it goes noisy, get straight back to Grillo at the accommodation. Leave Voss, Curtis and Van Rijn at the compound. With any luck, we'll produce a prisoner.'

Once the orders were complete, the teams moved away to make their own preparations. It had been decided that the point section would comprise of René Voss, Jimmy Curtis and Leo van Rijn. The point man would be Thomas the Tracker. It had also been decided that the op would take the form of a walk in; which meant exactly that. So, instead of starting with the usual bang of mortars or artillery, they would walk straight into the target using nothing more than audacity to achieve the element of surprise and success. The first the enemy would know of their presence would be when Curtis blew open the compound gate, by which time the teams would be all over them like a rash.

For Curtis and Kaminski, it meant a stroll along the track with Van Rijn, Voss and Thomas. They would walk straight up to the compound gate, with Thomas in front. Kaminski would come next who, when they got close enough, would begin to wave his arms about, remonstrating in Russian and basically giving the sentry a bollocking, terminating with a sound beating to silence the chap – in other words, to kill him.

Later, Curtis and Kaminski stood chatting about the virtues of walking into an enemy stronghold as if they owned the place. Kaminski speculated that once they'd managed to scale the wall of the ravine, and providing there was no sentry in the sentry post – the boys reckoned there would probably be no sentry there now that there was no longer a bridge to guard – they'd simply have several hundred yards of track to stroll along, before turning right into the garrison and doing the business. He speculated also that they had nowhere to go if they got bumped! Apart from back over the cliff, that is!

Curtis smiled one of his "what's the big deal" smiles.

Kaminski looked at Curtis' apparent lack of concern for the obvious and said, 'Jim, many, many long and complicated years of therapy is probably what you require, mate. I kid you not, boy. We could very easily end up in serious shit here, mate.'

'That's true, Dick. That's definitely true,' replied Curtis. 'We're going to require balls the size of melons! But don't worry, mate,' he paused, a thoughtful look on his face, 'we'll probably be dead before we get out of the ravine, ha, ha!'

Kaminski shook his head and resigned himself to the fact that Curtis was probably a hopeless case – a lost cause – but in spite of all that, if he was going to do this, there was no one he'd rather be with than Jimmy Curtis.

So the teams fanned out into patrol formation. Voss' team took point with Kaminski attached. Walking through the night towards their goal, they reached the ravine as planned and climbed down into its base, which was rocky and quite thickly overgrown. They moved slowly through the undergrowth through a thin mist, which added to the eeriness of their surroundings.

About 200 yards from the remains of the bridge, they began to smell the result of hundreds of corpses already putrefying in the wreckage of the train. As they got closer, the stench became stronger and stronger and by the time they reached the site of the previous day's attack, it was almost unbearable, causing some men to throw up.

They pressed on regardless, each team now going their own way. René's team reached the top of the ravine, sweating and feeling sick; but they ignored their discomfort and peeped gingerly over to see if the sentry post was occupied. Seeing it was deserted, they clambered over the edge and quickly moved the 100 yards along the track, stopping to compose themselves before starting the walk in.

From then on, using hand signals only, they moved on along the track, stopping every 100 yards or so to watch and listen. Soon, they reached the edge of the cleared area, which surrounded the buildings in the garrison. They took in their surroundings, peering into the darkness, looking for signs of movement. Then, the whispered voice of Schollonburg could be heard, confirming that he was in position and had the roving patrol in sight. René's team waited as the others confirmed that they were ready. There was a pause of about four to five minutes and then Schollonburg confirmed that the sentries had been dealt with. Two minutes after that came the order, 'Go, Go, Go!'

Curtis, Voss, and Van Rijn and Thomas, together with Kaminski, started towards the compound. Then, 30 yards from the main door, Kaminski started jabbering away in Russian. Voss, with his hands stuffed in his pockets, nodded his head vigorously, proclaiming *"Da da"* or *"Niet"* – the only Russian he knew. Curtis had slipped in close behind but was looking intently, straight ahead, at the guard, whose attention had been drawn to the approaching group from the darkness.

Kaminski began gesturing to the sentry now as they approached to within 5 yards. The man was obviously resigned to the fact that he was in receipt of an unsolicited bollocking and sprang to attention, just in time to receive the most viciously delivered right hook to the jaw with a knuckleduster from Kaminski. Thomas was onto him in a flash and Curtis was already fixing his small charge to the locked gate. He lit the 12 inches of safety fuse and they jumped back into cover, waiting for the explosion – twenty-two seconds later, up it went with a flash and a bang. Within seconds, the fireworks began as the other teams began their tasks.

Dashing back to the compound gate, the boys discovered that far from blowing open the door, the charge had simply removed the lock and by a cruel twist of fate, it had interlinked both iron gates like twisted fingers, refusing to leave go – they were jammed shut! Curtis cursed; Voss giggled and called him a tosser! Kaminski was running back to join Grillo. Thomas stood, shaking his head disapprovingly at Curtis.

Curtis wasted no time.

'Gimmee your fuckin' grenades, WP, all of them – quickly!'

After the others had handed them over, they watched as the quiet soldier changed into something else.

Curtis paused for a second and then turned away and ran back to the twisted gate, climbing up onto the wall of the compound. Almost immediately, he was spotted by the enemy, who rained fire at him from several different positions. But Curtis seemed oblivious – either that, or he just didn't give a fuck. Voss supposed the latter.

'Crazy fucker!' said Van Rijn.

'Yes. He's pissed off because he didn't manage to open the gate.'

A bullet tugged at Curtis' shirt, another drilled a hole through a water bottle on his belt and a third split the rubber on the heel of his boot. The firing was becoming more intense by the second. Voss, Van Rijn and Thomas just knew that Jimmy Curtis was going to die – and not for the first time, either! But still he pressed on, looking for an opening for the grenades. As he reached the end of the wall, he found a vent. Just then, he heard the sound of a tank engine off to his left. It burst from cover, traversing its main armament left and right. He unslung a 66, flipped off the end covers, extended the weapon, took quick but careful aim at the front-left drive sprocket and fired. There was a huge bang as the missile hit the target. The tank was disabled but the main armament was still in operation. He pulled the pins on the grenades and pushed them through the vent, jumping from the wall just as the tank fired again, punching huge holes through two walls of the compound. The grenades exploded and the fireworks began. Tracer criss-crossed the night sky as Curtis hit the ground and rolled, coming up onto his feet and running back towards Voss, Van Rijn and Thomas, who were crouched, watching his performance, barely able to believe he had survived.

As Curtis made his way towards them, a woman ran, delirious and screaming, straight past him to his right into a burning building. He instinctively changed course and ran after her, rugby tackling her just inside the door. The heat was indescribable. His skin began to blister and his hair caught fire. He dragged her to her feet and she dropped a bundle to the floor between them. It was a child of about eighteen months of age. Grabbing the woman by her burning hair and the child by the leg, he dragged, stumbled and fell back out of the door, where he was projected along with the woman and child into the pond. Then, almost immediately, the same strong arms pulled the coughing, choking trio back out and threw all three against the pond wall like a steaming pile of drowned rats.

Curtis' FN was thrust back into his hands by Leo and they began to make their way purposefully around the burning compound towards the tank. Then a bang from the left, followed by a huge explosion behind Curtis' group, swiftly followed as an RPG was fired in their direction. The blast knocked all three to the ground. As Curtis and the others composed themselves, he looked back towards where they'd left the woman and child. All that remained was a pile of bloody rags and body parts. They'd taken the full force of the missile. Curtis turned away, shook his head and pressed on.

Voss and Van Rijn thought it would be a good time to rip the piss out of Curtis' ability with the explosives.

'So, you can get into anywhere, can you? You fuckin' amateur!'

'Yeah, next time let's just ring the bell, eh, Einstein?' said Van Rijn. 'What a fuckin' tosser!'

Jim regained his sense of humour, stifling a grin.

'OK, OK. In future, I'll ask an adult!'

They pushed on around the back of the compound now and, peering around the corner of the blazing building, they saw the rear of the disabled T54, its main armament still traversing and firing at targets around the camp. Knowing it was doing some terrible damage, Voss was already gathering the remaining 66 mm for a further attack on the tank and they pressed on around the rear of the compound this time to engage the beast from the rear with a volley of three. Small arms fire flew in all directions and different coloured tracer stitched crazy arcs across the night sky. Grenades exploded and Curtis could hear Grillo and Kaminski shouting to each other in the darkness.

The trio continued on their way, scanning left and right for signs of the enemy. The sounds of battle and the smells of used ordnance filled the air; someone was screaming off to their left. The tank's main armament overpowered its engine sound as it fired. Then they had it in their sight and at 50 yards, the rear of the beast made a wonderful sight.

They stopped and wasted no time in preparing the 66 mm; each took careful aim. Voss counted down: 'Three ... two ... one ... fire!'. There were three simultaneous bangs, a whooosh, then a bang, bang, bang as the missiles struck home on the crippled beast.

They'd all aimed at the turret ring and the triple impact on the armour was enough to encourage the crew to bail out. As the first of the crew came out into the night air, two rounds hit chest and head and he dropped back inside. At that moment, Curtis started to run towards the tank, his FN slung across his back. He carried a grenade in each hand and, leaping onto the back of the tank, he pulled the pins on both grenades.

Voss was up beside him now on his left and Van Rijn was covering from ground level. They'd arrived in time to meet the second crewman's attempt to leave through the open cupola and Voss promptly drew his backup 38 and shot him in the head. He dropped back in a heap, rapidly followed by Jim Curtis' two grenades. The cupola was slammed shut and the grenades did their work.

Laughing, Voss and Curtis joined Van Rijn and went to ground behind a low, grassy bank, just in time to see the ammo compound explode in a display of smoke and flames; tracer and flying shrapnel made their heads buzz.

Their job done, they started back towards the target that Grillo and Kaminski had been given in order to extract a prisoner. They could see tracer rounds pouring into a sandbagged guard post. The occasional burst of automatic fire was being returned. Then a loud bang, followed by a much louder explosion, signalled the end for the enemy who occupied the post as it was taken out by another 66.

Immediately, Kaminski and Grillo burst out from cover like men on fire. Charging towards the bunker, they both reached it at once, firing several rounds point-blank into the already dying enemy. Once inside the guard post, which stood close to the front door of the accommodation block, they covered the front exit as the remainder of Grillo's team entered from the back of the building. Several grenades exploded, windows were blown out and fires started as WP ignited timber and furnishings inside.

After several minutes, four men dressed in combat kit were unceremoniously shoved out of the door on the end of McNiel's AK47. All were bleeding from various shrapnel wounds and one nursed a gunshot wound to the chest – he sank to his knees, coughing up pink bubbly blood.

Grillo waited until his team were all clear of the building and then fired a single round at the coughing, choking enemy soldier from about 6 feet, hitting him in the left knee. He fired a second into his right shoulder, knocking the man flat onto his back. Then, Kaminski put his lights out with a round to the head. Grillo and Kaminski were operating in the pissed-off mode now. The other three enemy – clearly petrified by the absence of the Geneva Convention and in no doubt that the boys meant business – stood, riveted and shaking.

Then, Grillo, with the memory of Kurt Willt clear in his mind, spoke in Spanish. *'Manos aribas, avanté. Pronto, pronto.'*

A Cuban sprang forwards from the group onto his knees, his hands clasped prayer-like, crying, looking up into Grillo's hard, cold face. Grillo sent a vicious kick into the man's jaw, knocking him senseless. Then he turned to McNiel.

'We'll take this one, Billy.'

McNiel kicked the unconscious Cuban onto his front and then secured his hands behind his back with 18 gauge baling wire.

Grillo nodded to Kaminski, who then stepped forward and spoke malevolently in Russian.

'Hello, my Soviet friend!'

Neither of the two men moved, but recognition of Kaminski's statement registered in the eyes of the smaller of the two, which gave the game away. Kaminski fired a burst from his FN into the other man's chest, who dropped like a sack of spuds. Then he butt-stroked the other in the face, smashing his nose in the process and knocking out several teeth.

Turning to Grillo, he said, 'This one's a Ruski.'

Grillo nodded to McNiel, who repeated the wiring process on their new best friend Boris.

It was a joy to behold. Both Grillo and Kaminski were feeding off their emotions, born out of the death of their friend Kurt Willt, thought Curtis. They were cold, hard bastards – perfectly cast for the job. But the same could be said for all the men and now they had what they came for.

130

Just the odd shot rang out around the camp now as men cleared the position. The sound of exploding ordnance in the ammo compound as it continued to burn echoed off surrounding hills.

The teams had re-org'd and were distributing ammo and weapons. Several wounded were being treated by medics and the group had lost four men, dead. The enemy body count numbered forty-two confirmed kills and once again, the bodies were piled high and burned before the helis extracted the men.

Jimmy Curtis was considering his future whilst he sat with his back to the large acacia, waiting for the heli. He was due out in the last lift, along with René Voss and Leo van Rijn. He stood up, brushing the dirt from his trousers, looking around at the damage they had done.

'Someone's getting their money's worth out of us, Voss!'

'*Oui. Oui,*' Voss responded, recognising an uncharacteristic unease in Curtis.

Voss stood and Van Rijn joined him. Then Voss placed his hand on Curtis' shoulder.

'What's wrong, *mon ami?*' he asked. 'What's wrong with the quiet soldier?'

Curtis pondered over the question before he answered. He loved Africa, the smells, the sounds, the space, the seasons – and he loved the Africans – he loved the wildlife and he loved his work, but he was torn between his desire to go back to Ireland and his love of the Dark Continent and the true friends with whom he'd encountered so much.

He knew if he left Africa he would never meet the likes of them again and he struggled with that. He thought of Kurt Willt lying buried on the knoll. We came to this place to make them pay, he thought, and we've done it.

He'd left Ireland when he was just 7 years old and he wanted to go back to find his roots – if there were any left. He'd never tried to keep in touch. No one would know him, or at least not many, anyway. There were bridges to build and there was the stigma of his service in the British Army; he knew he couldn't reveal that.

He turned to his two friends and said, 'Life's short in this line of work; sometimes very short. I have much to do in a short time, relatively speaking. I think I've done enough here and I think we've all done some good. We may even be remembered – at least by the enemy,' he sighed. 'But now it's time to go.'

Van Rijn and Voss starred at Curtis; all three were of the same mind.

They believed fervently in the freedom to live as you wished and that no person has the right to try to prevent someone from doing it.

They said nothing, although their faces spoke volumes. They offered no arguments and, in spite of all their own opinions, they respected Curtis' decision; but they were tremendously close and it hurt them all.

In the distance, the sound of the helis grew louder and five minutes later, they climbed aboard the heli and it took off. Turning south-east, they surveyed the scene below with silent indifference. It was a familiar sight. Curtis knew the next job would be his last and it seemed odd to be thinking about the end. How could anything else measure up to this? He knew nothing would.

The Last Shot

"Walk softly – but carry a big stick."

President Franklin D. Roosevelt

Jackson's Crossing wasn't a crossing at all. It was a railway junction which sat, literally, at the point where the rail tracks stopped abruptly at the bottom of a low hill. It looked as if the engineers who had built the line had reached the point where they would have to go round or go straight ahead through a tunnel, which had never materialised. That's Africa for you!

The military detachment, which many years before had accompanied the track layers, had reached Jackson's Crossing with the engineers. When the builders had left, an army outpost had been established at the site, housing up to 100 regular government troops. It doubled as a storage depot for the military, keeping a foothold in the region; in latter years, developing into a training camp for guerrillas.

There had, at times, been over 1,000 rebels sited there, ready to undergo basic military training. The usual communist indoctrination had been delivered by "Free Enterprise Russian Advisers", in preparation to go forth and kill anyone associated with attempts to resettle or stabilise the border areas in the absence of any governmental leadership since the collapse of governments in South Africa and Rhodesia. This included many White settlers, who could now no longer rely on military protection but who had successfully farmed the border areas for many years. A third force was at work – establishing power by eradicating freelancers.

Attacks on these homesteaders had become more and more frequent and extreme in their violence and intensity. Settlers were being butchered, literally. Children of both sexes were being raped and then murdered in front of their parents, who in turn, if they were lucky, would have their eyes gouged out, hands and feet cut off and tongues torn out; after which they would be nailed to trees by their legs to hang upside down until they died. Others were simply disembowelled and then beheaded. All in an attempt to force the settlers away from the border areas and their farms, to serve to achieve Soviet-style domination of the Dark Continent, to fill the vacuum fronted on the ground by Black indigenous troops and militia, plus the odd private enterprise. It was these that the teams were paid to fight. Many of these attacks originated from Jackson's Crossing and that's how it earned itself a place on the hit list.

A total of seven children had died in the last attack by insurgent troops. They had ranged in age from a 15-month-old boy up to 11 years of age; five girls and two boys. All were raped, including the baby, in the traditional fashion, and they were then beheaded and sat in the upright position. Their backs were leant against fence posts opposite the front of their tidy, Dutch-style farmhouse, with their heads looking out through lifeless eyes between their legs at the parents, who had been tied with barbed wire to the stair posts leading up the wooden stairs to their home's front door. Both parents were naked; the father'd had his genitals torn from his body and the mother'd had her breasts cut off. Just enough damage to allow time for them to watch the deaths of their offspring, before they, too, succumbed.

Intelligence indicated this latest outrage had been carried out by a renegade group operating with its militia, led by a pathological lunatic, who fully believed he was operating under the express direction of God.

God had apparently – during one of their personal meetings together – instructed the miserable wretch to rid the world of all he deemed unworthy and, in return, he would be rewarded with complete global domination for his trouble.

To the local megalomaniac, this seemed like a very nice deal and he set forth with his group of merry men and a copious supply of class A drugs to do just that.

Schollonburg, Voss, Van Rijn, McNiel and Curtis arrived the day after the attack and were standing between the two small groups of corpses.

There was an additional body now; that of a huge black vulture, which had its head rammed inside the abdomen of the farmer as the men had arrived. As it hopped, loped and skipped away – covered in putrefying gore and its mouth full of entrails – it unravelled several yards of intestine before being shot by Van Rijn. Not through hatred of the beast, it was just surviving in its natural way, but through respect for the owner of the offal.

The men were not turned by the sight before them. It wasn't new and they were hard people, moulded by the lives they now lived and of those they had lived in the past. They were the men who were reviled by the do-gooders and left-wing press; the civil rights organisations, which never seemed concerned with the civil rights of the type of souls who'd lived, loved and grown here and who had built their lives through hard work in peaceful toil on the rugged land. These contract soldiers or mercenaries, described by many as the real carnivores of the bush, were, according to some, not worthy to carry the description "human being".

Descriptions and opinions didn't concern the men, but what did was the fact that none of the people making the accusations and statements ever seemed to turn up at the business end of things to see what their "freedom fighter" friends were really up to.

C'est la vie. Curtis wondered if it would ever occur to those living safe lives what it cost soldiers to win battles. It was a fleeting thought which quickly passed, and so, with an enemy in front and another memory behind, the men moved off to track, find and eradicate the perpetrators.

Curtis, Schollonburg and Thomas – the Black Rhodesian tracker – were kneeling down over a set of tracks that looked like the retreat from Moscow.

'No problem, here,' said Jimmy.

'Right, mate,' replied Schollonburg. 'What do you think, Thomas?'

Thomas was the best tracker Curtis had ever seen – unbelievably talented – but it wouldn't take the skills of a gifted tracker to follow this rabble.

Thomas walked for about 30 yards, studying the sign.

'I think twenty-five people; maybe thirty,' he said.

He had estimated the number by laying his FN rifle alongside the tracks and then scratching a parallel line opposite the weapon about 18 inches apart, then another top and bottom, creating a box. Then, by counting the number of prints inside the box, he had come up with his figure. Schollonburg and Curtis had also done their own estimations and calculations and between the three of them, they had come up with the same squad average, agreeing on twenty-five enemy. Some wore boots; one had a deep V-shape cut in his right heel.

Thomas said, 'I've seen this one before. He was at the old SWAPO training camp last year. These are large feet, too, and the prints are deep. He's heavy ... big ... a big, big man!'

'There are women in this group, too. See here; smaller prints. And the toes turn in slightly,' said Curtis.

'Yes, I see. And look, car tyre sandals on this one. Looks like the majority are barefoot though. They've taken no care about covering their tracks, Jimmy,' said Schollonburg.

The three were moving slowly just to the left of the main group of tracks. The sign was rampant. Broken twigs and branches, half-smoked joints, upturned leaves, rocks rolled over by careless feet, leaving the darker sides uppermost, broken spider webs, crushed vegetation and insects, mud from the soles of boots left lying on bare rock in the shape of shoe tread or tyre-sandal tread, chewed grasses and human faeces. There were also the indentations left by someone's knee and the butt plate of their personal weapon as they'd knelt and waited. The weapon print had been identified as the usual AK47 and at least two GPMGs – good to know, he thought.

The men moved more quickly now after the tracker. Curtis and Schollonburg covering forward along the axis as Thomas read the sign. Forward and out to the flanks moved Grillo's team on the left, with Kaminski, now a team commander himself, on the right of the tracking group. They provided security in case of a head-on contact with the enemy. To the rear, a third team about 50 yards back moved in reserve. Every two hours, the left and right flank teams would move clockwise round the group, changing places with the reserve team. This way, the ratio of work-to-rest, relatively speaking, was equally shared, whilst maintaining forward momentum.

Mid morning on the second day, they came across the body of one of the people they were following. It was in two distinct pieces. The lower half, from the waist down, lay on the track; the upper torso lay about 15 yards off to the left. Signs indicated that it had probably been dragged here by wildlife before being disturbed by the men. Careful inspection of the scene by Schollonburg, Thomas and Curtis, showed that he had almost certainly been blown in half by his own grenades, which he'd probably been carrying in his ammunition pouch.

'Another gifted amateur!' commented Schollonburg.

There was no weapon or ammo to be seen and the corpse didn't appear to be booby-trapped and so, after a short while, the team moved on.

The body had revealed some interesting points. An old gunshot wound on the left leg and a newer injury from what was probably shrapnel. These showed firstly that at least this individual was not new to conflict, which would have a big effect on how he performed under fire; and secondly, the shrapnel wound had at some stage become infected, resulting in a rather amateurish attempt to reopen the wound to clean out the infection. This suggested a poor level of medical support. In the Western-European soldier, this can have a profound effect on morale. However, in the African bush, where the way of life for these already hardy people is extremely tough and unforgiving, it probably meant nothing more than dying an unpleasant death from sepsis – blood poisoning – or gangrene. In normal life, they suffered many indignities equally as bad as that – Dengue fever, AIDS, motabe fever, sleeping sickness, green monkey disease, malaria and Ebola virus – all of which are rampant in many areas and cut huge swathes through the indigenous population of the Dark Continent. Malaria alone kills a million people a year in Africa.

A quick look inside the open mouth of the corpse revealed several large cavities inflicted post-mortem. Curtis commented that they'd been the result of the removal of gold teeth – probably with pliers – and they'd be rattling around in someone else's pouch now. So this one had been well-off enough to be able to afford professional and expensive dentistry at some time.

'Therefore,' commented Schollonburg, 'it would also be reasonable to assume that he was privileged enough to be educated – he was probably a left-wing idealist, liberally indoctrinated with Moscow's values and military training.'

'Dead men speak volumes, if you know how to listen,' said Curtis.

Not just another stiff, after all; possibly a low-level commander. This was all valuable intelligence for the teams, he thought.

The sun climbed high in the sky and followed its regular journey back towards the horizon. Just before last light, the teams went firm amongst some very large boulders and shrubs. There were twenty men in total, including the tracker Thomas. Once the night-time routine had been established, Thomas, Curtis, Schollonburg, Van Rijn and Voss, after a quick brew and some biltong, moved off quietly to continue the track in the disappearing light. They would carry on until darkness, giving them a one and a half hour start on the main group and they could also act as early warning in the event of the appearance of the enemy.

At first light the next day, the main body would move off in the same direction and rejoin the Schollonburg team to continue the track. The night passed quietly and the tracker group slept in turn, two at a time.

Curtis and Voss listened to a lion in the darkness and timed its roar. Every seven minutes, it split the night and at one stage, they estimated it to be no more than 30 yards away as the majestic beast patrolled its domain beneath an inky-black, star-studded sky.

Daybreak on the fourth day was a revelation. Purple-green hues tinged with deep orange brushed the landscape as the leviathan sun strode across the horizon, bursting skyward in deep vermilion, casting its golden red net across the bush, tinging the tips of bushes with amber.

Dewdrop-spangled cobwebs shimmered like precious stones. The earth was coloured with pink rocks, which blushed and glowed like burning coals. Curtis and Voss watched, speechless. Curtis closed his eyes and felt its warmth wash his dirty, stubbled face.

Gazing out, Voss spoke first. 'There's no place on earth like this, Jimmy.'

Curtis paused, taking in a lungful of air. 'Yes, René, you're right,' he allowed.

Another African sunrise had touched the souls of the men. Africa can do that. Surreal, it eclipses any perceived or imagined vision; the birthplace of modern man.

An hour and twenty-two minutes later, the main body caught up with the tracking team. They exchanged a few pleasantries, before sorting out the order of the march and continuing on their way.

The track bore on through the bush and at one point, it passed between two pieces of elevated ground, like long spines running parallel to each other, about 200 yards apart for half a mile. The terrain between the two was covered with classic sparse vegetation. The ground was largely level and a narrow, dried stream bed cut a diagonal course between the hills.

The sign followed the stream bed, before passing into the valley. The tracker went to ground and waited for the flanking teams to move up onto the high ground each side of the flat plain. From these positions, they would dominate the high ground and be able to engage the enemy if required, ahead of the tracking team.

Once in position, the men moved forward. Almost immediately, Kaminski's voice came up, muffled on the radio. Schollonburg stopped the trackers dead. He listened intently to the tense message being transmitted. At the end of which, Schollonburg replied, 'Echo One. Roger. Out.'

Grillo sent, 'Echo Three. Roger. Out,' confirming he'd heard Echo Two; Kaminski's message to Schollonburg.

The message had been clear, concise and simple: non-tactical enemy group of three, 150 yards to your front. Two AKs and one RPG 7. Over.

Grillo had to move his own team a further 50 yards along the ridge, which he did on the reverse slope, before he could get an eyeball on the enemy. But once he could, he went firm and informed Schollonburg.

Kaminski's team presented a mirror image of Grillo's on the feature opposite.

Meanwhile, one man from Kaminski's team and another from Grillo's were sent alone along each opposing feature, a further 200 yards ahead and beyond the enemy, to act as flanking cut-off teams, in case any enemy managed to make a break for it. Radio traffic was minimised, as normal.

Back at Schollonburg's team, he was issuing QBOs to advance along the tracking route and engage the enemy as and when sighted. They had the drop on them now, but the men would leave nothing to chance, knowing all too well the dangers of underestimating the enemy. Graveyards are full of overconfident dead soldiers.

Their FNs were made ready, as always, but they'd decided to use crossbows to avoid alerting the larger force, which they knew were also held up somewhere up ahead. Tracking teams in the unit always carried the crossbows as a backup weapon for precisely these situations. The men they were concentrating on now were likely to be a poor example of a rearguard early-warning protection group, who felt safe enough to relax owing to the close proximity of Jackson's Crossing, now only 15 miles further on. They were about to meet the architects of their demise.

The trackers moved on – deep concentration etched on their faces – Thomas studying the ground sign, only 2 mph now; Curtis and

Schollonburg left and right of Thomas; Van Rijn and Voss to the rear. You could virtually hear them think. Then, 40 yards short of the enemy, the team could clearly hear them talking and laughing; not a care in the world. Twenty-five yards now and, just beyond the men, who were now in clear view of the team, a flock of African starlings burst up from cover. This got the enemy's attention. They stopped talking and looked; first towards the birds and then back towards the men facing them, 15 yards away now. The realisation of their desperate position replacing laughter with dread and fear; their feeble and futile efforts to react cut short by the whistling bolts, which struck all three with chest shots.

Before they'd fallen to the ground, Thomas was striding forward, machete in his right hand, to dispatch all three with a single blow to the back of the neck, using just enough force to sever the spine, without removing the heads. The bodies of the men spun round after each blow as the spinal cord whipped back down the spinal column like a snapped elastic band.

Schollonburg was already on the radio declaring job done, fast and clinical. Curtis sat down next to one of the stiffs, who was twitching away merrily on the ground – a natural bodily response to a rather fast and unexpected departure. He rooted through the man's pockets, pulled out a couple of joints and, splitting the outer covers and removing the contents, he rubbed them together in the palms of his hands, letting it fall to the ground, after which he checked the man's ammo pouches.

He removed a rusty, half-filled magazine from one and from the other he took a child's pink teddy bear.

There was dried blood on the face of the teddy and across its furry chest the name "KATY" was stitched. Curtis thought of the children back at the farm. The bear would have been one of theirs. He tucked it into the utility pouch on his belt.

Then, sitting on a small earth mound next to the twitching stiff, he rested his boot contemptuously on the face of his dying enemy and made himself comfortable, watching the others search the remaining bodies. Whilst he waited, he chewed a strip of biltong and amused himself, guessing how many times his footrest would twitch in one minute. Unfortunately for him, fifteen seconds later, it stopped, which put an end to his little bit of fun!

'Fuck's sake!' said Jimmy Curtis, lifting his boot from its resting place, frustration etched across his features. He spat into the vacant face as it gazed back at him. Returning its steady stare, he spoke quietly to the stiff: 'If there's any life left in you, you piece of fuckin' dog shite, then the last thing you're going to see before you leave this planet is my extremely right-wing capitalist boot in your paralysed fuckin' face!'

Then he lifted it up once more and drove it viciously back down into the centre of the dead guy's countenance. Continuing his vigil, he thought to himself, well, Jimmy lad, that's a step in the right direction!

The enemy weapons were gathered together and put out of commission by removing various parts from the firing mechanisms; apart from the RPG, which was checked over by Van Rijn and was carried forward to use against the enemy at the crossing. The move on from there took an even more cautious tone. Having already encountered the enemy – albeit on their own terms – the men moved more slowly and stopped more often to listen, watch and smell.

It was 09.30 hours the next day before they heard solid evidence of the enemy base. The track they had followed for the past five days had brought them to the reverse slope of the hill, which overlooked the unfinished rail track on its opposite slope. There were sounds of everyday life in a rear echelon military detachment camp, clear in the hot, dry morning air. Engines revving and the smell of exhaust fumes, thick in the nostrils of the men grouped together.

On the reverse slope of the hill in amongst the rocks and a thick patch of scrub, the teams waited in silence for last light. In the meantime, Curtis, Schollonburg, Van Rijn and Voss, plus Thomas – the tracker, moved slowly up the slope towards the top of the hill. Then, 20 yards from the top, they dropped from a walking crouch onto their stomachs and leopard-crawled the rest of the way to the top. Peering through the thick scrub, they had a commanding view of the camp laid out below them.

A man came out of one of a row of five latrines in the bottom corner of the camp about 60 yards below them. He fastened his shorts and then stretched his arms above his head. Van Rijn noted he wasn't carrying a weapon of any sort. Then the man waved to someone across a broad yard and a woman's voice replied with a laugh. Scanning the camp with his binos, Schollonburg, Van Rijn and Voss took in the layout as Curtis began a detailed sketch map, which would be used later to brief the rest of the men, in conjunction with a scale model, to show individual and team responsibility for the assault.

The railway line formed the spine for the plan of the camp. It had its own platform, which was about 40 yards long, and a single-storey tin and wood building ran the full length of the platform. To the rear of the building, laid out in a roughly rectangular shape, was the rest of the camp.

On top of the hill, which the men now occupied, was an old, disused bunker with commanding views of the surrounding landscape. Then there was the rail line, which faded into the north-west, and the camp itself. The men had cleared the bunker as they'd arrived and had quickly decided that the ramshackle state of the bunker was an indication that the garrison felt it unnecessary to watch from there and that probably meant they felt safe, which suited the teams just fine.

Curtis continued with his sketch of the site. At the north end was the largest building in situ; an open-sided, barn-like building, which was crammed full of what he decided was tentage. He decided its contents were probably turned out and erected when the camp was full. Trainees require accommodation and this was probably it. Next to the barn stood a large water tower and then down one side of the camp stood a row of wooden, shed-like buildings. There were twelve, terminating at the stripped down hull of a BRDM. The base of the rectangle was formed by a fenced-in transport yard with a total of six lorries and four off-road type vehicles. At the end of the row was a shining, black ZIL Russian limousine. This was housed in its own tin roof cover; wire-sided with a double gate opening onto the interior of the camp's rectangular parade-type ground. Bare-earthed like others, the teams had encountered the left-hand side of the rectangle, which was taken up largely by the backs of the platform buildings. At its centre was a double door that led out onto a wooden patio, skirted by wooden railings, where four steps led down from the patio onto a rough stone pathway, which continued straight forwards, terminating at the steps for a wooden saluting dais.

To the right of this was a flagpole fashioned from a single narrow tree trunk painted in red, green and black stripes. Curtis let his gaze settle for several seconds on the flagpole and a moving picture from his subconscious flipped up into the present.

He could hear small arms fire, saw a Russian from a past encounter and heard the high, thin scream of a terrified teenage girl as she plunged to her death; he recalled her broken body and the cruel grin on the face of the man in the door of the heli as it sped across the camp and away out of sight.

He was snapped back to the present by the sound of a woman's laughter off to the right. She emerged from a building on the right-hand side of the camp, carrying two large metal cooking pots – one in each hand – and balanced on her head was an even larger pot full of what he supposed must be water. She walked across the parade area and entered the building adjacent to the patio. About five minutes later, smoke was spiralling skyward from its thin chimney.

'That looks like a kitchen or dining hall area,' commented Schollonburg.

Curtis nodded.

'Thank fuck,' said Voss, 'I'm starving!'

They all smiled.

'Possible job opportunity here, boys,' said Van Rijn. 'If that's a communal eating area, it's a fine chance to take out the majority in one fell swoop.'

Schollonburg noted the time – it was 11.30 hours. After about two hours, the boys withdrew back down the reverse slope, leaving Curtis behind to complete his sketch and to observe the routine – if there was any – in the camp.

A further two hours passed and Curtis had noted that at 13.00 hours, a group of about fifteen, including four women, had appeared from various areas in the camp; some carried weapons, mainly AK47s. They made their way to the building on the platform, which the men had decided must be the cookhouse. Their observations had turned out to be correct and the smell of cooking and the clanking of metal plates emanated from the building and lasted for an hour, after which the group dispersed back to their original abodes.

There seemed to be no other routine of any sort about the place. Curtis noted that although the presence of the big black ZIL limousine had at first caught their eye, there were no signs of any Russians or Cubans. Curtis deduced that it was probably there for the use of the local commissar or adviser during his occasional stays. Although he couldn't imagine where it would be driven, apart from around the compound, that is. Still, that in itself would add to the air of importance of any visiting dignitary.

It was Van Rijn who relieved Curtis on the hill and Jimmy briefed him fully on what had been going on down below, giving him his opinions on the likely uses for various buildings on the site. Just before Curtis moved down, Thomas joined Van Rijn and stated that Schollonburg had decided not to attack tonight and to be prepared to remain in situ for a further twenty-four hours.

Van Rijn accepted the fact and he and Curtis slipped away to find out what Schollonburg's intentions were. When Curtis reached the main group again, he presented Schollonburg with the sketch of the camp and the details he'd gleaned during his time on top of the hill. Van Rijn, Voss and Curtis huddled together around Schollonburg, who quickly pointed out that his decision was made owing to the presence of the cookhouse area and the suggestion by Van Rijn that it was a good opportunity to whack the lot, or at least most of the enemy in one go.

He'd therefore need at least twenty-four hours to observe any further routine in the camp, around which he could formulate his plan of attack. And so the rest of the day and night passed quietly, with the men taking turns to watch the camp and noting movement of any sort to build up the intelligence picture. Schollonburg had decided that whatever happened down below, they would be putting in their assault by last light the following day.

He was slightly concerned that the three stiffs they'd left behind on the track might become conspicuous by their absence and raise suspicion in the camp that there was dirty work afoot. But he also hoped that whoever was in charge would think they'd probably jumped ship, which was a constant occurrence, given that many were pressed men or boys in the first place.

Daylight turned into night with a huge, full moon. The men on the hill continued to rest in turns and a constant watch was kept on the camp. Curtis lay on his back with his FN tucked snugly by his side and at 04.00 hours, Thomas returned from the observation position and lay down close to him.

'How's it going, Thomas?' asked Curtis.

'Good, mate, good,' replied the tracker.

Curtis smiled. He liked Thomas. He was a gentleman, noble, kind and wise; yes, wise, thought Curtis. Curtis had once asked Thomas his age and he had replied, 'I think 44 years, or maybe 50,' but he wasn't sure. Looking up at the inky-black sky, he picked out several constellations.

'The stars see all things,' said Thomas.

Curtis didn't reply.

'Curtis?'

'Yes,' said Curtis, turning to Thomas, 'what's wrong?'

'The man in the big boots ...'

Curtis frowned. 'Which man?' he asked.

'Remember? The one with the V-shape cut in the track.'

'Oh, yes, I remember now, mate – what about him?'

'I've seen him before, his track, and that V-shape. It's always deep, he's heavy, a big man!'

'I remember you said you'd seen it at the SWAPO camp last year.'

'Yes, Curtis. This is true, but before that, it was at the village.'

Curtis was intrigued.

'You mean, you know this guy?'

'No, not personally, but he was there when my family died.'

It suddenly dawned on Curtis what Thomas was saying.

'Thomas, is this one of the people who murdered your wife and children?'

Curtis was facing Thomas now, looking into his inscrutable ebony features.

Thomas gazed back and the tears that flowed down his cheeks across the tribal scars from his eyes, themselves a pool of bottomless sadness, shouted the answer.

Curtis nodded. He put his hand on the tracker's shoulder. 'If he's here, we'll find him, Thomas. We'll find him and whoever dies in this battle, he will most definitely be amongst them.'

Thomas turned onto his side and went to sleep, sobbing silently. Just before he dropped off, Curtis asked if he could mention their conversation to Chris Schollonburg.

'That would be fine, Jimmy,' replied Thomas. 'That'll be fine.'

First light saw the men stood to and the routine continued throughout the day. At mid morning, Curtis joined Schollonburg and relayed his conversation with Thomas. Schollonburg listened intently and nodded in agreement when Curtis suggested the fate of the big guy should be left to Thomas. The same information was relayed quietly to the rest of the team.

At midday, Schollonburg started to prepare his orders for the assault. The routine in the camp was slack, but Van Rijn had been right about the cookhouse. That was the only point where it seemed that the inhabitants of the camp gathered at particular times with any certainty.

So, Schollonburg's orders would centre on removing as many as possible in the cookhouse – and that would begin the assault. The rest of the camp would be quickly cleared by the rest of the teams. At 14.00 hours, Curtis was back at the OP watching the camp.

At 14.20 hours came the sound of shouts from the accommodation blocks on the right-hand side of the camp, followed by the sight of a boy of about 12 years old, running towards the saluting dais. He carried the usual AK in one hand and in the other was a large brass bugle.

Reaching the dais he jumped up onto its platform, cocked the AK and fired several bursts of automatic fire into the air, following it up with a musically incomprehensible blast on the bugle. This lasted for about a minute and a half and just about everything came out of the bugle apart from anything which could be remotely regarded as a tune.

After that, he completed his rendition by emptying the remainder of his ammunition skyward.

Within seconds, the camp was alive with people scurrying about everywhere. Making their way towards the dais, they formed themselves into four ranks, one behind the other. Curtis immediately began to count the occupants and gave three strong tugs on the communications cord, which had been laid from the OP to Schollonburg's position. He was rewarded with a single tug in reply and within one minute, he'd been joined by Van Rijn, Schollonburg, Voss, Grillo and Kaminski, in time to witness the proceedings down below. Curtis counted thirty-eight men and women and this included the six boy soldiers aged, he guessed, between about twelve and sixteen; including the bugler. They stood in silence.

Each carried weapons of Soviet or Chinese origin. The men on the hill looked on while the parade waited, the sun beating down on them.

Just then, an apparition appeared from the platform door and swaggered forward towards the parade, taking up pride of place in the centre of the dais. He stood, hands on hips, nodding agreeably. Master of all he surveyed; his bugler, dwarfed beside him.

'Holy fuck!' said Curtis.

'Shit!' said Schollonburg.

'What the fuck's that?' said Voss.

Many months later, recalling the day, Curtis described him thus: 'I am not joking; the twat was about 6 feet 10 inches tall, three days walk

146

across the shoulders on a fast camel. His head was massive, no fuckin' neck and it sat perched atop a barrel chest, fit to burst through his olive-green shirt. He had wild, staring eyes, set in a great moon face, with a mind of their own, peering out in opposite directions. He had arms like my legs and legs like the trunks of trees; he had a top hat and medals adorned everywhere. What an arsehole!

Curtis was entirely right in his estimation of the big guy. As the men continued to watch, it became apparent that the man was speaking to the group of people to his front, who stood rigidly to attention.

Periodically, he would raise his massive arm in the air, clutching an AK, and then he would shout something incomprehensible, at which point, the massed voices of his troops would return: 'All praise to Emperor Edi.'

He wasn't the first crazy African to bestow great status upon himself, thought Curtis. Idi Amin Dada VC, King of Scotland, etc. – some Mau Mau commanders like Dedan Kimathi Waciuri, who decided to become Field Marshal Kimathi, commander-in-chief, Mau Mau forces in the Aberdares region; Knight Commander of the African Empire; Prime Minister of the Southern Hemisphere. Not bad, for this ruthless, sadistic and mentally unbalanced ex-clerk. He was wounded and captured in a firefight with the SF on 21 October 1956 and later executed, after trial, which is far more than he afforded his unfortunate victims – man, woman or child – and these were many.

So, "Emperor Edi" ranted on and his bugler scampered off in the direction of the vehicle compound. Undoing the gates to gain access to the ZIL, he jumped inside, started the engine and then drove slowly towards the saluting dais. As he arrived, "the giant" stepped menacingly down to the car, which now had its front passenger door and the skylight, open. He bent over and squeezed his huge frame inside and out through the roof. The bugler closed the door behind him and galloped around to the boot. He ferreted about inside and pulled out something dark. Slamming the boot shut, he ran back to the side of the vehicle and, holding the item in both hands, he ceremoniously offered it up to the big guy who, with great reverence, took it and placed it on his head. The undersized top hat looked ridiculous, but failed to diminish the physical threat that the great brute exuded. The bugler bowed low and then jumped into the driver's seat and began the first of a couple of dozen circuits around the compound. Each time the vehicle passed the front of the group, up went the roar extolling the emperor's greatness. Then the group would immediately turn about face, in time to meet the vehicle passing behind them and give the boss two for the price of one as it were.

The men continued to watch the circus and it would have been an amusing afternoon had it not been for the knowledge of the trail of murder, rape, torture and destruction that these people had obviously left behind over a period of many months, if not years.

In the end, the ZIL came to a halt in front of the saluting dais and King Kong extracted himself from the vehicle. Swaggering across to the parade of minions, he walked straight through two ranks as if they didn't exist, knocking three or four flat onto their backs. He stepped in front of one of his unfortunate victims, his large, shovel-like hand grasping the man by his throat and lifting him bodily from the ground, like a rag doll. He then crashed back through the ranks to the front of the parade and began to rant and rave, punctuating every few lines with a long, arching swing of his arm, holding in his paw a Simonov rifle by the barrel, which he brought crashing down on the head and body of the hapless individual who had incurred his wrath.

After several vicious blows, the man was cast to the ground in a bloody mess and the remainder of the crowd dispatched to various parts of the camp, scurrying about like ants on an ant hill. Soon, the parade ground was deserted apart from the still form of the battered man.

Schollonburg said, 'Let's get this done.'

Once again, the men moved back from the crest of the hill.

Curtis began to build his model with the help of Van Rijn and Voss. Once it was complete, the team were called in to receive their orders for the assault, which was due to take place at first light the next day – breakfast time.

The model, as usual, was produced in detail by combining the model kits from several of the men. It showed, in miniature, everything they could see for real on the other side of the hill.

Schollonburg had decided that the assault would start with a bang – always a good idea – and that bang would be provided by Curtis, using a blast incendiary placed on the railway track side of the cookhouse, which would be detonated using an electrical initiation. The device would consist of a 5-gallon jerrycan of petrol, pilfered from the vehicle compound that night. A 15 lb charge of PE would be attached to the side of the can with baling wire, tamped with plywood. An electrical detonator would be inserted into the plastic and attached to a roll of twin-flex cable, which would be extended a safe distance to a firing point.

Curtis, Voss and Thomas would work as the demo team and once it went noisy, they would concentrate solely on finding the big man. Once done, it would be over to Thomas.

Looking at the demo team, Chris Schollonburg indicated with his pointer the buildings they were to clear and search.

'Take everything on the left-hand side of the camp, guys, and you start as soon as we go noisy, OK? Gus, your team will clear along the right side of the camp. The limit of exploitations will be the water tower, here.' He pointed to the top end of the model.

'Dick!'

'Yes, boss.'

'Your team will move in reserve with me and we'll clear straight through the centre here, destroying first any vehicles in the compound.

Then, using the water tower as our axis, we'll clear to the base of the tower. You'll also have the RPG. Leo, you and Willy Fallon will remain here on the hill and give fire support onto the target on request, covering the flanks as well. Any questions?'

The orders concluded with the synchronising of watches and ready-to-move order at 06.00 hours.

Voss, Thomas and Curtis sat together, cleaning their weapons and checking equipment, while two men from Willy Fallon's team soon returned with the 5-gallon jerrycan and delivered it to Curtis. He prepared the charge and attached it to the can, so all he'd have to do in the morning would be to place the device, insert the DET, run out the twin-flex and ... fire!

Once they'd completed all their admin tasks, they prepared a cold meal and sat chatting whilst they ate.

'Have you decided what you'll do when all this is done, Curtis?' asked Voss.

'What – you mean here – in Africa?'

'Yes.'

'Oh, I'll probably do some time wandering about, relaxing – you know – maybe do some sightseeing, that sort of stuff.'

'You're leaving, Curtis?' said Thomas.

'Yes, mate. I've decided it's time to go.'

Thomas looked at Curtis and said, 'All things come to an end. It's the nature of life. I'm sorry you're leaving, Curtis, but there is a time for everyone. Soon, it will be my time, too.'

But Curtis failed to realise the gravity of Thomas' statement.

'I think I'll get some kip, guys.'

He drifted off, thinking about his mother, and later, he dreamt fitfully about slums in Ireland, priests, nuns and being locked inside an under-stair cupboard, alone in the darkness.

At dawn, the men were wakened and prepared to move off to begin their tasks. Curtis, Voss and Thomas joked about the impending BBQ.

Then, as they set off, the mood turned serious – businesslike. René Voss carried the jerrycan on his shoulder, Curtis led the way and Thomas brought up the rear of their small group. They used the cover of the bush and the odd piece of dead ground to approach their target. On the route in, about 50 yards from the cookhouse, they decided on the firing point. It was a large boulder amongst some scrub and Thomas dropped off to wait as Curtis and Voss moved the last few yards to place the charge.

Further ahead to their left and right, Willie Fallon and Billy McNiel's teams moved very quietly into position to act as cut-offs, to prevent any enemy from escaping the camp.

Curtis and Voss reached the first building and stepped up onto the wooden platform. It creaked quietly as they took their final steps to the side of the canteen. Placing the jerrycan to the left of the door, Voss peered carefully through the dusty cobweb-covered window and caught his breath. Curtis noticed his reaction and drew his Browning.

Inside, a boy of about 15 years of age was moving about, apparently preparing for breakfast, and he was now approaching the door. Both Voss and Curtis pressed their backs firmly against the wriggly tin sides of the building and waited.

A key turned in the lock and the door handle rotated. Curtis' heart beat fast; the door moved inward, there was a pause, the sound of a yawn and then a stream of piss emanated from the open door. The boy was having fun making shapes and puddles and as he did so, it splashed, flowed and pooled on the wooden floor, before disappearing between the gaps. He then took one further step forward and two strong arms shot out from either side of the door.

Voss grabbed his hair and Curtis gave him a flat-handed belt, full in the face. The boy was dragged out with such force that his feet left the ground. Curtis deftly slipped behind him, his large, left hand over the boy's mouth and nose. Pushing forward with all his force, he projected both the boy and himself forward off the platform, bouncing the boy head-first into the iron-hard ground. Voss, having quietly closed and locked the door, was down beside them now and both he and Curtis dragged the semi-conscious form below the platform through the 18-inch high gap and out of sight. Then, silently and relentlessly, the boy was suffocated. Voss, with a neck lock, and Curtis by stuffing a large handful of dirt into his mouth and covering both mouth and nose, just to help things along.

They hung on for all of ten minutes and then left the lifeless form below the platform, returning the jerrycan next to the door. They stood, watching and listening, for a further two minutes, and then signalled to Thomas that all was well. Curtis continued with the task of attaching the DET to the charge and then he stacked three bags of maize around the device, before running the firing cable along a crack in the wooden platform and away towards the firing point, where Thomas watched patiently.

Settling down, they listened as each team confirmed they were in position. Then, in turn, Voss informed Schollonburg by radio that all was well.

Just over an hour later, the woman with the water entered the kitchen and soon, preparations were under way in the cooking department. Smoke billowed from the metal chimney pot and the sound of singing emanated from inside the building. Curtis and Voss, both bathed in sweat from their recent exertions of killing the boy, waited patiently as the minutes passed.

Sounds around the waking camp grew louder. The chauffeur wandered down to the transport area and gunned the engine of the ZIL into life, leaving it ticking over in the shed as he wiped the windows. Then, at 07.00 hours, groups of three and four started towards the kitchen to eat. Schollonburg had counted twenty-one, when he decided that was enough and broke radio silence with the command.

'Echo 21B,' – Curtis' call sign. 'Stand by. Stand by. Ten ... nine ... eight ... seven ... six ... five ... four ... three ... two ... one ... fire!'

The three men ducked down behind the rock as Curtis let loose Armageddon, pressing the button on the firing pack, which triggered the mind-numbing explosion, igniting the 2 gallons of fuel inside the jerrycan, which, in turn, roared through the building, incinerating everything and everyone inside.

The fireball reached high up into the morning sky and rolled outward in all directions as far as the large rock, behind which Voss, Curtis and Thomas sheltered. Then it extended out over the parade ground, turning the saluting dais into a pile of charred, burning wood. The cookhouse was no more; wood and tin rained down all around and out of the smoke and flames ran a human torch, arms and legs flailing all around. It ran blazing, directly into the barn containing the tentage, which caught fire as the torch bounced around and then fell, smoking and burning on the ground.

'Time to play,' said Curtis, and the three went in search of the big man.

Simultaneously, fire had been brought to bear all around the camp by the other teams and it wasn't long before the remaining enemy were returning it. Curtis turned right through the smoke and wreckage of the charnel house that was the canteen; charred and burning body parts lay all around. He stepped across the upper torso of a man, chest down, missing lips stretched back in an evil grin of death. Flames licked at naked flesh and body fluids sizzled as the heat cooked the corpse. Very apt, thought Curtis.

'Curtis – look!' shouted Voss as they stepped out through what was once the front entrance.

Curtis looked to his right as the ZIL, driven by the chauffeur, made a break for it across the square. He raised his FN. Voss and Thomas also engaged the vehicle as it tore across in front of them. The side windows shattered as the high-velocity rounds struck the moving target. Then there was a boom, followed by an explosion inside the vehicle as a rocket from the captured RPG hit the rear windscreen dead centre, lifting the limo off its wheels and dropping it back down again like a toy. It continued, careering forward, its momentum carrying it across the square, crashing into the water tower before it stopped. Smoke and flames poured fiercely from the car, but no sign of human life remained.

The legs of the tower caught fire as the fuel tank exploded. Bullets whipped and cracked everywhere. The three turned left again, working their way along the platform buildings. Voss dropped two enemy as they ran from the remains of the building next to the kitchen. Then, Thomas fell, struck by a bullet through the thigh. Voss and Curtis dragged him into cover and dressed the wound; a hole about the size of a golf ball had torn through the muscle of his thigh, but it had missed the bone and Thomas insisted on continuing, regardless.

Room-by-room, they searched, building-by-building. Most of the activity was going on across the parade ground on the other side of the camp. But, most frustratingly, there was still no sign of the big man.

Grenades exploded, smoke billowed and flames roared. Then, turning right at the top of the camp, they began to make their way towards the water tower, now blazing away fiercely. Gunfire could be heard coming from the cut-offs as they hunted down the runners. Passing a gap between buildings, they were pulled up in their tracks. First, by the sound of shouting – a loud, one-sided conversation – reaching them through the smoke; then, by the sudden realisation that they'd found what they were looking for.

Standing, bent over the body of one of his men, ranting, raving and wailing like a banshee, stood the giant. He held a large wooden club in his right paw. Voss, Curtis and Thomas stood, weapons pointed at the man as he acted out his farce. Clearly, a demented and confused soul and obviously unhappy with the stiff at his feet, he continued the one-sided oratory with the corpse. He gave no indication that he was aware of the presence of the three men.

'Perhaps we could arrange some sort of counselling,' jibed Voss out of the side of his mouth, grinning.

Then, Thomas suddenly spoke as he limped slowly forward between Curtis and Voss, who stared, surprised by the act. Thomas glanced down at a myriad of prints, including one set with a V-shape cut from the heel, which led straight to King Kong. He spoke as he walked and as he came up close to the big man, within about 3 feet, the giant stopped, realising for the first time that he had an audience. He turned, slowly, menacingly, towards the diminutive form of Thomas.

His crazy eyes, full of malevolence, stared out in opposite directions. Thomas continued to speak; lower now and in native tongue. Voss and Curtis could no longer hear. The big man stared down at Thomas, tilting his huge head first to one side and then the other, like a puppy-dog listening to a new owner, and his stance became less threatening.

Thomas spoke for several minutes. Then, out of the blue, he wrapped both arms around him like the meeting of long-lost brothers and the big guy reciprocated. Several seconds passed and the pair continued their embrace. Then, turning slowly, the pair moved around so that the "giant's" back faced Voss and Curtis, who both registered Thomas' clenched fists in the base of the huge back.

There was a metallic ping as Thomas released the levers on the two grenades which he held. He was giving Voss and Curtis the three seconds they had left to take cover.

'Shit!' exclaimed Curtis.

Both men dived and the grenades exploded, tearing both Thomas and the big man apart. Thomas had settled the debt he was owed.

'Jesus!' exclaimed Voss, visibly shocked by the unexpected outcome.

Curtis just stared at the jumbled mess of blood, flesh, bones and gore. The tracker was dead – Thomas had joined his wife and children. So this is what he had meant last night on the hill, when he'd said his time was up. Both men climbed to their feet, took one last look and then pressed on.

Not 20 feet further on, they came upon a wounded rebel soldier. He was lying in a semi-foetal position, clutching a gaping wound in his stomach, blood pouring steadily through his futile grasp. Curtis stepped across the man and stood, straddling him. Using the barrel of his FN, he pushed the man's bloody hands away from the wound and stood on his stomach. The rebel groaned as a string of entrails uncoiled themselves into the sandy ground. Curtis was thinking about the owner of a teddy bear as he looped a coil around the end of his FN barrel, guiding it up across the man's chest and, shaking it loose, he dropped the gory mess onto the man's pleading face. He paused and then fired a burst of three into his mouth. The man's head was snapped over at a crazy angle, his neck broken by the impact of the rounds. He lay still now, eyes staring at nothing. Curtis stepped over the stiff and nodded at the smiling René Voss.

The pair pressed on again. Within seconds, a boy soldier had run out of a gap between a hut and a pile of large tyres. He skidded to a halt before Curtis and Voss, with his AK at the aim. Curtis fired and so did the boy; the sound of a dry click emanated from the boy's AK – the magazine was empty. But not so for Curtis as a burst of rounds hit the boy, knocking him backwards to the ground.

Voss and Curtis spent the next ten minutes checking the last building in the area of their responsibility. Once done, they returned to the body of the boy.

Jimmy Curtis had fired his last bullet in the border war. It was 26 October 1979 – it was his birthday – and he was 25 years old. He stood, looking down at the body of the boy soldier, who was wearing a ragged green T-shirt with two bandoliers of ammo criss-crossing his narrow chest. Black oversized shorts accentuated his skinny legs. His lower jaw, shot away by Curtis' bullets, hung down in a pool of blood.

Curtis starred impassively at the lifeless form before him. He reflected that the worst atrocities committed by one human being on another, which he had witnessed here in Africa, had been committed by boys just like this.

Looking around, he turned to his good friend René Voss and said, 'Let's look for someone else to kill.'

Tearing the bandoliers contemptuously from the stiff, they turned back towards the water tower. Curtis swung his FN across the front of his body and was sent crashing backwards against the pile of tyres and oil drums as an enemy bullet hit the magazine housing on the weapon – his FN – which was struck with such a force that it was sent spinning off into the dust. Curtis lay on his back amongst the tyres. He tried to breathe but couldn't. His head hurt from the impact against the oil drum and he couldn't move his left hand. It started to go dark and he fought it, but he was slipping backwards, down a dark tunnel – the light faded and then went out – he was dead …

Then, there were sounds he couldn't make out in the distance. Voices he couldn't understand. They came closer, and so did the light.

He could hear Voss talking and then he felt him blowing air into his lungs; his chest hurt. Schollonburg's voice merged with Van Rijn and Voss.

'Come on, Jimmy boy,' he heard from Schollonburg.

'*Oui, oui, mon ami* – you'll be OK, Jimmy.'

Then he was carried back from wherever he'd been only to find the men laughing, all except for Voss, that is, who cried.

The enemy bullet that had mercifully hit Jim Curtis' weapon, sending it spinning away out of his hand, was also responsible for breaking three of his ribs, two fingers on his left hand, his left thumb and his wrist. Small price to pay, thought Curtis, as he sat thirty minutes later, with his back propped against a hut whilst Van Rijn made a brew. His fingers and wrist had been splinted and now rested in a sling.

'Where the fuck did that come from?' Curtis asked Van Rijn.

'Just a stray shot, mate. Willy Fallon took him out in the bush, back there.' He pointed outward, past Curtis.

'Did anyone else get hit?'

'Billy McNiel lost one of his new boys, dead, and there were a couple of others wounded. Voss told me about Thomas – bad news, man.'

'Yes,' allowed Curtis, 'it was.'

'You guys did a good job estimating the size of the enemy group, man. We've accounted for twenty-nine enemy, dead – including the bits and pieces from the canteen – and we don't think any runners got through, either.'

'Good,' replied Curtis, wincing at the pain in his chest.

The next two hours were spent liberally booby-trapping the local area before the team pulled out to the PUP. Curtis had been lucky, but everyone deserves a bit of luck, he thought. And besides, it wasn't the first time.

Curtis sat watching the camp burn and thought about all he'd experienced in the last two and a half years. He watched the teams as they re-org'd in the square parade ground. Enemy dead lay in various places amongst the familiar debris of battle. His gaze drifted across his fellow soldiers: Van Rijn, McNiel, Schollonburg, Voss and Kaminski – all field-stripping and cleaning their weapons.

Schollonburg was speaking on the radio; cut-off teams returned from their perimeter watch with belts of ammo slung across chests, belt orders with their pouches containing magazines, rations, medical kits, lengths of rope and carabiners fastened to ropes around waists, various types of footwear, camouflaged shirts and trousers, bush hats, dirty, stubbled faces – some bearded, and others, their wounds dressed with field dressings.

There was a great air of confidence and tremendous presence, professional to a man; soldiers, here to soldier for an unknown benefactor – a third force – neither enemy nor government. A third force with its own agenda; an agenda that mattered not a jot to Curtis. He came to fight, to soldier, to test himself in conflict, away from an army that considered itself the most professional in the world, but which spent year after year carrying out the policeman's job of internal security duties in the Province of Northern Ireland. Whilst important to the UK, this British Army was missing what it should have been involved in, which was genuine armed conflict worldwide. It seemed to Curtis that everyone knew about it but the Brits, and especially the Paras.

So, whilst this highly trained, highly motivated and committed professional army patted each other on the back in the pubs at night, singing each other's praises and waiting for a war, Curtis had slipped away to find out the truth about himself. To see if he could stand up and be counted as a true professional, with a genuine baptism of fire and the real experience of outright armed conflict, to be able to truly call himself a real and complete soldier and mean it. He had answered the call and the questions. He was a soldier and would always be so. He had proved himself; not for medals or accolades – for there would be none.

He had faced the enemy, stood firm and won. He remembered Big Brendan's words: "Last man standing, boy. It's all that matters".

'Time to go, Jimmy,' said Van Rijn.

Curtis looked up at the two men standing before him. Van Rijn and Voss helped him struggle to his feet and as they did so, off to their right came the sound of creaking, growing louder, followed by snapping timber and a great rumbling rush. They looked round in time to see the huge water tower finally tilting and collapsing in a shattering rush and rumble of wind. Van Rijn managed an 'Oh fuck!' before 36,000 gallons of water cascaded, rushing and roaring as it thundered across the parade ground in a torrential water wall of 4 feet high, sweeping all before it. A great melee of men, equipment, bodies and debris from the top to the bottom of the square, it piled its cargo against the perimeter fence before subsiding, leaving all and sundry in a huge, muddy, soaking mass, subdued at last. A few seconds passed as they gathered their thoughts.

'What a rush!' said Voss.

'Yep,' groaned Curtis, throwing a severed arm from the attack to one side. His ribs hurt like hell.

Eventually, the men regained control and Schollonburg said, 'Let's fuck off before the tide comes back in.' Then he led them out to the PUP and Jimmy Curtis' great African adventure had come to a somewhat ignominious end.

His belief in saying "You're not a soldier until you've shook hands with the old man with the scythe" had driven Curtis to his experiences in Africa and now, he could say he'd not only shaken hands, but danced with the old boy on many occasions. And the old boy may have stood on Curtis' toes once or twice, but he'd never managed to trip him up – he was happy with that.

The sun beat down and up above, great black vultures circled.

Curtis turned to Voss and said, 'Time for dinner!'

Roots

You can pick your friends,
But you can't pick your family!

(Anon.)

The middle of November in the south of England meant frosts and fog, low temperatures and wind down to Christmas. The contrasting drop in temperature hit Curtis as he stepped down from the South African Airlines 747 onto the tarmac at Heathrow. The flight crew stood at the exits, wishing people well, a safe journey and a Happy Christmas. He nodded, smiled at the pretty hostesses and walked towards Customs, carrying his worldly possessions in a small grip. He was eyed with ill-concealed suspicion by the customs officer and standing behind the officer was a suited man, whom Curtis decided was probably SB.

The suited man spoke quietly in the ear of Mr Customs and he dutifully pointed to Jimmy.

'You, sir. This way, please.'

Curtis complied, placing his bag on the counter and offering up his passport.

Mr Customs looked through Curtis' bag and the Branch man slowly but surely scrutinised the passport.

'How long have you been in South Africa, Mr Curtis?' he asked.

Curtis knew that the Branch man already knew the answer. After all, it was his business to know other people's business. But what else did he know?

'Two years or so,' replied Curtis.

'Can be hot out there!' said the man.

There was duality in the statement and it wasn't lost on Curtis.

'What was your business in the country?'

159

'Oh, this and that. Labouring mostly – picked some apples near Bloemfontein, built rhino fences in KwaZulu, did some bar work in Pietermaritzburg.'

The Branch man returned his level gaze, looking knowingly into Jimmy Curtis' eyes. He handed the passport back to him saying, 'How's the wrist?'

Fuck's sake, thought Curtis. He knows all right. Curtis smiled and made a wanking motion with his wrong hand.

'Seems OK.'

The Branch man returned the smile as Curtis turned and walked away, out of the airport. The man had made his point; they were both aware of Jimmy Curtis.

He passed through the exit and turned right and into a phone booth, arranging to meet a friend that night in a pub in Aldershot. Jumping into a taxi, he asked the driver to drop him at The Queens in Aldershot and they set off at a pace down the M3, turning south onto the A331 towards the Shot. The closer they got, the more signs of military they saw. Then, on a large road sign, as they passed alongside Queens Avenue sports fields, were the words: ALDERSHOT – HOME OF THE BRITISH ARMY.

Turning left down the slip road, they passed Depot Para on the left and the Para Bde on the right. The cab pulled up at the lights. Curtis looked to his left at a group of would-be Paras being beasted along by their platoon staff and PTIs.

Pulling away, the cab turned right. Curtis took in the two churches situated diagonally across the junction, then the Victorian buildings of HQ 4th Division on the left, fenced in as all the garrison camps were.

Barbed wire crowned the tops of the fences and guard boxes punctuated the perimeters. Armed guards stood sentinel at each post, but the only ones who ever looked like they meant business were the Paras, with their air of aggressive confidence.

Then it was up to the top of the hill with Maida Gym on the left and Knolly's Road entrance to Montgomery Lines on the right, with yet more Para guards. They negotiated the small traffic island, taking the first exit down to the town, past Salamanca Park married quarters on the right and Salerno on the left.

As they passed through the next set of lights, Curtis said, 'This'll do, mate.'

The driver pulled up next to the Princess Hall just over the road from The Queens. Curtis paid the cabby and gave him a £10 tip and then he walked across the road into the pub, up five or six steps, past the pool table on the right and turned right along the empty bar, where he took up his usual place in the corner. He banged the bell on the counter and the landlord Bob stuck his head out of the hatch and said, 'Well fuck my old boots! Give me a minute, you big Scouse twat.'

He disappeared and then two minutes later, he reappeared, slapping Jimmy on the back and shaking his hand warmly.

'How are you, Jimmy lad? You're well, I hope? What do you need, old lad? Anything I can do? Oh, just hang on a minute, boy. I'll be back in a tick … and wait till Sally hears you're back.'

He laughed and shouted up the stairs to his wife, then disappeared into his office. There was a muffled reply from above and then Bob returned with an envelope and handed it to Curtis. It had sat in Bob's safe for two and a half years; since Jim had given it to him for safe keeping the night before he'd left. Bob never asked what or why; he was a shrewd and honest bloke and Curtis knew he could trust him to produce the envelope and its contents, the £1200 "emergency fund", at the drop of a hat.

Just then, Sally appeared and jumped on Jimmy; and so did big Kenny Salway – the guy Jim had arranged to meet. Soon, they were torn into The Queens Hotel's liberal stock of Guinness and rum!

Curtis' battalion was away on a tour in Northern Ireland, which suited him for the time being. He just needed a couple of days in the Shot to sort himself out, before he journeyed to the south of Ireland to try to build some bridges.

Bob, Sally and Big Kenny kept Jimmy's presence in the Shot quiet and took good care of him for the next forty-eight hours, which passed in a drunken blur! When the time came, Jim was bundled into Kenny's 20-year-old Skoda for the trip to the Island of Anglesey and the ferry terminal at Holyhead, to catch the night ferry to Dunloughaire, just south of Dublin. Jimmy Curtis was going home.

He said his goodbyes to Big Kenny, who dutifully pointed him in the right direction before setting off back to the Shot, sworn to secrecy.

*   *   *

Curtis spent the night on board in the toilets, with his head down the pan, paying the price for his excesses over the past few days. It was a sorry sight that pitched up on the shores of Southern Ireland in search of his roots.

Some seventeen years had passed since he'd stood on Irish soil. But, as luck would have it, as he stood watching a string of lorries pulling off the ferry and queuing to turn onto the main road for their onward journeys, he read the liveries on the sides of the cabs as they pulled up close by. Smith's of Maddison, Eddie Stobart, McGuire's Haulage – Dublin, Christian Salvesen, Howard Tennant's Transport – Wigan, and then the one he was waiting for: "Willy Simpson Trucking" – Dundalk.

Curtis banged on the cab door. The driver wound down the window and shouted, 'Wanna lift, big fella?'

'Yep. Can you take me to Dundalk?'

The driver paused for a second, recognising Jimmy's accent, and then said, 'Sure, why not. Jump in, Scouser. I'll take you there.'

Curtis climbed up into the cab. It was warm, comfortable and modern – built by Mercedes – and it showed. CB radio, TV, double bunk, air conditioning … The owner driver was suitably proud of his machine and he talked endlessly about his job, the road, artics, traffic police, the price of diesel and illegal immigrants – who, he was convinced, waited behind every bush in preparation to leap aboard his wagon as it passed!

'That's a fine tan you've got there, boyo. Have you been on your holidays?'

'Yes,' replied Curtis. 'Spain.'

'Oh, whereabouts?'

'Er, Costa del Sol,' replied Curtis.

'Well, fuck me! There's a coincidence. I went there with the wife and kids only six weeks ago.'

Fuck's sake, thought Curtis – change the subject, quick.

'How far now, mate?'

'Not long, not long.'

And sure enough, fifteen minutes later, Curtis was jumping down from the cab and thanking the driver for his trouble.

Grey clouds hung low over the small town of Dundalk and drizzle filled the air. Jimmy quickly got his bearings and walked south-east along the coast road to find what he was looking for. Brendan Fearon Manor was the home of the other half of an unlikely friendship, which had grown over a period of two years between his starting school and moving to England.

Mrs Fearon Warner was the latest Fearon Warner in a long and distinguished family line, who had been the guardians of the family seat since it was built over 240 years ago. It sat proudly in its grounds of 300 manicured acres, in an imposing position atop of a piece of raised ground, overlooking the surrounding hills. Acres of the best apple trees ran away in all directions from the main house, which faced a 6-acre man-made lake, stocked with the best trout. There was the stream that fed the lake at one end and it ran out over a sluice at the other; eventually reaching the sea just half a mile distant. The lake was bordered by masses of rhododendrons, azalea and bougainvillea.

The Fearon Warner wealth stemmed from ball-bearings, mainly used in the engineering industry. Latter years had seen great inroads made into the ownership of race horses and a strong partnership had developed with a fabulously rich Middle Eastern oil sheikh.

In the days when Jimmy Curtis Jnr was avoiding the world of education like the plague, in favour of regular forays into the manor's orchards and running about with a cough, a snotty nose and no arse in his trousers, he'd been captured by the keeper and was handed over to the lady of the house to endure some suitable punishment. But far from being punished, young Curtis, the urchin who couldn't – at first – string a sentence together without the use of the word "fuck", found kindness he'd never before experienced. If he wanted apples, all he had to do was ask. "Without the use of any profane language, young man". The same applied to the poaching of trout from the lake.

Then, later, when Jimmy turned up for his regular official visits after Mass on a Sunday – bearing the signs of another beating from Big Brendan, his father – she would sit him on her knee and dab the bruises with witch hazel and lavender balm and the boy often dozed off in her arms in the glow of her huge, open log fire. Waking hours later, he'd see a table full of sandwiches and fruit – but never sweets. The woman always maintained they were "bad for a child".

Curtis arrived at the house at dusk; there was no sign of life; no lights and no movement. He rang the bell on the gate; no answer. He rang again; still nothing. Then there were the sounds of a car approaching in the disappearing light. It drew up close, stopping next to Jim.

Winding down the window of the green and white car, the policeman inside spoke.

'Can I help you, mister? You'll find no one at home now, not yet. Not until young Mr Fearon Warner moves in and that won't be until the legals have settled the estate, which won't be for another week or so.'

'Settled the estate? I've come to see Mrs Fearon Warner – Alice.'

'You're too late, lad. Are you a relative?'

'No, no, just a friend. What do you mean, late?' asked Curtis.

The policeman looked doubtfully at Curtis.

'Well, lad. I'm afraid Alice, that is Mrs Fearon Warner, passed away two months ago.'

There was a pause.

'Oh, right,' said Curtis. 'How? I mean – what was the cause?'

The policeman's tone softened now, seeing that the news had moved Curtis.

'Her heart, son, but there was no pain. She passed away in her sleep.'

'Right,' replied Curtis, nodding; and he began to walk away.

'Is there anything I can do, lad?'

'I need digs; somewhere to stay awhile,' said Curtis.

'No problem, son. Jump in and I'll drop you at Clancy's. They do accommodation.'

Curtis climbed in and five minutes later, he was outside his father's – Big Brendan's – favourite bar from all those years ago. Outwardly, it hadn't changed.

Curtis pushed the door and it swung open to reveal a home from home. Brass and pictures hung over the deserted bar, which glittered and shone with glasses and bottles. There was seafaring memorabilia commensurate with the pub's theme everywhere he turned. Paintings adorned the walls, depicting great sailing ships and seventeenth and eighteenth-century whalers. A narwhal tusk, over 6 feet in length, took pride of place above an inglenook fireplace in which a turf fire glowed, radiating a gentle warmth throughout the bar. There were several leather armchairs in green and deep red, and a couple of low-backed leather sofas, which faced each other across a low oak coffee table. Home-made rugs of various sizes and colours lay on the quarry-tile floor and the bar was lit by four standard lamps placed strategically about the room. The wall opposite the bar housed several oak shelves, which stretched from one end to the other and from waist height to the ceiling, packed with row upon row of books of all kinds from the Dickens classics to great tales of the sea and adventures of whaler-men of old. The room smelled of beeswax, cigars, turf smoke, leather, hops and age.

In the centre of the bar, facing across the room, was a ship's wheel and its spindles were made from the bones of whales, with an ivory hub at the centre; its steering grips fashioned from the teeth of an orca. A huge grandfather clock ticked away rhythmically in the corner, hypnotically drawing Curtis' attention. To its right was a framed portrait in oils of a ship's captain; his bearded and weather-beaten face the home of cobalt blue eyes, his skin burnished brown by the sun, salt and wind, a pipe clenched between tobacco-stained teeth. In the background, a huge wave topped with white horses hung, threatening to crash down across his shoulders. A brass plate echoed the words: Captain Cirus Clancy – Master of the Whaler *Songbird*. Killed by a whale in the Sargasso Sea, 18.02.1878. Gone to God.

Curtis sat in the chair nearest the fire and waited. The fire glowed and the clock ticked. Curtis picked up a book – *Moby Dick*. He read the front: by Herman Melville. Opening the front cover, he turned to chapter one and read the first line, but that's all he managed before nodding off.

Curtis woke and couldn't remember where he was for a few seconds, and then he was back. A man with a grey beard, leaning with one elbow on the fireplace, looking suspiciously like Captain Clancy, gently tapping the upended bowl of a Meerschaum pipe against his open palm, smiled at Curtis.

'Do ya' feel better now, son?'

'Aye,' said Curtis, rubbing his eyes.

'You've slept a while. It's 9.30, you know!'

'I'm looking for somewhere to stay. The Guarda brought me here.'

'Good enough!' said the man. He turned to the bar and shouted, 'Clancy!' No answer. 'Clancy, you have a guest.'

Curtis turned and looked over his shoulder as a man in an apron appeared at the bar, squinting towards Jimmy. Curtis recognised old Clancy immediately. A little thicker around the waist and almost bald on top; the rest, a silvery grey.

'How can I help you, sir?'

'Well, you can give me a pint of the porter for an old friend – and how are the roses, Clancy? I sure shovelled enough shite for you to have had one named after me,' Curtis smiled.

'And who would that be?' asked Clancy.

'Jimmy Curtis – Big Brendan's boy.'

'Holy Jesus! You're wee Jimmy Curtis. Look at the size of you now! How's your da? Is the old brute still with us?'

'Oh yes, and no change – just older.'

'What in God's name brings you back here, Jimmy? And what have you been up to all these years?'

'Well, Clancy, in answer to your first question – building bridges, looking for any family hereabouts; and in answer to your second question – I've been away at sea,' said Curtis, deliberately leaving out his army connections.

'Well now, there's a thing,' said Clancy, sliding a pint of Porta across the bar. 'On the house, Jimmy lad, as long as you're here. And there's a room above for you now – so come in, come in, lad. How's your ma? A lovely woman, so she is.'

'Clancy, do you know if any of my family still lives hereabouts?'

'I'm sorry,' said Clancy. 'I think they're all gone, lad – either died or moved away. In the years after you left, they began to drift away. Australia, New Zealand, Canada and, of course, America.'

Just then, the man with the pipe cut in. He'd been listening quietly to Jim's conversations with Clancy.

'Clancy, Big Brendan's father had a sister, who lived out at Seaview. She'd be your great aunt, Jimmy, but she's long dead now, boy; she's the only one that I can think of that didn't move away – her name was Anne Quigley.'

'Fat lot of good that is if she's dead, you old fool!' said the landlord.

'No, Clancy, that's not the point. Listen now … she – your great aunt, Jim – adopted a wee girl years ago; she'd be your second cousin through adoption. Her name is Anne Quigley, too. She turned out a clever girl and I'm sure she went to university and then on into the education system; then politics or something of the sort. The people of Seaview would know the answer, Jimmy.'

Curtis thought this news was encouraging and being second cousin through adoption or not, he'd still like to say hello.

'Thanks a lot,' said Curtis.

Then the landlord cut in, 'You look tired, old lad,' said Clancy. 'You should get some sleep. Tomorrow, it's breakfast when it suits you, lad – then we'll start asking some questions. How's that sound?'

'Fine,' said Curtis.

'Glory be!' exclaimed Clancy. 'Now off to bed with you.'

Curtis climbed the stairs to his room, undressed and fell into a dreamless sleep in a bed like a cloud. Some fourteen hours later, he was awakened by Clancy, suggesting that he showered and get himself ready for whatever the day held for him.

Feeling suitably refreshed with a good appetite, he skipped down the stairs to the kitchen which, like the bar out front, possessed that familiar home-from-home ambience. A woman's touch, thought Curtis, sitting at the dining table. It was big and seated eight chairs comfortably. The chairs, all heavy, old, farmhouse pine, matched the solid table, which stood firmly on a bare flagstone floor atop four great legs. The flagstones were worn in some places more than others, like in front of the stone double sink and the blackleaded range.

Solid copper pans hung in abundance and an open-fronted pantry displayed home-made bread and butter, new from the press.

There were jars of pickle and chutneys, home-made jams and preserves, and Mrs Clancy's classic, home-made hedgerow wines: strawberry, elderberry, blackberry, redcurrant, gooseberry, plum and many more.

Gingham curtains covered half the window with its pretty green-and-white check. Stoneware pots lined the window ledge and in another open-fronted pantry, next to the back door, hung cured hams and other meats.

Clancy walked over to the window and glanced up at the morning sky.

'Fine day, Jimmy, anything you don't like to eat now?'

'Not met any, Clancy. You serve it, I'll swallow it,' he replied, smiling.

Curtis remembered Clancy as a good and kind man, who had always treated him well as a boy, and the man hadn't changed.

Forcing the lid from an urn of fresh milk, Clancy turned to Curtis and said, 'This was in the cow in the field not forty minutes since, Jim.'

And, holding a one-and-a-half-pint stone drinking pot by its large handle, he sank it into the milk inside; then, taking it back out, he wiped the jug with his apron and delivered it to Curtis at the table.

Taking up the jug, Jim took three or four long quaffs of the cool, creamy drink and set the jug down. It was marvellous – the best he'd tasted for many a year – the simple act evoking many feelings, memories and emotions in him. He sat thinking to himself as he gazed out of the window and Clancy busied himself, cooking a breakfast fit for a king.

When they were done, Clancy produced another jug of milk and they sat chatting about the past and present. After about an hour, there were a couple of bangs on the door and in walked the man with the pipe from the bar the day before.

'God bless all here!' he exclaimed, warmly shaking the hand of both Clancy and Curtis. He got straight down to business. 'Jim,' he said, 'I've been asking a few questions hereabouts; up at Seaview, you know.'

'Oh, yes, right,' said Curtis. 'Any luck?' he said, not expecting much in return.

'Yes, I have, lad. I told you yesterday that I believed all of your kin were away now, abroad and the like.'

'Yes,' said Curtis.

'Well, that much, it seems, is true.'

Curtis sensed disappointment.

'It's true for all but only one, because I was right about Anne Quigley Jnr. She teaches up at Seaview Primary. She'll be there today, but not for long. She's a busy girl, but you'll be able to meet and maybe make some future arrangements, OK?'

Curtis was more than surprised and pleased; this stranger, who Clancy had still not introduced, had pulled a rabbit out of the hat.

Curtis tried to thank the man for his troubles, but he was on his way as quickly as he'd arrived, shouting "cheerio" to Curtis and his host and saying, 'Clancy knows where to go. He'll take you there.'

Curtis turned to Clancy, asking the man's name, but Clancy avoided the question, just saying, 'Ah, he's a good man … a good man, Jim, but very private, very private. You know the sort. Anyway, get yourself ready and we'll be on our way.'

'OK,' said Curtis, still watching the man through the window as he climbed into a green Austin Cambridge and drove away.

Some ten minutes later, Clancy and Curtis were on the road to Seaview Primary School, 8 miles away.

The kids in the school yard ran about laughing and shouting, playing football and talking in huddled groups; some walked arm in arm with the schoolteacher on duty in the playground.

Clancy had parked at the front gate and he asked Curtis to wait whilst he made his intros to the teacher. Curtis watched as they spoke and Clancy gestured back towards the waiting car. A couple of minutes passed and the children lined up ready to return to classes. A whistle blew and off they trotted. Clancy jogged back to the car and joined Jim.

'It's time, Jimmy. You're expected. Go in through that door, there. Turn right and her office is at the end of the corridor on the right-hand side. If you come back and I'm not around, I'll not be long. Just jump back into the car and wait.'

'OK, Clancy,' said Curtis and, feeling rather nervous, he climbed out and walked across the now deserted playground; he felt out of place in the school's innocent environment. He reached the entrance and pushed the shiny brass plate on the double doors, which opened inwards and swung shut behind him.

Floor polish and school dinners were the smells that spoke to him. It was a happy atmosphere and he turned right along a corridor. Along the left-hand side were windows, which looked out onto a grass triangle, in the corner of which stood an aviary with budgerigars and three rabbit hutches. There were four classrooms along the right-hand side and as he passed each door, he glanced in to see the children hard at work with the teachers holding court. The kids looked happy, thought Curtis – a sharp contrast to his own school days. The walls between each classroom door were adorned with examples of the children's work: coloured handprints, poems, short stories, paintings, echoes of school visits to working farms or the swimming pool and the local amateur dramatics production of *Arsenic and Old Lace*.

Then, Curtis found himself facing another door made of oak; the neat brass plate was engraved with the words: Miss A. Quigley BA BSc Hons, Headmistress. Curtis knocked tentatively, feeling butterflies for the first time in years.

A microphone spoke a tiny reply. 'Come in. It's open.'

He pushed the door inward and took in a patterned carpet, a bookcase full of books and the window looking out onto the car park.

He entered timidly, like a naughty boy, and then, there she was, standing before him – Anne Quigley, second cousin by adoption – and Curtis didn't like her!

She stood, silently, feet together, waiting as if for an explanation. Round-faced with grey humourless, piggy eyes and her hair snatched back to form a neat, round bun contained in a tight hair net. She was 5 feet 4 inches tall, dressed in a flower-patterned dress, worn beneath a grey button-up, cable-stitched cardigan. A neat white-collared, starched, cotton shirt was held closed at the neck with a silver butterfly brooch, small ruby stones adorning its wings and eyes. She wore thick brown woollen tights and sensible, highly-polished, flat-soled shoes. All this, contained her rather rotund body ...

She stepped forward and smiled a humourless smile. She held out her hand. 'I'm Anne Quigley, your cousin.' And before Curtis could reply, she confirmed, 'And you're Jim – Jim Curtis; home from sea to find your roots.'

'I am,' replied Curtis a little reluctantly, and then he attempted to offer up an explanation or conversation, or something.

She cut him short.

'Well, it's very nice of you to call, Jim. Or do you prefer James?'

'Jim's fine,' he ventured.

Again, she pressed on, this time shaking Jim's hand as she guided him back towards the door. Some reunion this, thought Curtis.

'I'm sure you understand, James.'

'No, it's Jim,' replied Curtis.

'I'm a very busy woman, James. It's hard to find time to socialise.' They were both out in the corridor now. 'But now you know where to find me; I'm sure it would be very nice on another day. You see, I have a prior appointment. Yes, yes, Clancy will arrange things. Goodbye, goodbye, it's been pleasant,' she said, sounding more as though it hadn't.

She turned on the heels of her highly-polished shoes and was gone.

'Well, fuck me!' said Curtis under his breath.

Retracing his steps back towards the car, he'd clearly been given his marching orders. Passing the classrooms, he turned out through the double doors, glanced to his left and saw Clancy about 100 yards away, gesturing to someone unseen. Then Cousin Anne appeared, striding out purposefully across the car park towards Clancy; or at least towards where Clancy was standing, leaning against a dark-blue Morris Minor.

Curtis kept on walking, occasionally looking back towards Anne and Clancy, who now both appeared to be in conversation with a third party in the car. Clancy was gesticulating as he spoke. Anne stood, holding her heavy-looking briefcase across her chest with both arms. Then, as Curtis got back into Clancy's car and his interest in the trio began to fade, the third party alighted from the Morris on the far side. He saw silver-grey hair, standing out, even at that distance, and he walked unsteadily, Curtis noticed, around to join Clancy and Anne.

Sore leg, thought Curtis ... then, no, no, it's a limp. His interest returning, he noted that he was walking with a stick, the seeds of vague recognition mixed with doubt, germinating in Curtis' mind. The man took the briefcase from Anne and shook Clancy's hand. Then, like a bolt out of the blue, Curtis remembered him; doubted again, then realised he was right.

'But it can't be,' said Curtis, half to himself.

He found himself climbing, almost involuntarily, out of the car again. Then, he knew it for sure; he knew he'd been right – the grey hair, the limp, the way he held himself, his great presence standing out even at that distance. He was looking at a ghost; a ghost from his past.

Long past – his African past. He was looking at Lt. Col Konstantin Alexandr Kashitskin. He stood, open-mouthed, staring at the Morris, which was driving away with Anne and Kashitskin on board.

Clancy was halfway back to his own car now. As he approached, Clancy could see the look of confused disbelief on Curtis' face.

Curtis looked at Clancy and, pointing in the direction of the disappearing Morris, he managed to squeeze out the question, 'That man! There, that man! With Anne, in the car. Who is he? What's he doing?'

'Oh, they're old friends. Don't you know? Very close. His name is Yuri; he's from the Ukraine. He's here to arrange educational school exchanges for the children. Annie's very much involved in that, too,' lied Clancy.

Then, at that moment, Curtis was certain. He knew it was Kashitskin.

He also knew then that there was more to Cousin Anne than met the eye; and he also knew that Clancy was far more deeply involved in something than he'd cared to admit. At the very least, Clancy had been economical with the truth.

Clancy was looking at Curtis now and he was instinctively aware that Curtis knew.

'Get in the car, Jimmy!'

It wasn't a request.

They drove on in silence for a few miles. Curtis could see that Clancy was troubled and then he spoke.

'Jimmy, I think you may have an idea about what's going on here, so I'll say only this, and I'll say it only once. Ask no more questions. When we get back to my place, pack your bag and get out. I'm telling you this out of respect for your father and yourself – don't dig any deeper – leave … leave now. There are forces at work here which you don't need to know about.' It was treasure and Jimmy knew it.

Curtis nodded and he made up his mind right there and then to return to the army. But before he returned, he would deliver his treasure to a man in SB and then visit some old friends … but Curtis was on his way back. Back home, with the germ of a plan to deal with Cousin Annie.

He had gold and he knew where to take it. Curtis was nobody's fool. It didn't take the brains of an archbishop to work out what was afoot. Cousin Annie had turned out to be a bad girl and cousin or not – he reminded himself he hadn't liked her from the start – he'd made the decision that she'd have to be dealt with; her fate was sealed and he was easily ruthless enough to terminate her activities.

In Africa, he and the others had demonstrated on an almost daily basis their ability to generate extreme violence whenever necessary to achieve their aims. No doubt, if you spoke to a trick cyclist about his willingness to end lives in the blink of an eye and not necessarily by anything that could be described as humane methods, they would produce endless, inane explanations in the form of top-quality psychobabble. These fuckin' clowns can give you the square-root of an orange, but they can't walk in a straight line – no common dog! The bottom line – blaming psychopathic madness. But there's a place in every war for what so-called civilised society term mad men. "They are the ones who keep you safe". He knew he was in a unique position vis-à-vis the PIRA business. The seed had been sewn and a plan was in its embryonic stages.

He had come in search of his roots and by a fickle twist of fate, he had found something else. He turned to Clancy. 'I'll leave, but there's one more person I need to see before I go.'

Clancy was becoming irritable.

'Who, Jimmy? Who?'

'Father Daly,' replied Curtis.

'Father Daly?' Clancy was incredulous. 'Why would you want to see that old bugger? He did you no favours.'

'I know, but it's water under the bridge. It's just for old time's sake. To clear the air.'

Clancy paused. 'You'll find him up at the chapel, if you're quick.'

They pulled up outside Clancy's bar. Jimmy stuffed his things into his bag and then hopped down the stairs, said his thank yous to Clancy, acknowledging his help and advice, and then started towards the door of the bar.

'Wait,' said Clancy. 'I'll drop you there – then the port.'

'Thanks,' said Curtis. 'Good man.'

A couple of minutes later, they reached the chapel.

Clancy said, 'I'll wait here. I've no wish to see the old dog.'

Jimmy climbed out of the car and stood for a moment, looking at the chapel, remembering! As he started towards the door of the chapel, a voice from behind a hedge on the left stopped him short.

'Can I help you?'

Curtis turned and looked towards the voice, but it was a cow that faced him across a gate into the field; and then, with a slap across the cow's rear, the priest made himself seen in the gateway. He was wearing a blue boiler-suit, a flat cap and wellington boots as he ushered the cattle away from the gate.

Then again, he said, impatiently, 'What do you want? I've no time to be wasting. I'm a busy man now.'

Curtis recognised the man immediately, many years older, well into his fifties, but still tall and strong, condescending and unpleasant.

'Oh, you'll find time for me, I'm sure, Father Daly. I'm Jimmy – Jimmy Curtis.'

The priest stared for a while and then recognition registered on his lined face. Curtis thought he saw a fleeting glimmer of guilt.

'Holy Mary, Mother of God! It's you, yourself!'

'Yes, it's me, myself,' echoed Jimmy.

'What brings you here after so long?'

'I just thought it would be nice to say hello, clear the air, you know. I mean, my last memory of you, of course, is the three or four hours locked in that dark cupboard under the stairs and a dozen or so lashes across me back to be going on with, just to help things along. Remember, Father?' Curtis wasn't smiling.

The priest stood, fidgeting and wringing his hands.

'Well, Jimmy boy, you were a Godless child now, uncontrollable. You had to be taught a lesson! We have a job to do, as you well know.'

The priest was looking nervous now. Curtis let him babble on awhile and then said, matter-of-factly, 'Ah well, Father, it's all in the past now, eh? Water under the bridge! And, after all, I just wanted to clear the air,' said Jimmy with a warm smile on his face.

The priest relaxed visibly.

'Anyway,' said Curtis, 'I'll not keep you; I can see you're a busy man like you said, so I'll be off.' He offered his hand in a parting gesture.

Father Daly stepped forward, accepting, and Curtis slammed a vicious headbutt, square into the centre of the priest's face. There was a sickening, thudding crunch and the priest collapsed backwards into a sea of cow dung. Blood gushed over his face and mouth as he struggled, stunned, to breathe through his shattered nose, wallowing in the filth.

Curtis looked down at the mess before him. 'Now you're where you belong, Father. Down amongst the shite! And by the way, that's from Billy Feany and me, for all your hard work.'

He turned and walked back to Clancy's car, slamming the door shut.

'Feel better now?' asked Clancy.

'Much,' said Curtis.

They drove on to the port and said their goodbyes and Jimmy Curtis was on his way. He smiled to himself, feeling a certain satisfaction in what he'd just done. So much for building bridges, he thought, laughing out loud.

He began to wonder who he would visit next. There were several names on his list, but the one he chose next was the most important. Curtis had never been inside a monastery before, but that was soon to change.

Change

"Kill them all – God will know his own"

Arnaud Amoury – Abbot of Citeaux

The building stood amidst tall poplars surrounded by a wall, a full 12 feet in height. It bounded a piece of land which the Trappists who resided there farmed. They grew all manner of fruit and vegetables and to the rear of the main building was a half-acre lake, thick with water lilies, which provided a constant supply of common carp for their menu. The monks toiled in silence, speaking not a word, except on one day of the year, when any with family connections in the outside world would receive a one-hour visit; after which the monks would return to their chosen world of prayer and toil in absolute silence. Their chosen life of solitude – the Trappist way – and worship completely replaced their old lives. They had forgone the trappings of the twentieth-century world; just as others had done for the previous 800 years. No signs of electrical equipment: no TVs, radios, telephones, kettles, cookers, microwaves; no double glazing or continental quilts and no central heating. Wearing only a long cloak with a hooded cowl, around their necks hung a wooden crucifix on a necklace of small stone beads. They wore no underwear, apart from cotton shorts and a rope belt.

Each monk lived in a brick-walled cell, painted white; 8 feet long and 5 feet wide. The cell door opened into the tiny world, its only concession to comfort was a single woollen blanket which, when not in use, lay folded neatly on the raised wooden pillow at the top of a stone bed. A wooden bedside table stood below a glassless, cross-shaped window, through which a cruel wind blew across a ravaged North Sea. The table housed a Holy Bible and a single candle on a small metal plate with a round finger-handle. If someone were to stand on the table and venture a peep outside, they would be rewarded with a bird's eye view of the great rolling waves of the surly North Sea, crashing relentlessly against the rocky base of the cliff 200 feet below. The same surly sea that wet Canute.

Droplets of rain skipped through the opening and exploded into an enamel bowl, half-filled with cold water, rippling outward across the surface to hit the sides and gradually dissipate; a microcosm of the world outside the window. The wind howled and moaned, blew and cried. Brooding black storm clouds lived in the sky and offered yet more rain.

Each cell lay off a long stone-slab-floored, unlit corridor, which turned sharp left at the large oak entrance door to the great chapel. Opening the creaking, ancient barrier, one would be greeted by a dimly candlelit hall; the central focus of which was a man-sized, elevated wooden cross, depicting the Crucifixion.

From the open doorway, visitors were drawn forward between two opposing long benches, with room enough to seat fifteen monks on each side, in silent prayer, four times a day. During the time between, each monk would employ himself at his given occupation: be it cook, plantsman, fruitier, carpenter, herdsman or whatever. The monks pursued God's way through silence, work and prayer. This was their world. Comfortless, austere, silent. On this particular day, at the foot of the cross, a man of 31 years lay face-down on the stone-flagged floor. His arms were outstretched; palms flat on the ground. His head faced down, lips kissing the ground, his legs lay straight and he clamped his knees together to try to remain still. It was four in the afternoon on a bleak November day. He had lain for seven hours now, without relief.

He shivered uncontrollably from the bone-cold, which penetrated his mortal being. He was completely naked. He had lain in situ since 9.00 a.m., praying for the soul of the visitor he was expecting at 5.00 p.m.

The gravel and stone footpath led northward along the Northumbrian coast towards the man's destination. He wore a woollen hat, a Gore-tex waterproof jacket, Lee Rider jeans and a pair of old German Army paratroop boots. Beneath his jacket, he wore a French Foreign Legion sweatshirt with the insignia of a winged dagger shot through with a lightning bolt and the letters 2REP. Across the back of the shirt, in large black letters, was the word: AIRBORNE, and below this: KILL THEM ALL, LET GOD SORT THEM OUT. He'd been given the sweatshirt years earlier by the man he was about to visit. Now, he was coming to the end of this particular journey as he trudged doggedly on through the storm.

He crossed the brow of a small rise and about half a mile ahead of him lay the monastery; its poplars cowering away from the icy sea wind.

He ignored the cold rain and wind. He defied it; yet at the same time, he loved it. His feet crunched along the gravel and splashed through puddles and mud.

He unconsciously felt at the two small packets in his pockets. He felt the outline of the larger of the two and registered the biltong he had brought as a gift, along with the small packet of mixed vegetable seeds to be grown in an allotment and suchlike.

Arriving at the great double gate in the perimeter wall, he looked up at the imposing sight. Taking a couple of steps forward and grasping an iron handle, he pulled hard downward. On the other side of the wall, a bell rang. He waited. Then, after a couple of minutes, a small shutter about 5 feet up on the right-hand gate slid open. He looked through at the ruddy face of a cheerful-looking tubby monk peering back from beneath a cowl. The monk said nothing, but raised his bushy eyebrows which spoke for him. They said, "How can I help you, my friend?"

'Oh, I'm here to see Father Benedict. I'm Jimmy Curtis.'

The monk slid the shutter closed and the great door opened out onto an open courtyard, surrounded by cloisters. Curtis stepped inside and he immediately felt the atmosphere of peace and serenity, despite the wind and rain. It was 4.55 p.m. when he entered. The door banged shut and the rotund monk led him along the cloisters into the long corridor, which led one way to the chapel and the other to the monks' sleeping cells. He was ushered into an unused cell and his wet coat and hat were taken from him. The monk handed him a small hand-towel and then disappeared without a word. He sat on the cold stone bed and wiped the rain from his hands and face.

In the darkness, behind the towel as he wiped his eyes, he saw a man hiding in his memory. He stood well over 6 feet tall and had the face and physique of a boxer. He was holding a GPMG effortlessly in both hands – rifle-like. He was standing on the other side of a car, in which lay the remains of Mr Mokese. He was talking to Dick Kaminski and smiling that handsome smile – the one the girls all loved. He was a warrior, a great warrior – one of many who had gone in search of that other life. But now things had changed, and so had he.

The man on the floor in front of the cross was touched on the shoulder by the tubby monk. He paused, and then stood, feeling the aches and pains of his now stiffened bones and joints complaining at the sudden movement. He crossed himself and then took two steps backward and quickly picking up his cloak and rope belt, he dressed and smiled to himself at the prospect of uttering his first words for a year. He passed out of the chapel and was soon standing in the door of the cell, looking benevolently down at the man sitting with his face in the towel on the stone bed. It had been a long, long time and now, after all they had done in the past, this context did, indeed, seem odd; or at least it would for Curtis.

The monk glanced down and raised his left sleeve slightly, exposing a multicoloured tattoo. It read: 2nd REP LEGION ETRANGER and translated to 2nd Regiment of Strangers Paratroops French Foreign Legion. He dropped the sleeve and then lifted the other, revealing a second which, had it not been slashed through by a long, jagged scar, would have read: 2nd BN PARA REGT. Needless to say, the man who had rammed the bayonet through his arm had quickly died at his hands, ruthlessly. He looked up and mouthed the words, "Hello, my son". But nothing came out. He tried again and this time his first spoken words came, hoarse but successfully.

'Hello, my son.'

The man dropped the towel, startled. Then he quickly rose to his feet. In front of him stood the great warrior with the handsome smile.

They stood for many long seconds, looking at each other. Both had lived several lives and both had been more than lucky on many occasions not to be dead and gone; many would have been grateful if they were. Then, the visitor spoke and stepped forward, open-armed, saying, affectionately, 'Hello, Billy.'

But the monk held up an open palm, stopping him in his tracks.

'I'm Father Benedict now, Jimmy, and my order forbids physical human contact – I am sorry.'

But far from feeling shunned, he immediately accepted the monk's commitment. Father Benedict gestured for Curtis to sit down, saying, 'We have little time together.'

The monk stood before Curtis. It was 5.25 p.m. now and he had two hours – two hours to talk about so many lifetimes – Curtis didn't know where to start.

But, as if reading Curtis' mind, Father Benedict said, 'To answer the obvious question – why? Well, it's quite simply this – I'm answering a call. But I've never forgotten the boys. I pray for you all every day. But this is my life now, Jimmy. I could never go back.'

And so they talked without a breath, about René Voss and Leo van Rijn, and Chris Schollonburg and the others – guardians of a thousand priceless memories unlocked in a torrent of words. They laughed and cried. But then, as quickly as it had begun, it was over and the great warrior was speaking his final words as Curtis listened intently, as the men always did to one of their own.

'When you have been a professional soldier, there is much to contemplate and for us,' he gestured towards Curtis, 'perhaps more than most. But ask yourself this as you live your life from now on: do you see the hand of God in anything you do? Ask yourself this question each day, Jimmy.' The monk made the sign of the cross in front of Curtis and uttered the words, 'Cloak of Mary be about you.'

And Curtis found himself answering, like an echo from his childhood, 'And about you, Father.'

Then, once again, the monk was silent. The handsome smile returned to his face and Curtis handed him the gifts.

The tubby monk returned, as if by magic. He helped with Curtis' hat and coat and then turned and led the way back towards the cloisters.

Outside, Curtis turned to speak to Father Benedict but he was gone. Then, the great gate was opened and with a creak and a bang, Curtis was back outside in the dark, stormy night. As his footsteps crunched along the gravel track, away from the monastery, he thought to himself: all things change.

Horses, Handbags and Van Rijn

Live by the sword,
Die by the sword.

(Anon.)

René Voss and Jim Curtis were chatting over old times on the phone and they were roaring with laughter at yet another revelation regarding Leo van Rijn and his rather eccentric sense of humour; a sense of humour that all the men shared. They laughed at absolutely anything and everything – nothing was sacred, including, and especially, other people's misfortunes. If one were to experience some sort of mishap, then sympathy of any sort, from any direction, would be the last thing to expect. Hysterical laughter, on the other hand, well, that would be the norm.

"If you're looking for sympathy, you'll find it in the dictionary somewhere between shit and syphilis!" was the order of the day in any, and all, circumstances. Everything was a joke! Even death – especially someone else's.

But the latest outburst was over a day out on horseback, taken by Van Rijn, Voss and Curtis at a farm outside Cape Town.

The day began normally enough when they'd arrived on site to meet the owner – a gruff Afrikaner – a religious individual, with little time for the likes of Curtis, Van Rijn and Voss. He hired out his nags to people with a penchant for the great outdoors; it was a good means of providing his family with some extra income and it kept his beloved horses in good health. After paying upfront and saddling-up, the chaps were briefed on safe conduct and care of the animals and were then left to continue onto the trail for the day.

Curtis and Voss climbed aboard their mounts and sat, watching monkey-head – Curtis' nickname for Leo – as he hopped round in ever-decreasing circles, with one hand grasping his snorting, bad-tempered, irritable mount's mane, trying to get a foot – any foot – into the stirrup. On it went, with both horse and Van Rijn exchanging increasingly irritable expletives and at one stage it saw both horse and Van Rijn standing nose to nose like prize fighters, each sizing the other up.

The stand-off went on for a good twenty-five minutes before Van Rijn decided he'd had enough. Grabbing the bridle, he turned and strode off back towards the corral, but the horse stood firm, gave one sharp toss of its head and projected the diminutive form of Van Rijn skyward. He landed with a sickening thud on the iron-hard ground in a cloud of dust to shouts of, 'Get up, monkey-head. Stop fuckin' around, ya fuckin' eejit.'

He climbed to his feet – his jaw set in grim determination – and then he began several more uninterrupted minutes of verbal abuse and rhetoric directed at any, and all, horse-life in Christendom. He pushed it, pulled it, coaxed it, slapped it and dodged the odd kick and bite, but all to no avail. Until, sweating profusely, he collapsed to the ground, sitting, legs spread, glaring up at the beast, which glared back with contempt at the little man in the dust. It would not be moved. The beast was going nowhere; or at least, certainly not with Van Rijn on its back.

But Van Rijn hadn't lasted as long in life as he had through being a quitter and in due course, he climbed to his feet. Patting clouds of dust from his clothes, he calmly strode around the side of the now apparently disinterested and victorious horse, unhooked his kit bag and, rummaging inside, he retrieved a large bottle of Coke. He unscrewed the top and took a long and refreshing draught. The horse looked away, a superior expression on its face. Leo stuck his thumb over the open end of the bottle, gave it several vigorous shakes and then, in one fluid movement and before the animal could respond, he lifted its tail and rammed the fizzing bomb up the horse's arse. The animal responded with a look of eye-popping surprise. A snort and a fart of unrepeatable magnitude projected the beast forward through the corral fence, across the yard of the farm, collecting two rows of washing on the way and disappearing into the middle distance, away and out of sight, leaving Monkey-head stood, hands on hips, with an expression of unbounded satisfaction in his funny little face. Curtis and Voss were in hysterics, even when all three were ejected from the farm by the farmer and his missus on the end of his shotgun. What a day! Memories are made of this, thought Curtis.

The list of events were far too numerous to list, but the exploits of the blokes were many and varied. Another worthy contender on the list of all-time greats involved Leo again and his unsuccessful attempts to get into the knickers of a large-busted barmaid in a bar in Pretoria. She had spurned Van Rijn's advances on several visits to the bar and in the end, she had sealed her own fate by taking Van Rijn's beer back off him and refusing to serve him again. The blokes watched Van Rijn surreptitiously from various parts of the packed bar as he sat there, well on the way to drunken oblivion, sulking on his bar stool. After some time, Van Rijn disappeared off in the direction of the Gents, returning to the bar several minutes later, observed by Curtis and Schollonburg, who fancied they saw, through the seething crowd of the smoke-filled bar, Van Rijn depositing something behind the counter.

Time passed and the bar buzzed with chatter and laughter as the patrons enjoyed the evening. Suddenly, there came from the back of the bar a scream and howl fit to break the clouds. Several dozen sets of eyes flashed towards the now demented form of Van Rijn's big-busted barmaid as she bounced around behind the bar, waving her handbag in one hand and a rather large turd in the other.

Van Rijn had struck again! Having been turned down by the lovely lady, he had become distraught. But when she'd removed his beer as well … well, that was it! A man can only take so much. Van Rijn had spotted his chance to strike a blow for mankind and removing the woman's handbag from behind the bar, he had retired to the John and had taken a dump the size of the barmaid's left leg into the bag and then returned it to its place behind the bar. And now, the uncontrollable ranting of old big tits was the result, along with a lifetime ban for all and sundry. Leo considered the act as one of his greatest works and he took great pride in recounting it on many a night out. Funny as fuck, if you like that sort of thing, and, of course, the blokes did.

'This phone call's costing me a fortune,' said Voss, laughing!

'Well, you can blame Monkey-head for that, mate.'

They chatted on for another half an hour or so, enjoying the memories, arranging visits and talking of the possibility of future employment in the most lucrative fields and the like. There was talk of an operation in the offing regarding a trip to a west coast "resort" to recover some rather attractive gems in the form of uncut diamonds. Preparations were well under way as far as reconnaissance and logistics and the team was all but selected. There was just the small matter of overthrowing the government first. There was a guaranteed place for him as well and Curtis had agreed to give it some serious consideration. There were, and still are, many opportunities for an enterprising chap to make money in Africa – big money. Of course, a lot depends on how big your "gang" is and whether or not you're prepared to go armed to the teeth into the jaws of conflict to take what you want from an unwilling donor, and then fight your way out again! It sounded just fine to Curtis and as far as he was concerned, they could count him in! But as things turned out, this time, Curtis didn't go and events conspired against the boys who took part. Treachery, greed and double-cross ensured things went tits-up and many ended up incarcerated in a small West African country. But that's another story. You don't get nothing for nothing.

This is what kept the contract boys in work year-in, year-out, decade after decade, on the African continent. There was never any shortage of wars and weapons arrived by the ship load to arm the warring factions. At the end of the Cold War, Jimmy remembered, over 20 billion dollars-worth of armaments of all shapes and sizes simply disappeared from the Ukraine and that sort of scam can only exist with the highest authorities at least being aware and willing to tolerate or turn a blind eye at a price, whilst the time was right for personal gain.

The vast majority of the Ukraine weaponry was destined for the African continent and was, no doubt, paid for by what is in today's jargon termed as "conflict diamonds". War for control, war for diamonds, war for gold, war for power, war for war. Monrovia, Liberia, Sierra Leone, the Ivory Coast, South Africa and Rhodesia to name but a few, where governments or rebels often paid professional soldiers to give them the edge. No wonder the place was bursting at the seams with contract troops, thought Jimmy. It's worth noting for people who consider mercenaries bad lads that the French Foreign Legion is mercenary and so are the Gurkhas in the British Army. No one complains about that!

René Voss and Jimmy Curtis had been chatting on the phone now for forty-five minutes or so on the subject of Leo van Rijn. They'd laughed at each other's reminders of some of Leo's exploits and both had marvelled at the little man's ability as a world-class mountaineer.

'He seemed to have no fear of heights at all,' said Curtis.

'Yes, I watched him on a rock face once,' remarked Voss. 'He was like a spider. The climb was graded as VVS, but he scuttled up it as if he were climbing a ladder.'

'Yes,' replied Curtis, 'and he was ugly, too! World-class ugly!'

They both laughed.

A couple of days earlier, Voss and Van Rijn had been drinking in a bar in Cape Town; they'd been shopping for a pair of jeans for Van Rijn and hadn't planned on stopping off for a drink. But the taxi they'd caught for the short journey home to the flat they'd shared had broken down soon after picking them up, so they ended up in the bar, chatting, eating peanuts, and waiting for the cabby to fix the vehicle, which sat outside, steam billowing from under the bonnet.

It was a quiet bar and they'd decided to stay on for a session and a couple of games of pool. They'd been in the bar for about twenty minutes, when a man entered and joined the only other occupant on a stool by the window. Voss had decided to nip out to buy a paper. Van Rijn sat at the bar, not taking much interest in anything in particular, but he noticed after a while that the conversation between the newcomer and the other man was becoming heated. Accusations were being exchanged – then threats.

Van Rijn, who was sitting close to the two men, decided to move to the other end of the bar, knowing from experience how easy it was to become mixed up in this sort of thing without trying. Glancing at the barman, he raised his eyes knowingly, smiled and moved to take up an unobtrusive position out of the way. Sitting in a small recess, he could still clearly hear shouting. He couldn't see the men directly because of his position in the recess, but a very large, highly polished brass ship's bell offered up a reasonably clear reflected view of the two antagonists.

Van Rijn sat there, supping his cool beer, satisfied that all was well in his world, waiting for Voss to return.

Back at the other end of the bar, things were not all as they should have been, for one of the men suddenly drew a gun and shot the other through the neck. He fell to the floor, clutching his throat. The bullet from the gun passed through the intended victim, travelled the length of the bar and, clipping the top from a bottle of scotch, it hit the ship's bell, turned 50 degrees to the right, continued its trajectory into the alcove and struck Van Rijn in the head. He died in the arms of René Voss three minutes later. Fate!

This was the news that the phone call had delivered.

And so, had the taxi not broken down, Van Rijn and Voss wouldn't have been in the bar, where the two complete strangers happened to be at the same time. Furthermore, if Van Rijn had chosen to remain at his original place at the bar, in all likelihood the bullet, if it had been fired at all, would very probably have missed him. If the bell had not been on the bar, the bullet would not have turned right and killed Van Rijn. But it was – it was Leo van Rijn's time.

He had weathered all manner of storms, as had all the men. But in the end, he had succumbed to a cruel twist of fate. He had died at the hands of a complete stranger, who had neither intended to kill him nor knew he had done so as, having fired the fatal round, he had run from the bar and hadn't been seen since – leaving in his wake not one corpse, but two.

"What we do in life, echoes in eternity."

Roman Army.

Trick Shot

It's made round to go round,
You reap what you sow.

(Anon.)

A trick shot is normally associated with snooker players, but there is also another type – sometimes it works, sometimes it doesn't. Anne Quigley hummed to herself as she sat patiently waiting for her three escorts: two bodyguards plus one. The third person, an art historian and sympathiser, would accompany the group to the meeting place at the Lion's Mouth on Black Mountain on the outskirts of Belfast. There was a fourth individual and it had been his job to arrange the meeting between the PIRA team and their opposite numbers in the UVF. It was in the interest of both sides to extend their endeavours to trade across the sectarian divide.

On this day, at least outwardly, neither side bore any animosity and over recent months, it had become routine for the groups to meet on a monthly basis, alternately choosing the time and place for the business transaction to take place. For that was what this was: business – not sectarian violence or political aspirations. It was business carried out on a quid pro quo basis and both sides had benefited greatly from the agreement.

Quigley had taken over where Brinton had left off and gain was the aim. Her place on the Army Council was now in the hands of another. Her responsibility lay clearly in the business world that Brinton and Co. had built up with such success. Her style was "hands on". She'd always preferred that approach, insisting that you didn't have to worry who could be trusted that way. She continued to sing now; the song was *Kevin Barry*. Smoke from her cigar filled the air and stung her eyes.

187

Occasionally peeping through the curtains, she looked for her transport. When it arrived, she quickly checked the Tokarev and pushed it back into the shoulder holster. She zipped up her leather jacket, stepped out of the front door, banging it shut behind her, and walked down the path to the car which sat waiting. She climbed into the front passenger seat, pausing briefly to greet the others before nodding to the driver to proceed. They pressed on through the traffic, heading away from the guest house in Falls Road towards their destination at Black Mountain.

At the same time, in the Protestant Shankhill Road area of the city, in the small enclosed rear yard of the Everton Club, four gentlemen of the Protestant UVF were charging the magazines of their personal weapons and climbing into their transport for their own journey to the monthly meet.

'I hate those Fenian bastards,' said Doherty as he gunned the engine.

Jimmy Queen, his front-seat passenger, said nothing. Neither did his two bodyguards, who sat in the rear of the Cortina as the car drove off along Shankhill to their shared destination at the Lion's Mouth on Black Mountain.

Doherty was a hot-headed, short-tempered bully. He was a junior commander in the organisation and he often had trouble thinking before he acted. But he was a true Loyalist, like his father and generations before him in the Doherty family, and Jimmy Queen, a highly experienced Coy commander in the UVF, had decided it was time to offer him a new experience in the way of dealing with their historical enemy from across the sectarian divide. After all, "peace reigned supreme" in the Province these days, allegedly, and business is business. A transaction of this sort would give Doherty an insight into the way in which things are done and with any luck, the experience may well help to temper his ways. All he had to do was watch and listen – that was his job – to just watch and listen and hand over the goods when Jimmy Queen gave him the nod.

Like previous liaisons, the groups would meet at alternatley chosen venues and an exchange would take place. All the transactions could take the form of verbal information from one side to another, or an arrangement to remove a particular individual who may have become a thorn in the side for someone; and so they would be suicided or disappeared. It may have been the delivery of a specialist weapon, say a

Barrett sniper rifle, or an exchange of drugs, or even an agreement to work specific turfs. Today, it was a straight swap – one item for another.

On the agenda today was £500,000 worth of cocaine, to be handed over by the PIRA in exchange for an artefact from the art world of greater value. The financial imbalance was irrelevant; it was all profit to the organisations and anyway, each group was in a better position than their opposite numbers to disseminate what each had to offer. At the end of the day, it oiled the wheels of power in their worlds.

All four carried shoulder holster Ingrams. Across the knees of one of the rear-seat passengers lay a 3 by 4 foot artwork folder, inside which was half of the day's transaction. It had come into the hands of the UVF as part of a deal with a Spanish organised crime network. In exchange, the Loyalists had handed over a valuable consignment of weapons and explosives, along with £500,000 to help the Spaniards to continue to broaden their own horizons across Spain. Also included in the deal was an agreement to "cultivate" the friendship in other directions. Business again!

The French port at Antibes is home to many of the world's jet-setters in their luxury super yachts; and it was into this jet-setters destination that the owner of the super yacht *The Coral Island* – a man of Middle Eastern origin – cruised and docked in readiness for his visit to local France before moving on.

The Coral Island was a gem and it was fitted out to the highest possible standards; it left the other boats in its wake. The owner, an art lover, decorated its bulkheads with various works of very valuable fine art. On one balmy evening, whilst the owner was ashore and the boat unmanned, thieves gained entry and made off with a Pablo Picasso abstract named the Dora Maas. The work had not been seen since. It had been painted by Picasso in 1938 and it is considered to be one of his finest works of the type. It had not been seen on public display for nearly forty years.

By fair means or foul, it had now found its way into the hands of the gentlemen of the UVF and it now lay concealed in the art file on the knee of the rear-seat passenger in Jimmy Queen's car. Only Queen was aware of the file's contents as the Dora Maas sat quietly on the bodyguard's lap.

Anne Quigley's group arrived at the RV first and they sat there, patiently awaiting the arrival of the other half of the business meeting.

Some ten minutes later, the car with Jimmy Queen and Co. arrived and pulled up 10 yards away, driver to driver. Quigley wiped the condensation from the window and peered out towards the Loyalists.

No one moved. She puffed away on the short cigar, while the art man stifled a cough.

After a further five minutes, she wound down the window and gave the thumbs-up to Queen, who nodded and climbed out of his car, preceded by his security men. The man with the painting remained in the car.

Quigley stood, facing Queen; both were flanked by their bodyguards, who eyed each other with ill-concealed suspicion.

Quigley spoke first. 'Good morning, Mr Jones. All's well, I assume?'

'All's well,' came the reply. 'Are we ready to proceed, Mrs Smith?'

'We are.'

'Then let us continue.'

Both nodded. Queen turned and gave the thumbs-up to Doherty, who took hold of the art folder and came to stand alongside Queen.

Quigley beckoned the art man forward. He came up nervously, carrying the small grip, which contained the drugs. Quigley and Queen looked at each other over a distance of 5 feet.

Doherty fidgeted nervously and then Quigley said, 'Proceed.'

The packages were exchanged and then Doherty walked back to his car and placed the goods on the bonnet. The art man did the same. Unzipping the file and taking out a large magnifying glass, he began to inspect the Dora Maas. He smiled to himself and as he turned back towards Quigley, the smile burst into a huge, satisfied grin.

'It's her,' he said. 'It's her.'

An air of relief settled across both groups.

Then, a single high-velocity shot rang out. The bullet struck Jimmy Queen square in the centre of his forehead. He stood for half a second – a vacant look on his face – and then his eyes rolled back in his head, his knees buckled and he dropped to the ground. The next second saw both groups transfixed on the scene; the next saw weapons dragged from shoulder holsters and Doherty shouting, 'We've been ambushed! The Fenian bastards!' at the same time waving his Ingram in a crazy arc and squeezing the trigger.

A line of bullets stitched the ground between the two groups; two of the rounds caught the art man in the stomach; a third hit Anne Quigley in the throat. She staggered back and dropped to her backside with her back against the front bumper of her car, coughing up a mouthful of blood. Now, the bodyguards on both sides joined in and automatic fire rained in both directions. Doherty managed to knock Quigley onto her side with a burst to the head and chest, before being hit in the face and killed. A couple more died firing at each other from no more than 6 feet; the Loyalist, holding weapons in both hands, managing to hit the drugs bag with a bullet from his pistol before falling onto his back. Windscreens, mirrors and headlights shattered. A hubcap spun off a wheel as a tyre exploded. Petrol sprang from a ruptured tank and then ignited in a ball of flame, sending another Loyalist spinning, rolling and screaming in agony – then silence. It was all over in twenty-five seconds; eight people lay dead – each side believing the others had tricked them. They were all wrong!

As the fire gained momentum, two men walked from the undergrowth towards the carnage; one carried a mini Ruger with a telescopic sight, the other appeared unarmed as they walked in a close circle around the scene, inspecting each body. When they reached Anne Quigley, Konstantine Alexandr Kashitskin stood, looking down impassively at her body. Blood stained the front of her shirt, pooled on the ground and dripped from the end of the short cigar, still gripped in the corner of her mouth. Her lifeless, vacant, piggy-eyes still wide-open.

The second man bent down and removed the small silver butterfly brooch from her collar. He wrapped it in a handkerchief and put it in his pocket. Both men then turned and walked away. Within twenty-four hours, Kashitskin's weapon had found its way into an IRA arms cache and he had begun his new life in the West at the end of a long and winding road. The trick shot had worked, this time.

Soon after, Jimmy Curtis received a package from his friend Inspector Neil Kilbride of SB. It contained a newspaper cutting from the *Belfast Telegraph*. The cutting spoke of a drugs deal between opposing extremist groups, which appeared to have gone tragically wrong. A gun battle had ensued, leaving eight people dead, including a head teacher from the Free State, who had been caught in the crossfire. It named her as Ms Anne Quigley from the Dundalk area. It was believed she was in the north on a birdwatching trip. But there was also something else in the package: it was a small silver butterfly brooch, with small rubies adorning the wings and eyes; it had flown a long way.

Curtis held it in the palm of his hand and smiled at Quigley's description as a birdwatcher. Who'd have thought of that one? He had his suspicions, but only Kashitskin's companion knew the answer to that and anyway, Jimmy didn't really care. He put the brooch into a Jiffy bag with a short note and posted it back to an official address in Northern Ireland.

On 5 May 2006, Sotheby's Auction House – New York – the real Dora Maas was sold at auction for £53,000,000. The professional fake was destroyed in the blazing wreckage at the scene of the shoot out. The real McCoy now rests somewhere safe, maybe for another forty years.

These Days

You may talk o' gin and beer
When you're quartered safe out 'ere,
An' you're sent to penny-fights an' Aldershot it;
But when it comes to slaughter
You will do your work on water,
An' you'll lick the bloomin' boots of 'im that's got it.

Rudyard Kipling; *Gunga Din*

Over the months and years following Curtis' return from Africa, he received many phone calls from René Voss, Gus Grillo and Dick Kaminski, trying to persuade him to return and to continue working on the circuit. But Curtis refrained. He'd done enough. He returned to the regular army to complete his service there, thinking ahead to the pension he'd no doubt need in the future.

The others carried on though. Voss took to "security" work like a duck to water, "taking care" of various high-ranking personalities either in foreign governments or industry. Now and again, he would pop off to involve himself in some "nice little war", usually with a "nice little earner" at the end. He spent quite long periods in Nigeria, usually in the Niger Delta area, protecting oil installations from attack by rebels and bandits. He also managed to get himself shot again in an unnamed Central or South American state.

'I've been shot before though,' says he. 'It's not that interesting!'

Not one to make an issue of something as trivial as a gunshot wound, he would brush it off, like a cold. These days, Curtis moves among people on a daily basis, who act like they're being shot when they've got a cold. Soft bastards. And snidey, too. If they can't do you a good turn, they'll go out of their way to do you a bad one, but not to your face!

They haven't got the bollocks for that! None of them are good enough to stand in the shadow of the men Curtis knew.

At the time René Voss was shot, he'd been working with Kurt Willt's brother, who'd had a certain axe to grind.

Gus Grillo, who had once made a serious offer of employment to Curtis, had tenuous family links with a notorious Columbian/American crime syndicate. He occasionally disappeared off the scene for months at a time, no doubt getting up to whatever you get up to in that line of work.

Dick Kaminski returned to the UK – allegedly – and rumour has it that someone very much like him took up a rather lucrative career robbing post offices across the country, before returning to the Dark Continent to rejoin Grillo on the contract soldiering circuit. It was a decision that would eventually see both men captured and incarcerated in an African dungeon for their part in the unsuccessful attempt to overthrow the cruel and corrupt government of a small West African country.

Curtis' spell of self-imposed absence from the regular army was repaid in full by his court martial in Portadown, Northern Ireland, early in 1980. During which he was described as a damned adventurer, etc., etc. No time for your sort, what! Damned cheek, eh. His battalion 2 PARA was on a two-year tour in the Province at the time and he had returned via the ferry from Stranraer to the Larne, followed by a train journey to Belfast. Then, walking from the train station to Oxford Road Bus Station, he caught the bus to the village of Clough. Having enjoyed a notable conversation with an old man who had served as a Black and Tan in his day amongst other things, he hopped off the bus and took his time walking down the country lane which led to Abercorn Barracks in Ballykinler, County Down.

He arrived at the gate with long hair and beard and, after confirming his ID with the bloke on the gate, he walked over to the guardroom window and stood, looking in at his old mate Kenny Royals, who was busy filling in the guard report.

Curtis tapped on the window and said, 'Eh, ugly. I hear you do bed and breakfast.'

Kenny looked up and nearly fell off his chair.

'Fuckin hell, Scouse! Where did you come from, you fuckin' big ape?'

These Days

Curtis was home again! But it was time to "play the game". "Yes, sir; no, sir" etc.; standing to attention when it mattered; get a brew on when it didn't; "Interviews without coffee" with the RSM, the adjutant and the CO; tap-dancing lessons with the provost staff and, of course, the introduction to your new "best friend" in any Para regiment jail – the 58 lb 120 mm drill round – which instantly becomes an extension of your body as a SUS. It goes everywhere with you. Everywhere, double time; except, of course, when you're humping a 6-foot steel locker around the assault course. It's all character building stuff and Paras take it all with a pinch of salt. The way it should be: run 10 miles, straight onto the assault course, straight into the gym, quick shower, thirty minutes for dinner, an hour's cobweb drill with your "best friend", weapon training field craft, a 5-mile run to wind down, personal admin, evening meal, personal admin again, kit inspections; then a fag if you smoke, a brew and bed. Shut your eyes, blink once and then you're up and travelling at 90 miles an hour through another day.

Civvies would die. Do-gooders and civil rights enthusiasts call it brutal. Load of bollocks. Treat soldiers like soldiers. If they do well, pat them on the back; if they don't, kick their fuckin' arses. Paras just get on with it and take it on the chin, because that's the way they are – hard cases in hard places – where civvies and civil right enthusiasts don't have to exist … and couldn't! They're too fuckin' soft. We don't fuckin' want the pencil-pushin', paper-shuffling fannies, anyway. Best they stay in their air-conditioned, centrally-heated office, "just in case you catch a chill, sweet-heart".

Curtis spent less than two weeks in the nick, before being released back to B Coy to carry on working, waiting for his date for court martial. A few weeks later, the day came and went with the award of what Curtis considered a very lenient eight months' detention in the jail at Colchester. The system at "Colly" works on a reward set-up, which revolves around military training. There are three stages – numbers one to three – in which life becomes progressively easier and inmates are afforded more freedom the further they progress through the three stages. Everything you do is graded. The higher and more constant the high grades, the sooner you progress to the next stage. In short, the harder you work and the better you perform, the sooner life becomes easier as you progress through one to three. Some soldiers never leave the first stage, completing their time served here. A very detailed report is produced and forwarded to each individual's unit at the end of his time served. Jimmy got up to stage three in six weeks and was released in less than two months, enjoying every minute of it, strangely enough. Returning to 2 Para, he was back in the swing of things in a flash. Promotion soon followed and life returned to a paratrooper's "normal", remaining that way until his time was up.

The years flew by. Two Para remained busy and finally got their war in the Falklands. Curtis' experience stood him in good stead. He worked hard in barracks and in the field and was a well-respected member of the unit, finishing his time in the rank of Sgt, missing promotion to colour Sgt only because of the effect of defence cuts. He'd been due a posting as a PSI at 15 Para – a TA Battalion. But the unit was disbanded, so he lost his chance, but he wasn't that bothered. It's just the way things go – the luck of the draw.

He was true to the promise he had made to himself. He finished his twenty-two years service in the Paras, completing eleven tours in Northern Ireland, but not before seeing even more action in the Falklands War, where his battalion fought with great distinction. He was wounded in the battle for Darwin and Goose Green, where 2 Para – outnumbered three to one – won the first major land battle of the war, which set the scene for the rest of the conflict. The South Atlantic beckoned and the Paras answered the call!

The Maroon Machine

Bent double, like old beggars under sacks, we walked
till on the haunting flares we turned our backs.

Wilfred Owen; *Dulce Et Decorum Est*

Jim played only a small part in the Falklands War and he had little
control over his own destiny during the conflict. Unlike in Africa,
where he could influence, to a good degree, the way things were done.
In Africa, Chinese parliaments were often called and individual ideas
and suggestions could be put to the test, often with great success. But
back in the British Green Army, he was part of someone else's great
scheme and once a unit is committed, individuals are automatically
committed also and they have little or no say in events. In essence, they
are no more than a small cog in the proverbial "Big Engine", swept
along by the tide of conventional warfare. He would take it all in his
stride. He had preferred his war in Africa, which had been
unconventional. He had liked that, often using guerrilla-style tactics to
great effect, but this war was different and it would test the flexibility
of the Paras to the core.

His journey to the South Atlantic and back almost came via the
Caribbean country of Belize. The British Army train and operate in
areas all across the globe from Northern Ireland to Borneo to the
deserts of the Middle East. In 1982, 2 Para were prepared and packed
ready for a six-month tour in the jungles of Belize. Indeed, so close were
they to moving out that the sea freight belonging to the BN was already
on its way and the BN had all but begun its embarkation leave prior to
flying out to begin its tour of duty in what was once known as British
Honduras before it gained independence.

Still a Brit protectorate, the army carried out operational duties there in support of the Belize government. Its neighbouring country Guatemala laid claims to access to the sea and was determined to have access via a proposed road through Belize. However, the Belize government was having none of it and the resulting threats from Guatemala and probing cross-border patrolling by its own Special Forces known as *Kaibils*, recognisable by their distinctive camouflaged berets, resulted in British Army presence in the country and along the border between the two countries as a preventative measure. This maintained a show of force and commitment to preserve Belize's sovereign stability and security. The boys were ready and well prepared, with case loads of holiday brochures for R & R excursions to Mexico and buckets and spades and Ambre Solaire; "Why should Britain tremble!"

But unbeknown to the BN, all was not well in the land of a chappie named General Leopoldo Galtieri, the self-imposed President of Argentina and head of a military dictatorship called the junta, which ruled with an iron hand in an iron glove and was famed for its brutal suppression of its own people. Murders, disappearances and torture were its trademark and it had imposed all three with gusto since a military coup in 1976–77 had overthrown the elected government. But the junta's human rights abuses had led to a rapid decline in its popularity to the degree that civil unrest was rife. Galtieri needed a way back into the hearts and minds of the people and he knew exactly what he had to do in order to get there.

The Islands of the Falklands lay 8,000 miles south-west of the UK; British territory since 1833 and populated by 2,000 fiercely loyal British nationals. On mainland Argentina, however, a several-hundred-year-old dispute over sovereignty of the Falklands burned fiercely in the hearts of every Argentinian. They are taught from day one at school that the Islands are Argentinian and will one day be returned to what they believe to be their true place. One thing guaranteed to raise the blood pressure of these over-excitable Latin Americans would be a declaration by the junta of its intention to take back the Islands by force and that Las Malvinas would be Argentine once again.

Galtieri wasted no time in declaring this intent and hundreds of thousands of people soon thronged and poured into the streets of Buenos Aires, waving their flags and beating their drums and willing the invasion to start a bit quick! After all, the Falkland Islanders must be falling over themselves with excitement, just waiting for the day they would be saved from British rule by their Argentine liberators; or so the population had been led to believe after many lifetimes of indoctrination. Big mistake. Claims and counter claims had been thrown backwards and forwards between Buenos Aires and others since at least 1790 and it had become a protracted and complicated issue. But the mid nineteenth century seems to be the date of most significance for us, for it was then that Britain formally seized the Islands with serious intent. To stay, Galtieri needed a victory to make the 5-year-old junta "popular". The return of Las Malvinas to Argentine sovereignty and the end of British colonial rule was just the answer he needed.

Galtieri believed, and rightly so, that in the short-term at least, the action would subdue unrest on the streets, draw attention away from a series of serious problems in the economy and quell the dissent, which was then evident even in the armed forces.

And so on 2 April 1982, the business end of the Argentine invasion of the Falkland Islands began. A short but savage defence of inner Stanley and Government House was fought out by Major Mike Norman's Royal Marines Garrison, who fought valiantly and gave an outstanding account of themselves inflicting heavy casualties on the enemy Special Forces *(Buzo Tactico)*, who attacked in overwhelming numbers. In the end, our marines' forlorn hope was doomed to failure and they were ordered, against their wishes, to surrender by the Islands' Governor Rex Hunt. It was the correct course of action in order to prevent further loss of life. There is no doubt that the marines would have fought to the end given the choice, but they lived to fight another day and it would be those very same men of the Naval Party 8901, who would hoist the Union flag outside Government House after the Argentine surrender in the middle of June.

But not before 2 Para had become the first to reach Port Stanley. It is also worth noting that 2 Para, apart from the SAS and SBS, were also first ashore, first to engage the enemy and first to win a major land battle of the war at Darwin and Goose Green. They also liberated over a hundred islanders in the process, who had been held captive in the Goose Green Community Centre in absolutely appalling conditions for over a month by their so-called "liberators" – the Argentine occupation forces.

And so the scene was set. Some bloke with attitude had the brass neck to deposit 10,000 foreign enemy troops on British soil, replacing our Union flag with an Argentine rag, and call it Argy territory. And he and his cronies were dumb enough to think they'd get away with it! What an arsehole! ... Stand by, thought Curtis. The Para Bde can move and be on its way to anywhere in the world at the drop of a hat and preparations were now well under way to get the gang on the move en route to the South Atlantic War.

Stocks of kit, equipment, rations, ammunitions, weapons, signals, clothing and much more was demanded by demented quartermasters and their overworked staff from depots all across the UK to feed the beast. By the time the task force was deployed to the Islands, they would be operating at the end of a very thin 8,000-mile-long piece of logistical string and many doubted the likelihood of its ability to remain intact.

But Britain's armed forces and its logistical support are nothing if not resilient and this resilience would be tested to the extreme.

Much has been written of the latter since the war and so there is no need to labour the point, but suffice to say that the earth was moved by many. Not least, by those unseen and often unheard priceless personalities who worked tirelessly behind the scenes to ensure the success of Operation Corporate.

Once preparations for the move were complete, the BN travelled to Portsmouth to embark on what was to become its home for the next three weeks on its journey south to war. The MV *Norland*, a North-sea ferry, had been requisitioned along with other merchant ships, including the *Canberra* and the *Uganda* – both cruise ships – the latter of which would become the force hospital ship for the duration. Its cabins and open areas being transformed into wards and operating theatres manned by doctors and nurses from all three services, whose experience dedication and determination saved many lives during the war; including Argentinian POWs wounded in the various battles ashore and aboard ships, which were constantly attacked by Argentine fast fighter jet aircraft.

Curtis was to share a cabin on the top deck just below the bridge with a couple of his mates, Cyril and John. It was cramped but comfortable and, after all, the only thing they really wanted was a bed and the foldaway bunks were just fine for this purpose.

The day soon arrived to set sail and the boys were seen off at the dock by friends and family. It's the lot of the forces wife to endure much, if not more than others on occasions without complaint. They definitely had the rough end of the deal. But that's life in the Paras. It is what it is and the old saying "if you haven't got a sense of humour, don't join up", stands true. And so life goes on. But, sadly, some lives wouldn't and that was the worry that the wives and girlfriends, families and friends would endure.

The journey south was virtually uneventful and things didn't really start to pick up until reaching the Island of Ascension in the mid Atlantic, where the support weapons platoons went ashore to test-fire various weapons. Curtis' company stayed on board, where weapons training, medical cadres, aircraft recognition, etc., combined with fitness training, were the order of the day. It was good to get out of the confined space of the cabin as often as possible to run around the deck and get rid of the old cobwebs. When the men weren't doing that, they were checking their personal kit and equipment and modifying it as required.

It's worth pointing out that in 1982, the kit, equipment and clothing that the British Army was expected to operate with in the Falklands, in weather which arrived direct from the South Pole, was exactly the same as that used in Aldershot and on Salisbury Plain. This was despite, in no small part, repeated requests over prior months and years made by the military and no doubt the Admiralty and the air force, for more and improved equipment to some shiny-arsed Civil Servant in Whitehall or wherever. These requests were simply ignored or refused; no doubt because of lack of "funds". How very convenient. Still, I'm sure the poor chap in question has more important things than the country's armed forces to spend money on – office furniture, perhaps. And besides, what's a bit of trench foot, hypothermia or frostbite between friends; after all, it wouldn't be his toes that remained inside your boots when you prised your feet out of them.

In 2006–07, the British Army was fighting wars on two fronts in Afghanistan and Iraq, severely undermanned and still suffering the same old problems with kit and equipment, or lack of it. In spite of all the political rhetoric to convince us otherwise, the armed forces shouldn't have to wait for a war to turn up before someone decides they might send them the equipment they will need. It should be in situ on each and every unit, ready for any occasion. But it doesn't take the brains of an archbishop to realise that top of the politico's UK agenda are defence cuts. You've only got to look at the way we actually got to the Falklands; like the poor relations we are, we begged, borrowed and stole. It seems not much has changed since Dunkirk. The Yanks must have been pissing themselves. Still, who am I to complain, that's just my opinion, thought Jim, and you know what they say about opinions – they're like arseholes – everyone's got one! And when all is said and done, thought Jim, it's the job of the armed forces to uphold the policy of the "government of the day" at home and abroad … full stop!

The daily routine on-board ship for Curtis and the boys was loosely the same as a working day would be back home. The bosses were aware of the need to balance work with the rest and time-off was respected. One thing that did change noticeably after the ships left Ascension was the weather. Curtis' experience as a merchant seaman meant that he quickly felt at home on-board ship and he soon found his sea-legs. But many found the three-week journey through the Atlantic Ocean in a North Sea ferry dismal in the extreme as the ship pitched and tossed; its flat bottom no match for the 60-foot swells as it slid from the crest of one of the big lumps, sideways and down into the trough, ready to start all over again. Over and over, up and down, side to side … boom, boom, boom, as the bows crashed headlong through the pitiless waves. Seasickness took its toll and was evident by the unattended mealtimes and toilets awash with spew! Curtis was lucky enough not to suffer with seasickness and his familiarity with the shipping also added a dimension of interest to the trip for him, which most of the others didn't or weren't able to experience. He spent quite long periods chatting with the crews about things that only merchant seamen have in common. So, all in all, Curtis' three weeks passed faster than most. Unlike the unfortunate Cyril, who spent most of the trip talking down the "big white telephone" to hueeeyughaah!

There were two notable incidents during the trip. The first occurred not long after leaving Ascension, when two huge Russian spy planes flew extremely low over the *Norland*; no doubt taking photographs and gathering electronic intelligence. They came and went and weren't seen again. But it was a brief interlude of excitement for all aboard.

The second was more unsettling and was preceded by an announcement advising that "This is not an exercise – repeat – this is not an exercise" and had all and sundry running to action stations and shutting watertight doors. From his position, Curtis was able to watch a helicopter taking off from the flight deck and flying off into the distance to carry out an anti-submarine task. He never did learn of the result, but clearly the *Norland* survived and the heli returned unscathed.

There is an interesting point here; B Company, 2 Para and its various attached arms were accommodated about as far down in the ship as you could possibly get and they were certainly below the waterline. The drill when announced – "Not an exercise" – resulted in the watertight doors on B Coy's deck being immediately closed by a member of the crew and 100 men of B Coy were sealed inside with no means of escape. They were, in effect, written off inside a steel tomb. This may well sound like a self-imposed tragedy which, indeed, it is, but in the cold light of day, logic dictates that it's a far better option to seal a sinking ship and save the majority, even at the cost of the lives of 100 men. Thankfully, it never had to be done, which pleased Jimmy no end, because Scouse Wiggins, one of his mates in B Coy, would have gone down with the ship, taking with him the twenty quid which he owed Jim! What a fuckin' tragedy that would have been, ha, ha!

The landings often seen on the TV news reports and in documentaries made since the end of the war, showing the Gurkhas and others walking ashore along the old jetty in San Carlos Water, and military mechanical equipment moving large stockpiles of stores inshore, actually took place many hours after 2 Para had gone ashore under cover of darkness at Blue Beach. This wasn't filmed, as landing craft crewed by Royal Marine coxswains did their best to provide the boys with a "dry landing"! More chance of a fuckin' audience with the Pope! Jim Curtis is well over 6 feet tall and it still reached above his chest.

Unbelievably cold, combined with a South Atlantic wind, it marked the shape of things to come. The boys got wet and cold and stayed that way for the duration. What a way to start a war! With your nuts up round your ears!

As the landing craft brought the men ashore, off in the distance the unmistakable sound of mortar fire and intense MMG and small arms fire could be heard as the boys from D-SQN 22 SAS malleted Fanning Head – a divisionary attack designed purely to draw attention away from the main landings; all part of the overall deception plan. It certainly appeared to work, as 2 Para were blessed with an unopposed landing, met only by guides from the SBS.

Once ashore, the BN quickly regrouped and began its 15-mile march towards the feature known as Sussex Mountain, where they were to dig in and begin the long process of hurry up and wait! They marched doggedly onwards and ever upward to their first RV, where each man picked up two 81 mm mortar rounds, each weighing 12 lb, to add to their already huge burdens. It was not at all unusual to see men carrying kit and equipment weighing upward of 150 lb. Indeed, some guys carried things like the Carl Gustav ATK weapon or an 81 mm mortar base plate or barrel easily exceeding 200 lb, surpassing their own body weight; testament to the grit strength and fitness, combined with grim determination, of the Parachute Regiment soldier.

The terrain was an endless wasteland of bog marsh and tussock grass, which conspired to either suck the boots off your feet or trip you up; pitching the men forward onto their faces every few yards or swallowing them up in the stinking mire. Struggling back to one's feet was no mean feat under the almost overwhelming weight of their packs; only to be rewarded with more of the same just a few steps further on. Streams interspersed the barren, treeless emptiness stretching outward in all directions as far as the eye could see, accentuating the monotony of war; most of which consisted of long periods of nothing, punctuated by the manic insanity of the chaos of battle. Then add to this the weather; think of the Falklands' summer as being best described as all seasons in an hour, literally. And the winter as altogether ungodly and bitterly, bitterly cold, with a howling wind, which cuts through clothing that is frozen stiff with ice or dripping wet from driving, horizontal rain and hail – which threatens to peel the skin from one's face – snow, ice and fog, with low black clouds descending all around. Then there are the frost-covered bewhiskered faces, frozen hands and ears, and stinging eyes – imagine all of this, with no end in sight, and you might be some way to understanding what weather, direct from the South Pole, can be like in this region.

But the Paras marched on; each step taking them a little closer to their goal to regain control of the Islands. They trudged on in silence; for tactical reasons, talk, other than that which refers directly to the mission, is kept strictly to a minimum. One's thoughts to the greatest degree are confined to the job at hand and one can, and does, go for days at a time uttering nothing other than short, clipped, military speak, with little or no opportunity to reflect on personal thoughts or feelings. Sleep is often uppermost in the list of priorities; coming a close second to anticipation of close action with the enemy and, of course, food and the ever-welcome brew.

Of all the senses, the ever-present malevolent fear that lies closest to the surface in all men must, above all else, remain suppressed. Easier said than done when one is required to advance into MMG, mortar and artillery barrages. All seem to cope in their own way, but others pay dearly many years after the event through mental anguish and collapse.

In years gone by this condition was termed "shell shock", but it is now known as PTSD. A new name for an old condition. The effects are the same, but are rarely understood by any except those unfortunate souls who experience it. PTSD should never be construed as weakness. Many have endured much that others could not, before they, too, succumbed. But there is a limit in all human spirit and it is often those who have endured the longest who finally pay the price.

Jim considered himself a lucky man to have fared well mentally through all he had seen and experienced in his military life. And he would, on the odd occasion when he felt the urge to complain about something of little consequence, say to himself that things are never as bad as they seem or as bad as they could be; some poor sod is always far worse off than yourself.

On and on the men marched, ever watchful, as darkness left them and like specks in the daylight they crawled up and up, one foot in front of the other, each a step closer to the summit. Then, off in the distance, they spotted a Pucara, slow-moving under its huge payload of bombs, rockers and cannon, capable of inflicting serious damage on troops in the open as it searched the hills. The boys went to ground, then suddenly, they saw a small puff of smoke from the distant aircraft, which signalled problems for the pilot. He'd been hit by a ground-to-air missile fired by a patrol from the SAS operating ahead of the BN. The weapon, a Stinger, took out the threat and Jimmy watched as a purple parachute indicated that the pilot had managed to eject safely and drift earthwards to whatever fate awaited him. Again, they pressed on, until finally they reached the top, to be rewarded with a South Atlantic vista to rival any other on the planet. The light and the space around them were awe-inspiring in the extreme.

Curtis and Cyril stood gazing out at the scene as the rest of the men moved tactically into position.

'Holy fuck!' said Cyril. 'Have you ever in your life seen a sight like that, Jimmy?'

205

Curtis smiled and thought of Africa and René Voss and a similar context; he didn't answer. He felt the sweat running down his back and, wiping the back of his hand across his face, he said, 'Time to dig, Cyril. You get a brew on, mate. I'll make a start.'

Curtis took out his digging tool and took one spade's depth of peat from the earth at his feet, which immediately started to fill with peaty-brown water.

'Fuck me!' said Curtis, half to himself and half to Cyril, as he sat down on his Bergen looking into the small hole at his feet.

'Ah well,' said Cyril, 'I've always fancied a waterbed, ha, ha!'

It was obvious from the start that the Islands were nothing more than a peaty sponge. There was no mileage in digging down, so they set about digging blocks of peat from the surface of the ground and built upwards. It wasn't long before they had created a four-walled shelter, over which they built a waterproof roof using an Aussie poncho supported by telescopic aluminium tent poles. Bog-standard fieldcraft no problem for the boys, it gave them cover from the wind and rain, but it would be of fuck-all use if they were attacked. Still, it was the best they could manage with what they had available to them.

So day one began and soon the routine in defence was under way. Curtis modified the "stately home" that he and Cyril had created; straightening walls, making parts thicker and occasionally pausing to take in the view either down into Ajax Bay or across in the opposite direction to the Choiseul Sound when, without warning and completely out of the blue, an A4 Skyhawk fighter-jet bomber appeared overhead.

He was flying so low that Curtis could see the pilot clearly looking down at him. The aircraft, which was almost certainly on a reconnaissance flight, was travelling so slowly, relatively speaking, that as it passed overhead, it seemed for a moment to just hang there. Then he hit the afterburners and with a roar, he was gone. No one had reacted to the aircraft this time, but there would be many more chances over the next few days on the mountain. It was the shape of things to come once Manuel reached mainland Argentina and told his mates about the BN and the appearance of our ships down in Ajax Bay, which would soon earn itself the nickname "Bomb Alley"!

Routine in defence means food, sleep – whenever possible – preparation of kit and equipment and personal admin. The tasks of manning sentry positions and carrying out clearance patrols also fall into this category. These patrols are carried out to ensure that no enemy forces are probing forward towards British positions and, if discovered, they would be engaged and dealt with – killed.

One fine day during the BN's stay on the mountain, a clearance patrol was deployed, led by a section commander – full corporal. The patrol consisted of six men and was briefed to clear out to 1,000 yards forward of the BN position. They moved out tactically, carefully searching for signs of the enemy. Initially, the patrol was uneventful and at one point, the section commander opted to go to ground for a short time in order to carry out a listening watch. It isn't clear exactly what happened next, but as the patrol started to move off again, they spotted movement, which the boys believed to be enemy. The section commander, already aware that several other units were operating locally, including Britain's own Special Forces, decided to confirm, by radio, that Britain had no friendly forces operating at the grid reference where the sighting had been made. The reply came back as negative and the section commander prepared to engage the enemy, who were by now only about 150 yards away and moving purposefully towards their own position. The lie of the land dictated his next move. To engage the enemy effectively, he would have to move his section into a better position, but as he began to do so, he was spotted and the game was on.

Both groups engaged each other with heavy and sustained small-arms fire. The section commander, in true Para Regiment fashion, automatically opted to put out a flanking assault. So, leaving a GPMG plus one rifle man to continue to subdue the enemy, he moved off from his position back out of contact and then round the right-hand side to assault the enemy from the right flank. Staying low and moving quickly, the assault went in. About 200 yards into the flanking move, the section commander dropped off another GPMG to continue to engage the enemy, thus increasing the fire being brought to bear on them. This is called winning the firefight and, in simple terms, means pouring more fire onto the enemy than they're currently pouring onto you. It was classic section level tactics used to neutralise and then kill the enemy on the assault, which was what the commander on the ground was about to do.

He was now within grenade-throwing range of the enemy and about to do exactly that, before leaping to his feet with the remainder of his team to assault and kill the enemy. Bayonets had been fixed on the route around and they were literally 10 yards and seconds away from releasing their grenades when, incredibly, they heard an English voice ... then another in reply.

The commander stopped dead in his tracks, calmed his men – no easy task in itself – replaced his discarded grenade pin with a large safety-pin and shouted, 'British Army. Who the fuck's that?'

There was a pause then the reply, '45 commando Royal Marines! Who the fuck's that?'

'It's 2 Para, you twat. What are you doing in our area?'

'We're not in your area, we're in ours!' came the marine's reply.

'Like fuck you are! Anyway, stand up and identify yourself,' said the commander from 2 Para.

There was another pause.

'Bollocks! You stand up. I'm staying here!'

And so the Monty Pythonesque conversation continued for some time, before the two opposing section commanders agreed to a simultaneous "stand-up", which did the trick. The problem was sorted out over a brew, apologies were exchanged and both patrols departed on friendly terms; the marines with slightly red faces, as it transpired that owing to a map-reading error on their part, they had strayed into 2 Para's area of responsibility after all. And so it came to pass that two sections from Britain's two finest fighting units had engaged each other for several long minutes with extremely heavy GPMG and small-arms fire and, firing four 66mm ATK weapons from a range of between 25–50 yards, they hadn't managed to hit a fucking thing! Good job that one didn't reach the BBC, ha ha!

This sort of engagement is known as a "blue on blue" and no matter how good the individual, the human element ensures that it can happen to anyone. On this occasion, the boys were lucky. But in a similar incident in 3 Para that wasn't the case. Both patrols called in fire missions from their mortar platoons and gun lines and the ensuing intense and accurate fire had resulted in four seriously wounded men.

One of the men was a friend of Jim's. His name was John Hare and he was a demolitions expert from 9 Squadron of the Para brigade's airborne engineers. They had been on their way to blow up an Argentine ammo dump. He passed comment to Curtis after the war that it was like being on a white square on a chess board, when all the black squares were being hit by mortars and artillery; not to mention the small-arms fire. Lucky for John, the artillery missed him. Unlucky for John, the small-arms fire didn't and he was shot in the arse, courtesy of 3 Para. John Hare, an excellent lad, has remained the "butt" of many jokes ever since!

Air raids on the mountain began on day one as waves of A4 Skyhawks and Mirage fighter-jets swooped low across Ajax Bay and San Carlos, bombing and strafing ships, flying at heights often lower than 50 feet in order to hit their intended targets. Indeed, since the war, Argentine pilots interviewed about their part in the conflict have stated that their altitude alarms in the cockpit of their aircraft, set to go off if the aircraft few lower than 30 feet, constantly signalled they had done so and given that these fast jets were travelling at 500 knots or more, it is testament to the skill and bravery of these excellent American-trained pilots. During each attack, they flew through an unbelievable amount of fire from ground forces and ships to deliver their bombs; often making two or three runs at the same target. Many were shot down and, in fact, Curtis himself would spend a week on the Uganda hospital ship in the next bed to a Skyhawk pilot, who had bailed out over San Carlos Water having had his aircraft shot out from under him. He and other Argentine POWs were treated with the same care, attention and respect as the Brits. A sentiment the pilot himself has voiced since the war ended.

The task force lost ships owing, in no small part, to the professionalism of the Argentine pilots. The list includes the *Coventry*, the *Sheffield*, the *Ardent*, the *Argonaut*, the *Atlantic Conveyor* and the *Antelope*. The trawler *Norwall* was attacked and the *Sir Galahad* and *Sir Tristram* were both bombed, claiming fifty-one lives; on the *Sir Galahad* alone, day one of the landings saw a total of seventy-two enemy aircraft in a dozen separate waves attacking the task force in and around San Carlos Water and its surrounding high ground, where the ground forces were deployed.

The attacks continued for the duration of 2 Para's stay on the mountain, but on 27 May, after six days in appalling wintry weather and following direct instructions from London to Brigadier Julian Thompson to produce a "victory" for the politicians, 2 Para set off to cover the 13 miles to the strategically irrelevant settlements of Darwin and Goose Green. It came as a great relief to the BN to finally get moving. Their time on the mountain had taken its toll. Exposure to the atrocious polar weather on an exposed, open feature had ensured at least half a dozen cases of trench foot in B Coy alone and the other companies fared no better.

The SAS were operating in the area off Darwin–Goose Green, gathering intelligence and passing a constant stream of information back for dissemination, and so the BN was unable to deploy its own patrols forward into that area. All they could do was sit and wait, twiddle their thumbs and fire the odd burst at the daily, regular Argentine aerobatic displays; not at all what paratroops enjoy. It is in the nature of the regiment to "go forward and do maximum damage" and now, thankfully, the game was afoot, the frustration was over and they were finally out of that hideous, bone-cold of the mountain. Frostbite or not, the men were pleased to be actively engaged in offensive operations, wherever that may lead them.

D Company led the way, clearing first to Camilla Creek House, only 2 miles short of Darwin–Goose Green. It was secured without incident and the remainder of the battalion joined D Coy midway through the night.

Camilla Creek House was a small, abandoned farmhouse with a cluster of tiny outbuildings surrounding the main house. Indeed, 2 Para managed to squeeze 400 men plus equipment into the buildings in an attempt to remain undiscovered; 400 men in a family farmhouse and a few small outbuildings! It just had to be worth a call to the Guinness Book of Records. Blokes were kipping on floors, on shelves, in hammocks, in cupboards and standing up. They were squeezed into every available space, but it did the job. The BN had arrived within very close range of its intended target without being detected. But that was soon to change. Curtis and Cyril collapsed in a heap and squeezed themselves into an outdoor toilet with two other blokes, where they sat quietly chatting about the march to Camilla Creek and the sporadic artillery fire, which the enemy had been delivering throughout the night. Most had fallen wide or short of the men.

At one point in the night, a deep, rumbling sound approaching the marching men had brought the boys into a state of readiness to engage what they thought to be some sort of enemy mechanised vehicle. It rumbled closer and closer, louder and louder as it came. The men tensed and, ready-prepared for action, light ATK weapons were made-ready and rifles were brought into the aim. Then, out of the mist, the culprits had appeared, roaring across the open ground ... a herd of horses, spooked by the sporadic artillery fire. The men relaxed and then continued on their way.

After a feed of hardtack biscuits and processed cheese, Curtis and Cyril dropped off to sleep in the cramped confines of the loo; however, before Jimmy drifted off, the phrase "in the shithouse again" sprang to mind!

During times of war, you fully expect to encounter enemy-generated intentions of all shapes and sizes in the form of infantry attacks, air strikes, artillery barrages, mortar fire, snipers, booby-traps and so the list goes on. You also expect to deal with any of the above as and when they materialise, or before if possible. What you don't expect is your own side to hand the enemy information likely to bring about death, injury or even failure on a grand scale.

But, at Camilla Creek, on 27 May, the men of 2 Para had their military radios tuned in to the BBC World Service; an excellent source of information for anyone hiding in a farmhouse on the doorstep of an enemy stronghold, which you are about to attack, whilst being 8,000 miles from home and without any hope of help. The World Service does exactly what it says on the tin. It broadcasts to the world. And so when the Paras heard the London defence correspondent's statement that 2 Para were within a stone's throw of Goose Green and poised to attack, the men were absolutely dumbfounded. The Argies, on the other hand, were absolutely delighted with the heads up. As a result of the politicians' impatience to broadcast some good news to the nation, no doubt to save a bit of face after our recent losses, they simply blurted out "Don't look now, Mr Galtieri, but the Paras are just over the hill (literally) and they're coming your way".

The result was a foregone conclusion and within a very short period of time, the garrison began to be reinforced from Mount Kent, and 2 Para instead of facing about 500 enemy, ended up fighting over 1,500!

The broadcast triggered the BN into action as they deployed over a wide defensive arc to dig in and await the pre-emptive enemy strike, which must surely come. Amazingly, it did not come and in due course, orders were issued to the BN to carry out an attack on the twin settlements of Darwin and Goose Green. Shortly before first light, Curtis' A Coy moved off towards the start line, which had been secured by C Coy. It was A Coy that led the way, with two platoons forward and one in reserve, with the Coy HQ roughly central. Curtis, now a Coy medic, moved with Coy HQ along with the Coy commander 2 i/c and Coy CSM and the company's other medic Paul, accompanied the signallers and Cyril.

The first target en route was a small house named Burntside House. SAS patrols from D Squadron indicated an enemy platoon in situ in and around the buildings and as the company advanced towards the start line, Star shells burst above the forward edges of the enemy perimeter.

Friendly artillery fire directed by forward observation officers struck home around the target. On the start line, Curtis knelt down next to Cyril and Paul and watched as a tremendous barrage of MMG fire struck home on the buildings around them. An outhouse out to the right caught fire and the men from the point platoons advanced down the steep, grassy slope into a shallow valley; its bottom a swampy mass of tussock grass and peat bog. The enemy were returning fire now and several rounds whipped by Curtis on his way down the slope. At the bottom, up to their thighs in stinking mud, they laboured on under the weight of their equipment.

Curtis turned to Cyril and said, 'It's like carrying a fucking garden shed, mate,' as they started up an almost vertical slope towards the house.

The point platoons had, by this stage, secured the outside of the buildings and at least four had entered the main house, clearing room by room with grenades. The house was like a sieve, riddled with small-arms fire and to the complete surprise of the men, they discovered four civilians, shaken but unscathed, hiding under a bed in a room they were about to assault. In fact, the only friendly casualty was their family dog, which had an injury to its jaw. The enemy had withdrawn as the assault went in, leaving several dead behind. The company reorganised itself then pressed on along its axis.

Curtis and Cyril got yapping about the BBC broadcast giving the game away.

'All this fuckin' way for Queen and Country and some fuckin' prick in London kills you from 8,000 miles away,' said Cyril.

Curtis laughed. 'That's life, mate,' he allowed.

'Well, if they didn't know we were here, they certainly do now.'

Jim was sat on his Bergen waiting to move off. For Queen and Country, he pondered over the thought that if the truth be known, that's a load of fuckin' shite. When the fighting's over you can call it what you like, but when you're doing the business and your life is on the line, and people are vaporised, shot and dying all around you, there is no Queen and Country. Soldiers fight for themselves and the bloke next to them; their mates and survival and that's it. Nothing as noble as Queen and Country.

Curtis reminded himself that even though he was himself a Royalist, he hadn't once thought about Her Majesty during the conflict. He smiled again, thinking she'd understand. God bless her.

Then came the order to move out and the men moved off, leaving the first task complete, and passed into the night, away from the smoking buildings and the burning gorse started by tracer and WP grenades. The rain got heavier and the men got wetter as they looked to the battle ahead and Curtis thought about his wife and his daughters ... and bacon butties!

The people in Burntside House had been terribly understanding, considering what had happened to their home, and the old boy had said he'd rather have a home full of British bullet holes than a garden full of Argies, ha, ha. Good man, thought Jim. Anyone who has ever watched soldiers walking to battle will tell you that you can't fail to be moved by their quiet acceptance of their possible fate and like wraiths in the mist, 2 Para moved doggedly on to whatever awaited them. Curtis remembered that whilst you don't know who, you do know that many had only hours of life left, just hours. With each step closer, an hour would become minutes. Then they would lie dead and cold in a field some 8,000 miles from home, whilst thefamilies and friends were themselves still wishing and worrying and willing the safe return of their loved one who, unknown to them, was already gone. And then the news would make its way to their door and lives would be shattered and dreams would be ended. Leaving a lifelong burden of sadness and grief, with only memories of the man, who now walked through his last few short hours of life along the way to Valhalla.

They reached Coronation Point as daylight was looming and ahead of them in the gloom sat the high ground of Darwin Hill and before them the featureless, coverless billiard table of open ground; a perfect killing ground for the enemy. A rutted track ran directly forward and then curved round to the Darwin settlements. The track bordered the bay, which hemmed the company in on the left. High ground on the right ensured the company's advance would be channelled through a bottleneck of open ground, about 150 yards wide, in a head-on assault on a well-dug-in, well-prepared enemy position in depth. There would be interlocking arcs and artillery and mortar fire support, as well as numerous medium MMGs, small arms, several snipers, anti-tank and anti-aircraft guns and minefields that were to be used to great effect against the advancing Paras; not to mention the odd booby-trap.

But this was the stuff of war and as movement was spotted on Darwin Hill, just a few hundred yards to the front, the sporadic artillery fire crept closer and became more accurate. Then news filtered through that fire support for 2 Para had been neutralised, because the chopper bringing ammo to the gun and mortar lines had been shot down. Then more news that the naval gunfire support from HMS *Arrow* had ceased, because the ship's guns had packed up out in Falklands Sound. Curtis crawled past Cyril towards the next figure in line.

'Who's that?'

'Corporal Melia,' came the reply.

'Hello, mate, it's Jimmy Curtis. Have you got any smokes?'

Between them, they scraped together a fag paper and enough baccy for a roll-up and they enjoyed a tactical fag before advancing towards the hill. They finished their fag and wished each other luck and Curtis moved back into his own position.

Then, twenty minutes later, CPL Melia was dead, and the company was under the most intense enemy fire, with nowhere to go except forward into the mincer. The point platoons were able to gain some cover in the gorse gully and were engaged in a fierce firefight with enemy positions along a shallow re-entrant. Steve Tuffen was almost immediately shot in the head. Steve Prior and Dave Abols ran out into heavy enemy MMG and small-arms fire to pick up Graham Worrall, who had also been hit, and then Steve Prior was hit, too. Chuck Hardman then rushed out to help Dave Abols with Steve, but on the way back, still under heavy fire, Prior was hit a second time and killed. And so it went on. Then Chuck Hardman was killed, along with Tam Mechan soon after.

Curtis, Paul and Cyril found themselves in the worst possible scenario. They were pinned down, had been spotted and were being engaged by what seemed like every Argy on the Islands. There was no cover in any direction; except to the left, where the shoreline offered some cover just beyond the track, but Curtis and Paul fully expected it to be mined.

The fire continued as bullets kicked up divots of turf all around them. It became even more interesting as the enemy began to fire rockets at the pair. Thinking back, Curtis thought of those knife-throwing experts sticking knives around the shape of there assistants; except these knives were exploding, sending great lumps of mud, earth and shrapnel in all directions. Curtis gazed forward through the smoke and noticed an enemy soldier appear out of a bunker, which must have been bypassed by the point sections. He fired five quick rounds at the running man, just inches above Campbell Brand's head, who was lying just ahead of him. The man dropped to his knees but continued to crawl on. Curtis took careful aim again and fired twice more and the man slumped forward, dead. But this just drew more attention from up on the hill and the enemy fire became even heavier. Then there was a brief whistle, followed by a thud to Curtis' left as a mortar round hit the track just feet away, without exploding.

On two occasions, Curtis and Paul were flipped over like rag dolls as rockets detonated perilously close to them in the soft, peaty ground.

Seconds later, another mortar round pounded the ground between the two men but again, luck was on their side as this, too, failed to explode. It just sat smoking in the ground; an unwelcome guest.

But the rockets kept coming and all around the bullets hissed, whipped and pinged. Then another rocket exploded just 3 feet from the mortar round, knocking it sideways.

'The metal to air ratio is extremely high now!' Curtis shouted to Paul. 'We have to get to that drop-off on the beach, mate!'

''Yeah. Maybe we can link up with One Platoon, Jim.'

There was a short pause and then Curtis said, half to himself, 'It's that twat with the rockets I want to link up with!' as another exploded nearby.

'Jimmy, that beach is probably mined,' shouted Paul.

'What's up, you fuckin' fanny? You've got two legs, haven't you?'

'What's that got to do with anything?'

'It's only a minefield! How many legs do you need?' shouted Curtis. Joke over, they got back to the business at hand.

'We'll have to go for it, mate. Mines or no mines,' said Curtis. 'Down there, we've got a chance. Up here, we've got none.'

After a short pause, they both agreed. Then Paul was shot in the back! Curtis crawled the 6 feet to where Paul lay; he was pale and in great pain, but he was also fit and powerfully built.

Curtis shouted into his face, 'We've got to go for it, mate. I can't help you here,' said Curtis. 'I'm going to count to three and then we're going to go for it; straight onto the beach and into those lovely mines!'

Some fuckin' choice!

Another rocket impact made them both wince and then Curtis grabbed Paul by the scruff of his neck and dragged him to his feet as both men ran. Paul stumbled but stayed on his feet. The fire was intense and bullets cracked all around them. Each step seemed like a mile, like running through treacle in slow-motion.

Curtis powered forwards across the 15 yards to the foreshore and the explosions came closer and then ... bang! Both men were cartwheeling through the air; both knocked into half unconsciousness by the blast. Curtis was lying on his back in the cold sea, now a few feet from the shore. He was gazing at the sky through bloodshot, stinging, blurred eyes. He was completely deaf and there was a strange taste in his mouth. The chainsaw in his head threatened to burst out through his skull. He didn't know where he was.

After several long moments, maybe minutes, he turned onto his side and, for the first time, he started to remember. His vision started to clear and he could see Paul lying face down in the water. He was struggling forward towards the shingle.

Curtis crawled over and dragged him onto his side and Paul spewed a mouthful of seawater onto the shingle. Curtis was severely concussed and he half believed he could stand but stumbled forward, falling on top of Paul, who let out an agonising groan. But Curtis didn't hear him, as he was still deaf. Then he threw up lots of blood. He staggered to his feet again and, like a drunken man, he swayed and swooned as he tried to focus.

Then he was slammed onto his back by the hammer-like blow in his chest! Not one to do things by half, he'd managed to get himself blown up and then shot in less than two minutes. This time, he stayed down. He felt strangely peaceful; no pain now, just the buzz-saw in his head.

A short while later, he struggled back to Paul and, after several attempts, he managed to dress his wounds, before collapsing next to his friend, exhausted and unable to move.

The fighting continued all around them, but Curtis couldn't hear it. The incessant "buzzzzzzzz" in his head filled his consciousness and he was sick again; more blood. His back hurt deep inside and he could only take shallow breaths. He remained constantly dizzy.

After a time, he began to feel the overwhelming urge to sleep. He fought to stay awake, but wasn't able to distinguish between consciousness and unconsciousness. He began to hallucinate.

Then Feany was with him, laughing and calling, and Jimmy was reaching … reaching … but he couldn't quite touch him. He felt himself being lifted and strong, caring hands were laying him down. The medics had hold of him and he was safe; and so was Paul.

Curtis had achieved his immediate aim of getting his mate Paul into cover to treat his wounds, even though he ended up doing it with the aid of the enemy artillery.

The soft, peaty ground over which the men had been fighting had almost certainly reduced the effect of the impact of the rounds and Curtis had escaped the shrapnel and taken the impact of the blast wave as the round had exploded, blowing both him and Paul onto the foreshore. The shock and concussion of the blast resulted in a series of internal injuries for Curtis, which included damaged kidneys and lungs, and a busted left shoulder and eardrum. He also suffered some difficulty maintaining his balance for some time after the battle but, on the whole, he didn't fare too badly. After about three or four hours, the buzzing sound was slowing down and Curtis was once more able to stand up without falling over, which was just as well, because he had to walk the 5 miles back to the aid post to begin his trip back to the UK.

Dulce et Decorum est Pro Patria Mori

I went into a public-'ouse to get a pint o' beer,
The publican 'e up an' sez, "We serve no red-coats here."

Rudyard Kipling; *Tommy*

For Jim, the war was over. His injuries were potentially life-threatening, so the tab back to the aid post was no mean feat. He walked alongside fifty-one prisoners captured at Darwin as they were escorted by a couple of blokes from HQ Company, Frankie and Yank. They were travelling in a captured Land Rover, which they used as an ambulance to carry other wounded men. They moved back across ground that they'd fought across overnight and the evidence of the BN's presence and effectiveness was there for all to see. There were weapons, craters, bunkers destroyed by L-ATK weapons and many, many bodies of enemy soldiers, testament to the killing efficiency of paratroops in offensive action – the maroon machine.

As Curtis walked among the bodies, he was looking for something in particular. He'd promised himself a souvenir of the war and he found it lying beside the body of a dead officer. He knew he was dead, because he had no head. His trophy was the officer's FN. It was an excellent example of a familiar friend in good nick, well looked after and not at all old. Curtis bent and picked it up. Then he asked one of the prisoner escorts to check it was clear and carried on. It was a good souvenir and when he got home, he would have it professionally decommissioned by REME and have it mounted in a glass-fronted cherrywood case. He would then hang it on the wall at home. Or at least, that was the plan.

Before moving off again, he stood for a while and looked back towards Darwin. He still couldn't hear, but he could clearly see the signs of continuing battle beyond the high ground of Darwin Hill as the boys pushed on into the Goose Green settlement beyond. Tracer of varying colours criss-crossed the sky, interspersed with the exploding anti-aircraft shells still being used against the Paras on the exposed forward slope of the hill. Jimmy swayed slightly on his feet and took a couple of backward steps to get his balance, and then he was sick again. There was even more blood this time and he felt weak as he walked on towards the aid post, 3 miles distant.

He shouted to the others, 'Hang on, I need a piss,' and they stopped the column of prisoners.

Someone was shouting to him but it was like being underwater, hearing sounds from the surface, and the buzz-saw was still there. He turned away from the biting wind, did the deed and was rewarded with a stream of red piss – more blood. Not good, thought Curtis. But not quite as bad as the donor of his FN though. Things are never as bad as they seem, he thought. In due course, they reached the aid post and Curtis stood, propped up against the captured blue-and-white Land Rover as the worst injured were removed from the back of the vehicle and from off of the bonnet and roof.

Then, after a short while, he was guided into the building and the men of the field ambulance took care of him, administering drips to get fluid into his body. Then he was aware that someone was writing something on his forehead.

Caring hands, gentle touches, reassurances, comforting smiles and life-saving treatment with minimal equipment. Outstanding!

A D-Company lad named PTE Parr was at the aid post with Curtis. He was receiving treatment for a stomach wound that he had received earlier in the day. He was told by the medics what a lucky fucker he'd been, as the bullet had whipped across his stomach, cutting the zip on his smock and gouging a quarter-inch deep furrow through the surface of his skin, but leaving no lasting damage. He was treated and, at his own request, he was returned to D Company almost immediately to rejoin the fight. What a lad! He had a ticket home if he'd wanted it, but in true Para Regiment fashion, he returned to fight on beside his mates.

On the night of 13 June, as the BN attacked Wireless Ridge, one of the features on the outskirts of Stanley, PTE Parr was killed by friendly artillery fire on the mountain. One of life's unfortunate "happenstances".

The next stop for Curtis was the field hospital in Ajax Bay, located in an old refrigeration plant. It was crowded full of wounded soldiers and they were treated by yet more medics and doctors from the task force. Commander Rick Jolly, a Royal Naval Surgeon, ran the place with great dedication, enthusiasm and professionalism and it's tribute to these traits that anyone who arrived at Ajax Bay field hospital for treatment alive also left alive. A tremendous achievement given the circumstances, conditions and restrictions on those supremely professional and valuable people, who performed endless operations of the most extreme variety, day and night, throughout the war. Indeed, they carried on regardless, in spite of a 500 lb unexploded bomb being lodged in a large walk-in industrial freezer at one end of the hospital and a second lodged in the roof, directly above one of the operating tables. Operations carried on in spite of this. "The sword of Damocles" springs to mind!

Curtis was delivered by heli not long after five marines from the Logistics Regiment had been killed there by a bomb which did explode; testimony to the dangers present, even at a field hospital. As he was sitting feeling sorry for himself, waiting for further treatment and watching injured soldiers arriving from the same battlefield that he himself had left earlier, he was touched on the shoulder gently by someone he never expected to see.

He was asked, 'Are you alright? Can I get you anything?'

The voice, which was full of compassion, belonged to Brigadier Julian Thompson.

The buzz-saw had gone now but he could still only hear, and with some difficulty, in his right ear. Curtis looked up, did his best to smile and asked for a fag.

The Brigadier left and some time later, he returned with a cigarette for Curtis before going on his way; no doubt to visit as many of the soldiers in his command as he could. Curtis suspected that the man probably felt that he belonged amongst his wounded men and it was a kindness that Jim has never forgotten and he hopes one day to be able to thank Julian Thompson properly.

He remained overnight in the field hospital, where the medics' assessment of his injuries indicated that further treatment was needed and for that he would be transferred by heli to the hospital ship, the SS *Uganda*. He was flown out the following afternoon during the daily Argentine air raids; the heli hugging the waves out into the Falklands

Sound to deposit him safely on board. He was given a thorough examination and a sedative and he woke many hours later in a real bed in a large ward in the main body of the ship, amongst many other casualties in neat rows of hospital beds. He hurt from top to toe and was surprised to find that he had a tube up his willy to drain the blood from his bladder as a result of the damaged kidneys he'd sustained in the blast. A drip in his arm continued to replace lost body fluid.

Curtis asked a medic where his souvenir FN was but was told that his prized trophy, which he had taken from the headless officer, had been thrown over the side of the *Uganda* into the murky depths of the Atlantic Ocean. The Geneva Convention dictates that no weapons of any description will be carried on a hospital ship, and rightly so. Any transgressions of this sort would obviously compromise the sanctity of these establishments, turning them into legitimate targets for the enemy. Nature of the beast. So over it went and that was that. The bedside manner of the military medics often involves "black humour", which you wouldn't find in a civilian hospital, and Curtis' searching questions were often received with sarcasm and piss-taking.

When Jimmy enquired about the tube in his willy and any possible side-effects, the straight-faced doc pointed out that, 'The side effects are minimal, but there's a slight possibility of you experiencing one or two.'

Further enquiries produced the answer, 'What sort of side effects, doc?'

'Oh, nothing to worry about, old lad. There's virtually never a problem!'

'Well, what if there is? And what is it?'

'Well, if you think you really want to know …'

'Yes, doc, I do really want to know!'

'Alright, then. In a very few cases, and it's a very, very small percentage …'

'C'mon, doc, just tell me, will you.'

'OK, if you're sure.'

'I sure am.' Curtis was getting impatient now.

'Right then, the last time I experienced the problem in a patient with similar injuries, when we pulled out the tube, his bollocks were still attached to the end!'

The doc's po-face broke into a huge grin as he registered Curtis' realisation that he'd been had.

Curtis managed a painful chuckle, the first time for some time, as he visualised the doc holding up the tube with his nuts swinging to and fro and shaking his head in disappointment. Suffice to say, all was well and Curtis has still got his nuts!

In the beds on either side of Curtis were other wounded men. The man on Jim's left was the co-pilot of Lt. Dick Nunn, whose helicopter had been shot down by a Pucara aircraft operating outside Darwin–Goose Green area. His name was Mick Belcher and he'd lost a leg in the incident as the Pucara had engaged with a 20 mm cannon.

The pilot Dick Nunn had been killed. They were responding to a request to pick up wounded and dead soldiers from Curtis' A Coy at Darwin Hill, among whom were the CO, H. Jones, Captain Dent, A Coy 2 i/c, and the battalion adjutant Capt. Woods and several others. But the end was in sight and at Darwin, at least A Coy was able to consolidate and reorganise, having accepted the enemy surrender on Darwin Hill. They remained under heavy mortar and artillery fire from the Goose Green settlement until the remainder of the companies were able to secure the settlement. C, B and D Companies fought out courageous and successful actions at the schoolhouse and airfield and the eventual complete surrender came after Major Chris Keeble, the BN 2 i/c, who had taken over from H. Jones, called in a Harrier strike, which was carried out with great precision on the enemy gun line.

Then, they sent two prisoners into the settlement to inform the visitors that the tourist season was over and that it was time to hang up the sombreros. It is an oversimplified account and much more could be said, but Curtis was no longer involved; he was on his way home.

The initial period on board was spent under sedation, but after five days on the *Uganda*, Jim was allowed to move around with some assistance from the nurses, so he decided to visit a couple of mates from C Coy a few yards along the ship in the next ward.

Jock had had a nice piece of shrapnel removed from his chest and it now sat in pride of place in a glass on his bedside locker, along with Jock's false front teeth. He had several tubes and drips inserted in various places, with one rather large calibre tube, which had been pushed through his ribs to assist his breathing, with a further one acting as a drain.

When Jim arrived, Jock was in the latter stages of a self-inflicted coughing fit and he lay there, wheezing and spluttering, with a pair of bloodshot eyes bulging like a set of racing dog's bollocks.

Jim sat himself on the edge of Jock's bed and proceeded to root through his bedside locker and personal effects. Jock's red eyes rolled over in Jim's direction and, without speaking, Jock said, 'What the fuck are ya's doing, arsehole?'

'I'm looking for something to rob. You're obviously going to die, so this lot's of fuck-all use to you, is it?! Ha, ha. How are you feelin' boyo? You look like shite.'

'Well, I'm no deed jist yet, ya twat!' replied Jock. 'Och, I'm nae sa bad, Jim. Bit ay've jest hod ma bollocks chewed by the duty staff nurse. I thought she wis goin' tae throw me ooverboard!'

'Why?' asked Jim. 'What the fuck have you done now?'

'Well, ay've bin dyin' fer a fag fer aboot a week the noo, bit they widna let me hov win.' Jock looked about furtively. 'So a weeted till the'd done the roonds. Then a m'ed messel' a roll-up an' hod a dam gud snort!'

Jimmy could see what was coming and was struggling not to laugh, for fear of choking himself. 'So what's the problem, Jock?' said Jim as he began to giggle.

'Well, as ye knoo, a've a chist-wound like yer sel', so it's feckin' verboten accorden tae the gruppenfuhrer!' said Jock, referring to the staff nurse. 'Onyway, ah hod a sneaky blow an' tick a fit o' coughin'. Jeesus, et near feckin' kilt me. Ah soondet like a shaggin' dunkey. Talk aboot gev the game away, ah couldnae breathe. Ah torned blue, green and purple. They hod tae git the emergency resus team in! Whit a feckin' performance. Ah tried tae bluff me case and said mebee ah swallowed a feather, or perhaps et wis the rool of the shep. But it didnae work, Jimmy boy. There wis nae foolin' the gruppenfuhrer. She went daft. She wis hovin' feckin' kerniptions.'

Jim was pissing himself by this stage. 'What gave the game away then, Jock?'

'Och, it wis these feckin' pipes, boy. They were full of feckin' smoke. Dead giveaway; like a feckin' chimney. They hod tae whip 'em oot and flush away the smoke. Whit a feckin' performance!"

'That'll teach you to behave, you fuckin' eejit,' said Jim.

'Anyway,' said Jock, 'talkin' aboot the rool oh the shep, come closer and lestin tae thess.' Jim moved up the bed. 'Now, stond up and pit yer ear next to yon ventilation pipe up there.' Jock pointed up above the bed.

Jim put his head next to the pipe and listened and as he did so, he heard a metallic rattle followed by a muffled bump, which did, indeed, repeat itself in time with the roll of the ship.

'What the fuck's that?'

Jock put his finger to his lips and took on a conspiratorial tone. 'Ssshhh ... it's a feckin' grenade. I hid it in the grating when they came to check oor kit, but et rooled doon the pipe an ae couldnae reach the fecker! It's ben roolin' aboot ever since.'

Jim stood, shaking his head and laughing. 'You'll have more than smoke in your pipes if the pin comes out!'

'You're no wrang there, mate,' said Jock. 'I havnae slept a wink since ae drapped it in there.'

Jim never asked why he wanted it in the first place; he just walked away laughing. It's probably still in there today "jest rattlin' aboot", as Jock would say.

Jim made his way further along the deck to the next ward, which housed many of the guys who were suffering from leg injuries, gunshot wounds, shrapnel injuries, traumatic amputations from blast or stepping on mines and that sort of common battlefield injury. He decided to stick his nose in to see who was there and, sure enough, there were several guys from the BN who he knew well. Mick and Tommy were in the beds next to each other; but only after a "long and bitterly fought campaign" as they described it, in their quest to be moved from opposite ends of the wards to their present position. The reason? Well, as they both explained to Jim,

'He's lost his left leg,' said Tommy.

'And he's lost his right,' said Mick.

'So we decided to launch our campaign to move nearer each other on the basis that, two legs being better than one, we'd be far more use as the full package, as it were!'

'Yeah. Him with his good leg and me with mine, ha, ha!'

Jimmy laughed. No looking for sympathy here, he thought. Typical Para Regt – just get on with it.

'Well, I guess there'll be other benefits, too, boys. Like buying a pair of shoes from now on, for example.'

'Like how?' said Tommy.

'Well, it'll only cost you half as much,' said Jim. 'You get the left, Tom, and Mick gets the right half of a pair each. Halve the cost each, good, eh?!'

Tommy and Mick beamed with delight, shook hands and wished each other well in their future shoe shopping expeditions, telling Jim what a clever fucker he was in the process.

'You'll just have to be careful you don't go home with the wrong shoe or you'll both be fucked, ha, ha!'

Black humour was the order of the day and, as always, it carried the men through the darkest of times.

Jim made his way back to his own ward and lay on his bed, worn out but thoroughly entertained by his trip along the deck. Soon after, he was informed by Staff Nurse Marian Stock that he would be starting the next phase of his casevac a day later. He lay back on his bed and gazed about the ward at all the other casualties of war and he found himself wondering what the future held in store for them.

In the bed on Curtis' right, lay an Argentine Skyhawk pilot, Lt Lucero, who had been shot down over San Carlos. He'd received fore and aft dislocations of both knees as he ejected and was fished out of Ajax Bay for his trouble. Jim made several attempts at conversation with him, but to no avail. He probably thought it was a surreptitious attempt at an interrogation!

When the day came for Curtis to leave the *Uganda*, he left the pilot some boiled sweets and he was flown out to HMS *Hydra* for the next stage of his casevac to the UK. After the war ended, Jim saw the pilot on TV on a couple of occasions talking of his own experiences at the hands of the Brits, as it had not yet ended when he left the ship. Hope you enjoyed the sweets, thought Jim.

Another journey by chopper saw Curtis transferred to the Arctic survey vessel *Hydra* which, in turn, delivered both himself and several others to Montevideo for onward dispatch to the UK via the VC10 hospital aircraft crewed by our own RAF, which finally delivered the wounded to RAF Wroughton in Oxfordshire.

Back in the UK at last, Curtis' part in the Islands War had lasted around five weeks but during that time, he'd been part of the biggest movement of troops into conflict over the longest distance since World War II. He'd seen attacks by hundreds of fighter aircraft on a daily basis after the landings and he'd taken part in the largest set-piece battle the British Army had been involved in since the Korean War and, outnumbered 3–1, had won. This was probably the last time a classic, set-piece, bayonets fixed, hand-to-hand engagement was likely to happen and they had, against all the odds – 8,000 miles from home and help – been victorious! Not renowned for being a religious man, Curtis recalled the saying "God is not on the side of the big battalions, but on the side of the best shots"; Darwin and Goose Green was testament to just that.

On the battlefield, along with everything and anyone that the soldier encounters there, including the very real potential for sudden death, the very real potential for sudden fun exists, too. And if you imagine the context, the following examples are a hoot!

When A Coy was en route to Goose Green, they'd carried out a night attack at Burntside House, as described earlier. During that attack, as the enemy withdrew and the boys closed in on the main house, a small group of the chaps had decided to "post" grenades through the window at one end of the building before following them in after detonation.

One of the chaps, a gent of Scottish origin, opted for WP which, when it exploded, produced clouds of instant white smoke and threw out pieces of phosphorous over an area of about 15 yards diameter. This phosphorus burns at a tremendously high temperature and would, if you were to get a piece in the back of your hand, for example, burn straight through and drop out of the other side. So the deal is, if you get a bit on you, it should be immediately dug out with something like a bayonet or be immersed in water, which stops it burning; but only until it comes into contact with the air again, which causes it to reignite and carry on burning. So, to continue, Jock produces the weapon, shouts "Grenade!", and he and his mates huddle up close either side of the window. However, it smashed the glass and then bounced straight back off the chicken wire, which the owner had nailed across the inside.

Surprise, surprise! The grenade then dropped at the feet of the horrified trio, who dove in all directions, but not quite quickly enough. The grenade exploded and everyone got a bit, with the result being that the three amigos were instantly transformed into a trio of gymnastic, smouldering, break-dancing strippers at various stages of undress. Clothing was flung in all directions, some on fire, to a chorus of "fuckin' hell, Ooo ya fucker, you jock twat bastard, maniac bastard", etc., etc.,

etc. The smouldering trio of professionals were rescued by their mates and survived the ordeal without too much physical damage. Their pride, on the other hand, had endured several long-lasting dents. If the enemy had seen the performance, they'd have died laughing … and saved us the ammo!

Another incident strangely enough involved grenades again and occurred during B Coy's murderous rampage across the isthmus en route to Goose Green. Some of the enemy bunkers were interspersed with small tents and all had to be cleared, along with the bunkers and trenches. This was done with automatic MMG fire and small arms, 66 mm ATK weapons and, where required, bayonets – savage stuff – and the Paras are excellent at it.

At one point on the advance, a section from B Coy's point platoon encountered one such offending tent and duly poured a high volume of fire into it. Then, one of the men eagerly leapt up close to the front of the tent, ready to "post" his grenade. Now, there are some simple rules to remember when "posting" grenades. Number one – remember the grenade is a double-edged weapon; it can kill you as well as the enemy. Number two – once you've pulled the pin and released the lever, warning your mates by shouting "Grenade!", you quickly "post" the grenade, ensuring you have "hard cover" between you and the exploding grenade; then, you wait for the bang, before entering the assaulted space to finish the job, i.e. kill any surviving enemy.

So the scene was set with battle raging all around and the fog of war in full swing, when our harum-scarum lad posted his grenade, having alerted his mates to his intent, and then stood with his back to the tent flap with about a sixteenth of an inch of canvas between him and possible sudden death! The grenade exploded, destroying the tent completely, removing our hero's trousers from arse to knee and depositing him face down in the dirt, with several nice pieces of shrapnel in his white spotty arse. Curtis knows the lad well and he's never been allowed to live it down. Suffice to say, he survived the ordeal and continued with a sparkling career in the BN.

Another example of black humour involved a support company soldier with a leg injury he'd "picked up", again in the Goose Green area. Once the enemy had agreed the formal surrender of the settlement and 2 Para had moved in en masse, the various departments of the BN set up house in the settlement buildings. At the aid post, medics and the BN doctor were busy treating various minor complaints, when a soldier limped in complaining of an injured leg.

'Hello, doc, can you take a look at this, please; it's fuckin' killing me.'

The doc agreed and approached the makeshift counter and stood patiently waiting as the soldier bent over and rummaged inside his Bergen. Then, standing up, he promptly deposited a human leg, with boot still attached, onto the counter for the doc to inspect. The ghoulish item had obviously been separated from its Argentine owner at some point and was picked up by the soldier, intent on using it in some sort of mischief. The act was greeted with roars of laughter and whoops of delight and it served to maintain morale within the unit. The doc, a damned good egg, as expected, took it well.

Another incident that took place in the settlement involved the use of a group of Argentine prisoners for various work tasks; including the clearance of ammunition to ensure it wasn't booby-trapped. The use of prisoners for this sort of work is allowed under the rules of the Geneva Convention and it assumes that enemy troops would be aware of the presence of their own booby-traps and could therefore be expected to point them out, to be dealt with by the relevant agencies.

During the clearance of a large stockpile of ammunition and artillery rounds, there was a large explosion as a result of one such booby-trap, resulting in the death of a number of enemy and extremely serious injury to one other, who incurred terrible injuries to his lower torso and legs, from which he could not possibly survive. The man lay rolling about screaming, with his entrails hanging out and on fire. The screams were unmerciful and rather than let him suffer for a moment longer, a soldier from the BN stepped forward and shot the man twice in the head. It was not an act of brutality. On the contrary, it was an act of kindness from one soldier to another to end the man's unnecessary suffering. An act borne out of compassion.

Jim pondered over the many incidents and acts worth remembering. For example, you could have chosen many people worthy of awards. But they would receive none. Secondly, it occurred to him that it's often the most unlikely of people who perform those most selfless and outrageously gallant acts. But sometimes even the highest of honours can be bestowed upon those who may not have performed as well or as bravely as others who would receive lesser awards. It seemed to Jim that there was "politics at work" here, or was it just the roll of the dice? Who can tell?

After a good stay in hospital in the UK, Curtis was released on leave. The BN returned victorious and life once again returned to a paratrooper's "normal". In short, that meant "back on the piss". And the return of:

> For it's Tommy this an' Tommy that, an' "chuck him out, the brute!"

> But it's "saviour of 'is country" when the guns begin to shoot; [...]

Rudyard Kipling; *Tommy*

Once again, life goes on. It was as if the past six months hadn't happened.

Jimmy was drunk. He'd been on the piss all day with his mates, who he was staying with in London, and they'd managed to become separated. But the homing pigeon gene had guided him in an ever increasingly circuitous route to Waterloo Station, where they'd all planned to be at the same time. The others, no doubt in their own drunken stupors, were taking equally unusual tactical approaches to their RV. Meanwhile, back at the station, Jim was giving an excellent impression of the drunken idiot that he was, by managing to fall arse over tit over a bench, coming to land in a heap. Covered in chicken fried rice and curried beef, he proceeded to devour it with gusto and a good old "look what a clever lad I am" grin on his face, which was now barely visible through the curry. Liberal globs and blobs of which were dripping onto his lap.

He felt super; totally at ease with himself and the world and completely satisfied with his performance so far. He was also completely oblivious to the presence of two police officers standing not 6 feet away. Their expressions betraying the abject disgust with which they viewed Mr Curtis Esq. Jim's arm was still in a sling as a result of his injuries in the Falklands.

'How'd you hurt your arm?' came a voice from above.

'Fighting!' said Jim, without looking up.

There was a pause before the next busy spoke.

'Well, there'll be none of that here, right?'

The officer, a sergeant who carried a large stick, poked Jim to gain his attention. Jim didn't respond. Another poke, only harder this time. He looked up and eventually managed to focus on the enemy. The sergeant looked at Jim as if he'd just crawled out from under a stone, the point of his stick still touching Jim's shoulder.

In a broad Scottish accent, he announced, 'There's a piece of shite on the end of this stick!'

Jim looked up into the face above and said, 'Not this fuckin' end, Jock!'

'Name, smart-arse?' demanded the sergeant.

Jim giggled. 'James Curtis, age 12, what's yours, sweetheart? Ha, ha.'

'Mind your manners, you!' cut in the younger of the two; a stroppy individual and evidently devoid of a sense of humour.

'Never mind,' the smart-arse remarked, 'just answer the question.'

'Sorry, Sherlock!' muttered Jim.

'What was that?'

'OK, cock,' said Jim.

He was duly hoisted to his feet and propelled towards the ticket barrier, just in time to catch his train to Aldershot. On the way to the platform, the younger of the two, obviously in a bid to impress Sgt Jock as well as Jim, made it abundantly clear that pond life like Jim weren't required on "his patch", ever!

'Anyway, what do you do for a living? Have you got a job?'

'Yes,' said Jim, indignantly. 'I most certainly have!'

'Well, what is it then?'

'I am employed by the dole office, one day a week, for which I'm handsomely remunerated.'

'Grrr,' said Sgt Jock.

'What's your purpose in life?' demanded the wee man, a smug look on his face. 'Apart from sponging off the state, that is?'

'To live as long as I can and to die when I can't help it!' said Jim.

Not at all entertained by Jim's rhetoric, both bobbies proceeded to lecture Jim on the virtues of getting a job and not living off the state.

Then they reminded him that "we've" just fought a war in the South Atlantic. Where were you when that was going on? National Service is what we need; sort out the likes of you!' Etcetera, etcetera.

They stuffed him into his carriage and as the train pulled away, Jim blew them both a kiss and gave them the finger. Oh well, you can't please all the people all of the time, he thought. Probably best I didn't mention the war; might be a bit too scary, bless them! Mind you, if I had told them, they may have been a bit more sympathetic, he thought. But then that wouldn't have been half as much fun, ha, ha. He fell asleep an instant later and dreamt of short-arsed coppers with an attitude and pointy heads to fit into their pointy hats. "We've" just fought a war, have we? I don't remember seeing either of them down there!

Thus ends another phase in the life and times of the Quiet Soldier. Water under the bridge. But National Service, mmm. Now there's a thing. Jimmy actually agreed with the busies' sentiments on that one and he knew he'd have loved it. Just like Colly!

He stumbled off the train in the Shot and his thoughts wandered back to Africa, as they often did, and he pictured Shollonburg back with the kids in the neat little school where he'd taught and he laughed to himself as he pictured his friend in that particular context. Hope he doesn't eat too many of them, the parents are bound to start asking questions, ha, ha!

Chris Schollonburg had returned to his pre-army days as a primary school teacher, educating the small children he loved. What a contrast! But then, in 1999, during a short reunion, both he and René Voss had climbed the knoll outside the town to the spot where Kurt Willt had been buried. They sat on a boulder on the top where, all those years before, they had sheltered from the rain before they had retrieved Willt's body from the town. A heat-shimmer covered the land and the town was barely visible through the haze. They sat for several hours and talked and listened, as old soldiers do, about their lives and exploits, past and present.

Late in the day, when the sun was way past its Zenith, they began to dig and, in due course, they retrieved the remains of their friend. Kurt Willt was returned to his mother in Pietermaritzburg, where he now rests in peace in the family plot. It was a promise kept. Many contract men went on to work for private "security" companies around the world and some died in Iraq in bombings and ambushes.

As for Jimmy Curtis: he writes books and remembers, with great affection, the other half of a most unlikely friendship. And he remembers the words Alice Fearon Warner once spoke to Big Brendan, showing no fear of the man. Quote: The one thing that this boy would have benefited from most would have been the attention of you – his father. It was the only time Curtis ever saw his da walk away from what he would normally have seen as a challenge, to be settled with his fists. Years later, in a very rare display of sentimentality, Jim found himself thinking, we could have been such great friends. Not Big Brendan's style though; so sad, what a waste.

In Northern Ireland, Jimmy was involved in several controversial incidents in the campaign against Republican groups and others. The Paras left their references on various parts of the conflict. At times, they, too, paid the price. But when the enemy eventually decided to capitulate, the Paras never did – they're still here, and they're still *Utrinque Paratus!*

"Alone" had been Curtis' friend for many years. But now, several lifetimes later, at the time of writing, "alone" is no longer there.

Looking up from the page, he always sees – standing somewhere close by or sitting in a chair opposite – Van Rijn and Willt, Willy Fallon and, of course, Little Billy Feany – still aged 7, with a snotty nose and no arse in his trousers, laughing. Billy Feany, killed in action, fighting the English!

All the others visit, too, large as life – all Curtis has to do is remember.

He sat thinking and listening to the record *Desperado* by the Eagles. It could have been written for him. He'd been told by so many people that he should write some sort of record of what he'd done in his life. Each time he'd said, "Yeah, OK. Maybe sometime", and then in the end, he decided he would.

But where to start? He was spoiled for choice. He doodled and drew pictures, paused for a while, had a brew, doodled some more and then he began to write: It was hot in the hide. The man lay motionless, peering through the bramble cover ...

In memory of the soldiers who died, and lastly, but not least, of Billy Feany, whose spirit lives in the great oak on the island in the lake.

> *From little towns in a far land we came,*
>
> *To save our honour in a world aflame.*
>
> *By little towns in a far land we sleep;*
>
> *And trust that world we won, for you to keep!*

Rudyard Kipling

THE END

Glossary:

Acacia	Large thorny bush/tree, prolific in Africa
AFV	Armoured Fighting Vehicle
AK47	Assault rifle
Armour Piercing	Type of bullet/projectile
ATK	Anti-tank weapons
ASU	Active Service Unit
Barrat 50 CAL	Sniper rifle
Bde	Brigade
Beasting	Army slang for a beating or a very hard run with kit
Bergen	Rucksack
Beyer Garratt	Steam train
Biltong	Strips of sun-dried meat
Binos	Binoculars
Bivvi Bag	Gore-tex sleeping-bag cover
Black and Tans	Auxiliary wing of the Royal Irish Constabulary (so named because of the colour of their uniform) now disbanded
BN	Batallion
box	To circle a location either to observe or avoid it
Box	Term used to refer to MI5 – derived from the department's address – being a Box No.
Browning High Power	Semi-automatic pistol
BRDM	Soviet-built armoured fighting vehicle

Chinese Parliament	An informal talk between soldiers of all ranks (say what you think). Usually to decide the way forward or form a plan – individuals offering up their own opinions
Chuff Chart	Chart used by soldiers to count down the days to the end of a tour of duty.
CIA	Central Intelligence Agency
Colt 45	Semi-automatic pistol
Cordtex	High-explosive detonating cord
Coy	Company
CPGB	Communist Party of Great Britain
CPL	Corporal
CSM	Company Sergeant Major
CTR	Close Target Recce
Cupola	Exit hatch in tank turret
Da Da	Yes, yes (Russian)
Dachas	Holiday homes (Russian)
Dead Letter Box	A place where items or information are deposited to be retrieved covertly
Det – Detachment	14th Intelligence & Security Company covert operations
DET	Detonator
Drill Round	Anti-tank round
Dulce Et Decorum Est Pro Patria Mori	'It is sweet and fitting to die for one's country' Poem by Wilfred Owen
DZ	Drop Zone
ETA	Expected time of arrival
E4A	Covert operations wing Royal Ulster Constabulary
FN	Fabrique National – assault rifle
FRV	Final Rendezvous Point
Glock	Pistol
GPMG	General-purpose Machine Gun
Ground Sign	Tracks
G3	Assault Rifle
Heckler & Koch G3	Assault rifle

Heli	Helicopter
HE	High Explosive
HQ	Headquarters
H + 01	Time to start proceedings
IO	Intelligence Officer
Ingram	M10 9mm sub-machine gun
in situ	In place
Int	Intelligence
IRA	Irish Republican Army
Jenny	Generator
KGB	Russian Secret Service
LAW	Light anti-tank weapon
LOE	Limit of Exploitation
LS	Landing Site
LUP	Lying Up Point
LZ	Landing Zone
Manos aribas, avanté.	Spanish: hands up. Come forward.
Pronto, pronto.	Quickly.
Malleted	Gave a good hiding
Motorman	Operation mounted by the army against Irish extremists in Northern Ireland
MI5	British Security Services
MI6	British Security Services
MMG	Machine gun
MP5	Sub-machine gun
NCOs	Non-commissioned officers
Niet	No (Russian)
NISS	Northern Ireland Surveillance Section
OC	Officer in Command (usually a major, commands a company group of about 60 men)
O-group	Operations or Orders Group
OP	Observation point
op	Operation
OS	Ordnance survey map
PIRA	Provisional IRA
PE	Plastic explosive

Poncho	Waterproof sheet (used to make cover)
Provo	PIRA (Provisional IRA)
PSI	Permanent Staff Instructor
PTE	Private
PTIs	Physical training instructors
PTSD	Post Traumatic Stress Disorder
Pucara	Ground attack aircraft
PUP	Pick Up Point
QBOs	Quick Battle Orders
QRF	Quick Reaction Force
Quid pro quo	You scratch my back, I'll scratch yours
R & R	Rest and Relaxation
RCIED	Radio/or remotely controlled improvised explosive device
Recce	Reconnaissance
REME	Royal Electrical Mechanical Engineers
Re-Org	re-organise
RLI	Rhodesian Light Infantry
RPG	Soviet anti-tank weapon (light)
RSM	Regimental Sergeant Major
RUC	Royal Ulster Constabulary (now Northern Ireland Police Service)
Ruger	Rifle
RV	Rendezvous point
SA	South African
SADF	South African Defence Force
SASF	South African Special Forces
SAS	Special Air Service (or "Troop")
SB	Special Branch
SBS	Special Boat Squadron
Security Service	MI5 and MI6
SF	Security Forces
Shebeen	Illegal drinking place (Ireland)
SILVA	Compass
Simonov	Rifle
Source	Informer
Special Forces	Special air service and the Det.

SNCO	Senior non-commissioned officer e.g. sergeant
SIS	Secret Intelligence Service
Stag	On stag – on watch – stag position; on watch at this position; sentry or sentry duty
Stinger	Ground to air missile/man portable
SUS	Soldier under sentence
SWAPO	South West African People's Organisation rebel army (Marxist)
T54	Soviet main battle tank
TCGN	Tactical Coordinating Group North responsible for the tactical coordination of ops in the north of the province.
TCGS	Tactical Coordinating Group South
Technical Attack	Method of intelligence-gathering using various technical methods and means
Teeth Arms	Units in the military who do the actual fighting in any conflict
Tokarev	Pistol (7.65 mm)
Tout	Informer
TCG	Tactical Coordinating Group
Ultrinque Paratus	Motto of the British Parachute Regiment: "Ready For Anything".
UVF	Ulster Volunteer Force/Irish Protestant extremists
VCP	Vehicle Checkpoint
VVS	Very, very severe/refers to degree of difficulty
Wings	Insignia issued to British Paras on completion of parachutist training
WP	White Phosphorous grenades
X-factor	Anything unexpected/not planned for: not a talent show on ITV!
ZANLA	Zambian African National Liberation Army (rebel army – Marxist)
ZIPRA	Zambian Independent People's Revolutionary Army (Marxist)
ZIL	Russian limousine

2 i/c	Second in command
2REP	French Foreign Legion Paratroops
58 pattern mug	Type of standard issue drinking mug/British Army
7.62 ball	7.62 mm ammunition for use with the GPMG (in linked/belted form) or individual rounds magazine fed for the SLR (Self Loading Rifle)/FN.
9 mm side arms	Pistol
14 int. Coy	Covert operators
27 KVA	Wheeled generator
38 Smith & Wesson	Revolver
482	Locomotive
58 Pattern	Type of equipment – pouches – belt order 1958 style design – standard issue/British Army. Now replaced.
66 mm Law	Light anti-tank weapon
81 mm	Mortars
303 Lee Enfields	Rifle

Poetry Sources:
Rudyard Kipling (1865–1936)
Robert Service (1874–1958)
General Douglas MacArthur (1880–1964)
Wilfred Owen (1893–1918)
Song – *Liverpool Lullaby* – written by Stan Kelly (b. 1929)